POINT BLANK

POINT BLANK

AN FBI THRILLER

CATHERINE COULTER

LARGE PRINT PRESS
An imprint of Thomson Gale, a part of The Thomson Corporation

Detroit • New York • San Francisco • New Haven, Conn. • Waterville, Maine • London

THOMSON
™
GALE

LIBRARY OF CONGRESS CATALOGING-IN-PUBLICATION DATA

Coulter, Catherine.
   Point blank : an FBI thriller / by Catherine Coulter.
     p. cm.
   ISBN 0-7862-8032-8 (lg. print : hc : alk. paper)
   ISBN 1-59413-159-7 (lg. print : sc : alk. paper)
   1. United States. Federal Bureau of Investigation — Fiction. 2. Sherlock, Lacey (Fictitious character) — Fiction. 3. Savich, Dillon (Fictitious character) — Fiction. 4. Government investigators — Fiction. 5. Married people — Fiction. 6. Large type books. I. Title.
PS3553.O843P65 2005b
813'.54—dc22   2005018772

ISBN 13: 978-0-7862-8032-2 (hc)
ISBN 13: 978-1-59413-159-2 (sc)
Published in 2007 by arrangement with G. P. Putnam's Sons, a division of Penguin Group (USA) Inc.

Printed in the United States of America on permanent paper
10 9 8 7 6 5 4 3 2 1

To Anton
We've got a winner here.
Thank you for being who and what you
are and thank you for being mine.

CHAPTER 1

Winkel's Cave
Maestro, Virginia
Friday afternoon

Ruth Warnecki paused to consult her map, even though she'd read it so many times it was worn and stained from use, with a smear of strawberry jam on one corner. Okay, she'd walked and crawled down this twisting passage exactly the 46.2 feet indicated on the map. She'd measured it carefully, just as she'd measured all the distances since she climbed down into that first offshoot passage at the end of the cavern's entrance. A narrow and twisty passage, smelling strongly of bat guano, some lengths of it so low she'd had to crab-walk, it had finally flattened out. So far the distances had matched those on her map to the centimeter.

At this point, there should have been a small arched opening directly to her right. She focused her head lamp some eight feet up to the top of the cave wall then slowly scanned downward. She didn't see an arch or any sign that there'd ever been one. She went over the directions again to this point, rechecked the distances, but no, she hadn't screwed that up. Again, she shone her head lamp on the cave wall, moved back and forth at least three feet in both directions. Nothing. She was in the right spot, she knew it.

Ruth rarely cursed when she was frustrated. She hummed instead. And so she hummed as she began to glide the palms of her hands slowly over the wall, pushing inward here and there. The wall was limestone, dry to the touch, eons of sand filming over it. Nothing but a solid cave wall.

She was disappointed, but she knew that was a fact of life for a treasure hunter. Her old uncle, Tobin Jones, a treasure hunter for fifty years, and something of a mentor to her, had told her that for every authentic treasure map, there are more fraudulent ones than illegal aliens in California. Of course that was because every fraudulent map was a treasure in itself if it sucked in the right mark. Problem is, Tobin had said with a shake of his head, we're all suckers. But that, he'd always believed, was better than those idiots traipsing over an empty ballpark or a beach with their metal detectors, looking for nickels.

Actually, she used metal detectors, had a portable one attached to her belt along with two more flashlights. Yes, she understood all about fake treasure maps, but she'd really been excited about this one. All her research had led her to believe it could be the real deal. Even the age of the paper, the ink, and the manner of writing tested out — about 150 years old.

But there was no arch. She felt the crash of disappointment again and kicked the cave wall. There was always frustration, and it wasn't as if she hadn't been taken before. There were the two fraudulent maps that had sent her after the guys who'd sold them to her; they'd known she was a cop, the morons. Then there was the Scotsman who sold her a map of a cave not a quarter of a mile west of Loch Ness. She should have known better, but he was so charming she believed him for one delicious moment.

She shook her head. *Pay attention.* This map wasn't a fraud, she felt it in her gut. If there was gold here, she intended to find it. If there wasn't an arch, maybe it had crumbled and filled in over the long years.

Yeah, right. She laughed at herself, an odd, creepy sound in the dense silence.

What an idiot. The arch certainly could have collapsed, but it would remain visible. Debris from a cave-in would remain *in situ* for longer than time itself. Nothing would magically occur to fill it in from bottom to top so seamlessly.

Only men could do that.

She stepped back, lifted her head so her head lamp shone directly on the wall. She studied every inch of it, pressing inward with her fist everywhere she could reach. Mr. Weaver had told her this part of Winkel's Cave had never been explored, much less mapped. Even though he appeared worried for her, he still had a gleam in his eye at the thought of splitting any treasure she found.

It was the feel of the cave, she thought, the way the silence felt, the hollow sound of her footsteps. She was sure no one had been in this cave for a very long time, perhaps since the gold was left here. Mr. Weaver had installed an iron grate to close off the entrance — fools injuring themselves, suing him, he'd told her. He couldn't find the key, but that hadn't mattered. The lock had been child's play to pick.

Finally, she stepped back and hummed some more. If someone had filled in an arched opening, they did it remarkably well. She could find no seams, nothing that looked out of place or staged. She sat back against the opposite cave wall and retied one of her walking boots. She realized she was tired. She pulled out an energy bar, her favorite peanut butter, and slowly began to eat it, washing it down with water from the plastic bottle fastened to her belt. Still sitting, she raised her head to train her lamp again on the opposite wall. She was beginning to hate that frigging wall. She began at the top, and slowly scanned all the way to the bottom again.

She saw something, about two feet above the floor, where the light reflected differently. She crawled to the wall and studied the thin shadow she'd seen. There, that was it, a line of dust and dirt about a half an inch wide.

Ohmigod, it wasn't just a line; it was shaped like an arch.

She felt her adrenaline spike. She looked more closely and saw that someone had gouged the arch deeply into the wall. She touched it with her fingertip, lightly pushed inward. Her finger sank easily through years of soft, thick dust, up to her first knuckle. She knew one thing for sure now. The accumulation of dust in that grooved arch was decades older than she was. She wondered how many more years would have to pass before the arch outline disappeared entirely. Who had cut this arch and why, for heaven's sake? Or was it a cover of some kind?

Ruth lightly pushed against the limestone directly below the top of the arch. To her astonishment, it gave a little. She laid her palm flat against the wall and gave a sharp push. The stone fell back some more. Her heart kettledrummed in her chest. The stone was light enough that she could dig it out. She pulled the small pick from her belt and went at it; the limestone crumbled, and suddenly she was staring at a small round hole.

She leaned forward, but the hole was too small for her to see anything in the chamber beyond. And there *was* a chamber beyond, the chamber she was looking for. Grinning like a madwoman, Ruth continued to use the pick on the limestone below the line of the arch. The stone broke apart, collapsing inward into the next chamber. When she'd cleared it out, it was no bigger than a St. Bernard doggie door, but it was large enough to look into. Shoving dirt out of the way, she stuck her head through the opening. She saw nothing but a floor. Pulling her second flashlight out of her belt she beamed both it and her head lamp straight ahead, then slowly to the right, then back to the left. The light faded into endless black, without reflection.

She pulled back and sat on her heels. The men who'd hidden the gold had cut this slab of limestone out of another part of the cave and fitted it in this space, to better hide the low entrance to the treasure chamber. She was so excited her fingertips were dancing: she was nearly there. She stuck her arm through the opening, felt nothing but the smooth dirt floor, solid and dry, the chamber the map showed beyond the archway. Everything was as it should be. So the precious map hidden in the age-dampened cardboard box of nineteenth-century books she'd bought off that old man in Manassas wasn't created two weeks ago in a back room in Newark and planted there. *Let's do it, Ruth.* It was a tight squeeze, but once she got her shoulders through, the rest was easy.

She swung her legs in front of her, raised her flashlight, and beamed it together with her head lamp around the space. According to the map, the chamber was good-sized, some thirty feet across and forty feet wide. She didn't see the opposite wall, she didn't see anything.

She pulled out her compass. Yes, the opposite wall had to be due east. Everything was where it should be. She realized in that moment that the air wasn't stale or dank, which one would expect in a cave chamber sealed for 150 years. She sucked in air that was fresher than the air in the main passage. Now wasn't that a kick — she had to be close to an unmapped exit, and wouldn't that have been handy for the men who hid the gold? Slowly she got to her feet and looked straight ahead. It was like standing in a dark pit, but she'd done that before, and with a head lamp you'd see the boundaries, wouldn't you? She sucked in more of the wonderful fresh air. There was an underlying scent, something rather sweet that she couldn't quite identify. For a moment she felt disoriented. She paused, and continued to breathe slowly and deeply, waiting for her head to clear, for the world to right itself. She felt a sort of dull heaviness in her arms and legs but then it was gone and her head seemed clear again. Time to move. She took a step forward, carefully planting her foot on the solid earth. What had she expected? To step off into space? She laughed aloud, to prove she could. Her own voice sounded fresh and alive, clear as Mrs. Monroe's when she called to Woodrow to finish his business and come in. What a strange thought that was.

She felt something familiar niggle at the back of her brain — excitement mixed with fear, she thought, and smiled. Oh boy, was she pumped, even a little dizzy with it. But not stupid. She had no intention of gaily striding forward and stepping into a pit right before the finish line. She had to be smart, like Indiana Jones. She had to feel for trip wires and booby traps. Now that was a weird thought. She felt a shot of dizziness that made her stumble. She eased down to her knees, laid her flashlight on the ground in front of her, and began to slide her palms along the floor. The floor, thank God, continued smooth and sandy, though it seemed to shimmy a bit when she got up close. There weren't any gnarled old vines tied across the chamber to unleash poison-tipped blow darts or to fire old rifles that surely wouldn't work anymore. She heard nothing but the sound of her own breathing. Truth was, she was so excited it was hard to keep herself crawling and not do a mad sprint to the short passageway just beyond the chamber. The gold was there, in a small alcove, waiting for her, untouched since those bone-weary soldiers had hauled it in and drawn the map so they could return for it. Only no one had.

She continued to ease forward on her hands and knees. Every little while, she moved the flashlight out ahead of her again. It seemed like she had crawled for a long time.

Too long a time.

She suddenly felt disoriented, again felt that strange heaviness in her arms and legs. She stopped, brought the flashlight up, and looked at the map. She could hardly read it and wondered why. She knew it said thirty feet to the opposite wall, she knew that, but for some reason she couldn't get her brain around the idea. Surely she'd crawled thirty feet. It seemed like she'd crawled forever. Well, all right, maybe she'd crawled for a good three minutes. She looked at her watch. Thirteen minutes past two in the afternoon. She looked at the map yet again, tangible, as real as she was, her guide to the underworld, her guide to the River Styx. She laughed, a harsh, ugly sound. Where had that come from? She tried to concentrate. She was in a cave chamber, nothing more, nothing less. She had to be near the opposite wall, had to be. Then she'd take those three long steps to the right and there would be a small passageway — it was a passageway, wasn't it? — and it led . . .

She heard something.

Ruth froze. From the moment she'd finessed the pathetic lock and begun her trek into the cave, there'd been only the noise made by bats and the sound of her own voice, of her own breathing. But now she held her breath. Her mouth was suddenly as dry as the sandy floor beneath her boots. She strained to listen.

There was only silence, as absolute as the blackness.

All right, she'd take silence. Silence was good. She was alone, no monsters hanging around at the edge of her light. She was freaking herself out for no reason, she, who took pride in her control. But why couldn't she see any cave walls?

She knew the rough distance of a foot, not much longer than her own foot, and started counting. When she reached about fourteen feet, she stopped, stretched out her hand as far as she could, and her flashlight and head lamp cut a huge swath farther ahead of her. No wall. All right, so her distances were off. No problem, no reason to panic.

But she'd heard something — for an instant. What was the noise she heard?

She kept counting and crawling forward. At least another twenty feet. Okay, this was ridiculous. Where was the opposite wall?

She rose to her feet, shone her head lamp and flashlight together in a circle around her. She pulled out her compass again and pointed it. She stared at the needle. West. No, that couldn't be right. She wasn't facing west, she was facing east, the direction of the opposite wall. But there was no sign of a wall in any direction. She shook the compass. It still read west. It couldn't be functioning properly.

She stuffed it back in her pocket and pulled her hefty twenty-five-foot measuring tape off her belt. She slowly fed out the metal strip in a line directly in front of her, into the blackness. Finally she reached the end of the tape. There was no wall.

She felt fear, raw and paralyzing, crawl right up her throat. Why was she feeling this way? She was a cop, for heaven's sake, she'd been in much tougher spots than this. She prided herself on her focus, on her ability to keep panic at bay, on her common sense. Nothing could shake her, her mother had always said, and it wasn't necessarily a compliment.

But she was shaken now.

Get back on track, Ruth, get back on track, that's what Savich would say.

All right, bottom line: The chamber was bigger than the damned map said it was. Another effort at misdirection, like the arched doggie door covered with a slab of limestone. So what? No big deal. She'd go back out of the chamber and think things over. How many feet had she come? A good long ways. She turned and fed out the measuring tape back toward the archway. Naturally, she couldn't see the arched opening beyond the dissipated circle of light from her head lamp. She crawled on the tape to make sure she kept in a straight line. When she reached the end of it, she fed out a second twenty-five feet. Nothing. Then another twenty-five feet. She shone her head lamp together with her flashlight all around her. Nothing at all. She looked at her compass. It said she was moving northeast. No, that was absurd. She was heading due west, right back toward the opening.

She looked up again, realized that her flashlight had faded away into a ghostly beam. All right, she'd walked a mile, who cared? And the compass was all screwed up. She didn't need it to make her think she was crazy. She stuck it in her pocket, picked up the tape and fed it out another twenty-five feet, sure she'd see the archway at any moment. She'd come a hundred feet. At any moment, the tape would slither right through the opening back into the corridor. She crawled more slowly. By the time she'd crawled the full twenty-five feet, she was shaking.

Stop it, stop it. She pressed the retract button and heard the hiss of the tape as it smoothly ran back in. She stood there, holding the tape, knowing she was afraid to feed it out again. What was the point?

No, no, that was stupid. She had to. She had no choice. She fed out the tape again, smoothly and quickly. But even as she worked it out to its maximum twenty-five feet, she knew in her gut it wouldn't touch anything. Still, she crawled the distance, then stopped, looked. She was nowhere, surrounded by black; she was being pressed in by black. *No, no, stop it.*

She knew she'd crawled in a straight line, but it was obvious now that she hadn't; it was the only explanation. She'd veered off to the left or right. But still, shouldn't the tape measure hit a wall? *Of course it should, but you're not near a wall, are you? You're not near anything at all.*

20

Ruth began to move in a circle, keeping the measuring tape fully extended. No wall, nothing.

She was losing it, her brain was twisted up, gone squirrelly. At a wave of dizziness and nausea, she sat on the floor, barely breathing now. She felt cold raw fear skitter through her, a deadly fear that made the hair on her arms stir. Her heart pounded, her mouth was dry.

And she thought, *I'm in the middle of a void and there's no way out because I'm trapped in a black hole larger than anything I can imagine.*

That thought, fully blown and as clear as bright headlights in her brain, shook her to the core. Where had it come from? She couldn't seem to draw a deep breath, couldn't seem to focus her brain. This was ridiculous. She had to think her way out of this. There was an answer, there was always an answer. It was time to get her brain working again. All right then. She was in a cave chamber. She'd simply crawled in farther than she'd thought, the ridiculous chamber was much larger than on the map —

She heard the noise again, a soft, sibilant sound that seemed to be all around her, but there were no visual reference points, like a snake slithering through sand, a snake so heavy it made a dragging sound as it pulled itself along. It was a snake that was coming toward her but she couldn't see it, couldn't get out of the way, couldn't hide. Maybe it was one of those South American boas, thick as a tree trunk, heavy and sinuous, probably twenty feet long, dragging itself toward her; it would wrap its huge body around her and squeeze — She jerked the compass out of her pocket and hurled it as far away from her as she could. She heard it thud lightly against the cave floor.

The sound stopped. Once again the silence was absolute.

She had to get a grip. Her imagination was having a hoedown.

Stop it, just stop it, you're in a damned squiggly hole deep in the side of a mountain, nothing more than a maze.

Maybe now she was at the center of the maze — bad things could happen at the center of a maze, things you didn't expect, things that could crush your head, smash it into pulp, things . . . She was lost in the silence, she would die here.

Ruth tried to concentrate on breathing slowly and deeply, drawing in the blessed fresh air, and that strange sweet smell, on cutting off the absurd images that wanted to crash into her brain to terrify her, but she couldn't seem to. She couldn't find anything solid, anything real, to latch on to. The fear danced through her. She yelled into the darkness, "Stop being like your father, stop it!" To her relief, the sound of her own voice calmed her. She managed to clamp down on the panic. All she had to do was follow the straight line of the tape measure. It was metal, it couldn't turn into a circle, for heaven's sake. She'd follow it and end up somewhere, because there had to be a somewhere. Her heart slowed its mad hammering, her breathing became smoother. She leaned down and spread the map on the floor, held the flashlight close.

The only crazy thing here was the damned lying map. After all, the arch wasn't where the map showed it to be. The arch, that was it, she'd gone through the wrong arch. Maybe, just beyond where she'd stopped looking, she would have found the arch the map showed and crawled into the right chamber. Or maybe the map was a trap.

But the fresh air, where was it coming from?

Where was a damned wall?

Ruth felt her head begin to pound, felt saliva fill her dry mouth, felt a scream bursting from deep in her gut. She knew in that instant she was going to die. She stood up, weaved a bit, and listened for the noise. She wanted that noise. She would go toward it; there had to be something alive, and she wanted to find it. It wasn't a huge serpent — no, that was ridiculous. Oh God, her head was going to explode. The pain nearly sent her to her knees. She grabbed her head with her hands. Her fingers sank into her head, into her brain, mixed with the gray matter, and it was sticky and pulsing, and she screamed. The screams didn't stop, just kept spurting out of her, louder and louder, echoing back into her head, through her wet brains oozing between her fingers. It took all her strength to pull her fingers out of her head, but they felt wet and she frantically rubbed them on her jeans, trying to wipe them clean, but they wouldn't come clean. She was crying, screams blocking her throat, then bursting out, so loud, filling the silence. Please, God, she didn't want to die. She started to run, stumbling, falling, but she scrambled up again, didn't care if she slammed into a wall. She wanted to hit a wall.

But there weren't any walls.

CHAPTER 2

Hooter's Motel
Pumis City, Maryland
Early Saturday Morning

Who were these people? *Moses Grace and Claudia* — those were the exact names signed on Pinky's kidnap note, the same as on the motel registry. Why would kidnappers advertise? They must have made up the names, Savich thought. Moses Grace and Claudia, whoever they were, didn't know the cops were there, waiting for them to come out.

Savich was so tired he could feel his thoughts falling out of his brain before he could quite finish with them. Only the bone-freezing bite of the swirling wind straight from the Arctic kept him from falling asleep. His feet were getting numb, and he stamped them hard. They'd been there since eleven o'clock. It was now nearly three on Saturday morning, and they were unable to hunker over their portable stove because Moses Grace and Claudia might see the light. They were hidden in the trees across from Hooter's Motel, out in the boonies of western Maryland.

Why this Moses Grace character had picked Pinky Womack to take was another puzzle. Pinky was a middle-aged part-time comedian at the Bonhomie Club who could spout thirty lame jokes in ten minutes if you let him. He didn't have much money of his own, and his only family was a single brother who had less than he did. He was unusual at the Bonhomie Club because he was one of Ms. Lilly's token whites. He'd been gone a day before his brother, Cluny Womack, found the note duct-taped to Pinky's kitchen counter. *Hey, Savich, we got Pinky. We'll be seeing you.* And it was signed *Moses Grace and Claudia.* The handwriting was a young girl's, all loopy, the *i*'s dotted with little hearts.

It was written specifically to him. Moses Grace and Claudia knew not only who he was but also that he performed at the Bonhomie Club, and they knew Pinky. What did they want?

They were stymied until one of Agent Ruth Warnecki's informants, who called himself Rolly, had called on Ruth's cell phone that evening. Since Ruth was out of town, he was forwarded to Agent Connie Ashley. Rolly was a street person, really quite insane, but he'd given her the real juice more than once. Ruth called him her psycho snitch because his information always came for the price of a pint of warm blood, O negative. Ruth had a deal with a buddy at the local blood bank to give her expired pints of O negative when she needed them.

Rolly told Connie how he'd been testing this new dark brew from Slovenia, or some such weird-ass place, rumored to have a nip of blood mixed in it, but he couldn't taste it, and, he'd added as an afterthought, he was standing on the east side of a 24/7 on Webster Street, N.E., when he overheard this old man and a girl shootin' the breeze not six feet away from him about how they'd scuttled old Pinky right out of his apartment as he was watching reruns of *Miami Vice* on cable.

Rolly said the guy sounded like an ancient old buzzard — Rolly had been too afraid to try to get a look at him — but he sounded like he was on the brink of death, coughing like he was going to puke out his lungs. The old guy called the girl Claudia and cutie and sweetheart. She spoke all jivey, sounded Lolita-young, jailbait, like

27

ripe fruit hanging off a low branch.

Rolly knew to his pointed canines that both of them were worse than badass bad, and they'd talked about hauling Pinky to Hooter's Motel in Maryland, and they'd laughed about Agent Dillon Savich and his Keystone Kops braying around like three-legged jackasses. Rolly didn't know why they'd picked a boob motel in the sticks of western Maryland. Claudia had laughed and said, "Well, Moses Grace, I'm goin' to butter Pinky up and stick him in a big toaster if the cops show their face." Why did she call him by his full name?

When Connie offered him another pint of blood, Rolly remembered they had talked briefly about taking Pinky out of the motel before dawn on Saturday, but they didn't say where to. Mostly they laughed a lot, weird crazy-like laughter. Even Rolly had shuddered as he said that to Connie.

It could be a setup. Maybe. Probably. But the FBI and the local cops were there because they had no other leads. They only knew Savich was at the center of it. On short notice they'd set up this elaborate operation — too elaborate, too compli-cated, Savich thought. And so they waited on a brutally cold winter night for Moses Grace and Claudia to leave their room dragging poor Pinky with them, FBI sharp-shooters at the ready.

Savich rubbed his hands over his arms, then raised his night-vision scope toward room 212, the last room on the second level of Hooter's Motel. Moses Grace's old Chevy van hunkered in the parking lot, so filthy they couldn't make out the license plate.

Raymond Dykes, the owner of the motel, had told Savich the girl signed both their names, with the same loopy handwriting. He couldn't describe her well since she never took off the oversized dark glasses that covered half her face, but she was white, real pale white, and he knew she was pretty, with all that blond hair, wild and blowy, and a blue fake fur over jeans and a top.

They'd come strutting into his lobby during the evening, he didn't remember the exact time. Maybe eight or nine, even ten o'clock, who knew? They were carrying bags of McDonald's takeout under their arms, and they told him they had a sick brother moaning in the back of the van. Mr. Dykes gave them aspirin for the brother. Moses Grace called him Pinky, a funny name, which was why he remembered it. He watched them haul Pinky and the McDonald's bags up the stairs between them to their room. He thought about the french fries and Big Mac and hoped Pinky wouldn't puke in the room.

When Savich, along with Sherlock and agents Dane Carver and Connie Ashley, had met up with Chief Tumi and half a dozen of his deputies, and given them instructions, Moses Grace and Claudia were already ensconced in their room with Pinky. By 12:15 a.m., agents had evacuated the motel's other three occupants.

At one a.m. Savich's directional receiver crackled, and he heard Moses Grace say in an old scratchy voice, "We ain't heard a single lame joke from the little loser, just look at him, sleeping like a baby." Claudia, sounding like a teenager, added casually, "I could wake him up with a little kiss of my knife in his ear, you know, dig it in a little bit, rouse him real fast." The old man laughed, and then he wheezed and coughed, phlegm rumbling low in his chest, and then there was nothing more.

Savich looked down at his receiver, as if willing the unit to come to life, but there was only silence again.

He heard a couple of yawns, a snort or two in the minutes that followed. There were the sounds of sleep, but could he trust them? A lone light still shone at the window, but he saw no movement of any kind.

At three o'clock, Savich heard Moses Grace say clearly in his aged, juicy voice, "You know, Pinky, I'm thinking I'm gonna stick my fingernail through your left cheek, poke it in deep, twirl it around in your sinuses." Nothing from Pinky, which meant, Savich hoped, that he was gagged.

Claudia giggled. "I wish we took your brother, too, Pinky. He's like a cute fat little pig. I could stuff him in the ground and roast him, pretend we're in Hawaii at a luau." She giggled again.

They wouldn't rush the motel room, not with just verbal threats. They had to wait, and Savich knew it was driving everyone nuts.

Agent Dane Carver whispered, "The old man sounds tired and sick. Claudia sounds hyper, talked so fast I could practically see spit flying out of her mouth. She's young, Savich, real young. What's she doing with that old man? What is she to him? They're mad, no doubt in my mind, like Rolly told Connie."

Savich nodded.

"Do you have any ideas yet who they might be, why this is all aimed at you?"

Savich could only shake his head. Mr. Dykes was the only one who'd seen them, and there hadn't been time to work with their forensic artist, not that Savich was holding out much hope since Dykes's descriptions were both too general and, frankly, lame. Surely he could have come up with something distinctive, if he'd tried. It made Savich uneasy, made him feel there was something wrong about Dykes. On the other hand, if everything went as planned, Savich would be seeing Moses Grace and Claudia for himself real soon now.

In the cold dark night, Savich knew that none of this made a lick of sense. There was no way Moses Grace was going to do what Rolly had overheard him say he'd do, namely take off early with Pinky stuffed in the back of that old Chevy van. And take him where? Something was seriously not right. Maybe Rolly had fed Connie what Moses Grace wanted them to hear.

At ten after four, Agent Connie Ashley appeared from behind Savich, dressed in black, as were the rest of her team, her face nearly completely covered with a black stretch hat and wool scarf. "I just got a call from Rolly. He wanted to talk to Ruth, but I told him she was still out of town, and besides, I was the one with the phone, and the blood now. Rolly told me he remembered something else this old guy said, about leaving with Pinky before dawn so they had plenty of time to get to Arlington National Cemetery."

"Rolly remembered this now? In the middle of the night?"

"Rolly said something woke him out of a dead sleep and *wham* — he suddenly remembered."

"How much more blood did he want for the information?"

"Two more pints."

Savich said, "I wonder why Arlington National Cemetery? To do what?"

"Rolly didn't know, said that's all the old man said. It sounds like Rolly is having us on, Dillon. It makes me itchy. I wish Ruth were here; she'd know if he was telling the truth or not." She paused for a moment, looked up at the last room on the second floor. The light still burned. "With those thick shades, it's impossible to tell if anybody's in there."

Dane whispered to her, "At least we can hear whatever they say. I think it's pretty cool that all Ruth's snitches have cell phones."

"She gave them all cell phones, told me

it paid off big time in the Jefferson case to have her snitch get to her right away, not in an hour or twenty-four. She laughed when she said Rolly really liked it, told her it was the new century and you had to move forward with the times. She enrolled him and all her snitches in a family plan. Anything at all out of those two up there?"

Savich said, "Not in the last couple of hours. But there's no way out except through the front door or the back window, which you guys are covering, so they're in there. Even if Rolly was shining you on about their leaving early to go to Arlington National Cemetery, they'll leave soon. We just have to stay ready."

Connie nodded and silently blended back into the trees that surrounded this end of the motel to make a wide circle back to the other agents and the local cops.

"I agree with Connie," Savich whispered. "This isn't right."

Dane was rubbing his gloved hands together. "But what else can we do?"

Not a thing, Savich thought, except wait. Why would Moses Grace want to take Pinky to Arlington National Cemetery? Savich frowned down at his hands, flexed his fingers to get the blood going. Nothing made any sense, and that scared him. He'd meant to ask Connie if Sherlock was okay, but of course she was. He hoped Ruth, at least, was having a better time than he was on her caving trip.

He frowned as he thought again of Raymond Dykes, owner of Hooter's. He'd been very cooperative at first, perhaps too cooperative, Savich thought now, only a bare minimum of complaining and general pissiness. Naturally they had told him he would be recompensed by the taxpayers for any loss of income, but still, he should have protested more. Savich suddenly remembered the small chipped red bowl on the end of the green-painted counter in the motel reception room. It held at least half a dozen chewed-up balls of gum, and wasn't that the oddest thing? Dykes hadn't chewed gum while they spoke to him to set things up. Were those chewed-up gum balls out of Claudia's mouth?

Savich looked at his Mickey Mouse watch. It was exactly three minutes later than when he'd last looked. He shivered as an angry slice of bitter wind cut through the wool scarf wrapped around his neck. He pictured his son, Sean, sleeping with his bear Gus wrapped in his arms, a soft blanket up around his ears, all toasty warm, dreaming about tomato soup with popcorn on top, his new favorite meal.

He looked over at Dane, hunkered down behind a trash can some six feet away, close to the thick black woods, and wondered what he was thinking after so many hours into this freezing stakeout. Dane wasn't moving a muscle. He was being a pro, taking no chances that if Moses or Claudia happened to look out the window they would see a flash of movement and Pinky Womack would be dead. Moses Grace and Claudia had to move soon, before dawn. The FBI sharpshooters' orders were straightforward — kill the old man and the female before they could kill Pinky. Savich knew this was Pinky's best chance to ever giggle out more blonde jokes at Ms. Lilly's Bonhomie Club.

A single, unsilenced gunshot popped, obscenely loud, in the night. Both Savich and Dane had their SIG-Sauers in their hands in an instant. But they heard no voices, no sound of a reaction or an argument from the directional receiver, only silence. Not even a whimper from Pinky. Was that single gunshot a bullet in Pinky's heart?

Savich knew the unexpected shot had instantly chased away the deadening cold and snapped everyone to hyper alert. But it was a surprise. Unless they'd killed Pinky and were now ready to head out.

Savich and Dane heard a low rumble of voices from the other side of the motel. No doubt Sherlock and Connie were having trouble with Police Chief Tumi and his men wanting to rush in, guns blazing. Savich said clearly into his wrist radio, "No one move. Is that clear? We can hear you. Stay put, no one talk."

Police Chief Tumi's voice returned through the speaker band. "You heard the shot, Agent Savich. They must have killed Pinky Womack. Let's get the bastards now!"

Savich said again, "Stay put, Chief. Agent Carver and I have it covered from here. I'll tell you when we move."

Chief Tumi was pissed, Savich could hear it in the manic breathing pouring out of his radio. "Give us a moment, Chief. A man's life is on the line here."

He looked at Dane, whose eyebrows appeared to be dusted with ice chips above the wool scarf tied over his face.

Another gunshot broke the silence, and then the sound of a groan through his directional receiver.

Savich whispered, "That's it, Dane.

We're moving." He added into his radio, "Chief Tumi, stay put. Agent Carver and I are going in."

They ran toward the motel together, their pluming breaths hidden behind black wool scarves tied over their faces, bent over nearly double to the ancient paint-pimpled green stairs that led to the second level of the motel. If they were spotted by either of the kidnappers right now, they were dead. Savich kept his eyes on the thick blinds that hadn't moved since they'd arrived. A trap, he thought, they were probably running right into a damned trap. Now here they were, in the open.

There was no movement from within room 212. Dane, his SIG in one hand and his ancient and beloved Colt .45 in the other, ran crablike under the single draped window.

Savich knew the room plan — fourteen by fourteen with a mattress-sagging double bed against the far wall, a small nightstand beside it, a thirty-year-old black-and-white TV on top of a three-drawer fake-wood dresser just to the right of the front window. There was another window along the back wall, looking onto the skinny back parking lot that touched the edge of the woods where Sherlock, three other FBI agents, and Chief Tumi and his deputies were hidden. There was a five-foot-square bathroom to the left, and since this was an end unit, there was a single high window off it that a three-year-old couldn't squeeze through.

Savich prayed they wouldn't find Pinky lying on the cracked linoleum floor, his head blown apart. What were they doing? There were two of them, they'd killed Pinky, no doubt in Savich's mind about that, and yet there was dead silence. Not a single muted breath, not a whisper, no old man's cackling voice.

He held the radio to his mouth and whispered, "Dane and I are going in. When you hear us break down the door, turn on the floodlights. Chief, use your bullhorn to order them to come out, the more noise the better. We know they're here. They've got no place to go."

Savich hoped the Pumis City police chief would do what he was supposed to and not hotdog it. He nodded to Dane, rose, and bashed his right foot against the doorknob. The door flew inward, slamming against the inside wall.

Dane was behind his left shoulder. He stayed high, Savich went in low.

They quickly canvassed the empty room.

Dane shouted, "Come out of the bathroom. Now!"

"There's no one here," Savich said. "No one is here," he said again more slowly. "I don't understand — how did they get out?" Then he knew, knew even before he saw the small red light on top of the night table, pointed directly toward the front door. He yelled into his wristband, "There's a bomb in here! Get down!" He and Dane were out the open door and leaping over the rickety second-floor railing when they felt a tremendous jolt and the whole building shuddered with the force of it.

CHAPTER 3

Savich and Dane landed ten feet away on the cracked concrete parking lot, rolled, and ran all out. A huge ball of flame erupted behind them, bursting outward from the room and through the roof like a volcano blowing. Suddenly the air was hot, a heavy pounding heat, and a noise like hell itself bursting apart. For a second the entire motel seemed to lift off its concrete foundation.

They heard the top floor crashing into the rooms below as they ran, trying to protect themselves from the exploded debris flying outward with the force of missiles. Huge pieces of wood and jagged chunks of glass speared high into the air away from the gushing flames and rained down around them. Savich saw a television set hurtle down to the parking lot and smash into bits on the concrete in front of them.

The heat was so intense Savich felt it searing the back of his thick wool coat, and wondered if he was smoking. Dane looked all right, so maybe not. He wondered if the Kevlar vests they were wearing had made the difference. When they'd dived into an ice-coated ditch some twenty feet beyond the parking lot, Savich yelled into his wristband, "Sherlock, are you all right?"

One second passed — too long — and then her voice came over, panting, "We're all okay, but it was close, Dillon. The main explosion was in your direction, not ours. We've got lots of flying debris — I'm looking at most of a bed, with the sheets still on it — but we're hunkered down behind an oak tree. Dillon —" He heard the fear in her voice when she swallowed. "You're okay? Dane?"

"Yes, we're fine, I promise. We jumped over the second-floor railing, managed to land soft, and rolled. All the padding we're wearing kept us from breaking anything."

She gave a shaky laugh. "What happened, do you know?"

"When Dane and I went in, the room was empty. I knew in my gut it was a setup even before I saw the device — sitting on the side table, red light blinking right at us — and we got out of there."

"Which means," Sherlock said slowly, "that Moses Grace and Claudia got out of that room without us seeing them, somehow hauling Pinky with them. They would have had a remote detonator, a timer, or some kind of trip device."

Connie said, "They had it all planned out. I'll bet you anything they used Ruth's primo snitch to set us up. She'll rip out his pointed canines."

Savich said, "That sounds right. We need to find Rolly, Connie, really get in his face. Put out an APB for him. We need to nail him as soon as possible."

Connie promised as she jerked out her cell, "I'll track him down as quick as I can. They must have gotten out before we ever got here, Dillon. They could have cut through the bathroom wall, since the building is so cheaply built, or maybe they just slipped out the back window in the dark and Dykes didn't see them. No way they slipped out after we got here."

Savich said, "Have Police Chief Tumi and his men spread out through the woods and see what they can find. They obviously stashed another car or van somewhere. There's an access road that runs behind the woods to the east." But he knew it was too late. They were long gone, enjoying themselves, probably thinking that the cops outside the motel were dead or injured. *That he was dead.* Savich looked over at the old Chevy van. It was flattened under smoking debris. "Sherlock, we need everyone out here looking for Moses Grace and Claudia. See who you can roust. Dane called nine-one-one, so the fire department should be here soon."

"Yes, I'm on it. Connie called nine-one-one, too, and probably every other deputy here. You swear to me you're all right, Dillon?"

He couldn't believe it, but he grinned into his wrist unit. He had been more scared for Sherlock than for himself. She was okay. "When this is over, I'll take you dancing."

He turned to Dane. "At least we're not freezing to death anymore."

Dane grinned, his face black with ashes, showing white teeth. "Wasn't that a kick. A well-thought-out plan, except for that small timing glitch. They wanted you, Savich. I wonder if they saw us jump or if they think you're dead."

Twenty minutes later, Savich stood in front of what was left of Hooter's Motel, watching the fire hoses douse the last of the flames. The smoldering carcass was puffing out black smoke, sending up little spurts of flame, the heat still too intense to get very close. The old building had gone up quickly. He'd had Chief Tumi send two deputies to find the owner, and at that moment he saw Raymond Dykes walking toward him, shoulders slumped, looking white and dazed. Savich wanted to kick the man into the frozen ditch where he and Dane had sheltered after the explosion. He heard Dykes say to himself, "Those bastards. Jesus, Mary, and Joseph, this wasn't supposed to happen. I'm a dead man walking when Marlene finds out."

The final piece slid into place. Moses Grace had double-crossed Raymond Dykes. It was all a setup, to kill him and as many cops as they could manage.

Dane walked up and stood behind Dykes. In a voice as nonthreatening as a nun's at vespers, he said, "I can see how you'd be shocked that they blew up your motel, Mr. Dykes."

"I've lost my livelihood here, my whole life."

"They lied to you and showed you some money and you decided to believe them, right?"

Dykes looked at the smoking bones of his motel. "Only information," he said, "that's all they wanted — information. They gave me five hundred dollars, that fast, all smiles — five hundred dollars for a phone call." He snapped his fingers and moaned, now holding his belly. "Nothing about an explosion. I'm a dead man. You don't know Marlene."

"Your wife?"

"No, my sister."

"So they paid you to tell them if the cops showed up? That was all?"

Dykes nodded, then as if suddenly realizing he was talking to an FBI agent, and saying things he shouldn't, he gulped and shut his mouth.

Dane said, a bit of threat in his voice, "Too late, Mr. Dykes. If you don't tell me everything now, we'll make it real hard for you. You phoned their room when we were getting into position outside?"

Dykes began to rock, his arms collapsed over his chest. He nodded.

"What else? What were you expecting to happen?"

"Nothing. They said they'd go out the back," Dykes said. "I'd let the phone ring three times, that's all I had to do, just warn them. Nothing more. I heard them laughing later about firecrackers. When I asked them what they meant, the old guy, Mr. Grace, he laughed some more, said he'd like to scare the bejesus out of the cops, if he could, said the lot of you weren't worth spit. If he only had one firecracker, that's all he needed, he said. But

46

he didn't have one, did he?" He looked at the burning heap of rubble that was, up until an hour before, his main support, then raised smoke-reddened eyes to Dane's face.

Dane wanted to smack him upside the head for being so greedy, so stupid. "He didn't lie. He didn't have a firecracker, what he had was a bomb."

Dykes whispered, "Why did they lie to me, Agent Carver? Why? I did what they asked, called their room when you showed up, let the phone ring three times. This was crazy, mean and crazy. They ruined me."

Savich said, "No, Mr. Dykes, you did this yourself." He was still trying to get his brain around what this man had done, for five hundred dollars.

"It was the girl with all that beautiful hair; she paid me to let them know if you guys showed up. But I wasn't born yesterday, people are always trying to stiff me because they figure the rooms are cheap, the name of the hotel is a joke, but look, I believed them. And she was so pretty, and she liked me. Her stomach was so white and — I guess I didn't call this one right at all, did I? I'm an idiot."

Dane said, "Yes, I'd say tonight you were."

Dykes, skinny as a nail, wrapped up in a coat two sizes too large for him, thick mousse glistening on the half dozen long gray hairs plastered down over the top of his skull, realized fully now that he was in deep trouble. "No, I — I — I'm not an idiot, and it isn't nice of you to agree with me like that. I didn't mean for anything bad to happen, Agent Carver, you've got to believe me. I didn't have a clue what they were planning. Oh Jesus, Mary, and Joseph, Marlene is going to kill me."

"You took five hundred dollars knowing that our lives were on the line." There was no rage in Dane's calm voice, but it was there, clear as could be, in his eyes, if Dykes had looked up at him. But he kept his eyes on his shoes, and shook his head.

Savich asked him, "They requested room two-twelve?"

Dykes nodded. "Yeah, that's a prime room since it's on the end and there's a window in the bathroom."

Dane said, "You realize now that they either cut through that thin back bathroom wall or they went out the back window and were gone by the time we walked into your office. They meant to kill as many of us as they could. The bomb was powerful enough. Do you have a family, Mr. Dykes,

48

or are you only at the mercy of your sister Marlene?"

"No, Joyce left me two years past for a trucker whose eighteen-wheeler smoked up every state he traveled through. I'll bet he told her he'd show her all the sights and the dip believed him."

Savich said, "Then you can think of Joyce enjoying the Grand Canyon while you're nice and snug in jail."

Dane said, "Maybe Marlene will visit you in your cell."

Dane accepted a pair of handcuffs from one of Police Chief Tumi's deputies, clicked them around Dykes's bony wrists, and handed him over to a deputy, who stared at Dykes like he couldn't believe what he'd done. He hauled him off, none too gently, to a cruiser. Chief Tumi called out, "Read him his rights, Deputy Wiggins. It's a right shame that stupidity isn't a felony." He turned to Savich. "So the two gunshots we heard — they really were gunshots, weren't they?"

"They were well timed, whatever they were," Dane said. "Maybe the arson investigators will find the remains of a tape recorder in the wreckage. Maybe the conversation we heard, as well as the gunshots, was recorded to play at a specific time."

Chief Tumi nodded, looked over at his deputy, who was stuffing Dykes into the backseat. "Roy, don't leave that yahoo alone. I'll be with you in a moment."

Savich said to Dane, "One thing we can bank on — they were long gone out of that room, with Pinky, before we heard the gunshots. They might have been watching."

Connie said, "You can fry Rolly when I reel the little bugger in." She shook her head. "This will sure shake Ruth's belief in her snitches. Do you know the little geek reminded me about his extra pint because he's throwing a goth party?"

Chief Tumi said to Savich, "My deputies are reporting no sign of them yet, but we'll find them. I've called the State Police, given them descriptions, told them about Pinky. We've done what we can."

Savich knew there was a lot more to do but mostly for the forensic team.

Connie said, "That old Chevy van over there — it was bait, the lure to keep us here. I wonder if they really are heading for Arlington National Cemetery."

"Or is it more misdirection?" Sherlock wondered aloud.

But Savich knew they had no choice but to run another complicated operation, and they only had about four hours to get everything nailed down. He couldn't imagine how much manpower they'd need to cover that huge expanse of land, with its thousands of white markers and monuments and rest areas. "I hate to say this, I really do, but I have a feeling they'll actually be there. Find Rolly, Connie."

"Dillon, do you want to call Ruth, bring her back in?"

Savich started to nod, then thought of how excited she'd been about the trip, about going into a cave this time, and just wait until he saw what she brought back. "No, let her have her time off. There are enough of us here. She'll be back on Monday."

They looked up to see an older woman striding toward them, boots to her knees, a head scarf tied tight around her face, a thick wool coat flapping around her calves. She stopped at the cruiser, leaned in, and screamed, "What did you do, Raymond?"

Savich cocked an eyebrow. "Marlene, I presume."

CHAPTER 4

Maestro, Virginia
Friday evening

Sheriff Dixon Noble shrugged into his leather jacket, pulled on his gloves, and left his office at Number One High Street just before five o'clock. It was colder than Brewster's nose against the back of his knee in the dead of winter. Snow was coming, forecasted to dump a good one and a half to two feet. He really didn't want to think about the phone calls it would bring, from downed power lines to car pileups, older citizens with no heat, sick folks without a way to get to the hospital — the list was endless. He'd learned a long time ago to have a solid number of what he called "disaster deputies" he himself had trained to handle the worst that bad luck and nature could throw at them.

It had been a slow February anyway, he thought, except for Valentine's Day. Will Garber had brought his wife, Darlene, a three-pound box of Valentine chocolates as an apology, but Darlene wasn't buying it. She grabbed up a handful of chocolates and rubbed them in his face, at which point he slugged her, slammed out of the house, got drunk at Calhoun's Bar, broke Jamie Calhoun's nose, and ended up in jail.

"Hey, Dix, anything going on this weekend for you?"

Dix paused a moment, nodded to Stupper Fulton, owner of Fulton's Hardware, as his father had been before him, and said, "Not so's you'd notice, Stup. Me and the boys will be sledding down Breaker's Hill along with half the kids in town if this storm coughs up enough snow. If it coughs up too much, I'll be all over town with a shovel, digging people out of ditches."

"Don't think I'd want to sled in a storm," Stup said. "At my age, I'd break bones if I hit a tree."

Dix saw Stup was obviously cold but he wasn't moving. "You got something on your mind?"

"Well, yeah, it's like this, Dix. Rafer wants a job."

"Rafe's fourteen, old enough, but his grades in English and biology stink, and I've already told him there'll be no part-time job until he gets both of them to a B average. I'm trying to help him out myself, helping him build a model of the double helix for biology in the evenings and even reading *Othello* with him for English. The guy's an idiot."

"Rafer? He's not an idiot, Dix, he just needs some good motivation."

"No, Stup, not Rafer, this guy Othello. You know, the guy who murders his wife in Shakespeare's play."

"Oh, well then. Rafer wants a job so much he even promised me he'd work extra fast, do all I asked him to do in half the time it would take anyone else, and then he'd study."

Dix laughed. "That kid's always got a line. What did you tell him?"

"That I'd speak to you about it."

"Tell him you pay by the hour, so if he does the work in half the time, he'll only make half the money. Let's see what he has to say to that."

Stup rubbed his arms and broke into a grin. "That's good, Dix. He's supposed to come see me tomorrow, so I'll try it."

Before he reached his Range Rover, Dix walked along High Street, as he usually did, and spoke to a half dozen more citizens of Maestro, including Melissa Haverstock, the local librarian, who asked him if he'd like to come with her to the First Methodist Church potluck supper on Saturday night. He kindly refused.

When he pulled into his driveway eleven minutes later, it was already getting dark. He was getting real tired of the long winter nights. It was cold, the naked branches shuddering in the frigid air. He sniffed the air. Snow was coming, all right, he could smell it, heavy and moving closer. The house was all lit up, and that meant the boys were home or they had left and didn't bother to turn the lights off. Who knew?

He heard Brewster bark, knew he was waiting beside the front door, his tail wagging so fast it was a blur. Brewster tended to pee when he got excited, so Dix speeded up, hoping to head off an accident.

It was Friday night and he'd have to nag Rob to do the laundry. The three of them had lived through pink shorts and under-shirts until Rob finally got clued in to colors running in the washer. Rafer had worn a bathing suit under his jeans for a good two weeks after the guys in gym class laughed their heads off at him for being a girlie-man.

Brewster, whose truly impressive bark exceeded his body weight by at least fifty pounds, tried to climb up his leg when he came in the house. "Hey, Brewster, you hanging in there, fella? Yeah, I'm home and we're going to have a fine old time. And you didn't even pee on my boots." He picked up the four-pound toy poodle and laughed when he wildly licked his five-o'clock shadow.

"Hey, boys, you here?"

Rafer sauntered in, shoulders slouched, yawning. "Hey, Dad. I'm here."

"Where's your brother?"

Rafer gave a trademark teenage shrug, *Like ask me if I care.* "Dunno, maybe he went over to Mary Lou's house. He said he wanted to get in her pants."

"If he tries to get into Mary Lou's pants her dad will skin off his face."

Rafer grinned at that. "That's good, I'll warn him, but you know, Dad, he gets this glazed look in his eyes when he's with her, like he's a little nuts. Oh, never mind."

"Yeah, you warn him, Rafe." Of course Rob was nuts, he was a teenager. Given those raging hormones, it was a blessing there were fathers like Mary Lou's. Her parents kept a tight rein on her, but he supposed he'd have to speak to Rob again, for the umpteenth time — the teenage boy and sexual responsibility talk, now that gave him a headache.

"Rob did the laundry," Rafer said. Dix

felt a leap of pleasure, but it folded when Rafer snickered.

"What color are our shorts this time?"

"A real pretty robin's-egg blue," Rafer said, "that's what Mrs. Melowski called it."

"Great. Wonderful. Why did you show Mrs. Melowski our blue shorts?"

"You know, she's always coming by, wants to see you, and Rob was holding a pair of his shorts and she looked at them and started laughing. She showed Rob what he did wrong."

"So have I, countless times."

"Well, yeah, she said they'd need another couple of washings with lots of bleach and the blue would come out. She left a lemon cake for our dessert tonight. Hey, Dad, what's for dinner?"

"Not pizza tonight, Rafe, hang that up. I made some stew Tuesday and froze it. I'll make biscuits to go with it."

"I'll see if we've got enough catsup."

"We do. I checked before I left this morning. Is there any of the lemon cake left?"

"I did eat a couple of pieces," Rafer said.

Dix could easily picture the gutted cake. He pulled his cell out of his jacket pocket and called the Claussons' house. Sure enough, Rob was there, playing Foosball with Mary Lou and her parents, who were

killers at the game. They had the fastest re-
flexes Dix had ever seen. Rob must have
been getting beat really bad because he
didn't sound at all sorry to come home to
dinner. "Hey, Dad, can Mary Lou have
dinner with us?"

Before Dix could answer, he heard Mr.
Clausson say in the background, "No, Rob,
Mary Lou's aunt is visiting us tonight."

"Come on home, Rob."

"Yeah, Rob," came Rafe's voice loud in
the background, "you don't want Mr.
Clausson to skin off your face."

It started snowing about nine-thirty that
night. Dix and the boys were watching TV,
he and Rafe having buried Othello and
Desdemona an hour before. Rafe, rightfully
in Dix's opinion, wanted to know why Iago
didn't get his guts ripped out, to which Dix
replied, "Hey, Shakespeare gave us a body
count of five. That's enough, isn't it?"

Rafe had finally said, "Yeah, I guess
enough of the cast did croak."

Rafe's model double helix was finished
and sat once more on top of his desk next
to his Titans football signed by Steve
McNair. They usually watched TV on
Friday nights. It was a treat for the boys
since he had a no-TV rule during the week.

Rafe fell asleep in the middle of *Law &
Order,* his head on Dix's leg. Rob, sixteen,
long and skinny, was slouched in his favorite chair, snoring lightly. His hair was as
black as Dix's but his eyes were his mom's
blue-green. *I'm the old man here in the
room,* Dix thought, *and I'm the only one
awake.* It made him wonder what the boys
had been up to today to wear themselves
out.

He got the boys off to bed at ten o'clock
and took Brewster out for his night run.
Since the snow had only just begun to fall,
he didn't have to worry about Brewster
sinking in over his head and getting himself in trouble, a very real concern in the
winter. He let him down on the front
porch and watched him leap joyfully off
the top step and race into the yard, barking
and yapping. He twirled back around,
bouncing like there were springs on his
back legs, trying to catch the snowflakes
with his front paws, his fluffy little tail wagging frantically.

Dix walked down the sidewalk and
raised his face to the sky. The snow was so
lacy and soft it dissolved the instant it
touched his face. He stood silently, smiling
at Brewster, letting the cold night air fill
his lungs. He realized he felt good, felt

more whole again than not, and that was surely a step in the right direction.

Brewster yelped three times at him and took off toward the woods.

"Brewster! Come back here, you know the woods are off-limits!"

But Brewster had the scent of some animal and wasn't about to give up the chase. Dix headed after him, pulling on the gloves he'd pushed into the pockets of his leather jacket as he walked. There were lots of feral animals in the woods, ninety-nine percent of them bigger and more vicious than Brewster.

Dix called the dog again and again, but all he heard were Brewster's yelps, growing more distant. He kept talking to Brewster, following the sound of his barks. He'd found something, perhaps an injured animal.

The night sky hung heavy, fat, bloated clouds waiting for some internal alarm to dump their snow, and no more of this penny-ante stuff. "Brewster!"

More yelps cut the night silence, not so distant now. Had Brewster trapped an opossum?

The snow was coming down a bit heavier now, but the trees were thick, shielding them. "Brewster!"

Brewster was barking madly at a dark

hump on the forest floor, something that wasn't moving, something that looked human.

Dix grabbed up his dog, stuffed him inside his jacket, and zipped it up. "Calm down, Brewster, and don't pee on my shirt." He looked down at a person lying in front of him, unconscious or dead.

Dix fell to his knees and turned the person over. It was a woman, her face covered with blood. He pulled off his gloves, scooped up some snow, and lightly rubbed it over her face. The blood came off easily. He saw a gash on the side of her head, bleeding sluggishly. He touched his fingertips to the pulse at her throat. It was slow and steady. Good. He leaned into her face. "Hey, can you hear me? You need to wake up."

Her lashes fluttered.

"That's it. Open your eyes, you can do it."

She didn't open her eyes but she moaned low in her throat. Dix methodically felt her arms, her legs, her torso, and nothing felt broken. Not that that meant anything. He pulled his gloves back on. Brewster poked his head out the top of Dix's jacket. Dix carefully lifted the woman in his arms. She was tall, lanky and heavy enough. He was afraid to carry her over his shoulder because she might be injured internally, so he cradled her in his arms.

As he walked out of the woods, the clouds let loose and the wind came to vicious life and blew blinding snow in his face. By the time Dix got back to his house, it was snowing so hard he could barely make out his porch light.

He stomped the snow off his boots and got himself, Brewster, and the woman quietly into the house.

"Okay, Brewster, you hit the floor and I'll get her onto the sofa." She wasn't particularly wet so he spread two afghans over her, unlaced her boots and pulled them off her feet. She was wearing thick wool socks, which were still nice and dry.

He pulled his cell out of his pocket and dialed nine-one-one. His dispatcher, Amalee Witten, answered. "Yo, Sheriff, what's up?"

"I found an injured woman in the woods by my house. I need the paramedics as fast as you can get them out here, Amalee."

Amalee was fifty-two years old and weighed 211 pounds, but when it was urgent, she could move out faster than Rob when it was his turn to clean the bathroom. "Hold tight, Sheriff."

"Hey, Dad, is she going to be all right?"

"I don't know, Rob, I can't get her to wake up. Go make some hot tea. Let's see if we can get it down her."

Not five minutes later, his son came into the living room cradling a cup of tea between his palms. "It isn't too hot so she won't scald her mouth."

"Good." Dix lifted her, pressed the edge of the cup to her bottom lip. "Come on, smell that Lipton's, best tea in captivity. Rob made it just right so you can open up and take a big gulp. It'll warm your insides."

To his surprise, her mouth opened and she sipped it. She opened her eyes, looked at him, and drank more tea.

"Are you in pain?"

She slowly shook her head. Her voice came out thin as thread. "Only my head." She tried to raise her hand, but Dix held it down.

"You've got a cut on the left side, above your temple. I'm going to leave it for the paramedics to do it right."

Brewster jumped onto the sofa and hunkered down next to her. "This is Brewster and he found you in the woods just before the snow started coming down hard."

"Brewster," she said, reaching out her hand to his little face, "thank you."

63

"I'm Dixon Noble, sheriff of Maestro. The guy who made the tea is my son Rob. Can you tell me your name?"

"I'm . . ." She nuzzled her chin against Brewster, who was licking her. "This is very strange," she said after a moment, turning back to look up at him. "Do you know, I really don't have a clue."

Dix stood slowly. She looked suddenly scared and the last thing he wanted was for her to freak out. He said calmly, "Whatever else happened to you, you got a big whack against your head. Maybe that could account for you not remembering. The doctor can tell us what's going on. I'm sure it's temporary, so try not to worry, okay? Let me check the pockets of your jacket for ID." He heard the ambulance sirens in the distance. "You don't seem to have anything at all in your pockets. Did you have a purse or a wallet with you, do you remember?"

He saw her eyes were dilated and that concerned him. "Don't worry about it. Maybe you've got something in your jeans pockets. They can check at the hospital. I don't want to move you around. Tomorrow I'll check the woods for a purse."

"This is nuts," she said, and he saw her wiggling beneath the afghans. She was obviously searching her jeans herself. Then she lifted her hand and checked the jacket herself. "I can't find anything. That doesn't make any sense. Where's my cell phone? Did I have a purse? No, that's not likely. I never take a purse."

He waited patiently.

"Never."

"But you know you had a cell phone?"

"Yes. Oh dear, I think so." She started humming.

Rob said, "Why are you humming?"

"I don't like to curse so I hum when I'm unhappy about something."

"That's cool," said Rafe, who was standing behind the sofa, looking down at her.

"That's my other son, Rafer. Okay, things are coming back. Don't push it. There's always an explanation for everything."

"What you just said — that sounded really familiar, like I say that to people."

The paramedics followed Rob into the living room. Ten minutes later, Dix and the woman were in the ambulance headed to Louden County Community Hospital, some twelve miles away. It was snowing really hard, so it took a good thirty minutes to get there. She was pale and her eyes looked glassy. He held her hand. She wasn't wearing any rings, only a no-nonsense multifunctional black watch. The emergency room wasn't a zoo yet, but everyone was preparing for the worst.

Dix sat himself in the nearly empty waiting room after they had wheeled her away, and prepared to read his way through a *National Geographic* magazine dated 1997.

He heard her cry out. He rose automatically, took a step toward the curtained-off cubicle.

"Sheriff, we need to do some paperwork here."

He did his best, but since he had no clue who she was or what her medical history was, there were mostly blank lines left on the forms after her name, Jane Doe.

Dix pulled out his cell and called Emory Cox for a status report. "This is weird, Sheriff, we've only had one call. It was a wrong number if you can believe that."

"No, I don't believe that. It was probably an abuse call, and chances are the wife will show up tomorrow with a broken nose and bruises everywhere. We'll see."

"So far everyone seems to be staying in tonight, not being stupid."

"Let's hope our luck holds up, Emory. I'm at the hospital. I do have something of a situation here." He detailed to Emory how he'd found the woman, knowing of course that Amalee had probably already told half the people in town all about it. "I want you to send two of our disaster deputies — Claus and B.B. Claus can drive his four-wheeler out to my property. They need to find the woman's car. . . . No, I don't know what kind of car she was driving because, as I said, she can't seem to remember anything right now. I want you to check around the county for any reports of missing young women. If she can't tell us who she is by tomorrow morning, we'll run her fingerprints through IAFIS; maybe we'll get lucky. Tomorrow, if necessary, you can take a photo of her, and we'll send it out. Check all the local B-and-Bs, hotels, and motels within a fifteen-mile radius of Maestro. All I can say is that she's in her mid-thirties, dark hair, light complexion, really green eyes. She's on the lean side, a runner maybe. Her arms and legs felt strong when I checked her for broken bones. She's tall, maybe five-foot-nine, -ten. Of course, the car would tell us everything we need to know. Her ID's probably in there, or we can identify her from the plates, so emphasize to Claus and B.B. that the car's the priority."

Thirty minutes later, Dr. Mason Crocker

came over to him in the waiting room. "She seems to be all right, Sheriff, at least physically. The CT scan was clear. There is no evidence of any anatomic injury other than that head wound. She may have suffered a concussion, but I think she's also got some drugs on board. Her eyes don't seem right to me; they're dilated and glassy. She's restless and her heart rate is up. I can't quite place it — it's not one of the usual drug effects we see. We've sent off a toxicology screen on her."

"Do you think she was drugged? Poisoned?"

Dr. Crocker shrugged. "I wouldn't discount it. She seems to be coming out of it. We'll need to keep her for a while, though."

"Yeah, check it out, that's good."

"You said you found her in your woods."

"Yeah. Brewster did, actually."

"No ID?"

"There could be a purse out there somewhere but she told me she never took a purse out — to do what, she didn't remember. I'll send my boys out to look tomorrow."

Dr. Crocker said, "She says she can't remember who she is, how she was hurt, or how she ended up unconscious in your woods."

"Do you think she's faking it?"

Dr. Crocker shook his head. "No, I don't. It could be what we call hysterical amnesia. Her memory loss relates to particular memories, and is sharply bounded. For example, she can tell me who the president is, she can talk about the pitiable state of the Redskins. Sometimes when people are badly hurt or terrorized, they need to forget for a while, to protect themselves. Hey, I hope she's not an escapee from Dobb's Women's Prison."

"I hope not, too. Tell you what, I'll give them a call, have them do a bed check. That was a joke, Doc."

"Maybe she was out camping, something like that."

"In this weather?"

"Hey, maybe she's from California. You know, Sheriff, if someone struck her on the head to rob her, they could have taken her ID."

Eyebrow up, Dix said, "Yeah, that occurred to me."

"So what are we going to do with her? If she does okay tonight, she can be out of here, medically, in the morning."

"I'll have to think about that. Hope you stay bored tonight, Doc."

CHAPTER 5

"Thanks for the lift, Penny," Dix said to his thirty-year-old deputy, who knew how to box and was married to the local funeral home director, as she pulled into his driveway. "Hope you got a lot of hot coffee."

"Tommy wouldn't let me out the front door unless I filled his super-giant-size thermos to the brim with the sludge he calls coffee. I'll be fine, Sheriff."

Brewster and both boys were waiting for him and wanted every gory detail. It wasn't until well after one in the morning that Dix, Brewster curled up against his back, finally got himself to sleep.

The snow was back to a light powder the following morning, with about a new foot on the ground. Dix made breakfast while the boys shoveled the driveway and looked in the woods where he had found the woman. Brewster supervised, which meant he ran around them in circles until he was exhausted. Rob brought him back into the house and left him in the kitchen, next to the warm stove. "He nearly bought it in a deep patch of snow, Dad. I think he's had enough. We didn't find the lady's wallet, or a purse, or anything. There's too much snow."

"I appreciate your looking. Come and sit down now, breakfast is ready."

If there was something Dix considered himself good at, it was breakfast. The house smelled of fried bacon, eggs over easy, brown sugar on oatmeal, and blueberry muffins.

By ten o'clock, the boys were off with their sleds slung over their shoulders to Breaker's Hill, where most of Maestro's teenagers would be congregated along with some of the hardier parents. Dix finished shoveling the driveway and drove to the hospital. On the way, he checked in with his deputies, who, thankfully, had nothing dire to report, no six-car pileups or downed electrical wires.

Nor had anyone found an abandoned car. Nor were there any local missing persons reported. And not a single woman of her description had registered at any B-and-B or motel in the immediate area. Dix supposed he'd expected her to be registered at Bud Bailey's Bed & Breakfast, where most people stayed if they visited Maestro. Someone had obviously hit her. Had they left her unconscious in his woods, or had she managed somehow to get away from them, and then collapsed in the woods? All he needed was her car. Could the people who whacked her over the head have driven it off? Hidden it somewhere?

Maybe she'd come here for a specific reason, a reason someone didn't like. Or maybe that someone had moved her a good distance away from where she'd been brought down.

The main roads were already plowed and the light snow falling wasn't going to be much of a problem. The forecast was for more snow, though, becoming heavy in the late afternoon.

Emory called to check in.

Dix said, "Someone's got to have seen her, sold her gas, supplies, something."

"Maybe she's here with someone."

"If that were the case, they surely would have called us when she went missing."

Emory sighed. "Maybe her old man is the one who tried to off her."

"She wasn't wearing a wedding ring," Dix said.

"I don't either, Sheriff, and I'm so married Marty can finish my sentences."

"It's odd, but she didn't seem married to me."

Emory wondered what that meant, but he let it go.

Dix found Dr. Crocker, more rumpled than he'd been the night before, a stethoscope nearly falling off his neck, at the nurses' station on the second floor.

"You ever go home last night, Doc?"

"Nah, I haven't left the hospital for six weeks now. Just kidding, Sheriff. Now, our girl is trying really hard not to show it, but she's scared — understandable since she had a pretty rough night of it and still can't remember who she is or how she came to be in your woods. The head wound's okay. Since it's the weekend, most of the toxicology screen won't be ready until sometime Monday."

Dix asked Dr. Crocker a few more questions, then he found room 214. It was a double room, but she was the only occupant. She was sitting up, staring at muted cartoons on the TV. There was a white strip of keri tape over her temple, nothing more. She wasn't moving.

When she saw him, she said, "Do you use meters?"

"What? Meters? Well, no, I think in feet and inches, like most Americans. Why meters?"

"It popped into my head a little while

ago. I realized I know all about meters and centimeters, how to convert back and forth. I don't sound like I'm from Europe, do I?"

"Nope, you're American to the bone. I'd say Washington, Maryland, around there."

"Maybe I'm a math teacher and I teach the metric system."

"Could be. Sounds to me like you're nearly ready to remember everything, but don't push it, okay? Just relax. How's your head feel?"

"Hurts, but I can handle it."

Odd, but it seemed to him she could handle about anything. He pulled a small black plastic kit from his jacket pocket, opened it, and spread out the paraphernalia on the bedside table.

She watched him a moment, said, "You're going to take my fingerprints?"

"Yes, that's right. This is my portable kit since you're not up to going to the station to scan them in. It could be you had a job that required fingerprints."

"Could I be in NCIC?" The instant the words were out of her mouth, she froze.

"NCIC — you know what that means?"

He could tell she was trying really hard, and he raised his hand. "No, let it go. I'm sending your fingerprints electronically to

IAFIS. That's the Integrated Automated Fingerprint Identification System. If you're one of the forty million folks in the civil fingerprint file, we should hear back within twenty-four hours."

"I forgot your name."

"Dixon Noble. I'm the sheriff of Maestro."

"Maestro. What a strange name, charming, but strange."

"I prefer it to Tulip, Montana."

She smiled, but it wasn't a simple smile, there were remnants of pain in her eyes. He knew that look when he saw it, knew it to his bones. And he could practically feel her controlling her sense of panic. "You want some aspirin?"

"No, it isn't bad. I heard the nurses talking about me earlier. They wondered what the doctors were going to do with me."

"Not a problem," Dix said. "I'm taking you home with me."

The hospital insisted she ride in a wheelchair to the front door. Once she was seatbelted inside the Range Rover, she turned to watch the sheriff as he pulled out of the parking lot and onto the highway. Then she stared out the window to watch the bright morning sun glisten off the snow. "It's beautiful, and it feels familiar down to my bones, so I guess I'm not from Arizona."

"Now that's interesting. Some deep part of you feels at one with this atrocious weather."

"Kind of sad, actually."

"My boys looked in the woods where I found you, but there was nothing there. More snow's forecasted for this afternoon, but it's beginning to look like the weather guys are wrong again. Emory's coming to the house later to take some photos. We'll show them all over the area. Someone had to have seen you, someone will remember you."

"I don't live around here, I'm pretty sure of that, so that means I had to have a room somewhere. I like your Range Rover," she said, surprising him. "They're really good off-road, but I think they make me nauseous when I'm a passenger and there are too many bumps."

"What do you own?"

"A BMW — oh, nice how you did that — but I'm not sure, sorry. BMW popped into my mind, so maybe. I sure hope you find my car, whatever it is, soon. You can find out who I am in about two seconds flat."

"How?"

"From the VIN, not to mention the license plate."

"Yes, that's right," he said. "I've got people out looking for your car. If the person who struck you tried to hide it, he's in luck. With all this snow it could be well camouflaged."

She cleared her throat. "Seems like someone tried to obliterate me, and sort of has."

"You'll be okay," he said matter-of-factly. "But I am wondering how you got to my house."

"Maybe the woods were just handy?" She didn't sound upset, and that was surely strange for a civilian. She sounded curious, not at all scared, like she had a problem to solve.

"Or maybe you managed to walk into my woods."

"Who knows?" She laughed, actually laughed. "Here I am as useless as a lifeguard who can't swim. What could I have been doing here to make someone go to all this trouble?"

"I can see your eyes nearly crossing. Stop straining. Relax. Stuff is coming back really fast now. It won't be much longer. Do you think your Beemer is one of those SUVs?"

"It's not an SUV, it's an SAV. It's not a pedestrian utility vehicle, it's an activity vehicle." She started laughing again. "Oh goodness, can you believe that?"

"Dr. Crocker told me, probably told you, too, that bits and pieces of things may float back to you, but some big chunks might stay out of sight for a while. Like I said, stop straining. When we find your wuss SAV, maybe you'll recognize it."

"Your wife must be a very tolerant woman."

"She was."

She didn't say anything to that. Her head was pounding again. To her surprise, before she could say anything, the sheriff handed her a thermos. "You're hurting. Take one of those pain pills they gave you."

She nodded, took two, drank them down with coffee, and leaned her head back against the seat.

She heard the loud barking as soon as she opened the car door.

"That's Brewster. He's quite a watchdog. Be careful he doesn't pee on you."

Brewster didn't pee on her, but within three minutes of her lying on the sofa, he was cuddled next to her, licking her chin. The sheriff pulled two handmade afghans over her. She wanted to sleep on this wonderful soft sofa for at least a day.

She awoke when she heard the sheriff saying, "Keep it down, boys. We have a guest."

"The lady you found last night, Dad?"

"Yeah, she's going to be okay, but there are things she can't remember yet, including who she is."

Dix saw she was awake and looking toward the doorway at the three of them. He introduced the boys to her again.

"I made you the hot tea," Rob said.

"Yes, I remember. Thank you."

Dix said, "I don't know what to call you."

"Hmm. How about Madonna?"

Rob said, "You don't have a space between your front teeth."

She brushed her tongue over her teeth. "Do you think you could pretend I did? Pretend I'm a blonde?"

Rob said, "Madonna changes her hair color all the time, that's no problem."

Rafer said, "Mom liked Madonna, said she was so loaded with imagination she'd just keep reinventing herself until she was eighty, maybe end up buying the State of Florida."

Unlike his brother, Rafe had light brown hair, and his father's dark eyes, an odd combination that would slay girls when he was a bit older. Both he and his brother were skinny as rails right now, but when they reached their full size, they'd be big men, like their father. And their mother?

"Okay," Dix said, "Madonna it is. Rob, you want to make Madonna some more hot tea, maybe a couple slices of toast with butter and jam?"

Rob looked at the woman lying on the couch. She looked really beat. "Sure, Dad."

There was a knock on the front door.

Rafer took off to answer it, Brewster barking madly at his heels.

It was Emory Cox, Dix's chief deputy. "I'm here to get the photo, Sheriff. Hi, ma'am."

Dix introduced him. "Call her Madonna for the moment, Emory." Emory took six Polaroid shots of Madonna, then Dix took him out of the living room, out of hearing.

Rafe stood in the doorway, watching her. He opened his mouth, closed it. "Ah, do you know anything about the double helix, Madonna?"

"Sure, Rafe, come here and we'll talk about it."

"Let me show you my model!"

CHAPTER 6

Arlington National Cemetery
Arlington, Virginia
Saturday morning

The light snowfall had stopped two hours before, at seven a.m. The sky was iron gray, the clouds thick and bulging with snow that was forecasted to begin again at about noon.

Agent Ron Latham was standing two feet from Agent Connie Ashley, who was perusing a map of Arlington National Cemetery. "Why would Moses Grace come here? I think old Rolly has got some expensive habits he needs to feed —"

"No," Connie said automatically. "Not feed — drink."

"The guy's an alcoholic on top of everything else?" Agent Jim Farland was pretending to speak into a cell phone.

"Well, I don't think so, no. I'll tell you later about his drinking habits."

Agent Jim Farland said into his cell phone, his voice loud enough to be heard ten feet away, "Hello, Mom. Yeah, we're going to go over to section twenty-seven, where all the former slaves are buried. . . . Yeah, that's where all the pre–Civil War dead were buried again after 1900. Listen, Mom, I've gotta go, a funeral is expected in twenty minutes. See you soon."

Ron said to Connie, "They put this op together so fast I'm not sure I'm clear on all the details. We're supposed to hang out here acting like tourists until Moses Grace and Claudia show up, for whatever reason we don't know, Pinky Womack in tow?"

"Yeah, that's what the psycho snitch told me. Ruth said Rolly's never let her down. He's reliable and we've got to go with that, until we know for sure. The only reason I've got her cell phone is because I'm a woman and Rolly doesn't relate well to guys. Anyway, time for us to get ourselves moving."

Ron said with a smirk, "I like that pillow tied around your belly, Ashley. Hey, how many kids you got?"

Connie waved both of them off and paused to rub her back. It wasn't just for show. She'd been walking around the cemetery for almost two hours, stopping to listen in at a funeral, speaking briefly to other agents, all of them dressed as tourists strolling through the huge cemetery. She'd read in her brochure the astonishing fact that more than two hundred and sixty thousand people were buried here. She wondered if she'd walk by every gravestone and monument and memorial before she was through. She thought of Ruth, hoped she was having a better weekend than she was. She would have liked to be in the wilds of Virginia with her rather than here, waiting for a crazy old lunatic to appear. Many of the agents and all of the snipers were from the Washington, D.C., field office, the snipers posted wherever they could find cover in the cemetery, in position since eight o'clock that morning.

Savich stood by the Memorial Gate in section 30 speaking on his cell to Deputy Assistant Director Jimmy Maitland, his boss. "There's no sign of them yet." Just as there hadn't been an hour before when he'd reported in, but he didn't say that. "There aren't that many real tourists around, understandable given the weather, and that's good since we can't do anything about it in any case. We're keeping an eye on them, while we all try not to do anything Moses Grace could spot easily."

Maitland sighed. "One of my boys is playing basketball today, his first time starting as Maryland's forward, and here I am sitting in a damned van waiting for a psychopath crazy enough to detonate a bomb on top of my agents in a frigging motel to show up here in the nation's biggest cemetery. I doubt Pinky's still alive. You agree, Savich?"

"You're right, not likely. Anyone who would pull that stunt at Hooter's Motel wouldn't bother to keep Pinky alive. I didn't tell that to Ms. Lilly, though. She's still hopeful. Pinky's such a piece of work, no harm in him, not really, just a big mouth, always saying the wrong thing to the wrong person. I've got an incoming call I should get. I'll call you back in an hour with a status report. Can you get your basketball game on the radio?"

"I'm counting on it, Savich."

Savich raised his face to the steel-gray sky, breathed that fresh wild air deep into his lungs. He could feel Moses Grace was close. He punched up the incoming call. "Savich here."

"Hello, boy. This here's your nemesis. Ain't that a grand word? Claudia read it to me out of a book, said that's what I am to you."

Savich stilled, his mind working furiously. He knew, he simply knew. "Who is this?"

84

"Why, this is the poor old man you're trying to hunt down and kill, and bury real deep, Agent Savich. I saw you on TV after our fun at Hooter's Motel — on a local channel, real early this morning. I'll bet you didn't get much sleep, did you? I'll tell you, I was impressed, no question about that. But you see, you've got all these rules and you stick to them like a stupid lemming. That'll do you in when it's crunch time between you and me. But hey, you sure talk good, boy, all cool and calm for someone who almost got himself blowed up. Too bad you didn't break your damned neck when you jumped off that balcony at old Ray's motel. Would have been easier. Claudia, that sweet little girl of mine, said you was an athlete, made her want to jump your bones. Flat-out embarrassed me the things she said she wanted to do to you. As for Pinky, I wouldn't say he's in such good shape now."

"What about Pinky?"

"Let's say the little schmuck is where he deserves to be."

Savich felt disgust, his belly slick with nausea. He wanted to squeeze the life out of this man, to shut up that illiterate drawl. "And where is that?"

Moses Grace's scratchy laugh made

Savich's flesh crawl. Could the evil old monster be watching him now?

"Well, it's like this, Agent Savich. Pinky is already underground. Why don't you find Private Jeremy Willamette's gravestone; young fellow died in Korea, aged eighteen. Exactly Claudia's age. She's the one who picked the spot where Pinky would reside until you guys hauled his carcass off to cut it up."

"How did you get my cell phone number?"

"From Pinky, of course. Turns out Ms. Lilly gave it to him, and guess what?"

Savich remained silent. He was thinking of Pinky, how he'd probably been dead since they hauled him out of Hooter's Motel. They buried him with a soldier?

"You want me to spell it out for you, boy? Well, here it is. No one beats me, particularly a loser cop like you." He laughed and Savich could hear the spittle hurtling out of his mouth. "You know Rolly, that little pervert who snitches to your agent Warnecki? I think you'll have a much harder time finding him.

"I hear that little redheaded agent who's standing over there is your wife. I told Claudia those cops had more guts than brains but she wasn't listening. Too excited about all this and who can blame her? Looks like you've gone to a lot of trouble to catch me, and I really appreciate that. It makes me feel important. How many of you are there? Twenty? Forty? All for me and Claudia."

The words were out of Savich's mouth before he could begin to censor them. "You're right about one thing, you crazy old man. I'm going to kill you and bury you real deep."

The old man guffawed and cleared his throat. Savich could hear a sticky liquid sound. Was he sick?

"Nah, you wouldn't shoot me for revenge, that's one of your dumb-ass rules. You'd take me in all polite and proper. You'd even help me get a nice ACLU-type lawyer who'd claim I heard the voice of my long-dead mother who locked me in a cellar until I was sixteen, and so I'm not responsible for anything. You wouldn't want to be cruel to a mentally disturbed person, would you? I might even end up in a nice hospital with a bunch of cute little nurses swinging their asses in my face. My, I do believe this sounds familiar, almost like *day-ja vou.*

"Thing is, boy, you don't have the guts to kill me, yet. Hey, would you look at your wife, so serious and alert, all that lovely red hair, thick and real soft, I bet. Claudia doesn't like her at all. Maybe I could fit her right in with Pinky once Claudia was done with her."

Then there was silence. Moses Grace had punched off.

Savich called Sherlock, who was checking the names on the headstones against a list she was carrying, a pencil in her hand. Moses was looking at her. She'd walked away from the Rough Riders Memorial in section 36, stopped to study the headstones around her. Not three yards from her was a real tourist all bundled up in the cold morning, blowing on her hands as she stood in front of a headstone and stamped her feet.

Savich was so scared he wanted to puke. Sherlock was a perfect target for anyone with a clean shot and a scoped rifle. He didn't doubt for a second that Moses had both. He didn't doubt that Moses could shoot. How far away were they and where? Savich gave a ferocious smile as her cell phone rang. "Agent Sherlock."

"Sherlock, down! Find cover right now!" But from where would a shot come?

In under a minute Sherlock was surrounded by agents in Kevlar body armor. A few minutes later, Savich, with Sherlock in lockstep beside him, walked quickly toward section 27, where the cemetery records showed that Private Jeremy Willamette was interred. To Savich's surprise she hadn't questioned him when he first told her to get down. And now she accepted the impenetrable shield of men and women surrounding her, all of them with guns drawn and held at their sides. When they'd quickly assembled, Savich looked at each of them and said, "Moses Grace just called me. He's here and he's crazy and I'd bet the farm he's got a scoped rifle. We've all got to be careful. And he talked to me about Sherlock, threatened her."

Savich didn't think he'd ever been more hyper-alert in his life. He was aware of every sound, every footstep, everyone around him. And Sherlock walked beside him, her eyes continuously scanning, assessing. At least there would be no more playing tourist in the cold; they could all move and focus on finding the monstrous old man and Claudia.

Savich said to his wife, "Mr. Maitland sent the ME over along with a forensic team and another dozen agents to canvass the whole area again. He knows Moses Grace is here and he's as worried as we are."

Sherlock nodded. "If they carted Pinky

89

in here early this morning, they didn't have much time. Maybe they left something," she said as her eyes searched the horizon, just as his were.

The agents ringed the grave of Private Jeremy Willamette. The headstone was identical to thousands of others. There were big carved letters that read:

JEREMY ARTHUR WILLAMETTE
BELOVED SON

PRIVATE U.S. ARMY
KOREA

May 18, 1935
September 10, 1953

No one said a word, but each felt the death of the young man so many years before, each felt he was one of their own.

Agent Connie Ashley, who'd removed the pillow from around her middle, said, "It looks real fresh."

Savich looked down at the loose snow-dusted black dirt with an obscene bouquet of wilted red roses lying squarely on top and felt a moment of sadness. He'd wanted to save Pinky, but that wasn't going to happen now. He picked up the roses, tied with a big gaudy gold bow. Another couple of degrees and the roses would freeze. He handed them to Agent Don Grassi. "Find out where Moses Grace bought these roses. He could have picked them up from another grave, but check with the florists nearby."

Agent Dane Carver said, never looking away from the loose black dirt, "Do you think Moses Grace and Claudia can still see us?"

Savich nodded slowly, scanning every tree in the area. "There are too many places to hide around here. It's two hundred acres — full of trees, memorials, buildings, monuments." He said to Agent Ollie Hamish, his second in command, "Ollie, call Mr. Maitland, tell him I'd like to saturate this place. Tell him to ring Fort Meyer, get soldiers here to help."

"Do you think Pinky's under there?" Dane had asked the obvious, brought it out in the open. Every agent standing there knew Pinky Womack was under that black dirt, but no one wanted to be slapped in the head with the gruesome reality they knew was waiting for them. No one answered. They all stood silently.

Savich realized they were waiting for him to direct them, but the thing was, he couldn't get his mind off that old monster threatening

Sherlock. He met her eyes over the grave.

"I'm so very, very sorry about this, Dillon. Poor Pinky." Sherlock suddenly leaned down. "Would you look at this? It's a ball of chewed-up gum."

Savich remembered the small red bowl filled with chewed-up balls of gum on the counter at Hooter's Motel — all that gum hadn't been there because Raymond Dykes liked to keep his jaw moving. Moses Grace had deliberately left it there, just as he'd left the gum here.

Savich said, "He left it for us, to taunt us, some private joke perhaps. It probably won't matter, but let's do the works on it, run it for DNA."

Savich watched Dane slip the gum into a Ziploc bag. Two of his agents led a crew of cemetery workmen forward.

They found Pinky Womack's body in the coffin with his eyes wide open, a bit of shock his only recognizable expression. He was lying on top of the uniformed skeleton of eighteen-year-old Jeremy Willamette.

It looked from the bloodstains like Pinky had been stabbed in the chest, probably the heart, so his death had been fast, at least Savich prayed it had. He didn't see any signs of torture, but it would take Dr. Ransom's autopsy to be sure of that.

Savich called Ms. Lilly at the Bonhomie Club right away to tell her. After she had absorbed the news, she said to him, "Poor Pinky. He wasn't bad, you know, Dillon? He could even make Fuzz the bartender laugh once in a while. Not often, mind. I'll tell his brother Cluny myself, don't you worry about that. Oh, Dillon, I hate this, I really do."

As he slipped his cell phone back into his coat pocket, Savich knew it would take him a long time to get Pinky's face out of his mind. He wondered where his wife had slipped off to.

He heard the sharp crack of a rifle, heard yells, saw agents running, guns drawn. He found Sherlock, once again surrounded by agents, kneeling over a fallen agent, her palms pressing hard into her shoulder. Savich shouted her name. She looked up at him, her eyes dilated, her face white as his shirt. "Connie wasn't standing two feet from me, Dillon."

She was all right. Thank God she was all right.

But Agent Connie Ashley wasn't. He was relieved she was conscious. When he came down on his knees beside her, she whispered, "Don't freak out on me, Dillon, I'll survive." Blood oozed between Sherlock's fingers despite her pressure. He gently shoved Sherlock away and pressed his wadded-up handkerchief against Connie's shoulder and put his weight on it. "Yes," he said, "you'll be fine. I'll freak out until the ambulance arrives."

Sherlock said, "I think the shot must have been fired from over there — the northeast, right through those trees, maybe from the second floor of one of those apartments."

Savich had her go over the exact position of both her and Agent Ashley at the moment the shot was fired. He nodded. He put the angle a bit higher, but said, "Close enough. That's quite a distance. Okay, let's see if we can't find them." He gave out assignments and yelled as the agents dispersed, "Everyone be careful!"

He knelt down again beside Connie Ashley. "We'll get him, Connie, don't you worry about that."

Sirens sounded in the distance. The snow began to fall more heavily.

Savich watched his wife wipe Connie's blood off her hands on the fresh-fallen snow.

Tourists were gathering closer now. He knew the media would be there in force at any moment. He hoped the ambulance would get there first.

He watched his wife as she held Connie's hand until they arrived.

CHAPTER 7

Maestro, Virginia
Saturday afternoon

Rafe chugged down half a glass of iced tea, swiped his hand over his mouth, and said to his father, "Madonna told me about this woman Rosalind Franklin who did a lot of the work on DNA and they gave her research away and she didn't even get recognized or win a Nobel Prize."

"Hmm."

"She died when she was a little bit older than Mom when she left. Isn't that something, Dad?"

"Yeah, Rafe, it sure is. You wonder what she would have done if she'd lived longer."

"That's what Madonna said. She said Rosalind Franklin was the one who actually took the first blurry picture of what the double helix molecule looks like."

Dix wondered why he'd never heard of Rosalind Franklin, but didn't say anything. He set a bowl of chicken noodle soup on the table in front of his son, then set another on a tray and took it to the living room. Madonna was propped up with three cushion pillows, Brewster on her chest, his face on his front paws. His eyes fluttered closed as she stroked his head. Dix would swear her eyes were brighter than an hour before.

He moved Brewster to the coffee table, set the tray on her lap, pulled up a chair, and sat beside the sofa. "This is Campbell's best. I hope you like it, my boys sure do. How many miles do you run a week?"

"Not more than fifteen miles a week, you don't want to blow your knees out and —" She slapped her spoon on the tray. "I'm a runner and my name is Madonna. Just great. Swell. Hey, maybe I'm even rich since it looks like I own a Beemer, you think?"

"Could be. I try not to run more than fifteen miles a week either."

She ate some soup, set her spoon down. "Sheriff, is there anything of interest around here? You know, tourist interest? I guess I'm the outdoorsy type. Is there something I could have come to see?"

"Beautiful scenery, which means you could have come to hike, or camp out, or maybe you came to go antiquing in some of the towns around here. If you do drive one of those SAV Beemers it's got lots of room to lug stuff around in it. The only thing is, this snowstorm has been forecast for a while now. I can't see you wanting to hike in a blinding snowstorm."

"No, I suppose not. So that's not why I was here." She finished her soup, sighed, and set down her spoon again. Dix put the tray on the coffee table and patted his knee. Brewster jumped up on his lap and nuzzled against his hand. Madonna turned to look out the wide window across the front of the living room. "I don't think it's going to snow anymore."

"Don't bet the Beemer on it. I was just outside and the clouds to the east are nearly black, really fat, and rolling this way. I think it might actually be pretty bad later on tonight. You warm enough?"

"Yes, I'm fine. How long have you been sheriff here in Maestro?"

"Nearly eleven years now. I was elected when I was twenty-six."

An eyebrow went up. "Oh? And how did that miracle come about?"

He laughed. "Actually, I married the mayor's daughter when I was twenty-two and newly assigned to the Twenty-seventh Precinct in Manhattan. After five years in New York, we decided to move back here.

Christie's father, Chapman Holcombe, or Chappy as he's called by everyone, offered the best inducement by backing me as sheriff. He owns half of Maestro, along with fistfuls of other business interests in Virginia, so winning wasn't that hard."

"So you call your father-in-law Chappy?"

He looked down at his low-heeled black boots for a moment, then shrugged. "Sure. The boys call him Grandpa Chappy."

Sounded like there was a problem there, something deep-seated the sheriff didn't want to talk about. Maybe something to do with his wife, Christie?

"Chappy has a brother he calls Twister, the only person who does."

She laughed. "Twister, that's a good one. However did he get that name?"

"Seems he was feet first in the birth canal. The doctor had to grab his feet together, turn him around, and then pull him out. Hard going, nearly killed his mother before they got him out of her. She was the one who gave him the nickname. Only his brother and mother ever call him that. She lived with Twister until last year when she died in her sleep at the age of ninety-six. Chappy still calls him that. He hates it."

"Do you ever regret coming here?"

"As in leaving New York? Sometimes. I loved the Mets games at Shea Stadium, always saw myself taking my boys to the games. I took Rob once to the Garden when the Knicks played the Boston Celtics, but he was only two. He threw up all over the guy sitting next to me.

"For the most part, though, I think this is a great place for the boys to grow up. We've got only a smattering of drugs, no gang stuff to speak of. Teenage boys drinking and joyriding and keeping the kids away from Lovers Lane are usually the biggest teen problems we've got. Fact is, we don't get a whole lot of crime out here in the boonies, but there's enough to keep our department busy and me on my toes. With Stanislaus here, we get a fair number of out-of-town visitors."

"What's Stanislaus?"

"Stanislaus School of Music, a university with about four hundred music students in attendance, nearly year around. It's known as the Juilliard of the South. If you drive anywhere near the campus, you can hear singing and musical instruments blending together, so beautiful you think you've died and gone to heaven. The director of Stanislaus is Twister — real name, Dr. Gordon Holcombe, Chappy's younger brother."

"Hmm. Two Holcombes and they appear to run lots of things around here. Stanislaus — something makes me think I recognize the name."

"It's pretty famous. Maybe you read about it before you came here."

She shrugged, reached her hand out to Brewster, who was lying on Dix's legs on his back with his paws in the air, and scratched his belly. "You've got what? Twenty deputies?"

He looked at her closely as he nodded.

"How many women?"

"Nine."

"Not bad, Sheriff."

"You're on the pale side again. Your head hurting?"

"Not enough for another pill."

"Fair enough. I know it's hard, but try not to worry. Dr. Crocker said your memory should right itself soon enough, and in the meantime, our deputies are showing your photo around everywhere. It makes sense you were staying somewhere around here, and chances are you had to buy gas. We'll know pretty soon who you are. Or maybe I'll know by tomorrow morning, if your fingerprints are in IAFIS."

She sighed. "I can't stop wondering what

I was doing here. Maybe it was to hike, camp out, and I ran into the wrong people at some campsite."

"We're checking all the campsites out as well. But again, there's the weather, not at all conducive to anything outdoors, except for snowmobiling or cross-country skiing. Do you ski?"

She paused for a moment, frowned down at her hands. "I don't know. Maybe. But you know, I doubt that's it."

"Why?"

"I'm not sure, really, but I feel like there are lots of people in my life, that the last thing I'd ever do is go off somewhere alone." She shrugged, smiled at him. "I guess I could be wrong though."

"Probably not. Why don't you rest, nap a bit. Dream about dinner — I've got really good stew left over from last night."

"Lots of catsup?"

"You and my boys," he said, and laughed.

Madonna fell asleep at nine o'clock Saturday night in Rob's bedroom, wearing a pair of his pajamas. They looked brand-new, which Rob told her was true because neither he nor his brother wore pajamas, for the simple reason that their father didn't, even in the dead of winter.

The pain pills put her into a deep sleep where dreams came in hard and fast. She was standing in a dark place, so dark she couldn't see her own hand in front of her face. Wherever she was, she couldn't get out, though oddly, it didn't seem to bother her. She stood cocooned in blackness, waiting for a man who was going to give her a million dollars. Why in the dark? she wondered, but again, it didn't seem to matter. She waited patiently, wondering idly if the sheriff wore boxers or jockeys, an interesting question, but then the image was gone, and she was still standing in the middle of nowhere, wondering where the man was. She couldn't see her watch so she didn't know what time it was.

She heard something and felt her heart speed up because he was finally here, the man with her money, a million bucks in gold bars, and it was all hers, she'd earned it, worked her tail off. She wondered how she was going to carry the gold bars, but she knew she'd manage it. She had a plan, didn't she? Otherwise why was she so happy and excited in the middle of a black pit?

She heard something again. Was it footsteps? The man carrying all those gold bars? But she realized in that instant that it wasn't a man's footsteps, it sounded indistinct, too hollow for that. She jerked awake, shot straight up in bed, and looked toward the window. All she saw was a veil of white snow falling thick and straight down. She looked closely at it.

The house was cool, but not uncomfortably so. She was wearing a pair of Rafer's socks, his donation to her, nice thick wool socks, so she didn't feel the cold of the oak planks beneath her feet as she walked to the window and looked out, thinking about the dream. She heard a scratching sound coming from below the window. She tried to look down but couldn't get a good angle. Curious, she opened the window and leaned out. Straight below her window she saw two men hunkering down over something, both of them swathed in heavy coats over jeans tucked into big army boots. Ski caps covered their heads, heavy gloves on their hands. They were nearly white with snow. She must have made a noise because one of them suddenly looked up to see her leaning out.

He said something, then moved so fast she barely managed to jerk back into the bedroom before a bullet splintered wood not six inches from her head.

Another two, then three rounds came

through the window. It was a silenced pistol, the muffled sound quite distinctive.

She looked around for her gun, but didn't see it. Where was her gun? She always had her gun nearby. Another bullet shattered what was left of the window. She ran to the bedroom door, flung it open, and yelled, "Sheriff!"

He was out of his bedroom at the end of the hall in seconds, his Beretta in his right hand, his left hand jerking up the zipper in his jeans.

"What is it? You all right?"

"Two men, on the ground outside my window with a ladder. I heard them and when I looked down, one of them fired four, five rounds up at me."

Dix was past her in a moment, racing to the open window. He kept out of the line of fire, eased himself to the corner of the window, looked down. The men weren't there now, no one was there, but there were lots of footprints in the snow, and a ladder lay on its side.

As he pulled the window down carefully in the shattered frame, yanked the curtains closed, he said, "I want you to stay right behind me, Madonna. Rob, Rafe, both of you, get back in your room and lock the door. Now!"

They obeyed him instantly.

Dix raced to his bedroom, picked up his cell from its charger and called his night dispatcher. "Curtis, two men are at my house, fired at Madonna. Round up everybody you can find and get them out here, fast. These guys are dangerous. Tell everyone to be real careful."

Dix hooked his cell on his belt, yanked on the rest of his clothes. While he was pulling on his boots, she told him what she could. He nodded. "Good. The first car will be here within four minutes. I want you to stay right here, don't even think of leaving this room, you got that?"

"But I — Give me a gun, Sheriff, I know how to use one."

CHAPTER 8

"Forget about it, Madonna. Just do as I say and get down over there behind the dresser."

She knew way deep that crouching beside a dresser for protection wasn't something she would do or anyone would ask her to do, but her head was pounding, and images of her dreams, of the man coming toward her in the blackness, were still scoring through her. She fell to her knees and pressed her palms against her head.

Downstairs, Dix lifted the edge of the living room curtain and looked outside. It looked like an Impressionistic postcard out there, pure white snow cascading down, blurring what was real, softening everything, but still menacing because it was hiding the men who didn't want to be seen. He saw nothing moving, but knew it would be foolhardy to venture outside and let one of those clowns pick him off. Dix knew the boys would do exactly what he'd told them to, but he didn't know about her, about Madonna. One minute later he heard sirens, then saw lights flashing through the snow.

He was in his coat and gloves by the time five cop cars pulled up along his street almost at the same time and overflowed his driveway.

"Everyone stay down!" he shouted, and then slowly, his Beretta sweeping the area, he walked out onto the front porch. He heard Brewster yapping hysterically and knew he'd pee, no way around it.

Penny shouted, "Sheriff, any idea where they are?"

He shook his head, then quickly told the deputies what had happened. "You're looking for two men. Listen to me now. They're armed and they've already shot to kill, so be very careful. We can follow their footprints in the snow until they reach the woods. If we lose them in the trees, we'll split up. I'm hoping we'll find them before they get out of the woods. Let's hurry before the tracks fill in with snow."

His deputies fanned out around the footprints where the ladder lay. They headed straight for the woods, still easily visible, but not for long in the snowfall.

"They were running at a good clip, Sheriff," Penny said. She and Dix waved all the deputies forward at a dead run into the woods.

They met up with B.B. and Claus, already in the trees, and the four of them followed what was left of the men's tracks. Instead of snow tracks, they soon saw small clumps of snow that had fallen off the men's boots, and lots of broken and partially naked tree branches the men had run into in their hurry to escape. It took time, with their four flashlights trained, as the obvious signs of passage faded away. The trail passed through to the western edge of the woods, then back in for about twenty more feet, then out again. "Listen," Dix said.

They heard an engine fire up, and broke into a run. They cleared a stand of oak trees to see a dark truck fishtailing its way onto Wolf Trap Road, one road over from Dix's house. Snow and gravel fantailed, spraying a huge arc. They were too far away, the snow too thick, to make out the license plate.

"It's a Tacoma," Penny said. "Tommy's got one. I've washed that sucker more times than I can count. It's black, or really dark blue."

Dix spoke quickly on his cell, then stuffed it back in his jeans pocket. "Emory will be here in a minute with a cruiser. We're going after that damned truck. B.B., you head back to the house and post a few of us there. You have enough cruisers to set up a perimeter. These guys are playing for keeps. Hey, keep my boys safe."

In under three minutes, Dix, Penny, Claus, and Emory were piled into Emory's squad car, Dix driving. Penny was leaning out the passenger-side window, trying to make out the truck's tire tracks.

"Straight down Wolf Trap Road, Sheriff," she yelled. "These tracks are a giveaway."

They skidded and slid from one side of the road to the other because they were moving so fast, but Dix managed for the most part to keep them on the pavement. They came up to Lone Tree Road.

"Left, Sheriff!"

He spun into the turn, nearly into a ditch. Dix, cursing a blue streak, managed to get the cruiser heading down the road again.

Dix heard Claus say over and over in the backseat, "We're gonna get 'em and skin 'em and fry their livers —"

"Good images, Claus," Dix called out. "Too bad it's not that kind of hunt. Penny, are you freezing out there?"

"I'm okay, Sheriff. Not good — we're nearing the highway. You know that

Doppler Lane on-ramp to Seventy East. If they get on that, we can put in a call to the Highway Patrol."

"Nah, we'll get them," Dix said, and sped up. "Hey, that may be them ahead of us." Dix pressed his foot on the accelerator. His deputies' cruisers were well built with new winter tires and lots of power under the hood, but he knew he was pushing the envelope at the speed he was going in the middle of a snowstorm. He doubted the men in the truck were doing as well. He looked over at Penny, who grinned at him as she tugged her wool cap down to her eyes, her face nearly covered with ice. "Hallelujah, I see the truck, not more than fifty yards ahead! We're going to get them, Sheriff!"

Claus stuck his head out the back window. "I can't see the license plate yet, but the truck does look like Tommy's Tacoma. For sure it's black."

The truck skidded around the eastbound on-ramp and leaped forward when it hit Highway 70 East, its rear end swerving violently to the right, then sliding nearly off the road. Finally the driver managed to straighten.

There would be few cars on the highway in this storm at one in the morning, a good thing, Dix thought, as he fought to keep the cruiser in the middle of the on-ramp, through the curve, and onto the interstate. "Emory, Penny was right. Call the Highway Patrol in, maybe they can cut these guys off ahead. Stumptree exit's four miles up."

Dix knew his speed was crazy in these conditions, but he didn't care. He wanted these men badly. They'd attacked his home, put his boys in harm's way, tried to kill Madonna, for God's sake. Who was she? What had she done, or seen? He should never have brought her to his house, to his boys. But how could he have known two killers would come after her?

He was doing eighty, but he couldn't see the truck. He supposed they might have cut their lights. "Penny, can you see the truck?"

"It's in and out."

"Emory, pass Penny your Remington so she can try to shoot their tires when I get us close enough. I want these morons alive." The Remington bolt-action was Emory's pride and joy, but he didn't argue since Penny could outshoot anyone in the department.

In that instant, a bullet slammed into the corner of the windshield, spiderwebbing the glass.

"Son of a bitch!" Emory yelled.

"Penny, pull back in!" Dix shouted as he slowed and swerved.

"Give me the rifle already, Emory. It's time for some payback!"

"Dammit, Penny, be careful."

She laughed, and checked that she had five live rounds. Penny was a lioness, Dix thought, no fear at all, and he sped up to get closer. He saw the truck, speeding as well, keeping the distance between them about constant. Penny fired once, twice, all five rounds, quick and controlled, into the dense falling snow.

Dix could barely make out the truck, but in that moment he saw a flash of light, low, near the back left tire.

He yelled to Penny, "I think you hit something, maybe a rear light."

"Yeah, I think so, too," Penny said as she jammed five more rounds Emory handed her into the Remington. "Hey, Emory, nice gun. This barrel is heavier than my mother-in-law."

Claus yelled, "There's a guy leaning out the passenger window. Watch out, Penny!" Penny had already pulled back in. They heard six rapid rounds, and the sound of two bullets pinging against their right fender and the front grill. Penny hung herself out the window again, fired another five rounds quickly. "We've got to get closer, Sheriff. I can't see well enough to hit a tire."

He was doing eighty in a near blizzard, and pressed the accelerator to ninety. He heard Claus shouting to Penny and firing his Glock out the driver's-side rear window to give her cover or at least to distract the guys in the truck.

Penny fired again after Emory fed her more rounds, slowly this time so she wouldn't drop them with her cold hands.

There was a ferocious roar. The flash he'd seen earlier flared up like a night beacon, a huge circle of blinding white reflected blue in the thick, spearing snow. Dix heard Penny cry out, saw Emory jerk her back in. A bullet had hit her just as the truck blew. The world froze, shrank to a pinpoint in the next second as he watched flames whip up through the thick swirling snow, orange as the prisoner overalls in the Louden County lockup, rip twenty, thirty feet into the sky, red and orange, thick black plumes of smoke rising all around them.

Dix was already pressing on the brake when the truck had exploded in a deafening roar that sounded like the thunder of drums. They drove right through the fire-ball with debris flying at them. A slice of black metal scraped along the top of the cruiser, without breaking through the roof. A foot lower and it could have killed all of them.

Dix kept pressing the brake, trying to hold it steady until the cruiser slid into a slow skid. Dix prayed as he lifted his foot off the brake and steered into the skid, and slowly, finally, straightened the cruiser again.

"Sheriff! Ohmigod!"

Dix thought his heart would stop. A flaming tire was rolling toward them at a manic speed. Dix spun the wheel to the right and the tire crashed into their rear end, slammed them forward, then sharply to the left.

"Everyone, hang on!"

They ripped through the guardrail still moving fast and plowed into a field filled with snow. Small bits of ash rained down around them.

The cruiser came to a stop ten feet from the guardrail on fairly level ground, luckily well away from the thick stand of oak trees on the side of the road. A snowbank a good four feet deep stopped them dead.

Penny was slumped in the front seat,

Claus's arms holding her back from the windshield. Her head was bleeding.

Dix felt a moment of dizziness, shook it off. He pulled off Penny's wool cap and pressed it hard against the wound at the side of her head. "Let's get her to the road. The cruiser's done. Claus, call nine-one-one."

They pulled Penny carefully from the front seat and Emory carried her back to the highway as tenderly as he carried his baby daughter.

They saw sparks flying from a live wire that suddenly leaped toward them, coiling and uncoiling wildly. The wire suddenly snapped at Claus, nearly got his leg before he jumped back. They watched the wire finally settle into the snow, sparks still leaping out of the end of it.

Dix said, "Everyone okay?"

"Just shook up a bit, Sheriff," Emory said as he leaned over Penny, checking her pupils. "But Penny, her head's still bleeding and she's unconscious. I don't like how she looks at all."

Claus cocked his head. "I hear sirens. We'll have help real soon." He looked at the flaming truck. "Nope, it sure don't look good for the bad guys."

CHAPTER 9

Madonna watched the sheriff hug his boys against him. They had been terrified for him, but they were boys and they were trying as hard as they could not to show it. They were silent, but they clutched their father so hard he must have had trouble breathing. She knew they weren't talking because they were afraid if they did, they'd cry. As for her, she felt helpless, useless as a eunuch on his wedding night, and hated it.

Dix spoke quietly to his sons, telling them he was very proud of them, and he thanked them for watching over Madonna, which made her smile for a moment.

Finally, Rob pulled away. He stared up at his father. "There's blood on your face."

"It's not mine, don't worry."

"You scared the shit out of us!" Rob drew back his fist and slammed it against his father's arm.

"Don't cuss," Dix said automatically. He rubbed his arm, grinned down at his boy. "Not bad. You're going to lay me flat in a couple of years. You guys give Madonna any grief?"

"Nah," Rafer said, taking a bit longer than his older brother to pull himself together. "She made cocoa and we told her the story about old man Steeter's house, how he used to steal little kids and hold them prisoner. She said she couldn't tell us any stories because she doesn't remember any."

Dix raised his eyebrows. "That story would certainly make her feel better tonight, made her wish she'd made up a story for you."

Rob said, "Madonna wants to see the house, see if there are any secret passageways."

Dix said to her, "Old Mr. Steeter died some ten years ago, left his big old Victorian house to a nephew who never came to claim it, lots of legalities preventing anyone from buying it and fixing it up. The kids around here make a big deal out of it."

Madonna said, "It would be fun to explore if you swear no kid-ghosts would come out after us. You want a cup of cocoa, Sheriff?"

"That'd be great." Dix stripped off his coat and gloves, excused himself to wash the blood off his face in the downstairs bathroom. When he came into the kitchen, he sprawled down in one of the kitchen chairs, Rob and Rafe closed in beside him.

"You're going to tell us all about it, Dad?"

"Did you get those guys who shot at Madonna? Where'd the blood come from?"

"It was pretty hairy, Rafe. We had a car chase on the interstate. Penny must have hit their gas tank because their truck blew up. The bad guys didn't make it. That was Deputy Penny's blood on my face. She took a head wound, she's in the hospital, resting comfortably. She's going to be all right. The fire department is bringing in the remains of the truck."

He'd given the boys enough to satisfy their blood lust, Madonna thought, but not enough to make it too real for them. But still, even those bare facts were terrifying.

"Did those guys get burned up?" Rafe asked.

"Yes, Rafe, they did." Blown up and burned up, Dix thought, can't get more gone than that.

Rob said, "Did Penny have to get stitches in her head?"

"Yeah, about ten, all set real pretty by Dr. Oliphant." Dix shook his head at Rafe, who looked disappointed, then yawned real big.

Dix said, "It's going to be light in a couple of hours. Let's see if we can't get some sleep, okay?"

"Rob and I could stay up all night and not be tired, Dad."

Somewhere inside Madonna there was laughter and it bubbled out. "Since I'm old, a little sleep sounds good to me." She let herself be herded upstairs by the sheriff along with his two boys. She thought about lying on her back in Rob's bed again, staring into the darkness, terrified of who she was and who she might turn out to be. She hoped that in the morning he'd tell her everything that had happened, not just the bare bones of it, that he'd know, most important, who the men were and why they tried to kill her. She hadn't been about to ask him in front of the boys.

Dix woke up at ten o'clock Sunday morning, felt a spurt of panic, and drew a deep breath. It was over, and they were all right. He found Rafe and Rob both still asleep together in Rafe's bed in the boneless way of teenagers, and he smiled. He checked on Madonna in Rob's room and saw that the bed was not only empty, it was nicely made. The bed hadn't been made that nicely since Christie — No, he wasn't going to think about her. Even with the broken window frame, the room wasn't cold since she'd kept the curtains drawn tightly over the window.

When he walked into the kitchen twenty minutes later, showered and dressed, she was pulling biscuits out of the oven.

"Hi, I heard you coming. Coffee's fresh, on the counter."

"I've died and gone to heaven," he said, eyeing the biscuits.

"It's Sunday morning, the only day of the week your arteries are immune to cholesterol. You like scrambled eggs and bacon?"

"I'll make breakfast. Come on, sit down and —"

"Sheriff," she said patiently, "I feel fine. I'm bored. Let me do something for my keep, all right?"

She fed him a decadent breakfast, butter and strawberry jam dripping off hot biscuits, and he thought this was exactly what a Sunday morning breakfast should be. It had been too long since he'd made biscuits for the boys on Sunday.

Dix took the last bite of his third biscuit, wiped his mouth with a napkin, and said,

"You remember anything more today?"

She shook her head, drank down more coffee.

"I know you're scared, Madonna. I know it's tough being in limbo like this, looking at a stranger's face in the mirror, but I'll be hearing from IAFIS real soon now and we'll know who you are. If your real name doesn't jog your memory, it'll at least give you an anchor. As a matter of fact, let me check with Cloris right now." He leaned over and picked up the phone on the counter.

"Hey, Cloris, I need some —"

She heard a woman's excited voice on the other end of the line talking right over him. She saw him grin, sit back, and listen. Finally, he was able to grab the conversation. "Thanks for all that, Cloris. Yes, what you said, that's close to what happened. I'll stop by the hospital to see Penny later. I'll bet her husband, Tommy, was ready to tear down the hospital he was so scared. That's great news, though. Okay, Cloris, now it's my turn."

He asked her about IAFIS, frowned at her answer. "Okay, but let me know the minute you hear, all right? I'll be in later."

He hung up the phone. "I'm sorry. But there's no word yet from IAFIS. Still, it is

Sunday morning, to be fair about it. Those Rob's jeans?"

She was standing at the sink, washing dishes, listening to him tell her he still didn't know who she was. And then, what did he say? She whipped around and gave him a blinding grin. "Rob kindly loaned them to me. You forget how skinny boys' butts are. They're pretty tight."

He smiled, stared into his coffee mug.

"Did you ID the men? Tell me what happened."

He shook his head. "No, we didn't. The truck was a fireball, but we were able to identify it. It was reported stolen from a dealership in Richmond yesterday. The men had no ID on them, and they were badly burned. Identifying them will take longer."

"It might not be possible," she said.

"That's true. How do you know that?"

She shrugged. "It seems logical, particularly if you don't have much to work with. A Beretta is too big for me. I don't like to use them."

His eyebrow shot up, but he remained silent. She gave a start at what she'd said and began twisting a dishcloth, frowning.

He threw Brewster a small piece of bacon. "What gun do you prefer?"

122

"A SIG. It has a little kick, but it's really well made and accurate."

He nodded. She didn't seem to find anything odd about describing her gun. Who was she?

"I'm sorry I endangered your boys."

He said mildly, "You were protecting my boys, keeping them safe and distracted. I really appreciate that."

"I know I should have been out there with you, not hiding behind a dresser. You're very kind, Sheriff. In my experience, not a lot of sheriffs are like you."

"You know a lot of sheriffs?"

"Well, there was this guy in North Carolina who —" She broke off, shook her head. "All I know is I wanted to smack him. Isn't that strange? I saw a glimpse of his face — all smirky, filled with attitude — but now it's gone."

"What were you doing in North Carolina?"

"I haven't the foggiest idea."

He rose and walked to her, laid his hand on her shoulder. "Try not to be scared, Madonna. It won't be long now until you know who you are. As for the rest of it, we'll find out who those guys were, then we'll figure all this out, don't worry."

Dix left for the sheriff's office before the boys were up and didn't return until the middle of the afternoon. When he walked in the door, he sloughed off his coat and gloves as he walked into the living room. "It's finally stopped snowing. Maybe this'll be it. The sun even came out on the way home."

Both Rafe and Rob were on him again. He hugged them and waited for them to break away, which they did soon enough, to hurtle more questions at him.

"We heard about that live wire that could have fried Claus's leg."

"What about that huge burning tire that was coming right at you?"

"And those guys who tried to shoot Madonna — nothing left but burned-up skeletons!"

"So someone's been telling you all about it, huh? I'm hearing some bits of exaggeration there. I told you the important stuff last night. You guys got your homework done?"

"Ah, Dad," Rob said. "It's Sunday. We're going sledding on Breaker's Hill again."

Rafe said, "Don't you remember, Dad? We finished with *Othello* Friday night. Madonna beat the wadding out of us at Scrabble. We learned a new word — *lichen*."

Dix opened his mouth to answer when he heard a car drive up. Now what? He looked at her and called out, "Your name's not Madonna. It's Ruth."

"*What?* What did you say? My name's Ruth? Ruth what? Who am I?"

There was a knock on the front door. Normally Dix would let the boys answer, but the previous night was still too fresh in his mind. He picked up a barking Brewster and strode to the front entry. "Warnecki," he shouted over his shoulder. "Your last name's Warnecki."

Dix held up his arm. "Just a moment, boys, stay back, okay?" They responded instantly to the tone of voice but Brewster strained to get away from him. "Calm down, Brewster, calm down."

Dix opened the front door to see a big man in a black leather jacket, black slacks, white shirt, black boots, and black leather gloves, standing with a woman beside him, also in black.

"Sheriff Noble?"

"Yeah. Who are you?"

"I'm Dillon Savich, and this is my wife, Lacey Sherlock. We understand that you have a woman staying with you who's having trouble remembering who she is. We'd like to see her."

"You related to her?"

"She works with us —"

"Dillon! Oh God, is it really you, Dillon? I remember you! Sherlock? Oh, thank God — you guys look wonderful. I'm Ruth Warnecki, and I remember! I can't believe you're actually here."

Savich quickly stepped forward into the entry hall as Ruth leaped at him and he caught her in his arms. She was laughing, kissing his cheek, letting him hold her close, her feet off the ground. She reared back in his arms, tears in her eyes. "It was so horrible. I didn't remember who I was and all these strange things just popped out of my mouth. This is Sheriff Dixon Noble, and he's been taking care of me. And Rob and Rafe, who've been taking care of me, too. The sheriff just heard from IAFIS, just this minute told me my name is Ruth Warnecki, and then I saw you both and everything came back again. It was real scary, Dillon. Sherlock, you look so beautiful all in black. You guys match so well. I am so glad to see both of you." And she kissed Savich's ear and his left eyebrow and held him like she'd never willingly let him go.

Dix and the boys stood back, Dix still holding a straining Brewster, who, oddly, wasn't barking wildly anymore, just seemed anxious to join all the hugging.

The big man, Dillon Savich, let Ruth down, but still held her against him as he turned to say, "Forgive us, Sheriff, but we were very worried when we heard Ruth hadn't checked in."

"Checked in with whom?" Dix asked.

Ruth said, "Oh, Luther Hitchcock called you, right, Dillon? He's a major-league worrier, for which I am profoundly grateful, this time," Ruth said, grinning like a loon at all of them impartially. "He couldn't come with me because he had that gallbladder attack and —" She broke off, her face suddenly slack and pale.

"What, Ruth? What happened?"

"Dillon, someone's trying to kill me and it must be because of the treasure in Winkel's Cave."

"Winkel's Cave?" Dix asked. "What treasure? Who are you, Ruth?"

Sherlock smiled at the tough-as-nails-looking man holding a little white ball of fluff under his right arm who was trying hard to jump at them, a teenage boy on either side of him, standing real close. "We're all FBI, Sheriff."

Ruth stuck out her hand. "Special Agent Ruth Warnecki, Sheriff Noble. A pleasure to meet you."

Dix took her hand, Brewster licked it.

She shook his hand up and down, she was that excited. He said, "So that's why you shoot a SIG."

"I also have a Glock seventeen."

"You're really an FBI agent, Madonna?" Rafe asked. "I mean, Ms. Warnecki, er, Special Agent Warnecki? A real FBI agent like they have on TV? Boy, it must have burned your butt when Dad told you to hide behind the dresser."

She laughed. "Not really, at least at the time. I'm sure he wouldn't ask me to do that now, he's not like that idiot sheriff in North Carolina. Come on, you guys, call me Ruth." Brewster started barking frantically. Ruth plucked him from Dix's arms and hugged him. "It's so good to be me again," she said, "as in back in my own brain. Much better than being Madonna."

Brewster licked her face, barking wildly between licks as he peed on Rob's sweatshirt.

CHAPTER 10

Ruth sat between Savich and Sherlock. She didn't want to let go of their hands.

"Tell us what you can," Savich said, "we'll help you fill in all the blanks, don't worry."

"The last thing I remember clearly is crawling through that low arch in the cave wall and into that chamber. Then everything starts to get confused and, well . . . black. I remember the feel of that blackness; it was exactly like in the dream I had last night — so maybe the dream reflects what happened to me."

"Then tell us about the dream," Sherlock said as she lightly squeezed Ruth's hand.

"You'd think it would have gone all blurry by now, but it hasn't. It's still as clear to me as when I was in the middle of it. Okay, in the dream I was standing in this dark pit of a place, alone, I couldn't even see my own hand, but I wasn't scared about that. I was waiting for a man to bring me a million dollars in gold bars. I know now I was dreaming about the treasure I was looking for in Winkel's Cave. I heard him coming but then I realized it wasn't his footsteps I was hearing, and I jerked awake. I'd heard those two guys outside my window. That was all the dream was, nothing more than that."

Dix was shaking his head. "I still can't believe there's a treasure hidden in Winkel's Cave. I've never heard anything like that." He looked up to see Rob and Rafe standing in the living room doorway, all bundled up and ready to take off for Breaker's Hill, their eyes focused on Ruth.

Rob said, "You know about a treasure in Winkel's Cave, Ruth? Is it pirate's gold? Doubloons?"

She smiled at both boys, shook her head. "Nope, it's better — a stolen gold shipment intended for General Lee in Richmond."

"Wow," Rafe said, taking three steps into the living room. "A treasure, here, nearly right where we live and we didn't know anything about it."

"But why Winkel's Cave?" Rob wanted to know. He took a matching three steps into the living room.

Ruth said, "Did you guys know that the main ingredient in black gunpowder is potassium nitrate? That comes from niter, or saltpeter, that's formed in cave deposits.

During the Civil War, they mined a whole bunch of caves in western Virginia for niter. I'm betting that's how the soldiers who stole the gold knew about Winkel's Cave. Maybe they even did some mining there, found the cavern and decided it was the perfect hiding place. That's where they hid the gold bars."

"A million dollars in gold?" Rob asked, moving to stand beside his brother. "How much gold is that?"

"It must have been a great deal since they went to all that trouble."

Both boys were nearly on top of Ruth now, their sledding forgotten. Brewster hopped onto the back of the sofa and barked at them until Rob picked him up. Ruth said, "Hey, guys, I'll keep you posted, I promise."

Dix broke in. "Okay, you guys, we need to talk to Ruth now, so off with you. Be careful. I don't want any more stitches."

The boys dragged out of the living room. "I wondered if they'd leave without a fight," Dix said, watching them go. "You really got their juices going, Ruth."

When they heard the front door open and close, Savich said, "Okay, Ruth, back up. Tell us all about this treasure map, where you found it."

"Okay. Last month I bought a collection of really old books at an estate sale in

131

Manassas. The books were all over a hundred years old, on every conceivable subject, as you might expect in an old home library. In a skinny little songbook with all the popular songs of the day, I found a map of a cave that clearly had to be Winkel's Cave. It showed what was labeled as gold bars hidden there by rebel soldiers who were supposed to escort it from the rail hub of Manassas Junction to General Lee in Richmond, like I told the boys. On July twenty-first, 1861, there was mass confusion when McDowell attacked at Bull Run — or Manassas, as it's called here in the South — and the soldiers must have taken advantage of the confusion and stolen the gold bars, brought them here to store temporarily.

"When the dust settled, there were reports of over a hundred pounds of gold missing from Harpers Ferry. Many believed Union soldiers had captured it. The rebel soldiers who secreted the gold bars in a niche in the cave drew the map so they could come back for the gold after the war, but I guess none of them survived since the map was still in that book. I had the feeling it could have been the only one made, left for safekeeping in that little songbook, maybe when one of the soldiers left the battlefield to visit his family. Obviously he didn't tell any of his family what he'd done, or about the map. Anyway it looked legitimate, the right age, at least the paper looked old enough, and the handwriting was appropriate for the time."

Dix said, "There could have been more maps. That would be too much trust among thieves."

Ruth shrugged. "Maybe. Anyway, it was sure worth a try."

"But since it looks like others were ahead of you in that cave," Savich said, "the gold is probably long gone."

"You're right, Dillon. And my map is gone. If they didn't have it before, they've got it now."

Savich said, "We'll go back to the cave tomorrow. We're going to find out what happened to you."

Ruth clutched at his hand. "The thought of going back there scares me, way down to some primal part of me. You know, like there are saber-toothed tigers prowling outside and I'm huddled next to a fire, but it's not enough to protect me."

Sherlock shivered, despite herself. "I wish I didn't understand, Ruth, but I've felt the same way about a place — that maze I was in — but never mind that."

Ruth settled Brewster back in her lap, caressed his soft ears, and stared at the brisk fire in the fireplace.

Dix leaned forward. "You okay, Ruth?"

"Yes, I'm sorry, I just spaced out for a moment. Everything that's happened since Friday — it's a little overwhelming." She dashed tears out of her eyes, then took on a defiant look. "I'm going to shut up about that now. I'm a hard-ass, I'm going to begin acting like it."

"You can howl at the moon if you want to." Dix laughed. "What you've been through, Ruth, it's enough to make my macho socks shake off my feet."

"The important thing is that we're all here and we'll get to the bottom of this," Sherlock said. She gathered Ruth in her arms and hugged her tight as Brewster pushed his nose between them. "You are a hard-ass, and don't forget it. Now, I want you to tell me caving isn't that hard. Neither Dillon nor I have ever been off the beaten tourist track in a public cave."

Ruth pulled herself together. "You have to be real careful. I didn't find many really tough spots to navigate in Winkel's Cave, even in the unmapped parts, and that's probably why the soldiers used the cave to stash their gold bars. The thing is, you're never supposed to cave alone, so I guess I'm an idiot. I was so excited about this, I told myself I didn't need to have Luther with me."

"Yeah," Dix said, nodding, "that about covers it. You were an idiot. I'm a rank amateur and you couldn't pay me to go into an uncharted part of a cave by myself, even armed with million-watt searchlights."

"Thank you, Professor Noble," Ruth said. She turned to Sherlock. "I love it when a man agrees with me. In any case, I'll guide you — even though I don't have the map, I pretty much remember the route I took through the cave. It won't be too bad, I promise. I've been in much tougher caves, like having to belly-crawl through cold water or rappelling down sheer walls and not knowing what's waiting for you at the bottom — praying there will be a bottom — or shimmying through passages that are too small for a twelve-year-old.

"There aren't even any real claustrophobic spots in Winkel's Cave that make your skin crawl, at least that I saw. I didn't see any bats or cave animals, and there are supposed to be Virginia big-eared bats in the caves around here. It will be chilly, fifty-four degrees is the average temperature, but we won't have to wade through any streams. We won't be down there long enough to worry about hypothermia. We'll need plenty of light, that's the most important thing."

She paused. "I have to know what I ran into when I was in that cavern. I wish I could remember. Was there something I wasn't supposed to see? Did someone pull me out of there? But if they wanted to help me, why did they hit me over the head and leave me lying unconscious in the sheriff's woods? Fact is, I probably would have died if Brewster hadn't found me. And then those two men tried to break into the house and shot at me. If they wanted me dead, why did they leave me alive in the first place?"

"Stop worrying so much, Ruth, we'll find out," Dix told her. "Hey, Madonna, we already found out what your name is."

It was lovely to laugh a bit, to let the terror of Winkel's Cave fade for a few moments at least. Ruth asked Savich, "How did you find me?"

Savich laughed. "Trust me, Ruth, lots of people know the sheriff found a woman in his woods. And everyone knows all about that high-speed chase on the interstate in the blizzard last night and how those two yahoos tried to kill the woman who was staying at the sheriff's house."

Sherlock added, "They even sent your picture out over the wires for identification." She patted Ruth's hand. "And now we're staying here until we figure everything out."

"But, Dillon, I'm the lead on the Tiller case."

Savich said easily, "I'll give Dane a call. He can handle it. Don't worry."

"But he's getting married in two weeks."

Sherlock said, "Then he'll be motivated to get it cleaned up, now won't he?"

Dix asked, "The Tiller case?"

Sherlock said, "A farmer in Maryland was tilling a new parcel of land he'd just bought and plowed up some human remains. We're just getting our bearings on what happened."

Dix said slowly, "I heard on the radio about you guys finding a kidnap victim dead and buried in a Korean War soldier's grave at Arlington National Cemetery. What's that all about?"

Sherlock and Savich exchanged glances. Savich shrugged. "Okay, maybe it's time we told you about Moses Grace and Claudia, Ruth. You know how you left your cell phone with Connie? Well, she got a call from your snitch Rolly."

He went on to tell Ruth and the sheriff about the fiasco at Hooter's Motel, finding Pinky's body in Arlington National Cemetery, Connie getting shot. "I'm sorry to have to tell you this, Ruth, but Moses Grace also intimated he'd murdered Rolly.

"We don't know much about who Moses Grace or Claudia are. We found out he used Pinky's cell phone to call me. The phone carrier confirmed the call was received through a cell tower in Arlington. We left the account open, in case he uses the phone to call me again. If he even turns it on again, we'll be able to track him. Despite the drawl he talks in, and all the bad grammar, I think he's pretty smart. He's probably dumped Pinky's phone already."

"He really tried to shoot Sherlock?"

Savich said, "He wants both me and Sherlock. We left Sean at his grandmother's before we drove here to Maestro." He added to Dix, "We've been through something like this before."

"I should have been there, Dillon. You should have called me."

"Nah, we screwed up things well enough on our own."

Ruth jumped to her feet and began to pace, Brewster straining in her arms. "I can't believe you guys came out here looking for me with all this going on back in Washington."

"Family is family, Ruth. Let it go. You're

right, Moses Grace is a very scary man, I'm quite sure of that from our short acquaintance. He's targeted me for some reason we don't know yet — maybe revenge — so we've started a good deal of spade work into my past cases. He's pretty old, I think, and he sounds sick — hacks a lot, really wet gravel in his voice."

Sherlock picked it up. "Claudia is young, draws hearts over her *i*'s, that sort of thing. He calls her his sweetheart. Maybe she's his daughter, granddaughter, we're not sure, or maybe she's a runaway teenager. Sit down, Ruth, you're making me dizzy."

Ruth sat, aware that Dix was looking at her. He was realizing he was going to have to adjust to this matter-of-fact cop talk coming out of Ruth's mouth. Not at all like Madonna. He said, "We're still trying to find Ruth's Beemer. I'll call in the license plate later, but at this point we know it's been hidden somewhere, or taken out of the area."

"Her SAV," Sherlock said, grinning.

Savich turned to the sheriff, who'd been studying each of them for the past few minutes. "I can't tell you how grateful we are that you found Ruth and kept her safe."

Dix waved it away. He was studying Savich closely. "I think I recognize your name, Ruth. A couple of months ago you were written up in the *Washington Post*, weren't you? You helped locate a math teacher before he was killed by some jealous old nutcase?"

"Good heavens, you remember that?" Ruth grinned. "That was Jimbo Marple. One of my boys saw this old guy take Jimbo right out of a shopping mall parking lot. He called me right away. Savich was so mad when one of the sharpshooters killed the old guy. You've got quite a memory."

"A whole lot of people are involved in every case we've handled," Savich said easily. "Ruth here is known for her snitches. She gathered them all when she was with the D.C. Police Department before she joined the FBI."

Sherlock said, "And shoots like a champ, Dix. Tells her Glock what she wants to hit and the next instant, it's dead center."

"I hid behind a dresser while he was out on that high-speed chase."

"Well," Sherlock said easily, "now you're back with us."

"A hard-ass," Ruth agreed, pleased.

Dix smiled a perfunctory smile that didn't show at all in his stiff voice. "So is the FBI going to take over here?"

Sherlock gave him her sunny smile. "Oh

no, Sheriff Noble, we're simply here to help. After all, Ruth is one of ours. Dillon called our boss, told him what we were doing. Mr. Maitland wants this cleared up as well. He hates it when someone tries to kill one of his agents."

Savich said clearly, looking Dixon Noble in the eye, "We have no intention of bigfooting you, Sheriff, banish the thought. We can help you with equipment, information, anything you need."

Dix still didn't look convinced, but he nodded. "Would you like more tea, Agent Savich?"

Dix punched off his cell phone. He was grinning when he walked back into the living room. "The boys got a better offer than Dad's leftover stew for dinner. They're having pizza at the Claussons' house with a bunch of other kids, bless the Claussons and all their ancestors, so we don't have to watch what we say. I twisted the truth a bit, told them you FBI big shots weren't staying long this evening, which meant they wouldn't be able to get much out of you. That and the 'Garbage Dump' pizzas turned the tide."

After they'd eaten the sheriff's stew for dinner, Sherlock watched Ruth, as natural as could be, fill the kettle at the sink and put it on the stove, and fetch tea bags from a big messy cupboard. "Hey, we've got some cheese and crackers for dessert. They're closed with a rubber band so they shouldn't be stale."

Dix laughed. "Sorry I didn't have more to offer you for dinner."

"The stew was excellent," Sherlock said. "You're a good cook, Sheriff."

"I learned," he said shortly, and put tea bags into two cups. "Ruth, more coffee?"

He was watching her as she nodded. "Ruth — I like that. I suppose it sounds more like you than Madonna. It's powerful, biblical."

Ruth smiled at him. "Sorry to switch names on you in the middle of the stream, Sheriff. Where do you think Dillon and Sherlock should stay in Maestro?"

"At Bud Bailey's B-and-B, right on High Street, half a block from my office. Oh, I forgot, Ruth. Tell me where you were staying. No one recognized your photo."

"I hadn't made a reservation anywhere. I thought after I got my treasure, I'd drive back home if it wasn't too late."

"Did you get gas anywhere?"

"Sure, in Hamilton."

The sheriff frowned. "That's a bit too far

up the road for us to have canvassed. Where do you live?"

"In Alexandria."

Sherlock said, "The men in the truck that blew up — have they done the autopsies yet?"

"We were lucky we could get the county ME to work on Sunday. Even though the men were burned real bad, he managed to pull up some partial prints, and some dental X-rays. They had to come from somewhere. We're hoping there'll be missing persons reports on them in the next couple of days. Unless they were brought in, and that would make them professionals. There wasn't much time for that, so that may mean some sort of local group is behind this, whoever they are and whatever this is. In any case, I've called in all my deputies, and now the FBI is involved. Any ideas you guys can come up with will be appreciated."

It was grudging, Savich thought, but it was a start, and the sheriff almost meant it. "We'll plan to head out to Winkel's Cave with you as our first stop tomorrow morning." He turned to Ruth. "You want us to bring anything?"

Dix said as he shook his head, "No, I can provide flashlights and head lamps and picks in case we need them. We have a stack of them in the department."

Savich nodded, and continued to Ruth, "I don't suppose you got permission from the Park Service to go into that cave on Friday, did you?"

"Good news. Winkel's Cave is on private land. Mr. Weaver, the owner, and I have already made a deal. He even had a locked gate in there, but no key, so I kind of picked the lock. It's what Indiana Jones would have done, isn't it?"

Sherlock rolled her eyes. "At least we don't have to worry about getting permission from the Park Service."

Savich said, "I bet it wouldn't have been a problem. I wouldn't be surprised if Mr. Maitland has a golf crony who's a higher-up in the Park Service." He shot a look at Ruth, thought of how close she'd come to death. "You're not going to be out of my sight in that cave, Ruth."

Ruth looked pleased about that. She said, "Oh yeah, Sheriff, Mr. Maitland has four boys."

Dix crossed himself.

"Oh dear," Ruth said, "I've got to cancel all my credit cards. I left my backpack and my wallet in my car."

CHAPTER 11

Winkel's Cave
Monday morning

Ruth said, "Okay, guys, we won't have any stretches of nice electrical lights the Park Service provides for their caves, and there won't be any well-marked paths. You've got backup flashlights in your belts, but right now we'll only need our head lamps."

The ceiling was high enough for a while so they could walk upright. With Ruth in the lead, they took several steps around the first corner, a couple of steps down some jagged rocks, and stopped for a moment in complete darkness, except for the light from their head lamps. The cave was eerily quiet, their breaths the only sounds they heard.

"Take a look at the cave formations here," Ruth said, pointing to a sweep of spectacular draperies, and then panning her head lamp toward a towering stalagmite. "Don't touch anything, and try not to bump into any of these formations.

145

They're really fragile. Stay close."

Since they didn't need lug soles in Winkel's Cave, they wore hiking boots. Still, each of them slipped a couple of times, but not badly. "Coming up on the left is a nice drop-off, maybe ten feet down, so stay in my footpath. The map was real specific about this, so maybe one of them took a header here. See that slab of limestone that looks like a commode?" All their head lamps swung to the right. "It's distinctive, so they drew it on the map. We're headed in the right direction, I'm sure of it. Okay, all of us but Sherlock will have to bend down some starting soon, and then we veer slightly to the left for another ten feet or so. Sherlock, your head will clear okay. It's narrower, too, but don't worry, it'll widen out again."

"It's so dark," Sherlock whispered. Her voice echoed back to her like a hollow reed. "It's like we're the only people in the world."

"We are, in this world," Dix said. "I've never particularly liked caves."

"Thank goodness Winkel's Cave isn't at all hairy, at least where we're going," Ruth said. "Like I said, you're not even going to get your feet wet. Mr. Weaver told me there's a stream, but it's in a lower passage, some twenty-five feet down. He said he'd heard it but never seen it. I, for one, wouldn't want to get lost down there." Her laugh echoed through the huge vault they were walking through. "If you want to freak out, I'll show you a copy of *American Caving Accidents* — people have fallen into pits, got tangled up in ropes, died of hypothermia from crawling in muddy water, even drowned. Now that I've scared you, caving isn't dangerous if you know what you're doing. Scrapes or bruises or sprains, that's usually the worst of it."

"Yeah, yeah, yeah," Dix said, "you've shown how careful you are in unexplored sections of unfamiliar caves around here. I'd call that pretty dangerous."

"Bitch, bitch, bitch," Ruth said. "Okay, we've got about twenty more feet to go before we crawl a bit to the right through a passageway that leads to pretty near where I think I ended up."

Dix cursed.

Savich said sharply as he swung his head lamp around, "What is it?"

"Stumbled on one of Ruth's loose rocks. It's okay. I have a little trouble with all this darkness."

"We've got an overhang coming up; lower your heads, guys." The men nearly doubled over.

147

"Another ten feet or so and it'll get bigger again and we'll be able to stand up." But after five more steps, Ruth stopped cold. "Hello, what's this?"

They moved up to huddle around her, training their head lamps straight ahead.

A huge pile of debris blocked the low passage, chunks of limestone and dolomite, dirt and rocks.

Ruth said slowly, "This is a cave-in, the result of a blast. Look at how far some of these rocks were thrown."

Dix made his way to the heaping pile, tested it with his hands. He pulled out a couple of rocks, knelt down, and pressed against it with his shoulder. "It feels solid. I don't think we're going to get through here at all, not without some heavy equipment." Still, he and Savich put muscle into it.

"You're right, it's solid," Savich said.

For several moments, they could think of nothing to do but stare at the obstacle in their path. Dix said, "I guess someone's pretty serious about keeping you out of here, Ruth. They must have blown it at night when no one was around."

Dix looked back at them, and thought they all looked like rejects from a B movie, with gas masks attached to their belts, staring at the huge pile of rock in front of them. "You know," Dix said, "maybe I've got a better idea than bringing in bulldozers, not that that's even possible. My father-in-law, Chappy Holcombe. He grew up here, used to tell me he knew the caves in this area, said he's explored most of them. He may know another way through here, another way in other than the main entrance."

"You're right, no way to get any big equipment in here to dig through this mess," Savich said.

Sherlock said, "I say we go talk to Dix's father-in-law. If he knows a back way into the cave, that would make things a lot easier."

Ruth said, "Sounds like a good idea to me. Let's go see him. Oh, and we've got to pick up more catsup. Rafe said we pigged it all down last night with the rest of the stew."

"Rafe likes catsup on his scrambled eggs," Dix said. "He had to do without this morning. Yeah, let's go. I think we'd all feel better getting out of here for a while, anyway."

"Let's do it then," Savich said, "before I get a permanent bend in my back."

Tara

Nearly an hour later, on the opposite side of Maestro, Dix pulled his Range

Rover through massive iron gates, impressively scrolled with the word *Tara*. They drove a quarter of a mile on a well-graveled road with stone fences running alongside, lined with oaks and maples, snow piled high on either side. They climbed steadily until Ruth saw what must have been the biggest house within fifty miles. It resembled a Southern plantation, a huge expanse of white with Doric columns lining the front.

"Some spread," Ruth said. "How old is Tara?"

Dix turned into the circular driveway large enough to park twenty vehicles. "Chappy built it in the late fifties for his bride, Miss Angela Hastings Brinkman of the New Orleans Brinkmans. He had the architect copy the descriptions of Tara from *Gone With the Wind*."

Sherlock asked, "It's obvious he's got money. How'd he make it all, Sheriff?"

As they walked up the wide set of six deep-set stairs, Dix answered, "He learned banking at his daddy's knee, he told me when I first met him. He owns a privately held bank, Holcombe First Independent, with a dozen branches in the area. He and his wife, Angela, had two children, my wife, Christie, and a boy, Anthony. Tony and his wife, Cynthia, live here with Chappy. Angela died when Christie was ten, of what I don't remember."

Sherlock asked, "Is Chappy into any other kinds of businesses?"

Cops, Dix thought, they had to know everything. He grinned at her vivid face framed by a head of curly red hair.

"He's done some real estate development in Virginia, Washington, D.C., and Maryland. Nothing big or splashy here in the sticks."

Dix hit the bell and they waited about half a minute before one of the mammoth oak front doors swung inward.

"Hi, Chappy. Where's Bertram?" Dix asked.

"Damned butler's got a bug in his gut, was puking up all over himself, so I sent him to stay with his doctor sister in Belleville.

"And who are these people, Dix? Oh, are you the young lady Brewster found in Dix's woods? You're the talk of the town." At Ruth's nod, he put his hands on his hips and shook his head. "You and Dix hooking up like that — and that wild Saturday-night truck chase with Dix and his deputies hanging out the windows of the cruiser like Dirty Harry; it's the only thing folks are talking about in town. I guess that makes you celebrities, Dix. How does it feel?"

"Chappy," Dix said pleasantly, "let me introduce you to FBI Special Agent Ruth Warnecki."

"Yeah, so I heard, Miss Warnecki. What a kick to meet a female FBI agent."

Ruth stuck out her hand to the old man still standing in the doorway in front of her. "Yes, a kick is a good way to describe it." She pumped his hand.

"Chappy Holcombe, at your service, ma'am. What do you think of my grandboys?"

"Well, I'm wearing Rob's sweatshirt, jeans, and coat, and Rafe's socks. I'd say that at this point in my life they're pretty indispensable to me."

Chappy showed lovely white teeth when he grinned at her. "You know, Agent, you have the look of my little sister, Lizzie. It was sad though. Died of leukemia when she was fifteen." He looked at Savich and Sherlock. "And who are these folks?"

After the introductions, Chappy stepped back and waved them into an immense entrance hall covered in twelve-inch black-and-white marble squares that gleamed even in the dull winter light. Because he'd kept them all standing in the open doorway for five minutes, it was ten degrees colder in the house than it should have been. They watched him push the great door closed.

"Three FBI agents in my house all at once," he said as he waved them into the living room, which was, surprisingly, very cozy. It was filled with family photographs, many of them going back to the turn of the twentieth century. "We get some of Dix's deputies visiting from time to time, but this is a first."

Dix said, "Where is everyone?"

"God knows where Cynthia is, probably at the new shopping mall over near Williard. Tony's at the bank."

"You're retired, Mr. Holcombe?" Savich asked.

"Nah, I won't hang it up until I start drooling on our big-gun bank clients. I can do most of my stuff here at home. Ah, here's Mrs. Goss. Would you bring some scones and drinks, dear? Everyone sit and you can tell me what this is all about."

CHAPTER 12

Tara
Monday afternoon

"And what is it you want to know about Winkel's Cave, Dix?"

Dix said, "Christie told me you've explored every cave in the area, Chappy. She said Winkel's Cave is your favorite, that you know every square inch of it. So I'm asking you to tell us whether there are any other entrances, other caves that communicate with Winkel's besides the main entrance?"

Ruth sat forward in a lovely Louis XV chair, her scone cupped in a napkin so no crumbs would fall on the green satin chair cover. "It's very important to us, sir," she added.

Chappy looked at each of them in turn and put his coffee cup down on the small table beside him, a very old and elegant antique, Sherlock noted, that shone with the high gloss of excellent care. He said, "Maybe there are. There are dozens of small caves around here, and some larger

154

ones, too, but I never found any I could get through to Winkel's Cave. Of course, those limestone and dolomite caves are incredibly complex, and some of them might communicate with each other through channels you'd never know about, much less get through. I don't suppose you're going to tell me why you want to know something like that. Why the devil do you want to get into Winkel's Cave through a back door when there's a perfectly good main entrance?"

Ruth realized in that instant that the arched opening she'd found probably hadn't been known to any other human being in a hundred and fifty years. She heard Dix say in that calm, measured voice of his, "I'd just as soon keep that close to my vest for the moment, Chappy, if you could bear with us."

Chappy chewed on his lower lip a moment, absently picked up a scone, and eyed it as he said, "Well, why shouldn't I help you? I could show you openings to some of the caves I know near there. It's not like I have to nail down my takeover strategy for Citibank in the next ten minutes. Hey, don't sputter your coffee on that pretty sofa, Dix — I was joking. But still, I don't understand any of this. These caves, why

155

do you want to get into them?"

Savich said, "We're following up on what happened to Ruth down there, Mr. Holcombe. She got into one of those caves somehow, through Winkel's Cave."

"So there may be both a front and back door," Ruth said.

"Maybe there's one that passes through to Winkel's Cave. I remember I stumbled across an opening into a large cave near there when I was a boy looking for arrowheads. Only thing was, it was a dead end, only the one cavern. But then again I don't remember if I looked all that closely through there, and I haven't been back in forty-odd years. The entrance I'm thinking about is over near Lone Tree Hill, in the steep side of a gully." He paused, pulled on his earlobe. "I'll have to show you, what with the snow covering everything."

Dix shot a look at Savich, who shrugged and nodded.

Ten minutes later, the five of them climbed into Dix's Range Rover pressed in between the caving equipment along with four lanterns from Chappy's stash of camping gear.

"A lantern and a flashlight is all you need. I never liked those built-on headlights," Chappy said to no one in particular.

"This is a sweet car," Chappy continued, patting the dashboard. "Christie loved this car, said the Brits got it right with this one. I bought it for her for Christmas three years back. It's the Westminster Edition, only three hundred of them imported that year. She liked this soft black leather, said she loved to get it up to ninety just to watch your face go red, Dix, and your fingers turn white clutching the chicken stick."

Chappy saw the closed look on Dix's face, the same look he'd worn for nearly a year now. At least it was better than the blank despair Dix had shown that first year.

Dix didn't respond. They both just looked out at the road in silence, and Ruth was left to wonder where Christie was. If she'd left, why hadn't she taken her prized car?

After a couple of minutes, Dix said, as he wiped his gloved hand over the bit of fog on the windshield, "You guys okay back there? Enough room?"

Savich laughed. "I've been trying to talk Sherlock onto my lap, but no go. Yes, there's plenty of room for us and all the lanterns, too."

Ruth said, "Hey, Dillon, when I get my

driver's license replaced, will you let me drive the Porsche?"

"You think I'd let someone drive my Porsche who didn't even know who she was until yesterday? Forget it, Ruth."

Sherlock said, "Your amnesia has nothing to do with it, Ruth. He won't let anyone drive that car."

Chappy turned in the seat. "A Porsche?"

"Yes, sir, a 911 Classic. Red, nearly as old as I am."

"You're a big guy — you fit in that thing?"

"He fits great," Sherlock said. "I have to beat the women off with a stick."

"More often it's the guys," Savich said, "with their heads under the hood."

Chappy had Dix turn right off Raintree Road onto a single-lane road that was covered in snow and badly rutted. Dix said, "No one's ever plowed this road. The snow looks pretty deep but I think we can get through. The Rover has never let me down."

It was slow going, the snow reaching nearly to the top of the Range Rover's wheels at times, but they kept moving. They passed a couple of old wooden houses set in hollows of land a good ways back from the road, surrounded by trees, snow piled high around them and over the old cars parked in the driveways.

Dix said more to himself than to anyone else, "That's Walt McGuffey's place. It doesn't look like he's left the house in a while. I'd better call Emory, have him check to see if Guff is okay." He pulled out his cell phone and called the station.

When he signed off, Ruth noticed how quiet it was out in the woods. The bright midday sun beat down, glistening off the white hills, sending drops of snowmelt falling in a rapid cadence from the naked oak branches.

The road dead-ended about fifty feet ahead. Dix said, "I don't think we should go off-road in this snow."

"Don't try, we're close enough," Chappy said. "We've got us a little hike now. Ruth, you up for it?"

"Yes, sir," Ruth said. "A little thump on the head wouldn't stop me. I'm up for about anything."

"Bring your shovel, Dix," Chappy said.

The snow was so deep it was inside their boots within fifteen steps of the road. They heard a rustle in the trees to their left, and a rabbit appeared, stared at them, and hopped back into the woods, up to his neck in snow.

"I don't think he's one of the bad guys," Dix said. "Look around you, it doesn't get more beautiful than this."

Chappy said, "Yeah, yeah, you're a regular PR guy for Maestro, and here you are, a city boy."

Dix rolled his eyes. "Not anymore, Chappy. I'll tell you, when I visited my family in New York City last year, it seemed like I'd landed on a different planet."

Ruth bent over to retie her boot laces. "How much farther, Mr. Holcombe?"

"Call me Chappy, Special Agent."

Ruth laughed. "I guess you'd best call me Ruth."

"I'll try, Ruth. But you know, that sounds like you stepped out of the Old Testament or should be home, spinning cloth in front of a fire." Chappy stopped a moment, scanned. "Over there, I think, another thirty or so yards," he said, pointing. "You can see Lone Tree Hill — that single oak tree standing on top of that rise? It's been standing sentinel up there longer than I've had feet on the ground. The snow's really changed how everything looks — the snow and all the years."

They trudged on toward that single oak tree. Nearly goose-stepping through the snow with the bright sun overhead, they weren't cold, but their feet were wet through. "Rob's got lots of wool socks he can lend us, if you need any," Ruth said to Sherlock. "Dix can see to Dillon."

Chappy held up his hand, stopped. They were standing some ten feet from the edge of a gully that fell at least twenty feet, forming a bowl of sorts some thirty feet across. The sides of the gully were covered with scraggly trees and blackberry bushes, all weighed down with snow. Lone Tree Hill stood to their left, upslope, the oak tree silhouetted against a cobalt sky, its branches laden with snow.

Ruth said, "It looks sort of like a Christmas tree. I'll bet it's a favorite for photographers."

"Yeah, but mostly from a distance. Few people come up here," Chappy said, wiping snow off his arms. "My wife loved to paint that tree, in every season. A lot of people can see it from all around here." Chappy pointed to the far side of the gully. "Over there, by that bent old pine tree, that's where the cave opening is. That old tree looked near death when I was a boy. It still looks like it's about to fall over."

Once they'd made it across the gully and climbed up some six feet, Chappy stopped.

"The opening must be right there, beneath all that brush."

The brush came away easily, too easily. Savich stepped back when Dix began to shovel away the snow that had fallen through the brush. When he hit solid rock, he looked over his shoulder at Chappy. "You're sure, Chappy? There doesn't seem to be an opening here. Should I try to the left or the right?"

Chappy shook his head. "Nope, right there, Dix, by the twisted old bush. I'm not totally senile yet."

"Wait a minute," Savich said. He squatted down and wiped away the remaining dirt and snow with his gloved hand. "Chappy's right. This is the spot all right. That brush came away awfully easy, didn't it, Dix? It looks like somebody's packed a bunch of rocks in here. To hide the entrance."

"They did a nice job of it," Sherlock said. "It's invisible until you brush it clean and look real close. This could be where you got out, Ruth. It looks like somebody's trying to cover up that cave from both ends."

"Dix, you think you can pry those rocks out of the way with your shovel?" Ruth asked.

"Let's give it a shot," Dix said. He wedged the shovel beneath the lowest rocks and shoved it down into the earth. It took a lot of muscle, but after five minutes, Sherlock had pulled out the last stone. They caught their breath, staring at a cave opening in the side of the hill, maybe four feet high, three feet wide. They looked into blackness.

"Just a moment, Dix," Chappy said, elbowing his way forward. "Let me check this out first." Chappy leaned down into the opening. "Yep, I remember now. There's the easy slope downward, to the right. You have to press hard to the right because two feet to the left there's a nearly sheer wall that plunges straight down. When I was a teenage boy with more luck than brains, I tried to rappel down. Maybe twenty feet later I freaked out because out of nowhere bats were swarming all around me, heading up to the cave entrance.

"I remember that right-hand passage led to one big chamber. I don't remember any connections to Winkel's Cave, but I suppose there may be some small ones.

"I'll go first. You follow close behind me, single file. I remember it widens out pretty fast."

Dix laid his hand on his father-in-law's

shoulder. "Ruth might have been exposed to gas in there, Chappy. There could be residue. I don't want you swooning away at my feet. Think of your reputation. I'd prefer it if you'd let me go in first. I'll be careful, I'll keep pressed to the right."

"I hate it when a snot-nosed kid plays sheriff."

Dix laughed. "I'm paid to push you out, old man, if it means keeping you safe." Dix lifted his flashlight to shine it down into the opening. It sloped down but the ceiling was more or less level, so it was well over six feet high very quickly. And it looked narrow, but not so much that he couldn't get through. He eased through the opening, climbed down five steps to the right, and called back, "It's seems okay down here so far."

They followed him in, Savich bringing up the rear. Dix stopped when the space widened enough for them to all stand together. They shone their head lamps around them in the small space, and realized they'd been walking along a limestone ledge.

"Well, that'll make your blood pump a bit," Ruth said. She walked over to the edge and panned her head lamp upward. She saw glistening stalactites spearing down from a ceiling that was another twenty feet above them. She couldn't see the bottom. "The limestone is stained. Look, it's been gouged out in places. I wonder why."

"It smells nice and fresh in here," Savich said, "which means all that rock and dirt wasn't piled in that opening for very long, not long enough for the air to go stale. Since someone went to all the trouble of hiding the entrance, this must be the place we're looking for."

They made their way slowly and carefully down the ledge. Ruth asked Chappy, "The chamber this passage opens into, do you remember how big it is?"

"Good-sized, maybe forty feet across, maybe five, ten feet more the long way. But there's this weirdly shaped limestone niche inset deeply into the back wall that makes it seem even bigger."

"I don't suppose you found anything in that niche?"

Chappy gave her a sharp look. "I remember as a kid thinking there should be Indian relics set in there, but I didn't find any." He shook Dix's sleeve. "Okay, you're going to twist more to the right, I think, and then this passage drops off again — pretty steep so be careful — and dumps you right out into the big chamber."

When they'd all stepped down into the chamber after Dix, Chappy asked, "Was this the chamber you were in, Ruth?"

"I don't know yet, Chappy. I don't remember much."

"Let's head in, see if we can find out," Savich said.

Dix stepped farther into the cavern, his Coleman lantern casting misshapen shadows on the walls ahead of them.

CHAPTER 13

It was like a large vault, the ceiling soaring upward, with myriad groups of stalactites of incredible shapes hanging like chandeliers above their heads. But many of those within reach weren't whole, more like jagged, broken spears, scattered chunks tossed about on the cavern floor. "What a shame," Ruth said. "Men did this."

It was odd, but when she turned her head lamp away from the formations, reflecting light at her, the chamber seemed dark, too dark, and quiet, her voice alien in the dead air. She realized she was afraid.

"You okay, Ruth?"

"Yeah, sure," she said a little too brightly to Sherlock. "Look at that weird formation. It looks like a casket."

"Thanks for pointing that out," Chappy said. "Makes me feel all warm inside. Beautiful, though, isn't it? Too bad some people can't leave beautiful things alone."

It was odd, Ruth thought, but she had to struggle with herself to walk forward, afraid to find out what had happened to her here, if this was indeed the chamber. But of course it was since someone had gone to all the trouble of sealing up the entrance.

"It's longer than you thought, Chappy," Dix said as he walked farther into the cavern, his head lamp lighting up the shadowy walls near him. "Ruth, you think the arch might be over to your right? You want to take a look?"

No, she didn't even want to move. She felt like she was buried alive and the air was running out and she would suffocate. She wanted to run back out of this airless black chamber with its secrets, wanted to run along that long ledge until she could climb back out into the daylight. She schooled herself not to breathe too hard. She stood very quietly, surrounded by the weaving splashes of light from all the head lamps, and made herself draw in air, slowly, and slower still. She felt a hitch in her throat and she shivered. It was cold in there, colder than it should be.

She drew in another deep breath. Good, she could do that. She was being ridiculous. She made herself turn and walk along the right-hand wall of the cavern. The arch would be there, and she would know once and for all if this was the place where —

What? There was still a black hole in her brain, as black as the hole in which she stood. She focused her head lamp on the wall but couldn't see any opening. She remembered taking steps before, too many steps that didn't lead anywhere. Circles, she'd probably taken steps in circles, gone round and round, faster and faster. She shook her head again. She remembered the steps ending, but how was that possible?

She stumbled, went down on her hands and knees, and felt a jab of pain in her palm. She'd hit a sharp piece of fallen limestone. She looked at her hand, shook it. It wasn't bad, she hadn't cut through her glove. Other than the scattered limestone, the floor was surprisingly smooth. There was something, a small round object, on the floor at the edge of her head lamp light. She crawled over it to get a better look.

It was her compass.

A vivid memory seared through her. Her compass. She'd thrown it away in a moment of what? Anger? Frustration? She'd thrown it away because it had lied to her, given her directions that were impossible. She'd thrown it away because she was afraid.

She called out in a voice that didn't

sound like hers, "I found my compass. I remember I dropped it here. This is the chamber all right."

They surrounded her in a moment. Dix took her hand and pulled her up. He took the compass from her, laid it flat on his palm, studied it. "It still seems to be working."

She swallowed. "When I was in here, it didn't seem to work." She was shaking her head. "No, it didn't work. I didn't drop it, I threw it as far away from me as I could."

Dix slipped the compass into his jacket pocket. He heard her harsh breathing, stepped over to her, and rubbed his hands over her arms. "Listen to me, it's okay. Whatever happened in this chamber, you survived it. It won't happen again, all right?"

She wanted to throw herself against him, let him protect her from the monster in this place, just for a while, but she knew she shouldn't. She held herself back. He sensed she was on the edge and pulled her against him for a moment. He said, "Savich, maybe you and Sherlock should look for the arch."

Chappy stood beside them, staring at Ruth. "What arch? I don't suppose you're going to tell me what's going on here?"

"Later, Chappy," Dix said.

"Here it is!"

Dix said, "Shall we all go see the arch?"

Ruth nodded her head against his shoulder. "Yes, okay. I'll be all right. Stupid, really, falling apart like this."

"Even a hard-ass can take a beating now and then," Dix said.

They watched as Savich and Sherlock crawled carefully through the archway. There were jagged pieces of limestone around it. After a moment, Savich called out, "Not six feet up the passage is where they set the charge for the blast. It's a mess in here."

Sherlock said, "There really is only one way out again."

Ruth said suddenly, "I smell jasmine. It's really faint, but it's there. I remember now I smelled the same thing on Friday."

"Fresh air I can understand," Savich said, "but jasmine? Like perfume?"

Ruth nodded. "But that doesn't make any sense, does it? I wasn't wearing any perfume. What could it be?"

Chappy said, "Yeah, I caught a vague whiff of something, too. I didn't know it was jasmine, just something sort of sweet."

Ruth said, "Chappy, could you show me the niche?"

He led her over to the far wall of the chamber as Savich and Sherlock began to walk the perimeter.

"Thanks, Chappy. Can I have a minute?"

Ruth ran her flashlight carefully along the walls of the irregular, deeply indented space cut in the limestone by water over thousands of years. It looked like it hadn't been disturbed for a millennium. She knew the gold bars had been left there. Her map said *Beneath the niche,* but there was nothing there now. Who had found them, and how long ago? She wanted to cry. She'd been so excited, so hopeful, and it was all for nothing. "It's empty all right, Chappy, you were right."

She turned away and walked along the back wall of the cavern, away from the others. She smelled jasmine again, stronger now, and there was something else she smelled in the air, something nasty, unwholesome. She kept walking, leaning over when the cavern ceiling dipped a bit.

The smells intensified.

She heard a noise, a sort of whispering sound, maybe the soft flap of a bat's wings. Maybe bats had flown at her when she was there before, maybe they knocked her down and she hit her head. Her eyes flew up and she panned the ceiling with her head lamp. She saw nothing, only the gleam of lacy limestone.

She took another step forward and stumbled over something. She went to her knees, threw out her hands to save herself. Her fingers fell on something oddly pulpy and cold.

In the deepest part of her, she knew what she'd touched. She screamed, fell back, her head lamp scattering light all around her.

She heard their voices calling out to her, heard them running toward her. She forced her head lamp down. She stared into the greenish bloated face of a young woman.

"Ruth, what is it? What did you find?"

She looked up at Dix. "She's dead, Dix. She's the one wearing the jasmine perfume. And that sickening smell, it's coming off her."

Dix dropped to his knees beside her. "Savich, Sherlock, I need more light here. Chappy, you stay back, you hear me? Don't you move an inch this way."

"I know her," Dix said as he studied her face. "She's a student at Stanislaus. I don't know her name but I've seen her around town from time to time." He touched his fingertips to her neck, her cheeks, and finally, her hands, folded neatly across her chest. She needed only a lily, he thought. She hadn't wandered in here by accident, alone, that was for sure. Rigor had long passed. "She hasn't been dead all that long. I'd say maybe three, four days."

Ruth said clearly, "I smelled her perfume when I came into the cave on Friday."

Dix continued matter-of-factly, "The time seems about right. Decomposition would slow in here since it's cool and dry. You add the really cold weather we've been having, and it would slow things even more, but decomposition has started. See that small discolored circle on her chest? It looks like she's been stabbed. I don't see a knife, do you, guys?"

"The smell," Ruth said. "Not the jasmine, that other smell, it's pretty foul."

"Yes, it is," Dix said. "There's something medicinal to it."

"No knife," Savich said, "but I suppose the murderer could have left it in here, tucked away somewhere. The forensic team will have a huge job ahead of them looking through this whole chamber."

Ruth looked down at the young woman's face, bathed in the light of all their head lamps. "She's been posed. Look how her arms are crossed over her chest, her legs straightened out, her dress smoothed down."

Dix slowly stood, stretched. "Must be some crazy loon here, guys. He kills her, poses her, entombs her here for all practical purposes. He couldn't have known there was another exit from this chamber. It could be out of Poe."

Sherlock was checking the young woman's pockets, gently running her hands under the body. "I don't see a purse. Two pockets, but they're empty. No ID."

Ruth looked toward the arched opening on the far side of the chamber. "Do you think she was killed in here?"

"I don't know," Dix said. "I don't want to guess, either. I'm grateful you didn't stumble over her when you were in here alone."

She was shivering, so cold her body ached. She rubbed her hands up and down her arms. She couldn't look away from that poor dead young woman. "I might have stumbled over her. It might have been what shoved me over the edge. I still don't remember."

Dix handed her the compass. "Hold it a moment, Ruth."

She didn't want to, but she took it and

held it in her open palm. She heard Dillon's voice. "That's it, Ruth. Just hold it. You've had it for a long time. You've used it often. Do you remember what you were doing the last time you held it?"

She dropped the compass. "I was . . . terrified. Something was coming toward me, a slithering sound pulling itself across the cave floor. I ran, I had to get away from it. And I was screaming."

Savich clutched her hand tightly. "That's good, Ruth, that's really good for now." He nodded to Sherlock, who pulled Ruth against her. He watched Dix pick up the compass and slip it back into his jacket pocket.

Sherlock said, "Let's head back outside. We need to get out of here to call for help."

Savich said, "Dix, did you say your uncle-in-law is the director of Stanislaus, Dr. Gordon Holcombe?"

"Yes. If we can't ID her real quick, he'll be able to help us."

At three o'clock in the afternoon, the body of Erin Bushnell, age twenty-two, a very talented violinist from Sioux Falls, Iowa, was zipped into a body bag in the back of the Louden County medical examiner's van and on its way to the morgue in the basement of the Louden County hospital. As they watched the white van make its way slowly through the now-slushy snow Dix said, "The ME, Burt Himple, he's good, Savich. I think he had some training at Quantico. After meeting you and Sherlock, he'll be real careful not to screw up anything."

Savich looked after the van. "I gave him Dr. Conrad's name and number at Quantico if he wants to talk anything over."

Dix said to Ruth, "I think you're right. Erin Bushnell was probably lying dead in there when you first crawled into the chamber." Dix paused, looked over at his deputy, Lee Hickey, a young officer who'd ticketed Erin Bushnell for speeding a couple of months ago and identified her immediately. "I asked her to go out with me but she told me she was seeing someone," Lee had said and been violently ill.

Savich said, "The murderer probably had just placed her there, posed her to suit some insane directive in his mind, and heard you come in, Ruth. It sounds to me like you were drugged somehow, or gassed — that he somehow rendered you helpless."

Chappy, who'd been sitting in the Range Rover, had come over to them when the forensic people had carried the body away in its zippered green bag. He stood watching the dozen or so people moving in and out of the cave entrance. "This has to be the strangest day of my life."

"It sure ranks up there, all right," Dix agreed.

"What I don't understand is why Ruth is alive."

Savich said, "If Dix hadn't found Ruth in his woods, we would have searched the cave until there wasn't a bat left who hadn't had his wings stretched and examined for clues. Maybe the killer didn't want to leave her here, knew since she was an FBI agent, there'd be a huge manhunt, centering right here at Winkel's Cave."

"Hello, people, it's me, Ruth. I'm right here. I'm alive."

Dix said, "And all of us are real happy about that, Ruth."

"You're going to go see that twerp-ass Twister now, aren't you?" Chappy asked.

"Yes. We also need to find out where she lived. Sorry, Chappy, but you can't come with us. Hey, why don't you go finalize a buyout of the Bank of America, okay?"

Chappy shook his head. "I know Twister, Dix, know him down to the molecules that make that shifty little pissant tick. You can't believe a word he says. I'll be able to tell you if he's trying to cover up, to protect that precious school of his. I knew every one of his tricks by the time he was ten."

"Chappy," Dix said, "Why don't you tell our FBI agents how you really feel about Uncle Gordon."

"He's a sly, twisted little weasel."

Sherlock asked, "Why on earth would your brother hide anything, sir? We're only seeing him first because he's the big cheese at Stanislaus, nothing more, and he can direct us to her friends and teachers."

Chappy opened his mouth, shut it, then gave a deep sigh. "I can't acquire the Bank of America. I tried a couple of months ago, but they've got a stranglehold on all the stock options and the CEO is more shark than human — hey, that was a joke. Damn, what a day. All right, I'm going, but I want you to keep me in the loop on this. You promise, Dix?"

Dix nodded. "I promise. Deputy Moran is going to drive you home. Ah, Chappy, don't get on the phone to Uncle Gordon, all right?"

The campus of Stanislaus School of Music was set some four miles east of Maestro, sprawled in its own private wilderness.

Mountains formed a line to the north, with thick forests of oak, maple, and pine climbing their lower slopes. Closer in were low hills, little humps of land really, covered mostly with thick blackberry bushes that thinned toward the east into a wide, flat valley hidden under snow.

In the late Monday afternoon light, the campus looked like a precious stone in a matching setting, its redbrick buildings clustered around a large main quadrangle, surrounded by trees whose thick branches were weighed down with snow. All the walkways were neatly shoveled. The sounds of a Bach Brandenburg Concerto wafted out of the main auditorium, Van Cliburn Hall, named after the famed pianist, whose trust had given a large grant to the school fifteen years before. They all paused, taking in the scene and those beautiful sounds.

"It's nearly four o'clock," Sherlock said. "I hope Dr. Holcombe will still be here."

"He should be," Dix said. "He's a pretty remarkable musician, a flautist and pianist. He's run the school for the past ten years. Before that he toured, primarily in Europe, and lived in Paris for a couple of years. His daughter, Dr. Marian Gillespie, also teaches here."

"Is Dr. Gillespie also a musician?" Savich asked.

Dix nodded. "She plays the viola, though Christie told me she didn't have anywhere near her father's talent, or his ability to deal with people or do administration. She's something of an old hippie — you'll see what I mean when you meet her."

Ruth asked Dix as they walked up the wide sidewalk to Blankenship Hall, the administration building, "What does Marian's husband do?"

"Marian's husband left her before we moved down here from New York so I never met him." He added to Sherlock and Savich, "I was with the NYPD, a detective in homicide for four years. When we moved here, thanks in part to Christie's father, I was elected sheriff of Maestro. The boys and I don't see Marian much, maybe once every couple of months over at Tara for dinner. Rob and Rafe call it circus night."

"Families are such fun," Ruth said. "So did your boys get any of this talent?"

"Rob plays the drums in a band put together by one of his high-school friends, a mixed blessing. Rafe plays a bit of piano. Whenever I mention taking lessons, though, he won't have any of it. We'll see."

Dix led them to a gorgeous walnut semi-circular information desk where two women watched them approach with a good deal of curiosity. Dix nodded to them both, said, "Mavis, I'm here to see my uncle."

"He's in, Sheriff Noble," Mavis said, eyeing Savich, "although he did say he wanted to leave early today. I think Peter Pepper nabbed him."

Mary Parton rolled her eyes. "If he's with Peter, I know he'll appreciate being rescued. Ah, who are these people, Sheriff? Wait, you're the woman the sheriff found next to his house, right?"

Ruth smiled really big and nodded. "Yes, I'm Special Agent Ruth Warnecki."

"Ah," Mary said, nodding, "so you work in private security? In Richmond?"

"Well, not really," Ruth said, "I'm a special agent with the FBI."

"Oh goodness, oh my, how very thrilling. Does a pretty girl like you have a gun and body armor? Well, I suppose that's top secret, isn't it? All right then, Sheriff, you take these people right ahead."

Dix thanked Mavis and Mary and turned to lead them down a long carpeted hallway. "I would have thought they'd have heard all about you by now, down to that mole behind your left knee."

Her eyebrow went up. "You must be thinking of the one behind my right knee."

They stared at walls covered with large autographed photos of famous musicians, singers, and conductors.

"Quite a rogue's gallery," Ruth said. "Goodness, is this Pavarotti? In the flesh? Right here? Yep, it sure is. Would you look at that signature. Not shy, is he?"

Sherlock said absently as she studied Luciano Pavarotti's photo, "Looks like this photo was taken in summer, maybe fifteen years ago, right here at Stanislaus, with a bunch of excited faculty and students. Hmm. I don't think Pavarotti has anything to be shy about. Did you know he's considered the only living operatic lyric tenor who's really mastered the whole of the tenor's range?"

Ruth said, "How do you know about his tenor's range?"

Savich said, "Sherlock was on her way to Juilliard to become a concert pianist once upon a time."

Ruth said, "I had no idea. I would love to hear you play."

Sherlock nodded. She seemed to draw herself up. "It was a long time ago, Ruth, but I'd love to play for you. Sorry, Dix, you were taking us to Dr. Holcombe's office?"

"It's right at the end of the hall. We have to get past Helen Rafferty, his personal assistant slash secretary. She guards him like the Secret Service guards the president."

Ms. Rafferty was drumming her pencil on a neat stack of papers in the middle of her desk, her eyes on the closed door to Dr. Holcombe's office. Dix cleared his throat. "Helen?"

"Sheriff Noble! You're with all these people I don't know. Well, er, all of you, sit down, please."

"Helen, could you please give us Erin Bushnell's address?"

"Why? I see, you don't want to tell me. Just a moment, I have a directory of all the students right here. I hope she's not in trouble. Not drunk and disorderly. Ah, yes, here it is." Helen Rafferty wrote down the address and handed it to Dix.

"Now we'd like to see Gordon."

"Oh dear, Dr. Holcombe is meeting with a student — but you know what, I'm sure he's had enough of that. It's time for Peter to hang it up for the day." She rose to her feet and marched on three-inch heels to a lovely mahogany door and knocked loudly several times. Without waiting for an answer, she opened the door, stuck her head in, and said in a loud voice, "I'm sorry to disturb you, but the sheriff is here to see you, Dr. Holcombe. He said it's *very* important."

A man's easy, deep voice said, "Thank you, Helen. I'll be right out."

Dix said over Helen's shoulder, "I've got three FBI agents with me, Gordon."

"One moment," Dr. Holcombe called out.

Helen stepped out of his office and turned to face them, her hand over her heart. "Oh my, you're FBI agents? Really? Here at Stanislaus? Oh yes, you're that woman Dix found huddled against his front door, aren't you?"

"Yes, ma'am," Ruth said.

"Don't worry about people staring at you, dear, you can barely make out that bandage beneath all that nice thick hair. You're really FBI agents? All of you?"

Sherlock said, "Would you like to see our ID?"

"It's really not my place to, but I've never seen FBI badges before."

"They're actually called shields, ma'am," Sherlock said, "or 'creds,'" and she handed over her ID.

Helen studied it for several moments. "Oh my, isn't this the neatest thing? Ah, could you please arrest the young man who will be coming out of Dr. Holcombe's office very shortly?"

"Sure," Savich said. "Do you want us to haul him out in handcuffs, maybe rough him up a bit first?"

"That would be a treat," Helen said. She listened for a moment, then stepped back as a thin young man with a starkly ascetic face, a rumpled shirt, and close-cropped hair walked through the office door, his shoulders slumped. Dr. Holcombe followed him, saying, "There's no such thing as name discrimination, Peter. You must rid yourself of this notion that if a conductor doesn't like your name, he won't hire you. Dix, I'll be with you in just a moment."

Peter didn't appear at all interested, and continued in a loud voice, "Dr. Holcombe, you can't overlook this. Two rejections! I've brought them to you so you can see the truth. The rejections are nice, certainly, but both of them don't want me. Both! You know very well it's because of my unfortunate last name. You put my two names together, and everyone busts a gut laughing, particularly conductors and those snotty folks on their boards. You have to read between the lines, but it's there. No one wants a violinist whose

186

name is Peter Pepper. Can you begin to imagine how many rejections I'll get after I earn my Ph.D.?"

Helen said in a helpful voice, "I know I'll think you're rich from all the money you make on soft drinks. That's a good start, isn't it?"

"Enough, Helen, please," said Dr. Holcombe, unable to suppress a small snort of laughter. "Peter, this has nothing to do with name discrimination; it has to do with their collective opinions that someone played better than you, nothing more, nothing less. I read both letters very carefully, there is no 'between the lines.' "

Ruth said, "Hey, why not change your name?"

Peter Pepper stared over at her. "I can't. My mother would kill me, cut me out of her will, then I couldn't afford the tuition here."

"Okay then, use a different first name when you next audition, then everyone will be happy. What's your middle name?"

"Princeton. That's where my mom went to college."

"Hmm. Okay, then, how about simply reversing the two names. You'd be Pepper Princeton. Now, that sounds extraordinary. They'll love it."

Peter, aka Pepper Princeton, looked deeply thoughtful, then he began to nod slowly, never taking his eyes off Ruth. "No one's ever admitted before that it was my name that was the problem, but of course I've always known. *Pepper Princeton.* Now that's different, and it won't make anybody laugh. Hello, my name is Princeton, Dr. Princeton. That has a ring to it. It sounds like someone famous. Hey, can I take you to dinner tonight?"

Ruth patted his shoulder. "I've already got a date tonight, but thank you. Good luck."

Dr. Gordon Holcombe watched the young man walk down the corridor, shoulders squared, lively now, a snap to his step. He said to Ruth, "That was brilliant. If only I'd thought of that six months ago. But it was better coming from you. May I take you to dinner tonight?"

Dix ushered them all into his uncle's office.

"Hey, what about me?" Helen Rafferty called after them. "Would someone like to take me out to dinner?"

CHAPTER 14

Dix had always thought that Gordon's office proclaimed the man. Sheet music littered every available surface, musical instruments leaned against three walls, and a black Steinway baby grand jutted out from the corner, lid closed, loaded down with music scores. The desk, Ruth saw with a smile, was there only as a delivery system for the computer and printer and still more sheet music. There were half a dozen chairs scattered around the room, probably so Dr. Holcombe could pick up random instruments with his students and play. There was no area to sit, only chairs and music stands. A French horn sat on one of the chairs, and others were covered with reviews from newspapers and more sheet music.

It was a warm office, Ruth thought, reflecting what was important to the man and not the administrator of Stanislaus School of Music. She found she was smiling at Dr. Holcombe when she said, "Maybe I will have dinner with you, sir. Do you like Italian?"

Dix frowned. "Not dinner, Ruth, it's not possible. I told the boys I was making all of us hot dogs, baked beans, and corn bread for dinner tonight. They're expecting you."

Dr. Holcombe started to say something, but Dix rolled right over him. "We need to speak with you about something serious, Gordon."

"Why? Is this about Chappy, Dix? What is that old peckerhead up to now? Did you know Cynthia came to see me last week, afraid Chappy was going to kick Tony out of his position at the bank? The boy should simply pick up stakes and leave here, he'd be much better for it. So has Chappy accused me or the school of something and sent you here to arrest me? You know he's always hated me, Dix. It's jealousy, all of it; he wants me dead or in jail, anywhere he can't see me and be reminded that all he's ever accomplished was making money."

Dix was the only one not appalled by this show of vitriol coming from the talented and sophisticated Dr. Holcombe's very nicely sculpted mouth. Dix grinned, shook his head. "Nope, not everything's about Chappy or his trying to make your life miserable, Gordon."

Dr. Holcombe leaned against his desk, arms crossed over his chest, looked from one to the other of them. "All right then, Dix, tell me what's going on. First off, why don't you introduce me to all these people?"

Dix made the introductions, Dr. Holcombe's left eyebrow rising each time the letters FBI were repeated. He shook hands with each of them, paused when he took Ruth's hand. "I realize now that you're the woman Dix found Friday evening, sleeping in his Range Rover, nearly dead of the cold, but about these other two FBI agents? Are you all investigating together? How on earth can I help you?"

"How well do you know Erin Bushnell?"

Dr. Holcombe looked momentarily startled, then said to Dix, "Why, Erin Bushnell — very talented, plays the violin with extraordinary verve and bombast. I've been working with her on her control and spontaneity, which sounds weird, doesn't it? After all, music is learned; music is practiced. But that's what a true artist does — he sounds like the piece of music is bursting out of him, like he's never played it before, but for these people, here is his gift, his blessing. You should hear Erin play Bartók's Sonata for Solo Violin. She's absolutely brilliant. You'll feel like you're the first human being to ever hear it.

"How else do I know her? She's in her fourth year, due to graduate with her bachelor of music in May. I believe she wants to remain for her master's. What's going on, Dix? Has Erin done something? I know she doesn't do drugs, maybe some marijuana, there's some of that on campus, but never anything stronger. She likes to drive that little Miata of hers real fast, too. Oh no, she didn't have an accident, did she?"

Dix said, "It's not drugs, Gordon, and it's not a car accident. I'm sorry to tell you this, but Erin Bushnell is dead. We found her body in a chamber in Winkel's Cave. As of yet, we don't know the cause of her death, but it looks like she was murdered and entombed in that cavern. The exits were covered up, the murderer probably hoping she'd never be found."

Gordon looked ready to faint, his sharp-boned aristocratic face as white as his knuckles clutching the edge of the desk. His mouth moved, but all that came out was "No, that can't be possible. No, Dix, not Erin. She was so very talented, you see, so fresh and young and promising. You've got to be mistaken. No, that can't be right. Are you sure it's her you found?"

Dix lightly laid his hand on his uncle's shoulder. "I'm very sorry, Gordon, but we're sure. We think she was killed shortly before Ruth entered that chamber on Friday. The killer probably dragged her in there right before Ruth arrived."

"Erin in Winkel's Cave? Why in heaven's name would she be there? I was thinking about calling her this weekend, arranging for her to give another concert before she graduates, but I got caught up writing this new sonata I'm working on, and I forgot. Oh, that poor child."

Ruth said to him, "We all feel very badly about it, Dr. Holcombe. But we need your help. Erin needs your help. Someone killed her. We need you to tell us about her — her friends, her instructors, boyfriends, her habits, whatever you can to help us. We need to know where she was on Friday."

Ruth saw he wasn't ready to deal with it yet. She couldn't really blame him. Violent death is always a shock if one knew the victim.

Gordon covered his eyes with his hands. "This is very difficult to accept. A student, one of my students, murdered. Things like that simply don't happen at Stanislaus. Oh dear. What will this do to our school, to our funding? You're not thinking that another student murdered her, are you? We breed musicians here, not murderers." He lowered his head, trying to get ahold of himself. When he looked up again, he was still remarkably pale, but his voice was steady. "Erin studied with Gloria Brichoux Stanford, an older woman, immensely talented, flamboyant, with a razor tongue. She's given a dozen performances at Carnegie Hall over the years, made many recordings, played with a number of orchestras around the world. You and Christie knew her in New York, Dix."

Dix explained. "Christie and Gloria's daughter went to school at Carnegie Mellon at the same time. Gloria accepted a position here at Stanislaus about six months after we left New York, which surprised and pleased us. Her daughter also moved here with her. So Erin studied closely with her, Gordon?"

"Since the beginning of the fall term in September, Erin studied with Gloria two hours a day, at a minimum. I'd say no one on the faculty knows Erin better than Gloria. She may be able to tell you, well . . . I don't know, but wouldn't she know about Erin's boyfriends, people she didn't like, if she's been worried about something, things like that?" His voice fell off and he stood silent, leaning against his desk, staring down at his lovely Italian loafers. "Erin was so very young, twenty-one, twenty-two? Have you spoken to her parents, Dix?"

"Yes, I did. It was very difficult. They couldn't think of anyone who disliked their daughter, much less enough to kill her. No recent boyfriend problems they were aware of. They'll be coming here to take her back home to Iowa. Helen gave us Erin's address. Do you know if she had roommates? Lived alone?"

Gordon shrugged. "I have no idea."

"No matter. Thank you, Gordon, for your help. I'm very sorry about this. I'm sure you'll have a lot to do now. Especially when this gets out to the media."

"Oh yes, the media will see to it that everyone at Stanislaus is crucified over this. I've got to take steps to protect my students from them. Well, we'll deal with it, no choice." He was no longer Gordon, he was Dr. Holcombe again. "Please keep me informed if you learn anything. I will call Erin's parents myself. We'll set up a memorial here for her."

Helen was silent when they came out. There were tears in her eyes. "This simply doesn't seem possible. Erin, dead. I'm so very sorry. She was a fine young woman, really nice at least around me. I was at a couple of faculty parties where she was present. She didn't drink much, I remember, seemed rather shy, but friendly if anyone made the effort. This is tragic, Sheriff, it really is."

Ruth lightly patted her arm. "Thanks for your help, Helen."

Helen said, "Erin didn't have any roommates. She lived alone." She handed Dix a card.

They watched her walk into Dr. Holcombe's office and speak quietly to him for a moment as they left. The air outside felt heavy, and cold.

"What's on the card Helen gave you?" Savich asked Dix when they'd climbed back into the Range Rover.

"Gloria Brichoux Stanford's cell phone number and address. We'll visit her tomorrow. Let's take thirty minutes now to stop by Erin Bushnell's apartment, see if we can find anything."

"Some torn-up love letters, signed, might be nice," Ruth said.

"I'll settle for some nice clear fingerprints," Dix said. A couple minutes later he turned onto Upper Canyon Road, only three blocks from campus. It was an old neighborhood lined with brightly painted wooden houses, some of them Victorians.

Ancient snow-laden oak trees filled the deep yards.

"She lives on the second floor. There it is," Dix said.

There was no answer when Dix rang the bell. He knocked, waited, and knocked again. He yelled out his name. Still no answer. He tried the doorknob, and it opened.

He said over his shoulder, "This trust in your fellow man is good for us. Let's go."

It was a large house, an apartment on each of three floors. There was no number on the second-floor apartment. He turned the knob. The door opened. "I can't believe she didn't lock her door," Ruth said. "The front door's one thing, but this is asking for trouble of a bad kind."

Sherlock said, "Maybe the killer took her here and he was the one who left the door unlocked."

They walked into a large, high-ceilinged living room with cushioned window seats lining a turret to the right, facing the street. The living room connected to a dining alcove and a kitchen on the other side of a long serving counter.

Even though no lights were on, it was bright and made brighter by colorful throw pillows and pastel walls covered with huge posters, mostly of Brad Pitt.

"Okay," Dix said. "Let's split up and check it out quickly. My deputies will be here to check for fingerprints when they're done at the crime scene."

They all knew what they were doing, and in ten minutes they were together again in the living room.

"She needed to go food shopping," Ruth said. "There was a packet of carrots and a carton of nonfat milk in the refrigerator. I didn't want to smell it. Only junk in the junk drawer, no memos, no notes."

The living room, the single bedroom, and the bathroom looked almost unlived in.

But not Erin Bushnell's music room. It was shuttered and small, but they could tell this was the room where the young woman spent all her time. There were piles of neatly arranged musical scores for violin and orchestra. On a chair sat an open violin case with her violin tucked snugly inside it. Sherlock eased it out of its case, held it in her open hands. She said, "It was made by Hart and Sons in London in the nineteenth century. You rarely see these. It's exquisite."

Sherlock glanced through the music, didn't see anything that didn't belong.

There was no address book, no diary, no stray pieces of paper with notes or names for appointments. She did have a small laptop and Dix took it with him. "I'll have our resident Weenie check it out." At Ruth's raised eyebrow, he smiled. "His name is Allen. Everyone calls him Weenie. He actually likes it."

Ruth closed Erin's apartment door behind them. "The only thing really personal about the place was her music and her violin."

"I think we'll have to look elsewhere for why she died," Dix said. As he pulled away from the old house, he added, "Okay, we'll have to knock off for the night. The boys will be wondering where I'm hiding you guys. Too, I hate to have them at home alone for too long after school. They're beyond excited that you FBI agents will be at the house again."

"Yep, I guess they're the Big Dogs now at school," Ruth said. "Bet they promised all their friends they'd dig secrets out of us tonight."

Dix honked his horn to alert a car turning in front of him. He said to Ruth, "Be careful Brewster doesn't pee on you again."

Ruth grinned. "I know to be careful now. I couldn't go out to dinner with any of my admirers if he did. And I may be wearing the last of Rob's clothes."

Dix's cell rang as he was negotiating the Range Rover through a three-foot pile of snow blocking the middle of Stumptree Lane. Someone had put a ball of snow on top of it with a carrot for a nose. "I wouldn't be surprised if Rob and Rafer were involved in that stunt." He answered, "Yeah? Sheriff Noble here."

He listened for a moment, pulled the Range Rover to the side of the road, and said, "Tell me you're kidding. I really need you to." He listened awhile longer, rang off, and slid the phone back in his jacket pocket. He said, "That was the medical examiner, Dr. Himple. He says Erin Bushnell had a drug in her system that he identified with his spectroscopy unit. He thinks it's a chemical called BZ, and it may have incapacitated her. Then the murderer slid a thin blade or a needle into her chest." Dix drew a deep breath. "But it's what he did to her after he killed her — damnedest thing I've ever heard of."

Ruth leaned over and touched his arm. "What, Dix, what did he do?"

"He embalmed her."

CHAPTER 15

Savich sprinkled salt on his corn on the cob, bit into it, and sighed with pleasure. "Rob, we liked the snowman you guys built in the middle of Stumptree Lane. That old carrot was a good touch — it would have brought most cars, except your dad's, to a humiliated stop. He plowed the Range Rover right through it, probably would have eaten the carrot if it hadn't looked so gnarly."

The boys exchanged looks before Rob cleared his throat. "Well, it was a whole bunch of us, you know? A lot of kids from the sophomore class walk home near there," he said with a look toward their father. "It really wouldn't be fair to single any of them out, Dad. The thing is, they closed down school at three and none of us wanted to go sledding again. The snow on Breaker's Hill is really trashed, you know?"

"You guys want another hot dog?" Dix asked them, and both boys smiled at him, limp with relief.

Rob asked carefully, a potato chip suspended an inch from his mouth, "You're not pissed, Dad? You're not going to ground us?"

"Hey, Earth to Dad," Rafe said, and snapped his fingers toward his father.

"What? Oh sorry, the snow pile. I remember we did the same thing once only it was in Queens, and the beat cop took half a dozen of us down to the precinct house to scare us. My dad tanned my butt. You know, you guys aren't too old for me to hide."

Rob said, "We're too old, Dad, really. Besides, you always say that then never do." He grinned. "If you really want to teach us a lesson, why don't you toss us in jail for a night? That would be the ultimate punishment, you know?"

"Punishment as in really cool?" Ruth asked.

Dix rolled his eyes. "You were lucky I was the first one through your little snow fort and flattened it out for everybody else."

"Bummer," Rob said around a hot dog loaded with French's mustard and sweet relish.

"We had our test on *Othello* today, Dad," Rafe said. "I think I did really well. I think I knew the answers to all the questions."

"That's great," Dix said. "I've told you you have your mother's brains."

"Yeah, well," Rafe continued, "if I get at least a B minus can I take that after-school job at Mr. Fulton's hardware store?"

Dix's cell phone rang, and he stepped away to answer it. When he returned, he pointed his finger at Rafe. "No part-time job until you have at least a B in biology and a B in English, as we agreed. Not a B minus, a good, solid B. Your report card's out in three weeks, so you've got a goal. And don't whine about it. Sherlock and Savich have a little boy a lot younger than you guys, and we don't have to show them what's in store for them."

"We're not that bad, Agent Savich," Rob said. "Dad just pretends we are."

Rafe shot his brother a look, then leaned forward, his eyes on his dad's face. "We heard about you finding that murdered student in Winkel's Cave. Everyone's talking about it — first those two guys who tried to kill Ruth on Saturday night, and now this girl. What's happening, Dad?"

His father said, "Yes, we found a body in Winkel's Cave. It wasn't pleasant."

"You sure are lucky you've got FBI special agents here to help you," Rob said.

"Yeah," Dix said, his voice dry as a bleached bone, "I'm very lucky."

"Do you see dead bodies all the time,

Agent Savich?" Rob asked.

"Not all the time, no," Savich said easily. "Actually I do a whole lot of work on a computer, a laptop named MAX. He and I have tracked down a good number of bad guys over the years."

"As for us," Sherlock said, "Agent Warnecki and I have noses like bloodhounds. They just set us on a trail, and we sniff the bad guys right out."

"Dad, this is pretty scary," Rafe said. "What happened to that girl?"

"I've got to keep some things close, boys. I don't want the media to get ahold of everything I've got."

"But —"

Dix shook his head. "I've got some questions for Ruth about treasure hunting. Are there clubs, newsletters, that sort of thing?"

She nodded, more to the boys than to their father. "Yes, there's all of that. Have you guys ever heard of the buried treasure at Snow Hill Farm, about a mile south of the village of New Baltimore, right here in Virginia?"

The boys, who'd been sprawled long and skinny in their chairs, sat up and leaned toward her, Rafe's chin on his hands. "Silver coins," she said, "gold ones, too, valued at about sixty thousand dollars."

"Who buried it?" Rafe wanted to know. "Did you find it?"

"A Scottish pirate named William Kirk buried it back in the 1770s for safekeeping. But when he died, there was no sign of the treasure, and his widow sold Snow Hill Farm to Colonel William Edmonds, whose heirs still own the property. People have looked over the years, but still no sign of it, only an occasional eighteenth-century coin."

"I could find it," Rafe said, "not just one or two stupid coins."

Rob punched his brother in the arm. "There isn't any treasure, Dumbo. It's a myth, otherwise someone would have dug it up by now."

"But that's the thing about treasure," Ruth said, her voice dropping low, "sometimes you wonder how all the talk of a treasure even started. An old guy in a tavern two hundred years ago spun a story so he could get a free mug of ale? And then you sometimes wonder if it isn't all magic. When you think it's magic, you're ready. You go to Fauquier County and find William Kirk's will that's still there, and read that he not only left his wife a large property, he also left her a big bundle of currency. Where is it?"

Rafe said, "Didn't the wife know her

husband was a pirate? Everyone knows pirates always hide their gold, like Captain Kidd did somewhere on Long Island. She shouldn't have sold the farm, she was stupid."

Ruth grinned. "Maybe. Or maybe she didn't believe there was a treasure, like Rob. Or maybe she believed, she simply didn't know how to find it."

Dix said, "Knowing Ruth for only three days, boys, you can already tell the most important quality of a successful treasure hunter: you've got to believe. You've got to be the eternal optimist, and you have to stand lots of disappointment." He cocked his eyebrow at her.

Ruth stared at him, lounged back in his chair, his fingers laced over his lean belly, his long sleeves rolled up to his elbows.

She started to say something, but found she had to clear her throat first. "Well, yes, that's about it," she admitted.

"So you think the gold's still there, Ruth?" Rob wanted to know.

She nodded. "Oh yes, it's there. I think it was in leather pouches, a number of them, and some of them have split open, scattering the coins. But the big cache is under there still, waiting."

Dix rose. "With that, it's time for some

carrot cake from Millie's Deli. You can each take a piece, then it's off to do your homework. We've got some work to do down here ourselves."

Rob stopped long enough on the bottom step of the stairs to tell Ruth that Billy McCleland had come by today to fix the window frame in his bedroom. "No more cold leaks," he told her.

When the boys were out of earshot, the four adults moved into the living room, taking coffee and tea with them. The house was warm and quiet, except for Brewster's snoring from his seat of honor on Ruth's lap. Savich began, "So Dix, you told us the doctor at Louden County Community Hospital did a toxicology screen on Ruth when she was admitted. You hear from him yet?"

Dix nodded. "Actually, it was the ME who called earlier. He ran what was left of your blood sample, Ruth. You had the same drug in your system that Erin Bushnell did — a drug called BZ."

Sherlock said, "I don't know much about it except I think it's a gas they used in Vietnam that affects the nervous system. Did he tell you more about it, Sheriff?"

Dix paused for a moment, smiled at her. "Actually, Sherlock, while Savich's corn on the cob was boiling, I Googled it on the Internet. I printed some of it out, so you can look at it later. It's officially called quinuclidinyl benzilate, but for obvious reasons it's known simply as BZ. It's a colorless and odorless gas that's usually delivered as an aerosol and was developed for the military in the 1960s. It works fairly quickly, causing increased heart rate, blurry vision, lack of coordination. The unusual thing is that it's what they call a psychochemical — it affects perception and thought, causes hallucinations, confusion, forgetfulness, and eventually stupor.

"BZ didn't turn out to be much use in war, though, because the effects are unpredictable, ranging from overwhelming fear and panic to all-out rage that led exposed soldiers to attack without regard for their own safety.

"The Russians used an agent similar to BZ against the Afghan guerrillas during the eighties, and get this — it's possible they pumped this gas into that theater during the hostage crisis in Moscow, probably in really high concentrations because they ended up with hundreds of people dead."

"But Erin wasn't dead when she was stabbed," Sherlock said.

"No, but there was a lot of it in her system, more than in yours, Ruth. From what you told us about how terrifying it was for you in that cave chamber, how you were imagining God knows what coming after you, I hate to think what Erin Bushnell went through."

Ruth let out a long breath. "So I guess I didn't just go crazy. But how does anyone get ahold of a gas like this?"

Dix shrugged. "The ME said chemicals like this are available from pharmaceutical companies and on the Internet. Apparently they have some legitimate uses for research. It's unusual enough to warrant looking into but it's unlikely the BZ is from a nice, clean local source that would identify our killer."

Savich nodded. "Since you got a lower dose than Erin, Ruth, you probably got the residue from the gas he used on her. Maybe he came back later to check on his handiwork and found you, freaked out, maybe unconscious. Maybe he bashed you on the head or he found you already injured, and hauled you out of there."

"But why not simply kill me and leave me in there with Erin?"

Savich said slowly, "Because that was her tomb, Ruth, not yours. All hers."

"That would be really sick, Dillon."

"Yes," he said, "it would be."

Sherlock sat forward, her teacup balanced on her knee. "So you think this tomb idea has something to do with his embalming her?"

Dix said, "Dr. Himple said he didn't actually embalm her. He said it was the strangest thing he'd ever seen. I'll try to explain this correctly." Dix pulled a sheet of paper out of his shirt pocket, perused it for a moment. "Okay, when a funeral home embalms a body, they make small incisions in the carotid artery and the jugular vein, thread a tube into the carotid to pump in the embalming fluid, and drain the blood out through the jugular vein. It takes about three gallons of embalming fluid to thoroughly disinfect and preserve a body. They also put fluid in the body cavities, a mixture of formaldehyde, methanol, ethanol, and other solvents.

"The thing is, our murderer didn't do a thorough job of it. He made the small incisions in her carotid and jugular, pumped in about a gallon of embalming fluid, let a bit of blood drain out the jugular vein, then called it a day."

Sherlock said slowly, staring into the fireplace, "So he either didn't know how to

210

do the procedure correctly or it was some kind of ritual, enough to give him the taste of the process, to give him the satisfaction."

Savich nodded. "Yes, and he posed her. He may have considered it part of a ceremony, probably done with a good deal of gravity on his part, almost reverence. He may have wanted to preserve the body for a while before he buried it somewhere."

Dix said, "I don't like the sound of that. A ritual? I was thinking this guy may have done this before, but I was hoping you'd disagree."

"We don't know for sure, Dix, but it's got all the earmarks," Ruth said. "Did Dr. Himple tell you if the incision sites were sutured?"

"No, I don't think so. But he did mention that the stab wound in her chest had no blood on it; it had been swabbed clean."

"Part of the ritual then," Ruth said. "He did a thorough job. So, Dix, are there any funeral homes in Maestro?"

"Of course. Tommy Oppenheimer is director of Peaceful Field Funeral Home, on Broadmoor Street. He's my deputy Penny's husband, a good guy, a bit high-strung, overprotective of Penny, but okay.

I'll ask him if he's had anyone asking questions about embalming, or if he's heard anyone in his business mention any strange employees they might have now or recently fired."

Sherlock said, "If I were you, I'd tell Dr. Himple to threaten all his techs with pain and dismemberment if any of them open their mouths about finding embalming fluids in her."

Dix shook his head. "Unbelievable, the loony actually performed an embalming rite on her. That is something her parents will never find out about."

Sherlock said, "You should go personally and speak to the techs, Dix. That might keep it under wraps longer, particularly if you guilt them about the parents finding out, and what it would do to them. Dillon will get MAX on the embalming process, and find out if this MO has ever appeared before."

Dix stretched his back, crossed his legs at the ankles. "When I left New York, I thought I'd left the crazies behind. Was I wrong, or what? If Ruth hadn't gone into Winkel's Cave treasure hunting on that particular day, Erin Bushnell would have simply disappeared forever. No one would have had a clue what happened to her —

did she pick up and leave with no word for anyone, or run off with some guy no one ever saw, or . . . did someone take her away?" He stopped dead, looked down at the floor, his hands frozen in fists on his thighs. Ruth saw that he was pale, markedly so. There was something very wrong here. Then she knew. "Dix, what happened to your wife, Christie?"

Dix didn't answer for the longest time, didn't move, didn't look at any of them. Finally, he looked up at Ruth standing beside him. "My wife . . . Christie . . . she disappeared nearly three years ago."

"And you don't know what happened to her, do you?"

He shook his head. "She was simply gone one day, like Erin Bushnell would have been if you hadn't happened along. We conducted a huge criminal investigation, did everything humanly possible — I even hired a private detective I'd heard about out of Chicago — but no one ever found a single clue, a single lead, nothing. For nearly three years."

He looked up then at Savich and Sherlock. "From the minute Ruth found Erin Bushnell, I've been asking myself if this was what happened to Christie."

Savich cleared his throat and glanced

briefly at his wife. "I can't imagine what it would be like to live with that uncertainty, the pain of not knowing. It's got to have been really rough for you and your boys. But you've done a remarkable job with them. And I'll tell you the truth: I'd be thinking along the same lines as you if it were Sherlock. But the fact is, I think it's highly unlikely that Christie's disappearance had anything to do with Erin Bushnell's murder."

Ruth felt tears burn her throat and swallowed them. She smiled at him. "Dix, did I ever tell you how very grateful I am that they dumped me in your woods? Hey, I never would have met your boys otherwise and had the opportunity to bleach the blue out of your boxers."

There was quiet laughter. Ruth thought it felt very good.

As he helped Sherlock on with her jacket, Savich said, "We have a very unbalanced individual here, guys, but someone functioning normally enough to send those two men here to the house after you. It would behoove all of us to be very careful, you in particular, Ruth. He's tried to kill you once, and he may try again."

"What would be his reason now?" Ruth asked. "We found his cave, we found Erin, and I've told you everything I know. Why would he mess with an FBI agent now?"

Dix said, "Savich is right. You're being logical, Ruth. I doubt we can say the same thing about someone who pumped embalming fluid into Erin's body. Fact is, we can't be sure about anything he might do."

"That's a cheery thought," Ruth said.

Dix said, "Savich, what are the chances of your profilers at Quantico taking a shot at this?"

"I'll call Steve in the morning."

After Savich and Sherlock left, Dix walked Ruth to Rob's bedroom. He paused by the closed door of Rafe's room to listen. "It's too quiet," he said. "Usually I can hear at least one of them snoring."

She lightly laid her hand on his arm. "I am very, very sorry about Christie. You believe she's dead, don't you?"

He nodded. "Yes, I know she is. There is no way Christie would leave me and the boys. Not willingly. Someone took her, someone killed her. I just don't know who."

There was nothing she could say, and so Ruth simply pressed against him, held him for a very long time.

When she finally stepped back, she kept her hand on his arm for a moment. "You don't think there's any danger from me staying here tonight, do you?"

He heard the hint of fear in her voice and shook his head. "I'm thinking you could kick your way out of a bar fight, Special Agent. But I'm not about to take any more chances with you or the boys. I've got my deputies on a rotating schedule. They'll be checking the house every hour, not to worry."

She nodded. "I need to pick up some clothes tomorrow, Dix. Rob needs his stuff back."

"No problem," Dix said, and turned away. He paused, turned back. "You okay, Ruth?"

"Sure, I'm fine. Are you okay, Dix?"

He said nothing, merely nodded.

When he lay in his bed, Dix listened to the familiar sounds of the night and wondered what was happening to his peaceful town. And he thought of Christie. He'd never before spoken of her as he had tonight. Somehow he felt comforted, a bit freer of the numbing pain, a bit more open to life again. He still had Christie's photo on his desk at work, taken with his boys only a month before she vanished. He looked at her every day, and every day he wondered what had happened to her.

CHAPTER 16

Maestro, Virginia
Tuesday morning

It was ten-thirty Tuesday morning before the four of them met for a late breakfast at Maurie's Diner on Main Street. Savich sipped tea, set down his cup. "MAX found us instances of stabbing and gassing, of course, even embalming, by a parade of psychopaths you don't want to know about, but never all together, at least that we know about. I make that caveat because if not for Ruth, we might never have found Erin Bushnell."

"You don't sound surprised," Dix said as he spread butter on wheat toast.

Savich shook his head. "I've learned that the killers among us have limitless imagination."

Ruth laid down her fork, leaned her chin on her laced fingers. "And that's the whole point. It's his own special deal, his way of making himself unique, his own creation."

Savich said, "I agree, Ruth. It's usually a

script the killer must follow to the letter if he's to consider his act a success. He didn't want his handiwork discovered, that isn't what he's about, what he's after. It's the process — that's what's important to him."

"More tea, Special Agent?"

Savich smiled up at Glenna, the waitress. "Yes, thank you." When she'd left, looking over her shoulder at him several times, Savich asked Dix, "Did you meet with the techs at the morgue this morning?"

"Yep. I threatened them with whatever I could think of." He shrugged. "They all agreed, but who knows? None of my deputies know a thing about it, either. Only the four of us, Dr. Himple, and the three techs. I also called Dr. Crocker at Louden County Community Hospital." Dix's cell phone rang. He pulled it out of his pocket, said, "Sheriff Noble here."

His expression lightened as he listened, and then darkened, and his hand fisted on the tabletop. He looked very angry. "Is this your idea of good news, bad news, Emory?" He listened for quite a while, the three agents sensing the deputy calling was trying to calm his boss. He looked ready to eat nails when he flipped off his cell phone.

Ruth said, "Well?"

"My deputies found your Beemer in the

shed behind Walt McGuffey's house, Ruth. Remember the house we passed on the way to Lone Tree Hill? And I saw that the snow didn't look like it had been disturbed at all, and called to have my people check on Walt?" He paused, and there was such a look of helpless rage on his face that Ruth laid her hand on his arm.

"What happened, Dix? What's the bad news?"

"They didn't stop by until this morning. Walt was dead, probably since Friday. Murdered, more than likely by the same monster who murdered Erin and tried to murder you. He hid your Beemer in the shed."

"How was Mr. McGuffey killed, Sheriff?"

Dix got ahold of himself at the sound of Savich's voice. "Stabbed through the heart with one of his own kitchen knives."

Sherlock said, "Walt wasn't part of his ritual. It was expediency, nothing more than that. Maybe the old man saw something he shouldn't have."

Dix nodded. "Maybe he needed very badly to hide Ruth's car in a hurry, and simply dispatched Walt quickly because he was in the way. Maybe we'll find something in the car."

Dix dropped a twenty alongside Savich's money on the table. He helped Ruth on with Rob's old leather jacket. She said, "I'm really sorry about this, Dix. This Walt McGuffey, have you known him for a long time?"

He nodded. "As long as I've lived here. Walt was eighty-seven years old, bragged about it, lived here all his life. Chappy told me he used to be the finest furniture maker in the state, liked to build with bird's-eye maple the best. His wife, Martha, died in the seventies, cancer I believe. Christie used to invite him over for Thanksgiving dinner, and . . . well, I've had him over myself for the past two years."

Since Maurie's was across the street from the sheriff's office, Dix walked right over, ready to ream out Emory for waiting so long to get out to McGuffey's place.

Penny Oppenheimer was sitting behind the information desk, a large bandage wrapped around her head. Dix was surprised to see her at work. She was supposed to rest for the next few days.

Before he could say a word, Penny said, "The reason Emory didn't send deputies out to the old McGuffey place sooner, Sheriff, is because we've all been working overtime guarding your house and working on the three deaths we already had, not to mention the downed power lines from the storm. Emory's also been dealing with the hundreds of calls we've had from people asking about all this, not to mention fending off the press, and three DUIs, all of them teenagers."

"The press?"

"Yes, sir. Milton has been bugging us every five minutes for updates, said it's the public's right to know and he wants up-to-date details for his deadline on Wednesday."

Dix snorted, said to the three of them, "Milton Bean owns and operates the *Maestro Daily Telegraph.* He's seventy-four, hacks nonstop because he smokes cigars. He hasn't had a byline in fifteen years."

Penny said helpfully, "He swears he's writing one right this instant, if only our office would cooperate —"

"I'm surprised the real press hasn't arrived yet. Then you'll really have your hands full. Where is Emory?"

"In the men's room, I think," Penny said. "On top of everything else, he was talking about diarrhea. He's really sorry, Sheriff, feels really bad."

"Yeah, I'm gonna make him feel a lot worse."

Ruth grinned. "But you, Penny, did a great job breaking all this to the sheriff. Everyone knew he wouldn't get mad at a poor deputy whose head is all bandaged up from risking her life for him." She added to Dix, "You've got a pretty smart staff here, Dix."

Dix asked abruptly, "How is your head, Penny? Maybe you should still be home. Did Emory get you in here to keep me from kicking his butt?"

Penny shook her head. "Believe me, I want to be here. At home Tommy makes me lie on the sofa and watch TV. I couldn't take it anymore. I'm only doing desk duty — taking calls, that's all, answering questions if anyone comes in, I promise. Hey, everyone's really upset about this. Walt was a neat old guy."

"He sure was," Dix said, and stomped away to his office.

Sherlock said to Deputy Penny Oppenheimer as she walked by her desk, "Nice touch, that lovely huge bandage. No man could withstand that. No man would have even thought of it."

"Thank you," Penny said. "I figured I had to do something or the sheriff would kick in Emory's kneecaps. Hey, he doesn't seem to mind you guys being here. I guess

222

you're not trying to tromp him under your big Federal shoes."

"An occasional toe nudge is all," Sherlock said. She nodded at the large room through a glass partition behind Penny, where half a dozen deputies were trying to look busy, but naturally were focused on the three interlopers. And Ruth in particular, who was dressed in Rob's jeans, a flannel shirt, and an old leather jacket. She followed Dillon into the sheriff's office.

"Nice office," Sherlock said.

Ruth was surprised, truth be told. Covering an entire wall was a photographic pictorial of Virginia, from the old town in Alexandria to the sweeping white paddocks of horse country. There was a large black-and-white print of the fog-shrouded mountains and color blowups of incredible green valleys, wildly beautiful in the middle of summer with thick pines, maples, and oaks. They were framed in black like the photo on his desk of a woman and two boys. It must be Christie, she thought. She saw he was looking at her and smiled. "She's lovely, Dix."

"Thank you." Dix tucked some papers in his pocket he'd pulled out of his desk drawer. "Okay, let's go out to Walt's place."

Fifteen minutes later, after Dix had spoken to four of his deputies who had marked off the perimeter of the McGuffey property from sightseers, they stepped into Walt McGuffey's 1940s bungalow that looked like it hadn't been updated since it was built. The furniture, though, was amazing. Walt had kept his best pieces, all of bird's-eye maple and exquisitely made — a sofa, a table, six chairs, several side tables. The unfortunate 1970s burnt-orange shag carpet, however, didn't enhance the setting. Dr. Himple was there with the forensic team from Louden, the county seat. The forensic folks looked tired. Dr. Himple stretched as he stood up, and nodded in their direction, but his eyes were on Dix. "I'm really sorry, Dix. Walt died easily, if it makes any difference. The knife killed him fast; he probably hardly felt it. There aren't any defensive wounds. He probably didn't even see it coming. But that's preliminary, you understand. I'll do an autopsy immediately and let you know."

Savich said, "So Mr. McGuffey knew his murderer — he let him in, welcomed him."

Dr. Himple nodded. "Yes, I would say so."

Sherlock said, "Mr. McGuffey probably invited him into the kitchen, say for a cup of coffee. The murderer knew he was going to kill the old man, probably looked around for a weapon, saw the knife on the counter, and used it."

Dr. Himple looked from Sherlock to Savich and slowly nodded. "That could be about right."

"Fingerprint everything," Dix said to Marvin Wilkes, head of the forensic team. "Especially around the kitchen."

Dix knelt down next to the old man, who, in truth, resembled a bundle of old clothes wrapped around bones. He lightly laid his hand on the old man's shoulder and closed his eyes for a moment. He pictured Walt grinning up at him with his six remaining teeth, asking if those gall-derned boys of his had given him any gray hairs yet. Now there was a look of surprise on the old man's face, no pain, only blank surprise.

He felt tears sting his eyes and swallowed. He rose quickly, said to Dr. Himple, "Treat him well, Burt, he was a grand old man. My boys are going to be very upset by this."

"I'll take care of him now, Sheriff."

"He doesn't have any family. I'll set up his funeral myself."

They searched Walt McGuffey's house, but found nothing of note except an ancient wooden box that held photos of Walt and his wife, and a young boy, taken in the forties. "His son?" Savich asked.

Dix shook his head. "I don't know. If so, he must have died real young. Walt never mentioned any children." Dix paused, then tucked the box under his arm. "I think Walt might want to be buried with this."

In the old shed at the back of the house they found Ruth's Beemer, nice and clean since the murderer had hidden it there before the snow started. Her wallet lay on the front seat, her duffel bag on the passenger-side floor. The Beemer's keys were in the ignition.

You'll have to leave all this here for a while, Ruth," Dix said. "The forensic team needs to go over everything."

"Of course, no problem."

"The boys will probably bug you to drive them around in it later," Dix added wearily. "All right. If everyone wants to pile back into the Range Rover, we'll go to meet the famous violinist."

Gloria Brichoux Stanford lived on Elk Horn Road, not a quarter mile from the Stanislaus campus, in a one-story ranch-style house with a very big footprint, surrounded on three sides by woods. The three-car garage was tucked away in the back and connected to the kitchen. It was in a lovely setting that once belonged, Dix told them, to an old gentleman who'd been the head bookkeeper for Chappy at the Maestro First Independent Bank before he retired. He'd inherited the property and house from his great-aunt. When he died, his heirs sold it to Gloria when she retired from public life and accepted a position at Stanislaus.

"What's she like, Dix?" Ruth asked as they walked up a well-shoveled front walkway.

"I told you she and her daughter moved here about six months after Christie, the boys, and me. Her daughter is a lawyer here in Maestro, does primarily wills, trusts, and estate planning. Christie said Ginger always bragged about not having a lick of musical talent, thank the Lord."

"Why was she happy about that?" Sherlock asked.

Dix turned to Sherlock. "Ginger felt like her life was in constant upheaval, with her mother always traveling, always per-forming, leaving her at home. When Gloria wasn't touring, she was down for the count with exhaustion or shot through with adrenaline about her next performance.

Ginger's father took off when she was about ten. Ginger says all she needs is a will to draw up in peace and quiet and she's a happy camper."

The front door was opened by a plump older woman who appeared to be the housekeeper. They were shown to the living room and politely asked to be seated. They were all speaking quietly and looking out over the beautiful front lawn when Gloria Brichoux Stanford made her entrance. She was wearing ratty old sweats, sneakers, and a headband, and was toweling off her face. "I see Phyllis gave you the formal treatment," she said in a deep, booming voice. She tossed the towel on the floor and walked to where they stood, her hand outstretched.

Dix accepted a kiss from her on his cheek and made the introductions. She said to the rest of them, "Welcome, all of you. You're here about my poor Erin. Gordon called me right after you left him, Dix. I've been running my feet off on the treadmill trying not to think about it." She pressed her palm over her mouth for a moment, as if catching a sob, and turned back to them. "Forgive me. She was like a daughter to me. She had such talent, such passion and life in her music, but none in her own life — a very strange thing, I always thought. She poured everything out of herself into her music. She was acquainted with a lot of men, but rarely dated, and no, she wasn't involved closely with anyone. I would know if she had been.

"I hope you don't mind, Dix, but I called Ginger. She'll be over soon, after she finishes up composing one of her very important wills." She rolled her eyes and wandered to the fireplace, fingering the Hummel figures that stood in a line across the mantel. "Gordon said you would want me to tell you everything I know about her. Well, as I said, she didn't talk about any men in her life. She had no time for them; every bit of her passion went into her music. I could close my eyes while she played a violin solo from Schumann or Edvard Grieg and be reminded of Yehudi Menuhin or myself playing it. She could be that good."

Gloria paused, pulled the headband off her forehead, and ran her fingers through her thick, sweaty salt-and-pepper hair. She wasn't wearing any makeup, or she'd sweated it all off. She'd always worked out, taken good care of herself, Dix thought. She was big-boned, firm, her color excellent. What a change from how he remembered her years before. She'd been much thinner, drawn so tightly she could snap at you like a violin string.

Gloria said, looking off at nothing in particular as far as Ruth could tell, "Erin always wanted to study here at Stanislaus, never Juilliard. She hated New York, thought it was dirty, too big and loud, and didn't like some of the people who lived there." She paused for a moment, sighed. "Her idol was Arcangelo Corelli, though of course she never heard him play since he performed in the seventeenth century. She read a contemporary poet's description of his playing and swore she wanted nothing else."

She turned suddenly, and there were tears in her eyes. "Gordon is devastated. I am devastated. When Erin graduated, she would have been one of the top violinists to come out of Stanislaus in many years. In time, she would have taken her place as first violinist in one of the finest orchestras in the world. I do not understand why anyone would want to snuff out her life and her immense talent."

"How old was she when she began to study violin, Ms. Stanford?" Ruth asked.

"Three, I believe, the usual age if the

parents are intelligent and observant."

"Was she close to her family? To her siblings?" Sherlock asked.

"She was an only child. Before you arrived, her parents called me. I could hardly understand her mother she was crying so hard, poor woman."

"You know of no one who was jealous of her? Hated her because she played so well? Saw her as competition to be eliminated?"

She looked at Agent Savich, who'd asked the question in a deep, soft voice but looked so hard and competent, and dangerous. She saw the wedding ring on his finger and felt a moment of disappointment. "I'm sorry, Agent Savich, what did you say?"

"Jealousy, ma'am. Can you think of anyone who could have gone over the edge because of jealousy?"

Gloria said matter-of-factly, "Let me be clear here. Schools like Stanislaus and Juilliard have only exceptionally talented young people, and every student is in competition with every other student. There aren't that many occupational avenues open for violinists other than performing unless one wants to teach in some high school in Los Angeles. It is cutthroat, sometimes heartbreaking, and it can bring out a person's darkest passions. But musicians learn to focus on themselves and the music when they are challenged, not on each other.

"I cannot imagine a single one of the dozen violin students here at Stanislaus who would have considered Erin such a threat to their own future that they would consider killing her. I've never heard of such a thing. How strange it is that she died in a cave. Do you know she once visited a cave near her home in Iowa so she could hear how her violin sounded deep underground?"

Dix asked about Erin's professors, if she knew anyone living in Maestro. He told her to call him if she thought of anything at all, and because he realized she needed it, he spoke to her of Rob and Rafe, about their sledding on Breaker's Hill and Rafe's double helix project. She was smiling when they left ten minutes later.

Sherlock rose on her tiptoes and said into Savich's ear, "I thought there for a while that she was going to jump you."

He looked startled, automatically shook his head. "You are such an innocent." Sherlock squeezed his arm, and then she noticed the twinkle in his eyes. "Dillon, I'm going to have to punish you for pulling my chain like that."

"How long have they been married?" Dix asked Ruth as he opened the passenger-side door for her.

"Forever," Ruth said. She watched Dix looking at Savich and Sherlock, his gaze unreadable.

CHAPTER 17

At six o'clock, as everyone filed into Dix's kitchen to eat his homemade meat loaf, mashed potatoes, green beans, and a Boston cream pie from Millie's Deli, Savich's cell phone sang the opening lines of "Georgia on My Mind."

Savich excused himself and walked to the kitchen doorway. He looked down at his cell phone screen. It read *Private.* He said, "Savich here."

"Hello, boy, been too long since I checked in with you, now ain't it? Hey, you miss me and my little pranks?" Moses Grace's scratchy old voice sounded happy and so clear he could have been at Savich's elbow.

Savich quickly stepped over to his laptop, MAX, sitting open on the sideboard in the dining room, and pressed ENTER.

Savich had been waiting for this, had expected Moses Grace to call again, and here he was, only four days since he'd first heard the old man's voice. Savich walked into the entrance hall, he didn't want anyone to overhear the conversation. "So, you're blocking Caller ID, Moses. That's cute. Did you kill someone else for this phone?"

An obscene laugh sounded in his ear, ending in a phlegm-filled cough. "Hey, you're the cop, boy, you're the one who's supposed to be able to pinpoint a flea on a sand dune. But you know what? You couldn't find me if I drove up and waved in your face. You want a hint?"

"Yes, give me a hint."

"Maybe I will. Hey, how's that precious little wife of yours?"

A flash of rage poured through Savich. "She's well out of your reach."

"You really believe that? I was thinking about taking that little wife of yours and giving her a shove off a nice steep cliff, watch her roll over and over and pound herself into pieces, watch her sprawled out dead at the bottom. You can watch, too, from the top, boy."

Savich hated this, hated it to his soul. But words couldn't kill and he needed Moses Grace to keep talking. "You still sound pretty bad, Moses. I suppose you're too far gone for any drugs to help you?"

"Me? Not well? Just a little tobacco cough, is all. For a sick man, I did pretty well against all of you comic FBI agents at

Arlington. How about I go shoot up the FBI building?"

"Yeah, why don't you? Or maybe you should first come after me again, you evil old bastard."

The old man was silent for a moment.

"Me? Evil? Yeah, well, meybe so. Meybe my pa poured Drano on Mama's face when she sassed him once too often. Always had a mouth on her, Mama did. Daddy socked her upside the head so many times it knocked her brains squirrely, but she kept on mouthing off at him.

"Hey, what do I care if I'm evil, anyway? The good Lord can take care of His, and I'll take care of my own. Ain't you glad to hear from me, Special Agent Savich? Special Agent — I like that, like all you baboons are worth spit. Four whole days and none of you have gotten anywhere close to me and Claudia. She laughs and laughs whenever we drive by a cop, even flips some of 'em the finger. A finger from my cute little dolly always makes the cops gape at her — they can't believe someone so young and sweet-looking would do such a vulgar thing. She pushes the envelope when meybe she shouldn't. Meybe she's not the brightest child in the world, but she's mine."

"What do you want?"

"I done told you," Moses said, his drawl stretching out endlessly. "I wanted to check in with you — ah, ask you a favor. I want you to call that Ms. Lilly at the Bonhomie Club, tell her what a lovely memorial party she threw for Pinky last night."

Moses Grace and Claudia hadn't been in the nightclub the night before. Six undercover agents were there, hidden cameras everywhere. But they were outside, watching who went in.

"Your boss, D.A.D. Maitland, looked really nice in his dark suit and that yellow tie with the black squiggles on it."

"Yeah, tell me what James Quinlan was wearing."

"Dark suit, red tie with blue triangles on it, looked pretty somber for someone carrying a saxophone. I enjoyed listening to him play. Surprised me — there were lots of folks weeping. It was affectin', real affectin'."

Savich drew a deep breath. They'd been talking a good long time now. Maybe long enough, but he wasn't sure. Best to keep him talking as long as possible, to make certain. "Tell me, Moses, why are you so interested in me? Me in particular? What did I ever do to you?"

Moses was silent for a moment. "So you think this is personal, do you, boy? Well, fact is, you're right. I got more hate for you stored up inside me than Lucifer."

"Why?"

"You hurt her, boy, hurt her so bad she was screaming with it." He broke off. Savich heard the old man's breathing quicken.

"Who was that, Moses?"

"I might tell you before you die, boy. You know my Claudia still wants you, don't you?"

All right. Moses was not going to tell him. He decided to shake the old man. It might be the best way to keep him on the line. Savich said in an amused voice, filled with contempt, "You think I'd actually have down and dirty sex with that bug-eyed crazy teenage slut? I bet Claudia drools, she's so far gone, particularly since she's with you." Savich laughed, vicious and nail-hard. "Hey, I'd kick that crazy bitch in the head before I'd let her get near me. What is she, old man, your grand-daughter? Or is she some pathetic drugged-out teenager you picked up?"

Blank surprise, Savich heard it in the cold, dead silence. He waited, finally heard a wheeze, as if Moses Grace was going to start hacking. He'd been as crude as he could manage — was this teenage girl old Moses's lover?

Then Moses Grace wheezed out a laugh that made gooseflesh rise on Savich's arms. He said in that wet drawl, "Must have been real tough for you, boy, talking all dirty like that. Let me tell you, you'll change your mind if Claudia has a shot at you. I've seen my little sweet cakes diddle a woman before I told her enough was enough and to dig out the old girl's eyes then kick her out of the van."

Yes, tell me more, you insane old man, yes. "Yeah, right, you old liar. That's about as believable as Hollywood throwing a ticker-tape parade for Schwarzenegger."

He looked up to see Sherlock standing ten feet away, watching him. He said very deliberately, "It must be tough for you, Moses, knowing you're too decrepit, too diseased, to screw your own wife."

Savich felt cold dead rage blasting at him. Then Moses Grace chortled, a disgusting, juicy sound. "I don't like a dirty mouth on you, boy, it don't seem right somehow. You know, Claudia's got her fantasies about you and I've got mine. We'll see what you say when I watch your life drain away. I'll win and you'll know it. See you then, Savich."

There was the silence of dead space. Moses Grace had disconnected.

239

Sherlock walked to him, nosed against his shoulder. "I've never heard you speak like that before."

"It surprised old Moses, too," he said as he saw Dix walking toward them.

Savich nodded to him, then speed-dialed the communications center in the Hoover Building. "This is Savich. Did you locate Moses Grace's cell phone?"

He heard a man shouting, "I need the location now!" Then a voice came back on the line, panting, "He's within a two-mile radius of a semi-rural area west of Dulles, heading toward Leesburg. We just dispatched local police and agents to the area. He was moving, and unfortunately knew enough to turn the phone off, so we've lost his signal. You kept him going a long time, Savich, but he didn't make it easy on us. He was using a different carrier than yours, so we had to track him down through Sprint's Automatic Number Identification system, using your number as the target phone. That took a while. We'll keep you posted."

Savich punched off his cell, turning to Sherlock and Dix, "Moses is headed towards Leesburg. Cops and agents are on their way, but it sounds like a crapshoot."

Sherlock said, "A pity he's not at a nice warm motel, all tucked in for the night."

"How did you track him from way out here, Savich?" Dix asked.

"MAX helped," Savich said. "I had him set up to instant message our communications center in Washington if Moses called again. MAX recorded the call, too, through a Bluetooth transmitter I have wired into my phone.

"Since the Patriot Act was put into place, we've been able to get wiretap warrants for all calls made by an individual suspect, not just a particular phone number. So it doesn't help them to just ditch a phone and get a new one. So, wherever Moses goes, no matter what cell phone he happens to use, we go with him. He used Caller ID blocking, which slowed us down at bit. If we'd known his number right away, we could have located him in about fifteen seconds."

"Do you think the police and agents will catch him?" Dix said.

"We should be so lucky," Savich said, and sighed. "He was driving while he talked, and probably kept driving after he turned the phone off." To Sherlock he said, "Do you know he bragged how he and Claudia were at the Bonhomie Club last night for Pinky's memorial? There was no way they were inside, that's for certain.

They had to be hiding outside, watching who went into the club."

They stood silently for a moment before Savich spoke again. "It kept him talking, though, and he may have given me a lead without realizing it. We need to find a woman who was probably kidnapped and eventually dumped on the side of the road, with possible eye injuries. I'll call Mr. Maitland, give him a heads-up. Moses still sounded like he was wheezing; he can't disguise that. You guys head into the kitchen, play it light. I'll be back in a couple of minutes."

Sherlock nodded. "When we get back to the B and B, we'll get MAX started on finding this woman." She rose to her tiptoes, kissed his mouth. "Okay, don't be too long, there are two growing boys in there. No telling how long that meat loaf's going to last."

"One more thing, Sherlock. Moses said I hurt a woman he cared for. That's why he hates me."

Bud Bailey's Bed & Breakfast
Tuesday night

Savich got the call that the roadblocks hadn't turned up anyone resembling Moses Grace or Claudia. The cell phone

242

belonged to a woman in Hamilton whose purse had gone missing. He wanted to kick something.

Instead, he put MAX to work. When Sherlock came out of the bathroom fifteen minutes later, Savich said, "Her name is Elsa Bender, forty-five, divorced a little over a year, kids grown. About two months ago, she was kidnapped right out of the parking lot at her local supermarket — only one witness. The guy said he heard a woman scream, saw a dirty white van screech into the street. Elsa was found the following morning by a farmer driving a tractor on a country road only three miles from her home in Westcott, in western Pennsylvania. She was naked, dumb with pain, her eyes gone. There'd been a warm spell, thank God, or else she'd have died. As it was, she nearly died from shock.

"She's now living in Philadelphia with her ex-husband, who's evidently been a stand-up guy since this happened. I think we need to go see her, Sherlock. I called the chief of police in Westcott, finally convinced him I was for real and asked him to read her description of the kidnappers. He said he didn't have one; she couldn't remember what had happened from the moment she drove into the supermarket parking lot until she woke up in the hospital. He didn't know if she was telling the truth or was just scared, and he couldn't do any follow-up interviews because the ex-husband took her out of the local hospital and his jurisdiction and back to Philadelphia. The Philadelphia police know about it, but so far, the chief said, they've got squat. The last time the local police spoke to her was four weeks ago. There's been nothing since."

Sherlock was excited. "How lovely of that mad old man to tell you about her. We could be there tomorrow."

He nodded slowly, rose and stretched.

"Hey, sailor, you wanna dance?"

He laughed, pulled her to him, and hugged her hard. He said against her ear, "We can be back in Maestro by tomorrow evening. Maybe we'll want to dance again."

"What if Moses and Claudia do —"

"It's okay. If they act, we'll deal with it. I'll be surprised if they don't do something. Old Moses called me to brag, and he needs something new to brag about. He's not well, Sherlock. I'm thinking this may be his last hurrah."

CHAPTER 18

Maestro, Virginia
Wednesday morning

"Hold up a minute, Ruth," Dix said. He and Ruth waited by the Range Rover for Tony Holcombe to cross Main Street. He was focused on Dix, looking straight ahead ignoring the slushy ground, nearly sending an old Ford Fairlane skidding into a parking meter to avoid hitting him.

Ruth watched the beautifully dressed man hurrying toward them. He was tall and fit, probably in his early forties. He looked like a fashion plate out of *GQ*, his thick light brown hair beautifully styled, shining in the morning sun.

"Hey, Tony," Dix called out. "What's up?"

Tony Holcombe came to a stop not a foot from Dix's face. "I — I heard about Erin — that is, Dad told me what happened. I can't believe it, Dix. Erin was the sweetest girl, never did anything to anybody, only wanted to play her violin, there was nothing else in the world for her but her music."

Ruth came around the Range Roger and nodded to the man bundled up in the thousand-dollar black leather coat and soft leather gloves.

Tony Holcombe turned his large dark eyes to her face. "You're the woman Brewster found in Dix's shed, aren't you? Are you still staying at Dix's house? I was wondering how it might look if my sister —"

"That's enough, Tony."

"Sorry. Yes, all right. Dix, do you know anything about who killed Erin?"

Dix said, "Why don't you come into my office, I'd like to warm up a bit."

Tony had the Holcombe body — long bones, no extra flesh, a strong jawline. His dark eyes were a dramatic contrast to his light hair. He looked remarkably like Chappy, his father, but wasn't as graceful as he, a man as lithe as a dancer despite his age. Tony walked awkwardly, his arms moving in a different rhythm from his legs. It was curiously charming.

In the sheriff's office, Dix spoke to half a dozen people before he opened his office door and ushered the two of them inside.

"Now, let's get official here. Ruth, this is my brother-in-law, Tony Holcombe,

Chappy's son. He runs the local Holcombe bank. Tony, this is Ruth Warnecki, FBI."

They shook hands. Tony had a nice firm grip along with his well-manicured nails, and his beautiful eyes met hers directly. She wondered if his sister's eyes were that color, her coloring that dramatic. She hadn't been able to tell from the photo on Dix's desk.

"Call me Tony, please. Why are you still here in Maestro?"

"I'm here to find out who tried to kill me. It appears that the same person also killed Erin Bushnell."

His face tightened. "I can't believe she's dead. My dad told me and my wife, Cynthia. She's really upset. She and Erin were like sisters."

This was odd, Dix thought. To the best of his knowledge Cynthia Holcombe had never liked anyone of her own sex, beginning with her own mother and two sisters, whom he'd heard Cynthia refer to as the old bitch and her two whining whelps. Her dislike had extended to her sister-in-law Christie, whom she'd called a gun-toting right-wing redneck. Christie a redneck — it still boggled his mind. As for what Cynthia thought of him, he wasn't about to go there. She was like a sister to Erin Bushnell?

247

"How is Cynthia?" Dix asked, holding out a mug of black coffee with two sugar cubes to his brother-in-law, and waiting for him to pull off his gloves.

"Distraught, as I said. She wanted me to find out what you're doing, what you know. I heard you found her in Winkel's Cave. Do you have any idea who might have done this?"

"Yes, Tony, we found her in Winkel's Cave, where her killer left her. How did Cynthia meet Erin Bushnell?"

"At a concert at Stanislaus last year, but that's not important now. Dix, if you hadn't gone to Winkel's Cave, if my father hadn't shown you that back entrance, no one would ever have known she was dead."

"Very true."

"She would have simply disappeared, like Christie."

Dix's face was impassive. He nodded.

Tony turned to Ruth, who was sipping her own coffee. She'd laced it liberally with cream, realizing quickly if she didn't, it would clot blood. "I heard you were hunting some kind of treasure, that you found a cave chamber no one knew was there."

"That's right," Ruth said. So bits and pieces had gotten out, which wasn't too bad as long as it didn't go any further.

Chappy had given Tony a few facts, Dix thought, but not everything, thank the good Lord. Chappy never could keep his mouth shut, except when it came to money. He could tell Ruth was assessing Tony, like a cop would a suspect in a crime. He watched her push her hair behind her ear, a habit of hers. It took only a moment for her hair to swing back again. Thick, dark hair, with a bit of a curl to it. Dix watched Tony focus all of his bred-to-the-bone intensity on Ruth, then he eyed both of them in frustration. "Dad asked me to drop by and invite the two of you over to lunch, said you wouldn't be available for dinner because the other two FBI agents are coming back this evening."

"How does your father know that?" Ruth asked. Without thinking, she took a sip of coffee, and shuddered.

"Dad spoke to Rafer this morning, caught him as he was going to school. Told him Agent Savich and Agent Sherlock were going to fly in a special FBI Bell helicopter up to Philadelphia on a case. He didn't know what it was, but he said they would be back for dinner tonight."

Dix grunted. He'd have to speak to both his boys. He wondered if either of them could even spell "discretion." He'd give them the loose lips talk.

"Why did they take off for Philadelphia all of a sudden?"

"That's an FBI matter, Tony," Ruth said. "I'd like to have lunch with your dad. Will you and your wife be there as well? She could tell me all about Erin Bushnell and their sisterhood."

Tony Holcombe's eyes darkened, suspecting sarcasm, but not hearing any he finally nodded and set his mug on Dix's desk. "I must get to the bank now." He pulled on his soft-as-sin black leather gloves.

"How's the banking business, Tony?"

Tony Holcombe shrugged as he opened the office door. "Things are going quite well, but you know Dad — he'll never admit it, says everything's been going to hell in a handbasket since I've been running things."

They heard him greet some of the deputies on his way out.

"He seems quite likable," Ruth said. "I'd sure hate to be in his shoes."

Dix said, "Tony's always had to walk in Chappy's long shadow. If I'd been born in Tony's shoes, I'd have left the state a long time ago, made my own way as far from

Chappy as I could get. Now, I want to head over and meet with Ginger Stanford, Gloria's daughter, see what she has to say about Erin Bushnell. So far, Erin is a beloved, talented sister to my sister-in-law Cynthia, and believe me, that's both scary and unbelievable."

Ginger Stanford owned a four-story red-brick Georgian sandwiched between Angelo's Pizza and Classic Threads. On their short walk there, everyone seemed to want to speak to the sheriff and to inspect Ruth, as if an FBI agent had an extra arm or two heads and needed a closer look. Dix was patient but tight-lipped, doing a much better job than his sons of keeping quiet about their business.

Ginger's secretary was an ancient old man who was hunkered down behind a huge mahogany desk. A wooden name plaque set in the center of the desk read HENRY O.

"Sheriff," the old man croaked, nodded to Ruth, and looked back at his computer screen. "I got me a real puzzle here," he said. "Five words and each word contains three different words. You know, like 'splice.'"

"I don't think 'plice' is a word, Henry. We're here to see Ginger. Buzz her, please."

"You're right, it isn't. Drat. Ms. Ginger's writing up old Mr. Curmudgeon's will."

"I've never actually heard of anyone named Curmudgeon," Ruth said.

Henry O rose slowly. He was wearing a starched white shirt and natty black pants belted up near his chest. "That's just what I call him, miss. It's Amos McQueen, older even than me. I can't believe he's still breathing. Shoulda croaked in 1971 when his hay baler rolled over on him, but he walked away from it. Durnedest thing." Henry tottered toward a closed door and knocked. Ruth saw he was wearing new Ferragamos on his small, narrow feet.

"Come."

Henry opened the door, stuck his head in. "Ms. Ginger, the cops are here, acting all friendly so's I'll cooperate."

They heard a woman's laugh. "Show them in, Henry, show them in. I'll cooperate, too."

Ruth stopped cold at the sight of Ginger Stanford. She was a stunning woman, there no other word for her, her cheekbones high and sharp, her natural blond hair coiled at the back of her head. When she rose, Ruth thought she must be near six feet tall, with long legs that looked like they ended at her earlobes. She gave Dix a lovely big smile as she walked around her desk, her hand extended. Ruth didn't miss the look in Ginger's eyes. She really liked the sheriff.

They exchanged pleasantries. When Dix introduced her to Ruth, Ruth was aware of her quick, assessing glance, a look every woman recognizes when she's seen as a possible poacher.

Ruth said, "I'm an FBI agent, Ms. Stanford."

"Yes, so I heard. I don't see any sign of a head wound."

Ruth automatically touched her fingertips to the small Band-Aid hidden beneath her hair. "Nearly gone now," she said.

Dix shook his head. "Everyone in this town hears everything."

"Ain't that the truth," Ginger said and waved an elegant hand toward the sofa. "I heard Brewster found you behind the woodpile at the side of Dix's house."

Ruth wondered how many places to date Brewster had found her on Dix's property.

Once seated again behind her desk, Ginger steepled her fingers in front of her and said thoughtfully, "Mother is miserable about Erin, Dix. I spent last night with her she was so upset. She couldn't stop crying. Please tell me you've discovered who's responsible. And now Walt McGuffey. What's going on here, Dix?"

He shrugged. "I'd really like you to tell us about Erin Bushnell, Ginger."

Ginger sat back in her chair, closed her eyes for a moment, snapped them open, and blinked as her mouth formed a slow smile. Ruth wondered how that series of attention-getters played with a jury. Probably drove the guys wild. She finally said, "Other than the fact that she had the hots for Dr. Holcombe, she was pretty smart."

"What?"

"I know, I know. He's old enough to have been her daddy, but there it is. She was always hanging around him, offering to do things for him — put new reeds in his woodwinds, tune his harpsichord, polish his French horn, whatever. She audited all the classes he taught, even went mooning over to his house a couple of times, or so my mom told me."

"Your mother didn't say anything about this to us."

"She wouldn't. She just waved it off, said it was infatuation, nothing more, and that's why it didn't bother her. She saw Dr. Holcombe as being a safe lover who understood his role and could easily be left behind when Erin was ready to hit stardom road. I tried to tell her that Erin was gone over Dr. Holcombe, that she'd lie down in front of his car to get his attention, but Mom didn't buy it. She'd always shake her head and say no, Erin was going to tour the world, nothing would stop her." Ginger paused, looked at one of the African masks on the opposite wall. "She won't now, Dix."

"You think you could be wrong about the depth of Erin's feelings for Dr. Holcombe?"

"Me? Of course I'm not wrong, I'm a lawyer."

Ruth laughed, couldn't help it. "That was good," she said.

Ginger gave her a gracious nod, but her eyes weren't at all friendly. "When are you going back to Washington, Agent Warnecki?"

"If I can keep her here, she's staying until we catch the murderer," Dix said.

Ginger wasn't happy with that news. She pushed her chair back and crossed her legs. "I heard you found Erin in Winkel's Cave. I also heard that's where you'd been, Agent Warnecki. So you think the two men who shot at you killed Erin?"

"Could be. Maybe not."

"That's very proficient cop talk, Agent."

Ruth smiled, nodded, and said, "Thank

you. I'm very good at it."

Dix asked, "What else should we know about Erin, Ginger?"

"She was a dream on the violin. Incredible, but you know that." Then she gave Dix The Look, though he didn't appear to pick up on it. Instead he frowned down at his short black boots and said, "Did she go out with any guys her own age? Classmates?"

"Nary a one, as far as I know, and believe me, I know everything about Erin because of Mom. When Erin woke up to the guy factor, it was Dr. Holcombe from the get-go."

Ruth sat forward in her chair. "Did Dr. Holcombe reciprocate her feelings?"

"I don't know. You'd have to ask Gordon's dragon, Helen Rafferty. She knows all, and I mean that literally. The word is that she and Dr. Holcombe had a hot thing going maybe five years ago, and he was the one who called it off. Evidently he's quite a smooth talker, convinced her to stay on as his personal assistant, which indicates to me he's pretty selfish, and she's got the self-esteem of a gnat. She'd know exactly what his feelings are — were — toward Erin."

They left ten minutes later to drive out to Chappy's house for lunch. Ruth said as she buckled her seat belt, "Curiouser and curiouser. What do you think about Erin Bushnell, age twenty-two, in the throes of unrequited passion for Chappy's brother, a man more than twice her age?"

"We need to find out if it was unrequited," Dix said.

"Maybe what he felt was lust for her talent — the guy might have a thing for talented women, sees himself as a Svengali. No, that doesn't work. There's Helen Rafferty, his personal assistant, in the mix."

Dix said, "Helen Rafferty plays the piano beautifully."

"Hmm. I wonder what Dr. Holcombe will tell us about this."

"It'll be interesting. Chappy told me one of the reasons he calls his brother Twister is that he can writhe and wriggle out of anything."

Ruth looked out the window at the lovely expanse of white pristine snow. Two hawks cruised overhead, their wingspan impressive against the clear blue sky. When she lost sight of them, she said, "If I've got this right, Erin Bushnell wasn't only a brilliant music student at the Stanislaus School of Music, she was also in love with the director and the best friend of the director's niece-in-law."

CHAPTER 19

Chappy Holcombe sat at the head of the spit-polished Chippendale dining table. "Well, how about it, Cynthia, do you think Twister was sleeping with your good friend Erin Bushnell?"

Cynthia Holcombe finished chewing her breadstick, swallowed, and regarded her father-in-law as if he'd made a tacky joke. "No, I don't," was all she said. She picked up another breadstick, as if in self-defense.

Chappy waved his fork at his daughter-in-law. "Fact is, I don't, either. Cynthia, you're the one I'd swear old Twister wants to sleep with, given all those lusty looks he tosses your way."

"Dad, please," Tony said, but his voice was more resigned than angry or embarrassed.

"All right, all right," Chappy said. "Mrs. Goss, where's our lunch?"

"Yours is right here, Chappy." Mrs. Goss, fiftyish, was blessed with striking, heavy black hair she wore loose and curling down her back, like a gypsy. A long bright yellow velvet skirt swished gracefully around her ankles, a peasant blouse, cut low, the final touch. She leaned down to set a platter of shrimp salad at Chappy's right hand, her cleavage not three inches from his face.

"Looks good," Chappy said, "even the salad."

"Just control yourself," Mrs. Goss said and swished back to the kitchen.

"You're in for a treat, Agent," Chappy said to Ruth. "Mrs. Goss makes the best shrimp salad in Virginia, and she knows it."

"That may be," Cynthia said. "But she should wear an apron over her ridiculous hippie outfits."

"She's a gypsy, not a hippie," Chappy said, annoyance in his dark eyes if not in his voice. "She doesn't press her bosom in your face, Cynthia, only mine. Otherwise I wouldn't see any bosoms at all. Leave her alone."

Mrs. Goss finished serving, seemingly oblivious, and left them to it, her large silver hoop earrings flashing in the sunlight.

"Cynthia, tell me about Erin Bushnell," Dix said. "Tony said you two were like sisters."

Cynthia replied calmly, "Tony is out of

date. Erin and I got along nicely until she started eyeing my husband. Her death, well, it's a great shock, as you can imagine, because at one time we were quite close. I still grieve for her."

Dix said, "So Tony didn't know how you felt? He saw your grief and believed you and Erin were still as close as before?"

"Erin never came on to me, Cynthia, never," Tony said.

"I saw her pull you into the moonlight last Tuesday night at that cocktail party Gloria Stanford threw. It was cold that night, but that didn't stop either of you."

Tony speared a shrimp on his fork and stared at it. "I don't even remember that. I'm surprised you noticed, since you were flirting with Uncle Gordon."

Chappy set his fork on his plate, leaned back in his chair, and laughed until it was the only sound in the dining room. He said to Ruth on a hiccup, "You look shell-shocked, Agent Warnecki. It's always a circus between the two of them."

One of Dix's black eyebrows shot up. "Add you to the mix, Chappy, and we've got the wild animal act."

"Nah, I'm as tame as your little Brewster."

"Brewster thinks he's a Doberman."

Tony asked Dix, "You find out yet who hired those guys to kill Agent Warnecki on Saturday night?"

The question brought the conversation to a halt. Ruth could hear Mrs. Goss humming in the kitchen.

Chappy said into the heart of the silence, "Dix probably doesn't want to talk about it, Tony. Fact is, identifying them may not be possible. I heard the bodies were badly burned. That right, Dix?"

Dix shrugged. "We'll see. The FBI forensic lab is using their fingerprint recognition program on the partial prints we have. We're looking for where the men might have come from. We may have something more to go on soon."

"But you've got no leads now, right, Dix?" Chappy asked him.

"Oh, we're managing to keep busy," Dix said easily, sitting back and lacing his fingers over his belly.

Chappy suddenly said, "Dix, I heard you found poor old Walt McGuffey murdered in his own house. Another shock like that and you'll have to bury me. Who would want to kill him? Oh, I see. Someone must have thought Walt saw something he shouldn't since he lives near the other entrance to Winkel's Cave."

"That's possible," Dix said. "Walt was a fine gentleman, and Christie really loved him. He was devastated when she disappeared." He didn't mention finding Ruth's Beemer in the shed. He turned to Cynthia. "I find it surprising that you and Erin Bushnell were such good friends. I haven't seen you make friends with any women in town."

"I grew up with three women at home, Dix," Cynthia said, "and they were world-class bitches all, if that gives you some idea of why I never bothered. I believed Erin was different, but she wasn't. Yes, she made a show of affection for Uncle Gordon, but only to throw me off her real objective, which was my own husband. That's why she spent so much time with me here, at Tara. She wanted to see you, Tony."

"Or maybe," Chappy said, voice sly, "both of you had the hots for old Twister."

"That's not funny, Chappy. He's nearly as old as you are," Cynthia said. "How much longer before you grow up?"

Dix said quickly, "So you think Ginger's wrong about Erin loving Dr. Holcombe, Cynthia?"

Cynthia shrugged one of her thin, elegant shoulders under her dark red St. John knit top. "Ginger would say anything to make you happy, wouldn't she, Dix? Everyone but you knows she'd love to jump your bones. Now, her mother, Gloria Stanford, she's another matter."

After dropping that bomb, Cynthia gave her full attention to her shrimp salad.

Ruth took a sip of her white wine. "What about you, Chappy, do you know if your brother was sleeping with anyone else, say?"

Dix shot her a look, a ghost of a smile on his mouth before he speared a water chestnut out of his shrimp salad.

"Gloria and Twister sleeping together? Nah, maybe a long time ago, but she's way too old for him now," Chappy said. "Fact is, Twister likes 'em young. Even Cynthia's long in the tooth for Twister's tastes. You best accept the end is in sight, Cynthia."

Ruth said, "So Erin Bushnell was the right age for him?"

"Early twenties? Yeah, that's right, but what do I know, Agent Ruth? Really, what do I know? Me and Twister, we haven't gotten along since before you were born — too much alike, I suppose, and it makes our pots bubble and boil. Sounds like it's time you ask him, watch him sputter a bit." His smile was malicious.

After Mrs. Goss had cleared off the table, she brought in a big New York cheesecake and set it with some panache in the middle of the table, and handed Chappy a knife. As he cut them all slices, Ruth said, "I really like your house, Chappy. Why did you name it Tara?"

"Because when I brought Tony and Christie's mama here I told her she'd never be hungry again."

Tony said to Ruth, "My mother had a trust fund the size of the Rhode Island state budget."

Chappy laughed. "Makes a cute story. I like the name Tara. It appeals to something way down deep inside me. The architecture's real close, except, of course, we've got lots of nice big bathrooms."

Thirty minutes later Dix pulled out onto the long driveway. Ruth said, "We've already got fingerprints for those two men and IAFIS is trying to match what we've got. Why all that fancy talk about the FBI?"

Dix grunted, shoved on his dark aviator glasses.

"Setting a cat among the pigeons, were you?"

He grinned at her. "Who knows what might come out of that? The three of them always, I repeat, *always* put on a show for visitors. You start them on a topic and they'll go with it. I know it's hard for you to believe, but they were really rather tame today. Erin Bushnell's death took a lot of the fun out of it for them. Walt's death, too."

Ruth nodded. "I agree there were strong feelings about Erin, but I couldn't figure out who felt what."

"These folks are good. They've had years of practice."

"I've seen dysfunctional families before, and I'm probably part of one myself, but those three are champions."

Dix laughed. "You might have asked Chappy about him and Erin, to see the looks on their faces."

"I hate to ask you this, but do you think one of your family could be involved in Erin's murder?"

He was silent as he turned onto Mount Olive Road. "When Christie disappeared, I thought about every possibility, including someone in the family being involved. And after all these years they'd have to do a whole lot to surprise me. But I don't see any of them killing somebody. And yes, I've been wrong lots of times."

A short time later, they stood in front of

Helen Rafferty's desk. Dix slipped off his aviator glasses and smiled down at Helen, who looked harried.

Dix said, leaning close, "I need to speak to you, Helen. Five minutes, in the lounge?"

"I — Well, I don't suppose you'll take a rain check, Sheriff?"

"I would prefer now. This is very important."

There were two employees in the Stanislaus administration employee lounge, hunched over a green Formica table, a bag of Fritos between them. Dix flipped out his badge and waved them out.

Ruth sat beside Helen and looked at her for several moments, judging her mood. She turned on her FBI interview voice, calm, inviting. "Tell us about Dr. Holcombe and Erin Bushnell, Ms. Rafferty."

Helen looked from Ruth to Dix, who was standing with his shoulders against the wall, arms crossed over his chest.

She burst into tears.

CHAPTER 20

Philadelphia
Wednesday

Savich and Sherlock sat opposite Elsa Bender in the starkly modern living room of Jon Bender's home on Linderman Lane on the Main Line. Although it was very warm in the living room, a cashmere afghan covered her legs, a thick wool sweater draped over her hunched shoulders. Her brown hair was pulled back from her face, fastened in a clip at the base of her neck. Her hands clasped and unclasped ceaselessly in her lap. Savich saw that she wasn't wearing a wedding ring. The room was brightly lit, but Elsa Bender seemed to sit in the midst of shadows.

Her eyes weren't bandaged now, but she wore dark glasses. She was too thin, and unhealthily pale, as if she never went outside. However, they saw her smile up at her exhusband, who stood at her side, his hand resting lightly on her shoulder. According to the papers, Jon Bender was a successful

267

real estate developer who had traded her in for a younger model, namely his personal assistant, two years before, but didn't marry her. And he was here now, a big man, stocky, tough jawed, his blind ex-wife again living in his house.

Savich introduced himself and Sherlock. He said without preamble, "The old man and the young girl who bragged to me about taking you — their names are Moses Grace and Claudia. We don't know her last name yet, or her relationship to the old man. They're the same ones who buried my friend Pinky Womack in a grave in Arlington National Cemetery."

Mr. Bender looked from Savich to Sherlock, obviously wondering if he should be alarmed. He nodded slowly. "We heard about that. We had no idea until you called this morning . . . Well, now there are actual names attached to their faces. I assume you've spoken with the local police?"

"Yes, we did. We're here because we need your help, Mrs. Bender. You're the only one who can provide us with a description."

Mr. Bender answered for her. "Elsa still can't remember what happened, so she can't help you."

Savich sat on the hassock at Elsa

268

Bender's feet. He took her left hand between his two large ones, felt the chill of her flesh. She'd turned inward, he thought, and that was the wrong direction. He said, "I appreciate your agreeing to speak to us on such short notice. Do you mind if I call you Elsa?" At her faint nod, he continued. "We know how badly these people hurt you, Elsa. We don't need to focus on that. I know you want these monsters caught and punished for what they did to you. They've done terrible things to other people, too. You're one of the lucky ones; you survived. We need your help so that other people can survive, too."

"I wouldn't call this surviving," Elsa said, and Savich continued to hold her hand as the bitterness flowed through her.

He said, "I would. There's something else, Elsa. These people who hurt you, they're calling me, they want to kill me. They've also threatened my wife, and my little boy. I desperately need your help to protect them."

Her hand fluttered a moment, then settled again. "It's been a horribly painful time for me, Agent Savich. I don't know if I can ever think about what happened. I don't want to face those monsters again."

"Elsa doesn't need to be tortured with

this again, Agent Savich," Mr. Bender looked ready to muscle Savich out the door. He said, "Listen, she's gone through enough. We're sorry about the threats to you and your family, but Elsa can't help you. We'd like you to leave now."

Savich didn't look away from Elsa. "I imagine the doctors told you that when you begin to remember what happened, it's important not to block it out again. Remembering it, talking about it, will only lessen the pain. Tell us about it, Elsa, tell us and you can send it into the past, where it belongs. You survived. Never forget that you survived."

To Savich's surprise, Elsa said, "Jon was in the past. And yet he's here now. Isn't that strange?"

Savich saw Mr. Bender flinch, heard him say, "I'm not going anywhere," but Savich had no idea if she understood his words.

"We have children ourselves, Agent Savich, Jon and I. But I can't talk about what they did to me, I simply can't."

"I don't need you to, Elsa, although I'm convinced it would help you."

Elsa said, "The fact is, I've remembered almost all of it." She heard her husband's quick indrawn breath, but didn't pause. "The girl Claudia called him her sweet

270

pickle. He was a filthy old man with a hacking cough. She tied my hands behind my back in that dirty old van, told me that he wanted to see her with a woman and that he picked me because she'd told him I looked like her, like I could be her mama and wasn't that the coolest thing? Then he told her to pretend she was diddling her own mama. The old man blindfolded me and then the girl started." She began to cry quietly. She swallowed hard and whispered, "The oddest thing is that I didn't feel the pain in my eyes until later, in the emergency room."

"You were in shock, a good thing."

"I suppose it was." She lifted her glasses only enough to lightly daub the edge of a monogrammed white handkerchief to her eyes. She straightened her glasses again and said, "It doesn't hurt so much anymore when I cry."

Jon Bender said, "Tell them about the farmer, Elsa."

"The farmer who found me. He visited me in the hospital every single day, brought me roses. He'd sit by my bed and tell me about how he grows barley and oats. Jon came late that night, and three days later, he brought me back here, to our old home, only I can't see what they've done to it since I left."

"Ask him, Elsa. Simply ask him."

Jon Bender looked like he wanted to burst into tears. He said, "I didn't do anything, Elsa."

"Good." For the first time she smiled a little. "I hate fussy things. I'm glad you left it clean." She let Savich ask her questions for several minutes and gave the best description she could of Moses and Claudia. She agreed to talk to a sketch artist later in the day. She told Savich about how Claudia did indeed look like her daughter. She smiled toward her husband. "Jon, give them that photo of Annie throwing the beach ball. Remember, I sent you a duplicate? The resemblance is really quite striking."

While Mr. Bender was gone, she said, "Tell me more about your boy, Mr. Savich." Her hand still rested comfortably between his.

"His name is Sean, and he's a pistol." He watched her face as he told her about Sean's third birthday party, where Savich's sister Lily chased around twenty small children, her feet in gigantic clown shoes. He told her how Sean loved to barrel at him the moment he walked through the front door every evening. Hearing this, she was smiling, breathing easily.

Jon Bender broke in when he returned. "I've been trying to talk Elsa into giving me another chance, Agent Savich."

The hand in Savich's stiffened a bit, then relaxed. She wasn't ready to let go of him yet, and that was fine.

"I've promised her over and over I won't ever be an asshole again."

And glory of glories, Elsa Bender laughed. She looked up in the direction of her husband's voice. "Perhaps you won't," she said. "The kids seem to think you're not. Perhaps."

Sherlock looked closely at Jon Bender's face, studied his eyes as he looked at Elsa. "You know what, Elsa? I think this guy of yours has learned what's important to him."

Ten minutes later, Savich clasped Elsa's hands in both of his and pulled her slowly to her feet, letting the afghan pool at her feet. She wasn't quite steady.

He said, "You're going to be fine, Elsa. Jon is going to bundle you up and take you for a nice walk, maybe make some hot chocolate when you get back. It'll put color back in your cheeks."

It was nearly nine o'clock Wednesday night when Savich knocked on Sheriff Noble's front door. They heard Brewster's big-dog bark, footsteps running to the front door before it was flung open, Rob and Rafe elbowing each other to be front and center.

"Hello, Special Agent Savich. Hello, Special Agent Sherlock. Did you shoot anyone today?"

"Oh yes," Sherlock said immediately. "It was all blood and gore. Took me forever to wash it all off."

"Dude! Really, tell us everything you did. Not just the boring stuff like Dad does, but the cool stuff?"

Savich smiled for the first time since leaving Washington hours before. He hugged both boys quickly, breathing in their excitement, their teenage love of anything gruesome. In ten years or so would Sean be asking the same things?

Rob said, "We waited dinner for you until Dad said he was going to gnaw on his elbows if he didn't eat. We had bouillabaisse, Ms. McCutcheon brought it over because she knows Dad likes it. It was okay if you like fish."

"Dillon, come on in the living room," Ruth called out, before appearing in the doorway, Dix at her shoulder. "We've got some delicious tea, some scones that Millie of Millie's Deli made herself, just for the

Feds, and Dix and I had something really interesting happen today, but never mind that just now. Boys, bring in the Federal agents and let's eat."

"So how was your day?" Dix asked as he handed out scones.

Sherlock smiled as she took a cup of tea from Ruth. "Actually, our afternoon was great. We took Sean out to build a snowman, poured hot chocolate down his gullet, and listened to him talk nonstop about his grandmother's new puppy." She rolled her eyes. "I have a feeling there'll be barking in our house very soon now."

"Dogs are good," Dix said as he gave Brewster a pat. "This little guy keeps my neck warm at night."

Rob and Rafe finally went off to bed after nearly an hour and four more scones, Savich and Sherlock having filled their ears with horrifying, thoroughly fictional tales of mayhem in the suburbs of Philadelphia. Dix waited another couple of minutes until he was sure it was quiet upstairs, then nodded. "Okay, they're down for the count. Tell us what really happened in Philadelphia. Could that poor woman tell you anything about Moses Grace and Claudia?"

Savich said, "Yeah, she did. Her name's

Elsa Bender. She's going to be all right. I mean, I think the future looks pretty good for her." Savich looked over at Dix and Ruth, who were sitting on the sofa opposite him and Sherlock, Brewster sleeping between them. He pulled a photo out of his shirt pocket. "This is the Bender daughter, Annie. She's seventeen in the photo — tall, slender, nearly white-blond hair, big blue eyes. Elsa Bender says she looks like Claudia."

Ruth studied the photo. "She looks like a cheerleader whose biggest problem is deciding who to go out with after the football game on Saturday night. You've already got this photo out all around the Beltway, haven't you, Dillon?"

"Oh yeah."

Sherlock said, "Elsa said Moses Grace is as old as he sounds, at least seventy. His face is all leathery from too much sun, which suggests he could have spent a good deal of his life on a farm, an oil rig, a chain gang — take your pick. Elsa said he's lean and wiry, but he didn't look fit, he looked sort of gray. She said Claudia's voice was sweet one minute, shrill the next, with a midwestern accent. As for Moses, we've heard his deep drawl, the excessive bad grammar that simply doesn't feel right.

Elsa also said he had a hacking cough, and was always spitting up. That was two months ago. He sounds much worse now."

Dix sat forward, cuddling Brewster in his arms. "You had a productive day —"

Ruth cut in, the enthusiasm bubbling out of her. "But maybe not as exciting as ours. You're going to love this. I'll start you off with Ginger Stanford, and then move on to lunch with Chappy and the little rascals."

"Then," Dix said, "our *pièce de résistance* — Helen Rafferty."

CHAPTER 21

". . . When we got to Stanislaus, we took Helen Rafferty into the employee lounge. Ruth didn't give her a chance to settle, to get herself ready. She asked her point-blank about Dr. Holcombe and Erin Bushnell."

Ruth smoothly took up the tale, as if they'd worked as a team for a very long time. "She actually started crying, and only got ahold of herself after I reminded her how important it all is, now that Erin is dead."

Dix said, "After she dried her eyes, the first thing she did was ask us if we'd like some coffee. I said yes to give Helen some time to collect herself."

Ruth said, "She apologized to Dix because she knew Dr. Holcombe was his uncle, but she had thought about it, and had to let it out. The bottom line is, Helen Rafferty admitted she and Dr. Holcombe — that's how she always referred to him — were lovers for perhaps three months about five years ago. She said it was in the summer, when there weren't many students around. He broke it off, told her that being with her drained him. You're going to like this — he said being with her had been sort of like attaching himself to an ancient blessing that had lost its power over the years, and now it was suffocating him and he couldn't continue to be intimate with her. Fact was, she told us, Dr. Holcombe had this compulsion — she'd known about it since before their affair. He'd slept with a number of very talented young women at Stanislaus over the years, and he seemed not to want to stop. She confronted him with it, and he said he supposed that deep inside his spirit he needed their nourishment, their innocent love of music and life, or he couldn't create, couldn't compose his own music, didn't think he could go on at all. She smiled a little and said she knows what that sounds like, but that he believed it, she was sure of that.

"Helen still thinks of him as a great man with a sickness, a harmless infirmity, not an old lech. So she bought into it. Because she had to, I guess, because she still loves him and admires him tremendously. She said Erin Bushnell was just another girl in a steady stream of talented young students who found themselves ministering to Dr.

Holcombe's spiritual needs. Again, her words."

Dix sat forward on the sofa, clasped his hands between his knees. "Then she frowned, said maybe she was wrong, maybe Dr. Holcombe had felt more about Erin than about the others. It was creepy, guys, the way she spoke of him and his philandering, as if it was all right as long as it inspired Uncle Gordon's music. She forgave all of it."

Ruth picked up the story. "She said Dr. Holcombe had incredible energy, he composed the most amazing music in the past few months. But now, she said, he is destroyed, a shell of himself, and she is very worried about him. I mentioned he didn't seem all that destroyed when we told him about Erin's murder, and she told us he would never want to burden others with his pain." Ruth snorted.

Sherlock asked Dix, "Did you get the names of the other young girls who 'ministered' to Dr. Holcombe over the years?"

"Whoa —" Dix pulled out his notebook, thumbed through the pages. "Okay, over the period of time that Helen has worked for Dr. Holcombe — fourteen years, four months — she thought he had affairs with about eight female students — that is in addition to Helen — both graduate students and undergraduates. I believe that would be up to the advanced age of twenty-three or -four. She gave me some of the names — none of them are at Stanislaus anymore — and said she'd look up the rest."

Ruth marveled aloud, "Imagine, a man my father's age believing I was too old to sleep with. She said that when Dr. Holcombe 'disengaged' — her word — from a student, they didn't leave Stanislaus, except when they graduated. They all seemed happy to remain, somehow simply taking it as part of their educational experience. Maybe they even enjoyed themselves, knowing they had made the great man shine again, who knows?"

Savich said slowly, "It would seem Dr. Holcombe had very good judgment about whom to pick, an excellent talent for self-preservation. It must also have helped over the years that as director of Stanislaus, he had great influence over their professional futures. I'm surprised other people in the school didn't know about Dr. Holcombe's predilections, then certainly there would be gossip, some bad feeling from students who couldn't compete, maybe even a bit of huff from colleagues who found his behavior inappropriate."

Ruth said, "Helen told us she actually thought no one except the girls involved over the years knew about it. She certainly never heard any rumors."

Savich shook his head. "That's hard to believe. Usually if more than two people know about something illicit, particularly something as juicy as this, it starts coming back to them in embarrassing detail."

"Helen told us she herself had helped him quite a bit to protect his privacy," Ruth said. "Translate that to 'helped him keep his dirty little secret.' "

"He lives alone," Dix said. "And I know he's owned a place outside of town for many years, converted it into a studio. He may have spent time with them there. And another thing: if Chappy were aware of this, every single soul within a hundred miles would know about it. And the way Chappy would tell it, his brother wouldn't have had a chance of staying on at Stanislaus. Maybe some of the students know, some of the professors, but no one outside Stanislaus."

"He must be the smoothest talker around," Sherlock said. "I hope all those other girls are all right."

"Yes," Dix said, "we wondered that, too. We already located two of them, and they're fine. As soon as we get the rest of the list, we'll track them all down."

Ruth said, "We asked Helen not to speak to anyone about our conversation, particularly Dr. Holcombe. We asked her for Dr. Holcombe's schedule on Friday, and when she last saw Erin. At that point her eyes nearly bugged out of her head — she realized that we might be thinking he killed Erin Bushnell. She started babbling, saying over and over that he didn't have that kind of illness. Dear Dr. Holcombe wouldn't even bang down hard on a piano key, there was no way he'd hurt anyone, particularly a Stanislaus student. She was sure of that, only told us all this because she didn't want to lie to the police, and it was probably better for Dr. Holcombe that it come out right away. She knew he didn't tell us when we talked to him on Monday, and assumed he hadn't even thought of it because he was so distraught. Then she went on with this sappy spiel about how Dr. Holcombe's precious students play all over the world, and inspire beauty and understanding, maybe even world peace."

Sherlock said, "Is she nuts?"

Dix said, "I think she's got a big blind

spot when it comes to Uncle Gordon. She said he hasn't eaten since he found out about Erin, stopped composing and playing his instruments, is silent, unable to deal with the world or his job. She felt terrible for him. As to what he did on Friday, Helen claimed he was closeted in student meetings all afternoon and he never left the campus. Then she gave us a look of triumph because she'd given him an alibi. Is she telling the truth?" Dix shrugged.

"What did Dr. Holcombe say when you asked him about his whereabouts?" Sherlock asked.

"We haven't talked to the man today," Dix said. "Helen had convinced him to attend a rehearsal he had scheduled. We'll talk to him, and Helen again, in the morning." Dix turned to Ruth and said suddenly, "Ruth, how are you feeling? Do you have a headache?"

She blinked at him, smiled. "A tad of pounding behind my left ear. It's nothing, Dix."

"Let me get you some aspirin. Better to cut it off before it digs in." He walked quickly from the living room.

The phone rang, but only once. Dix must have grabbed it. Savich looked at Ruth, an eyebrow raised.

To his surprise, Special Agent Ruth Warnecki, tough, seasoned, and sharp as a tack, blushed.

Life was sometimes unutterably cool, Sherlock thought as she took Dillon's hand and rose. "It's getting late and we're both pretty tired. We can get an early start in the morning."

Dix came back into the room, handed Ruth two aspirin and a glass of water, and stood over her while she swallowed them. Then he turned to Savich and Sherlock. "You'll want to hear this before you go. I just this minute got a call from a Detective Morales in the Richmond PD. He told me that two known lowlifes didn't turn up where they were supposed to. No one's heard a thing from them. One of them, Jackie Slater, is wanted on suspicion of auto theft. The other one, Tommy Dempsey, has a girlfriend who's been badgering the police since Sunday morning, claiming he's missing, that someone must have hurt him.

"Detective Morales heard what happened here Saturday night — about the stolen Tacoma exploding, and the two guys who were killed, and wondered if it could be them. My deputies faxed him the descriptions and a picture of a ring one of the men was wearing, and the girlfriend identified it. It was Tommy Dempsey."

Savich said, "Detective Morales said they were lowlifes? Does that mean incompetent, or cheap to acquire?"

"Slater got out of the Red Onion State Prison four months ago, was probably trying to build up his business again. Dempsey was a wannabe. They think he might have been involved in some local burglaries, but can't be sure."

Ruth asked, "What was Slater in for?"

"Felony assault on a police officer and resisting arrest on a grand theft auto charge. About ten years ago he was arrested for felony homicide in the course of a robbery, but the evidence wasn't there and they had to drop the charges. So Detective Morales thought Slater was fully capable of planning what happened here and drafting Dempsey to help him. Both were violent and reckless. I asked him to see if he could find out who they worked for recently.

"When I told him they tried to kill an FBI agent, he nearly fell off his chair. He told me, 'I never thought the two of them were that stupid.' "

Ruth rubbed her hands together. "Hurray for Detective Morales. I'm putting him on my Christmas card list."

Savich said, "Our local field office can give Detective Morales all the help he needs, Dix. They can start at the prison, talk to Dempsey's girlfriend, track down their associates."

"I'm sure he'd appreciate that. It would save us having to drive over to Richmond ourselves."

"When would you like us to be here in the morning?"

Dix said, "The boys leave pretty early, so breakfast will be on by dawn. You're welcome to join us."

"That was pretty good, Dix," Ruth said. "Okay, guys, anytime after eight. I'm making scrambled eggs."

"Oh, I forgot, Dix," Sherlock said. "You mentioned Dr. Holcombe has a daughter?"

"Yes, her name's Marian Gillespie, lives in a little bungalow in the Meadow Lake section, teaches music theory and clarinet at Stanislaus. Christie always liked her, said she marches to a different drummer. Yes, you're right. We should talk to her tomorrow, once we're done with my uncle."

Savich asked thoughtfully, "Have you ever noticed anything off between father and daughter, Dix?"

"No," Dix replied. "Not that I remember."

★ ★ ★

Dix's phone rang a little before six-thirty Thursday morning. He jerked up in bed, afraid it was something bad.

It was. Helen Rafferty had been found dead by her running partner and brother, Dave Rafferty.

CHAPTER 22

Wolf Ridge Road
Maestro, Virginia
Early Thursday morning

Dix couldn't seem to stop muttering to himself. He felt like an idiot for not seeing that he'd placed Helen Rafferty in danger. Was she dead because someone knew she'd spoken to them or was afraid of what she knew?

He and Ruth arrived five minutes after Savich and Sherlock had streaked in, Savich at the wheel of his Porsche. They found Dr. Himple and the Loudon County forensic team in the bedroom where her brother had found her.

After Dix and Ruth spoke to Dr. Himple, they joined Dave Rafferty in the kitchen with Savich and Sherlock, drinking a cup of black coffee. He was somewhere in his late forties, with a runner's lean build and thinning light brown hair. His face was covered with stubble since he hadn't yet shaved. He was badly shaken.

To help ground him, Savich asked, "Mr. Rafferty, what do you do for a living?"

"What? Oh, I teach science at John T. Tucker High School in Mount Bluff. It's maybe twelve miles from Maestro."

"Why were you here so early?"

Dave Rafferty motioned to his sweats and running shoes. "Helen and I run three days a week. She didn't answer the door when I rang at six. I really didn't think anything about it — you know, she over-slept, maybe she was tired. Oh Jesus, I was calling out for her to get her butt out of bed, come on, time's a-passing, but she couldn't hear me, couldn't talk. This is going to bury Mom. She and Helen were so close."

He swallowed, drank some coffee, and took a deep breath. Sherlock laid her hand on his shoulder, and he raised his head. "When I saw her in bed, I still thought she was sleeping, you know? 'Hey, lazy bones,' I yelled out, 'you're done sleeping, Nell. Come on, move your butt.' But she didn't move. She was lying on her back, the covers to her waist. She was wearing that blue flannel nightgown. Her eyes were open and she was staring up at me. I tried to wake her, but of course she didn't move, her eyes just kept staring. Then I saw the marks on her neck. It's crazy. She never hurt a soul." He shuddered, dropped his head to his folded arms and sobbed. "She's dead, dammit, my sister is dead."

Without hesitation, Sherlock wrapped her arms around him and held him tight. "I'm so sorry, Mr. Rafferty. We'll find out who did this." Savich knew she'd take care of things. He, Dix, and Ruth left the kitchen.

Dix was muttering again under his breath. "I'm dumb as that fence post on Moose Hollow Hill. It's my fault, no one else's, mine."

Savich said matter-of-factly, "None of us realized Helen Rafferty was in any danger. You told her not to talk to anyone. You think someone overheard you and Ruth with her in the employee lounge?"

"I've got to say it out loud," Dix said. "Helen might have called Gordon to warn him about what she told us."

Savich said, "And maybe about what she didn't tell you. It's certainly possible. And it's certainly true both of them — Erin and Helen — had been intimate with Dr. Holcombe. I'd say that puts him squarely at the top of our list."

"If he's not at Stanislaus this morning, we'll have to find him and bring him in,"

Dix said. "Now we can't break Helen's alibi for him on Friday."

He saw Sherlock speaking with Dr. Himple. She nodded, shook his hand, and walked over to them. "The doctor says she was strangled. There are no defensive wounds because whoever killed her probably crept up on her while she was asleep, garroted her, and it was over quickly. I'll bet she called Dr. Holcombe, Dix. Out of love or loyalty?"

Savich nodded. "That's what we were saying. We need to trace her movements, Dix, after you left her yesterday. You got a couple of good people to put on this?"

Dix nodded. "When we saw her at Stanislaus, Uncle Gordon wasn't there, as I told you. He was over in Gainsborough Hall, the big performing auditorium, listening to some pieces to be played at the concert next month. We'll find out who saw her before she left the campus. We can check her phone records — maybe she called him at the auditorium."

Ruth said, "Maybe Helen called someone else, maybe she couldn't remember all the names and she knew of someone else who knew, or she called one of the women."

Dix pulled out his cell and punched in

his office. He said to his dispatcher, "Amalee, get Penny, Emory, and Claus in. I'll meet them at the office in twenty minutes." He paused for a moment, listening, then flipped his phone shut, and pocketed it. "Amalee already knew," he said. He shook his head. "Of course she knew." He scuffed the toe of his boot against the living room rug and cursed under his breath.

They searched Helen Rafferty's small three-bedroom house thoroughly. There wasn't much to see because she'd simplified her life some time ago, according to her brother, preferring to have few possessions. But she loved photos. They were everywhere, on every surface. Mostly family. They did find some five-year-old notes Dr. Holcombe had written to her in a little box with a ribbon tied around it in her underwear drawer. Not hot and heavy love notes, but things like *Dinner tonight, at your place?* or *Meet me at my house at six o'clock.*

It was all incredibly sad, Ruth thought.

Helen Rafferty's empty desk at Stanislaus was pristine, not a loose paper anywhere. Her computer screen looked polished. Since Dr. Holcombe wasn't there, they took the time to go through all her desk drawers, but found nothing of interest. Soon everyone on campus would want to know what had happened. Everyone would be upset and confused — first Erin Bushnell, now the director's personal assistant. Soon, Dix thought, everyone would be scared.

Dix was starting up the Range Rover when his cell phone rang. He hung up a moment later. "That was Chappy. He said Twister is at Tara, drinking his Kona coffee, eating Mrs. Goss's scones, and is of no use to anyone at all. He said Twister told him about Helen being strangled, and now Twister is crying and sniffling. Chappy sounded disgusted."

The sun wasn't shining. The sky was steel-gray, heavy snow-bloated clouds dotting the horizon, and it seemed as cold as the South Dakota plains Dix had visited years ago with Christie and the boys.

Dix kept to the back roads and pushed the Range Rover well beyond the speed limit. Seeing Ruth hug herself, he turned the heat on high. "Snow," he said to no one in particular. "Probably by afternoon."

They pulled into Tara's long drive twelve minutes later. "I wonder where my law enforcement officers are," Dix said. "I was over the limit the whole way. Usually if there's someone speeding, they know it."

"You're the sheriff," Ruth told him. "They gonna pull you over? I don't think so. When was the last time one of your deputies came after you for speeding?"

"Point made."

As Dix pulled the Range Rover to a stop, he said, "If you guys will bear with me, I want to hold off asking my uncle about his affairs with Erin and the others in front of Chappy. He'd probably howl with laughter, say he thought Twister was impotent or something, and go on forever. We really can't interrogate him here. I want to confront him about Erin and Helen when he's away from his brother."

"He's your uncle, and it's your investigation, Dix," Savich said. "Your call."

Chappy answered the doorbell again, wearing a pale blue cashmere sweater, black wool slacks, and loafers.

"Is Bertram still sick?" Dix asked him.

"Yeah, he's still sniffling around her house, his sister told me, complaining he hurts all over when he gets out of bed. Not a good patient, is Bertram. It's about time you got here, Dix. I know Twister killed Helen. Come in and handcuff this pathetic wuss, get him out of here, he's making me sick. I see you're still towing the Feds around." He stepped back, waved them all in.

Gordon Holcombe was standing by the fireplace, a cup of coffee in his hand. He looked like an Italian fashion plate in a dark gray suit, white shirt, and a perfectly knotted pale blue tie. He looked sad and also somehow stoic, a strange combination, Ruth thought. Was he really sorry Helen was dead? Or relieved?

Gordon didn't say a word when they walked into the living room, and merely stood watching them.

Dix said, "Gordon, I'm very sorry about Helen."

"Why are you telling him you're sorry?" Chappy bellowed, waving his fist in his brother's direction. "This mewling little psychopath probably killed her. I already told you he did. Go on. Ask him!"

Ruth asked, "Did you kill Helen Rafferty, Dr. Holcombe?"

Gordon sighed, set his coffee cup on the mantel. "No, Agent Warnecki, I most certainly did not. I was very fond of Helen. I've known her since I first came to Stanislaus. She was a remarkable woman. I don't know who killed her." Suddenly, he looked spiteful. "Why don't you ask Chappy while you're at it? He's the loose cannon around here. How do you think he got so rich? He's stepped over some bodies. Ask him!"

"Ha! That was weak, Twister, real weak. As if I'd kill your former mistress. The good Lord knows you're the only one with a motive, not me. Er, what was your motive?"

Dix said, "How did you know she was dead, Gordon?"

"I called Helen because I wanted to ask her about some details concerning Erin Bushnell's memorial service. I got her answering machine, and I thought that was strange because everyone knows Helen is always at her desk by seven-thirty, so I called the reception desk in Blankenship and asked to speak to her. Mary said she hadn't seen her. When I called her home, her brother answered. He was crying, poor man. He told me she was dead, that she'd been murdered, said you guys had just left.

"I was upset, bewildered. I didn't know what to do so I came here." He shot his brother a vicious look. "Am I an idiot or what? No sympathy from Charles Manson here, the cold-blooded old bloodsucker."

Savich stepped right in. "When did you last see Helen, Dr. Holcombe?"

"Yesterday afternoon, for only a moment after I got back from Gainsborough Hall. I was upset because they'd had to replace Erin with another student who simply isn't in her league. Usually Helen would stay if I did, but this time she didn't. She left, barely spoke to me at all. Naturally, I thought she was troubled over Erin's murder.

"I remember watching her walk to where her Toyota was parked, thinking she'd gained a little weight. I watched her get in and drive away." His voice broke. "I never saw her again."

Chappy made a rude noise. "That was real affecting, Twister, gloomed my innards right up."

Mercifully, Mrs. Goss appeared in the doorway carrying a large silver tray.

Sherlock found herself staring at the lovely Georgian silver service, so highly polished she could see her face in the surface. When Mrs. Goss left, she turned to Chappy, who looked as satisfied as could be, sprawled in his chair, his long legs crossed. "Why did you say your brother was crying, Mr. Holcombe? I don't see a single tearstain."

Chappy only shrugged. "Because he was crying before you showed up, croc tears. Twister never cries about anything in his useless life unless it's over something he wanted and didn't get."

"Well, I didn't want Helen dead," Gordon said, his voice flat and too calm. "And well you know it, Chappy. You're trying to cause trouble for me, nothing new in that, but this isn't a joke. You little sadist, Helen's dead, Erin's dead. Even Walt's dead. Someone tried to kill Special Agent Warnecki. Don't you understand, you old geezer — everything's gone to hell!" His voice had risen steadily until he was shouting. Chappy merely grinned at him.

Ruth asked, "Dr. Holcombe, where were you last Friday afternoon?"

"What? What is this? Erin — You think I had something to do with her murder, too? God almighty, this can't be happening."

"What were you doing Friday afternoon?" Savich repeated.

Gordon waved his hand. "I don't know. I don't remember — Wait, wait. I was stuck counseling a procession of idiot students all afternoon. They were driving me wild."

Gordon turned on Dix. "I didn't kill anyone! You're the bloody sheriff. Who is going to be next? What are you doing to catch the monster who's doing these things? I'll tell you, it's someone who hates me, who wants to destroy me and Stanislaus."

Ruth asked, "Did Helen call you last night, Dr. Holcombe?"

"Helen call me? Why, no, she didn't. As a matter of fact, I considered calling her, but I didn't, more's the pity."

"Why did you think to call her?"

Gordon shrugged. "I was depressed. I suppose I wanted her to cheer me up, but I didn't call. I don't remember why I didn't."

Dix waited a beat, then asked, "Do you know Jackie Slater, Gordon?"

"Jackie Slater? No, I don't. Why should I? Who is he?"

"How about Tommy Dempsey?"

"No, dammit. I don't recognize either name. Why are you asking me?"

"They're very likely the men who tried to murder Special Agent Warnecki Saturday night."

"Wait, Dempsey — that name sounds familiar . . ."

"Jack Dempsey was a famous boxer, you ignoramus."

"Shut up, Chappy. Why are you asking me these idiot questions? For God's sake, Dix, get out there and do your job!"

Savich said, his voice suddenly hard as nails, his face as hard as his voice, "Tell us where you were last night, Dr. Holcombe."

Gordon stopped in his tracks at that voice. He looked at Savich, turning even paler. "You want me to give you an . . . *alibi?* Me? That's ridiculous, I — I . . . Very well, I'm sorry, it's just . . . Okay, I understand, this is standard procedure and I did know her very well. I had dinner with my daughter, Marian Gillespie, at her house. We dined alone, I stayed until around nine o'clock, played the piano while she tried to sight-read a clarinet solo composed by George Wooten, a musician from Indiana who sent it to her yesterday. She got through it before I pulled out my fingernails. It was perfectly dreadful."

"Marian plays like a dream," Chappy said. "Twister here is a snotty perfectionist. No one can do anything well enough to suit him."

"The music was dreadful, you fool, not Marian's playing. Wooten believes anything dissonant means genius — you know, like those modern artists who smear anything at all on a canvas. Before you croon to me about being a perfectionist, Chappy, look how you treat Tony, who's doing so well running your bank."

Sherlock cut him off. "What did you do then, Dr. Holcombe?" She pointedly ignored Chappy, looking intently at Gordon.

"What did I do? I didn't do anything. I went home, that's what people usually do when they're ready for bed. They go home. Like I said, I was depressed and angry because some maniac murdered Erin. I kept thinking of her, couldn't get her out of my mind. It really hit me that I'd never see her again, and never hear her play again."

Savich's voice sharpened even more. "Please tell us what time you got home and what you did."

"Okay. All right. I got home at around nine-thirty. I looked through my mail since I didn't have time to do it before I went over to Marian's. I watched the news on TV, drank a scotch, went up to bed. I tried not to think about Erin. I had trouble sleeping so I watched a bit more TV, but I couldn't get Erin out of my mind. And now Helen is dead, too."

"Can anyone verify this, Gordon?" Dix asked.

"No, I live alone, as you well know. The help isn't waltzing in and out after five o'clock in the afternoon."

There was a moment of silence, broken by Ruth as she looked from one brother to the other. "The two of you look remarkably alike. Bear with me, but I'm new here, and I've never seen two brothers treat each other the way you do. Why, Chappy, are you accusing your brother of murder? Can you explain this to me?"

Chappy laughed, clutching his hands over his belly. "Come on, Agent Ruth, look at that pompous, affected academician. Can you blame me? The pathetic liar's never done a decent thing in his life, except play the fiddle." He hiccupped, slapped his hand over his mouth, and hiccupped again.

Gordon said flatly, "Please disregard that jealous baboon, Agent. After our parents died, he decided he'd be my daddy, and did he ever do a job of it, until I could get away from him. The only thing that means anything to him is money." He jerked his head in his brother's direction. "I plan to bury you in a casket filled with one dollar bills, Chappy, let them keep you company."

"Now, make that thousand-dollar bills and you might have something, you cheap bastard," Chappy said, kicking the toe of his loafer toward his brother.

Ruth cleared her throat. "Yet you came here, Dr. Holcombe, when you didn't know what else to do."

"Even though I've had to put up with this overbearing jackass all my life, the fact is, I like his coffee." He saluted his brother with his coffee cup.

CHAPTER 23

Marian Gillespie didn't answer the knock on her door, a young man did. He was barefoot, dressed in jeans and a gray sweatshirt with STANISLAUS across the front.

"Yeah? Who are you?"

Dix smiled as he stepped forward, pushing him back into the house. "I'm Sheriff Noble. Who are you?"

"Hey —"

"Who are you?"

"Sam Moraga."

"This is Professor Marian Gillespie's house. What are you doing here?"

"Marian is giving me private tutoring," the young man said, and yawned so wide his jaw cracked.

"In what?"

"I play the clarinet, among other instruments. I had to come over late last night because Dr. Holcombe — he's her father — was here and she couldn't get rid of him before nine o'clock."

"You saw Dr. Holcombe leave?"

"Yeah, that's right. He drives this stuck-up silver Mercedes, thinks he's better than all the peasants. Thing is, though, he's got the talent to pull it off."

"Where is Dr. Gillespie?" Dix asked him.

"She left a little while ago, said she had to e-mail this composer who sent her some clarinet music. She thought it was great. She's at her office at school."

Dix continued, "You must be the only sentient human being in the area who doesn't know. Helen Rafferty was murdered last night."

Sam Moraga nearly fell over. Dix grabbed his arm. "You knew her, I gather."

"Oh man, sure I knew Ms. Rafferty. Man, everyone is dying. I can't believe this. She was nice, wouldn't hurt anyone, always great with Marian's dad. . . . Murdered? She was like a mother to Marian, to all the students. Who killed her?"

"We're working on it," Dix said. "I gather you and Dr. Gillespie are sleeping together?"

Sam Moraga nodded absently. "Helen is dead. I can't get my brain around that. It's horrible. First Erin, and now Helen. What's happening, Sheriff?"

"Come into the living room."

They spoke with Sam Moraga for another thirty minutes. He was nervous about the FBI agents, stammering the answers to their questions. Sherlock thought he might be spooked about having some marijuana in the house. They left him at the kitchen table, a mug of cold coffee between his beautifully shaped hands.

Dix and Ruth walked toward the Range Rover ahead of Savich and Sherlock, who'd slowed to confer.

"Sam was frightened about you Feds, and he probably thought I was a joke," Dix said. "You guys got to see me bumbling around."

"Dix, you realized as well as I did that Sam's not a player in this. Whoever's doing this is smart, and so far he's playing us like a pro."

He called out to Savich and Sherlock, "Let's go track down Dr. Gillespie." Suddenly he smiled at Ruth. "Hey, wanna go skating when this is over? Honeyluck Pond's been frozen for the past two weeks."

"Skating? Well, sure, I'd like that. I haven't skated in years but I used to be pretty good."

They ran Marian Gillespie to earth in the faculty lounge on the second floor of Blankenship Hall. She was alone in the plush, dark wood–paneled room, sipping from a mug as she stood at one of the multipaned windows, staring at the snow-covered hills in the distance. It was easy for Ruth to see she was her father's daughter and Chappy's niece. She was tall, slender, dressed in a beautifully cut dark blue suit, stiletto boots on her long, narrow feet. She had thick, light hair and dark eyes, like Tony's.

"Marian," Dix said to her from the doorway.

Her head came up fast, a long hank of hair falling forward. "Dix! Oh goodness, you're here about Helen, aren't you? Oh God, what's happening?" She set her mug on a table and ran to him, threw her arms around him. "I simply can't believe it; no one would want to hurt Helen. She was almost like a mother to me, always so sweet, listened to all my troubles. She wrote me when I was at Juilliard, did you know that?"

"Yes, Christie told me how close you two were. We need to talk, Marian." Dix introduced the three FBI agents.

She motioned them to join her. Once seated, Marian said, "I heard about those men trying to kill you, Agent Warnecki. Then there was poor Erin Bushnell and poor old Walt McGuffey. Now Helen. Who's responsible, Dix? Who is killing our friends, ruining everything we've worked for?"

"We're close to finding that out, Marian, but we need your help."

Savich said, "We spoke with Sam Moraga at your house earlier."

She didn't look embarrassed, not even much interested, only shrugged. "Well, Sam's a talented boy who has a brilliant future, if he can keep himself focused on what's important. We'll see. He learns quickly, I'll say that for him. And he's eager."

No one was about to touch that morass of double entendres, and Savich wondered if she knew about her father's affairs with students. Was she throwing this back at him?

Sherlock said, "We're very sorry about this, Professor Gillespie. We spoke to your father as well. He was over at Tara with Chappy."

"So my father knew and didn't bother to call me. That's par for the course. I'm not surprised he was with Uncle Chappy. I'll bet they were fighting, right?"

Sherlock said, "It seems to be the only way they communicate."

She shrugged again. "It's been that way forever. I never pay attention to their dramatics anymore. Sometimes the yelling breaks through, but usually not."

Savich brought her attention back to him. "Dr. Gillespie, did you know that your father and Helen Rafferty were lovers at one time?"

"Sure, she told me. It was no big secret. I would have thought you knew, Dix. I'm sure Christie did. Now, you're not thinking Dad had anything to do with this, are you?"

Dix held silent, continued to look at her.

Marian flipped her hand. "Listen, that's nuts. Dad needed Helen, probably more than any other human being in the world. He didn't love her, like sexually, but he needed her. She used to play the piano while I played my clarinet. She never tried to drown me out like some pianists do, she —"

Dix patted her hand. "I know it's hard, but let's try to stay on track, okay? Please tell me what you know about it."

"All right, all right. Dad and Helen. When Dad broke it off, Helen nearly went round the bend. I was really mad at him. I called him on it, told him she was already like a mother to me so why didn't he just make it official? I told him he was being cruel to her, and selfish." She sucked in a big breath, gathered her control together. "Do you know what he did? He laughed, actually laughed. He was tired of her as a lover, told me her talents were in administration, not in bed. When I asked him what his point was since he wasn't such a young rooster anymore himself, he walked out of the room. Later, after I apologized — yeah, I know, still trying to please Daddy — well, he told me she was too clingy, and just plain too ordinary, that was the word he used.

"I tried to help Helen get through it, I really did, but you know what? Whenever I told her what I thought of his behavior, she defended him. Can you believe that? She actually defended him!"

No one said a word. Marian drew a deep breath. "She left her job for about six months, but didn't tell anyone at Stanislaus why. I thought, good, Helen's ready to move on, ready to leave my father behind her, but you know what happened? He got to her, convinced her to come back as his personal assistant. I would have fed him his balls, but Helen bowed her head, let him walk all over her, and went back."

Marian shook her head and drank more tea. "She told me she still loved and admired him, that his genius set him apart, made up for everything else, and he still needed her. Can you believe that?" She paused and looked at each of them. "You want to know what the sad thing is? I'm thirty-eight years old and even I still want him to notice me, tell me he admires me, tell me how talented I am. Am I pathetic, or what?"

Ruth looked puzzled. "It is a little hard to understand. Why, if you feel as you do about him, do you want to work for your father, and continue to live in the same small town?"

Professor Marian Gillespie didn't act defensive. What she did was give them all a big smile. "I told you, Agent Warnecki, I'm pathetic. To balance it all out, there's a love pool of nice young men here."

"What became of your mother, Professor?" Sherlock asked, steering the subject back.

"Please, call me Marian."

Sherlock nodded.

"My mother? Oh, Dad divorced her when I was a baby. After that, she left and I never heard from her again. From then on it was only Dad and me."

"Do you know where she lives?" Dix asked.

"I don't know. Maybe Uncle Chappy knows, but I wouldn't count on him to tell you anything close to the truth. All I remember is Uncle Chappy didn't like my mother. I guess my dad didn't either, since he divorced her."

Savich said abruptly, "Did you know your father was sleeping with Erin Bushnell?"

She was shocked and clearly appalled. She was either a remarkable actress or this really was news to her. "That's a stupid lie." She jumped to her feet, her palms flat on the table. "Why would you say such a thing? It's ridiculous. Sure he slept with Helen, but she was closer to his age. A student? Erin Bushnell? No way."

Savich said, "It's true, Marian. Ginger Stanford knew about it, and so did Helen Rafferty."

"Helen told you that? Are you sure, Dix? Erin was much younger than I am, for goodness sake. She's Sam's age. No, I can't accept that, I simply can't."

"You're going to have to accept it," Dix said. "Helen told us everything. What I find interesting is that you knew all about your father's affair with Helen Rafferty, but you didn't know about Erin Bushnell."

Marian slowly shook her head. "Not a clue. On the other hand, I doubt my dad knows about Sam Moraga. But for heaven's sake, he's my father!"

Dix said, "Sam Moraga was really upset

about Helen's murder, more so than I thought a student would be about the death of an administrative assistant. Why?"

She shrugged. "Maybe he thought of her as his mother, too, I don't know. We never spoke about her. Actually, it was Helen who introduced Sam to me. He was in one of my music theory classes, but I hadn't really paid much attention to him. Then at one of those interminable professor and student get-togethers my father insists on throwing every couple of months, she introduced us."

"Does anyone know about Sam?"

She shook her head at Dix, worried at a fingernail. "We're discreet." She finished her tea. "If Sam hadn't been at my house, you wouldn't have known I was anything but the celibate everyone believes me to be. There were a couple of others before Sam, both of them out in the world now. My father called me a shriveled-up prude last year. I remember I'd gotten only two hours' sleep the night before, so I simply laughed at him. He couldn't understand that laugh and I didn't enlighten him." Her voice turned bitter and low. "Maybe I should have told him. It looks like we could have compared notes. We make quite a pair, don't we?"

Dix saw the tears in her eyes, and waited

for her to recover. He'd known her since he and Christie got married, and yet . . . He shook his head. Who ever really knew what another person was about?

Marian looked at the rest of them, her lips twisted at their carefully expressionless faces. "Were there others? Others besides Erin Bushnell?"

Dix said, "You need to talk to your father about that, Marian. We're going over to see him now. If you think of anything else, give me a call right away. I've got the same cell number."

"Is there some sort of serial killer on the loose here, Dix?"

"What we're thinking is that whoever tried to kill Ruth probably killed Erin Bushnell, and that opened Pandora's box. He may be trying to do damage control."

"But why Helen? Does that make any sense to you?"

Dix said, "Tying it together will be the key to all of this."

Marian walked to the window, turned, and looked back at them. "So much pain to bear now. I suppose I'll have to deal with Sam's pain, too. How can he possibly have loved her as much as I did? I wonder, Dix. Do you think my father cared at all?"

"Yes, Marian. I think he did."

CHAPTER 24

Dix called the deputy assigned to follow Gordon Holcombe when he left Tara.

"Where is he, B.B.?"

"Weirdest thing, Sheriff. When Dr. Holcombe left Tara, I thought he was going to Stanislaus, then he seemed to change his mind. He drove straight out to the Coon Hollow Bar. He's been in there nearly two hours. You told me I shouldn't try to keep out of sight and I didn't. He knew I was following him, and it didn't seem to bother him. Right now I'm tucked in a mess of pine trees across the street."

Dix told him to stay put, they'd be there shortly. He punched off his cell. "Gordon calls this place his sanctuary. It's a pre–World War Two relic, all weathered wood, dark glass in the windows, and a rutted parking lot in front."

Coon Hollow Bar was only a mile or so out of Maestro.

"It looks like a treat," Sherlock said, admiring the old dark charm of the place. "A good number of customers," she added, waving at four other cars in the parking lot.

There was no sunlight inside Coon Hollow. It smelled of beer and salty pretzels and cigarettes. There was one glowing sign for Bud Light above the bathroom door on the far wall. Gordon Holcombe was bellied up at the bar, head down, shoulders hunched. There were maybe six other folks at the bar, either talking in low voices or as silent as Gordon.

Gordon glanced up when the front door opened and sunlight poured in. He watched the four of them approach. Fact is, Ruth thought, he didn't look the least bit interested in anything except the drink he was sloshing around in his glass.

"Gordon," Dix said.

Gordon glanced at Dix briefly before looking back down. "Since you're all cops, I doubt you know what this is." He held up the glass, swirled the scotch around. "This is The Macallan, Highland scotch whiskey, eighteen years old. It's considered the Rolls-Royce of single malts. Our barkeep's father orders it special for me. My last bottle is low so I can't offer you any. Dix, if you find out who murdered Helen, I'll buy you a bottle of The Macallan for Christmas. Any of you want a beer?"

"No, Gordon."

"Then perhaps, Dix, you can tell me why you've got B.B. following me? He's sitting in his cruiser right across the street. Afraid I was going to take off since I'm so damned guilty?"

Dix said, "Tell us what Helen said to you when she called you last night."

"Helen called me often."

"Last night, Gordon, or do you want me to get a warrant for the phone records?"

Ruth thought she saw Gordon flinch, and then he stared down into his glass again and swished the scotch around, watching it film the sides of the glass.

"All right, so she called me. I didn't tell you in front of Chappy. He would have laughed his head off while promising to visit me in jail. He'd also volunteer to stick me with a lethal injection."

"Helen's call, Gordon."

He suddenly looked old, and somehow smaller. He sighed so deeply it made him cough. "It was only a short phone call, Dix, nothing more. God in Heaven, I can't believe she's gone. There's some maniac out there, some crazy man who hates me, who hates Stanislaus, who wants to destroy everything."

Ruth said, "How very odd, Dr. Holcombe. You believe it's all about you,

317

and no one else. Don't you think that's a rather narrow view? After all, you're sitting here drinking your fine single malt scotch, quite alive, while Erin Bushnell, Walt McGuffey, and Helen Rafferty are dead."

Dr. Holcombe looked confused for a moment, then said, "Of course I care, dammit. I didn't mean . . . Are you sure you don't want something to drink?"

Savich said, "No, thank you, Dr. Holcombe. Why don't we all go over to that booth?"

There were half a dozen ancient booths lining two sides of the room. The vinyl was slippery and cold, the cracks so large one could easily lose a wallet. Ruth allowed Dr. Holcombe to scoot in first, then essentially locked him in by sitting next to him on the outside. He didn't appear to notice.

"It's going to start snowing soon," he said into his glass. "I'm wondering when I leave here with all this scotch in me whether I'll be able to get back to Stanislaus. You know the media are there, Dix. Soon our donors will be on the line, asking to talk to me. What am I going to tell them? That their director is a murder suspect? I can't even imagine Helen being gone, much less dead." He raised pain-glazed eyes to Dix's face. "She's always been there for me, my guardian angel. After I left Tara, I was going to my office, but I couldn't stand the thought of it. Helen wasn't there, you see. You've got to believe me, I didn't kill her." He lowered his forehead to the table.

Savich went to the bar and asked for three coffees and a cup of tea.

"If that's true, Gordon, you'd best start convincing me you didn't. Tell us about Helen's phone call."

"I want another drink first."

When Savich came back to the booth, he heard Dix say, "No more, Gordon. You need to stop with that stuff. Here's Agent Savich with some coffee."

Savich handed him a cup. Gordon stared at it, gave a little shudder. He picked up his scotch glass, tipped it, but it was empty.

"Talk to me, Gordon. Don't even consider lying, or I'll give Chappy a free pass to have a field day."

"All right. Helen was whispering on the phone — it was absurd, really, her whispering like that. She told me she was worried for me, that I had to be careful. She told me you and Agent Warnecki and the other two FBI agents were snooping around, asking her about our affair."

No one spoke: they simply waited.

Gordon sipped at his coffee, unaware of what he was doing.

Ruth finally said, "This is a nice quiet place, Dr. Holcombe. I can see how you could view it as a sort of sanctuary, a place where you can be by yourself, away from students and colleagues. Do you always come here alone?"

"Sure, always alone, Agent Warnecki."

Dix asked him, "What else did Helen tell you, other than to be careful and that we're snooping around?"

"She said you told her that you knew about my relationship with Erin and some of the other students, that she'd already given you some names but you wanted all of them. She said she didn't have a choice but to help you. She started crying, begging for my forgiveness."

There was only the soft sound of Dr. Holcombe's palms rubbing the sides of his scotch glass.

"That's a pretty sturdy motive, Gordon," Dix told him. "Your ex-lover spilled the beans, starting a scandal that might get you fired from your prestigious job, and giving parents an excellent reason to yank their kids out of Stanislaus. I could arrest you right this minute."

Gordon nearly knocked over his glass.

He grabbed it, righted it. His breath was coming hard and fast. "I didn't do it, Dix, I swear to you. I couldn't kill Helen. I loved her, in my way."

"What is your way, sir?" Ruth asked.

"She was my anchor. She knew people, understood them in ways I couldn't begin to; she gave me comfort and advice. I'll never forget how I was interested in this viola student, and Helen told me she wasn't stable, that she'd cause scenes and probably hurt me, so I stayed away from her. A couple of months later, she accused a boy from town of rape."

"I remember that," Dix said. "Kenny Pollard, but he had a rock-solid alibi. Seems clear to me now, Gordon, that Helen actually helped you seduce your own students."

He shook his head back and forth, obviously shaken.

"When you realized she had told us about you, you killed Helen for revenge, didn't you? That, and you couldn't stand the world knowing you're a philandering old fool." Savich's voice was so hard, so brutal that Gordon froze like a deer in headlights. Savich sat forward, grabbed Gordon's wrist and squeezed. "You will tell me the truth, you perverted old man.

Why did you kill Erin Bushnell? Did she of all the music students see through you? Did she threaten to tell the world what you are, want to see you humiliated and run off campus, stripped of your power and prestige?"

Suddenly, the man who'd hunched over his drink, desperate and pleading, was gone. In his place was Dr. Gordon Holcombe, director of Stanislaus, back in all his dignity, his patrician face set in arrogant lines again. He looked at each of them in turn with disdain and a superior's patience. "I will tell you the truth about Erin. I first became involved with her on Halloween when she showed up at my house to trick-or-treat, dressed like Titania from *Midsummer Night's Dream.* She called me her Oberon later that night."

The expression on Ruth's face never changed, although Dix fancied he saw her shudder.

"Erin was the most talented violinist I've heard in a very long time. Gloria Stanford was convinced she'd be known the world over someday. She had glorious technique, could make you weep listening to her play. The three violin sonatas composed for Joseph Joachim by Brahms — she was transcendent. I was blessed by her company,

322

I reveled in it. But I did not kill her, there was no reason. I didn't kill Helen Rafferty, either. I loved both of them, in different ways.

"Whatever you may believe about my personal ethics and behavior, none of it concerns you unless I did something criminal, which I did not. Dix, you are the sheriff of Maestro. Everyone says we are lucky to have you. Well, prove it. Find out for all of us who killed two citizens of our town in under a week."

"You forgot Walt McGuffey, that kind old man who never harmed a soul in his life."

"I heard about him. You want to lay the old man's death at my door, too? Fact is, I didn't know him well, he meant nothing to me. Why would I kill him?"

"His house is on the way to Lone Tree Hill and the other entrance to Winkel's Cave. Ruth's car was hidden in his shed. That's why someone murdered him."

"I don't know anything about her car! I haven't seen Walt in months."

Dix said, "When did you last see Erin alive?"

"On Thursday afternoon, at Stanislaus. She was working hard rehearsing for the upcoming concert, and we had no plans to see each other over the weekend."

"But you did see her on Friday, didn't you, Gordon? You took her to Winkel's Cave, to murder her."

Gordon looked like he might faint. He paled, and his eyes nearly rolled back in his head. Ruth stuck her coffee cup under his nose. "Drink."

Gordon was babbling now, waving his hands at them like a drunk conductor. "I didn't, really, there's no way I could do anything like that. I didn't —"

Dix splayed his hands on his seat cushion and leaned toward his uncle. "Let me tell you what you're going to do for us, Gordon. You're going to give us written permission to search your home, your office, and your studio. If you cooperate, we'll do it discreetly as part of the investigation. If not, we'll get search warrants and post flyers on every tree on campus about the women you slept with, then subpoena each of them to come back to Stanislaus and talk to us — and the board of directors.

"You know now that you can't expect to keep your affair with Erin under wraps for long, but they might let you keep your job, or help you get another one somewhere, if you tell them yourself. Think about it.

"And you're going to tell us all about

your other affairs — the names of the students and how we can reach them. We can turn the records at Stanislaus upside down to find them if we have to. Don't make us do that, Gordon."

Ruth pulled out a pen and a small notebook. "All right, I'm ready, Dr. Holcombe. Tell us about your talented Lolitas."

"It wasn't like that! You make them sound like teenagers, and they weren't. They were all accomplished musicians. No, it was never like that. I loved all of them, in their time."

"In their time," Savich repeated slowly, his eyes steady on Gordon's face. "Who lasted longest, Dr. Holcombe?"

Gordon froze. "I don't want to talk about this. Dix, make them stop. I haven't done anything."

"Ruth has her pen ready, Gordon. Give her names. Who was before Erin Bushnell?"

There was a moment of tense silence. Gordon drew in a deep breath and said to Ruth, "Before Erin, there was Lucy Hendler, pianist, lovely long reach, incredible technique and passion, perfect pitch."

A litany of attributes, nothing about Lucy Hendler the woman, the individual. "What were the dates?"

"What do you mean, dates?"

Ruth said, "Dr. Holcombe, surely Lucy wasn't all that long ago."

"She performed Scarlatti exquisitely in a recital a year ago February. She got a standing ovation, difficult to do, let me tell you, in an audience of accomplished musicians. She told me later she actually hated Scarlatti, that he was dated and boring, far too predictable. I thought it amusing and sweet, her lack of historical context. I mean, how could anyone dismiss Domenico Scarlatti, for God's sake? She was only twenty-one. What did she know?"

Ruth said, "So you booted her because she wasn't a Scarlatti aficionada?"

"No, of course not. Our relationship deepened. I remember we got a little cross with each other before she graduated. It was May Day and we had a Maypole on campus. I thought it would be lovely if we had a choral group seated around the Maypole singing Irish folk songs, and other students could dance around the pole, dressed up in peasant costumes. She laughed at me. Can you imagine that?"

"Where is Lucy Hendler, Dr. Holcombe?"

"She graduated in June. She was accepted into our performing graduate program, but she didn't stay."

"Let me guess, she changed her mind after the Maypole."

"No, I'm sure that had nothing to do with her decision to leave Stanislaus. She had a friend up in New York she went to visit and decided to stay. Last I heard she was enrolled at Juilliard."

Ruth nodded. "And do you feel responsible for Stanislaus losing a graduate student?"

Dix kept his mouth shut. Ruth was handling this like a pro, reeling Gordon in, getting him to spill information Dix doubted he'd ever be able to get out of him.

When she got him back on track, Gordon told them about Lindsey Farland, a student about two and a half years ago, a soprano with incredible range he met when she sang the role of Cio-Cio-San, the betrayed young wife in *Madama Butterfly*. She hardly looked the part, since she was black, but when he heard her sing and she hit the high C in "Un bel dì," he fell in love.

"That is one of my favorite arias," Ruth said, and everyone at the table knew she meant it. She paused, then asked, "Where is Lindsey now?"

"I don't know. She graduated two years

ago. She hasn't kept in touch."

"It won't take us long to find her."

Ruth got six names out of him but he remembered few facts about the women. His recollection of the dates was also sketchy. "I can't remember anymore, Agent Warnecki. Wait, wait, there was one more. Her name was Kirkland. Her first name was unusual, something like Anoka. And then, there was . . . No, that isn't at all relevant. Look, I'll need to look through some school records, find out what her first name is exactly."

It was Sherlock who nailed him. "Tell us who you're leaving out, Dr. Holcombe. Why don't you want to tell us about her? Who is she?"

Dix shook his head. "I know why he doesn't want to tell us. She's local, isn't she, Gordon? She's from Maestro."

"No, there isn't anyone else. Now, Dix, I assume you'll be calling these ladies to verify what I've told you. May I contact them first to make it less alarming for them?"

"Not yet, Gordon. I'll be with you when I decide it's the right time to make any calls.

"Now, I want you to stay here and think about the woman whose name you're not telling us. Of course she's local. Is she married? Did she swear you to secrecy? I want her name, Gordon. You've got until tomorrow morning or I'm coming after you."

"There isn't another damned woman!"

Dix said flatly, "You give me her name or I'll arrest you."

"How can you say that, Dix, for pity's sake, I'm Christie's uncle!"

Dix slowly straightened. "Maybe that's why I'm making the mistake of not arresting you right now, Gordon, and taking your Italian-suited self to my nice warm jail. As for now, B.B. will keep an eye on you. I hope you don't disappoint me."

CHAPTER 25

Bud Bailey's Bed & Breakfast
Maestro, Virginia
Late Thursday afternoon

"I need a shower and a shave before we head over to Dix's house." But Savich didn't move to get up. He nuzzled Sherlock's neck, loving the feel of her hair against his face.

"Since I don't have any bones, you can go first." She bit him lightly on his shoulder, kissed him, then breathed in deeply, taking in the scent of him. "I'm thinking maybe I'm not through with you yet."

"You think?"

Fifteen minutes later, Sherlock was doing stretches, her mind automatically working the angles, thinking about the people they'd interviewed, wondering if Gordon Holcombe had told them everything.

She smiled when she heard Dillon singing "Baby, the Rain Must Fall" in the shower in his beautiful baritone. She was about to join him, to see if he was interested in some more quality time, when his cell phone played "Georgia on My Mind." She picked it up.

"Hello?"

No answer, only the sharp sound of breathing.

"Who is this?"

"My oh my, what an unexpected surprise this is. My lucky day."

A woman — no, a girl, a bouncy young voice. "Claudia? Is this Claudia Grace?"

"You win the prize, girlfriend. I was actually calling to speak to your man — you know, get him all hot and bothered with some of my great phone sex, but hey, I can do him later. It'll be fun talking to you. Cool name, Claudia Grace, don't you think? Maybe I should go ahead and marry Moses and make it legal. He's a cutie, no doubt about that, but the thing is, he has a tough time getting it up, even when I walk around in the buff for him. I fed him some of that Viagra, but even that didn't stiffen him up. So he got bored and went out and got this phone to call you guys with. I figured why should he have all the fun?"

Sherlock heard voices in the background. So they weren't driving around this time. Her fingers tightened on the phone. "Where are you, Claudia?"

Sherlock heard the shower turn off. She walked to the bathroom door, opened it to see Dillon stepping out of the shower stall. He frowned at the phone at her ear.

She mouthed, *Claudia.*

He nearly dove at her, his hand out to take the phone, but she shook her head and mouthed, *Not yet.*

Dripping, he walked past her to MAX, pressed several keys, and plugged a wireless earphone into his ear.

"Where am I? Question is, where are you guys? Moses says you're hiding from us. Are you?"

"No, Claudia, not in this lifetime."

"Come on now, sweet cakes, how is Moses going to give you the business if you disappear, and we can't find you? Hey, is your man there? We could get together if you're close by."

"Sure, my man's right here."

"Well now, that's good because Moses wants him close. Did Moses tell you what he's planning for you?"

"I really don't care, Claudia. Where are you and Moses, by the way? Under an extra-big rock so you can hide together?"

"We don't do no rocks, you little bitch. We're in a nice big Hilton, in a suite. I can hardly throw a football across the living room it's so big. I'm going to make you scream through that smart mouth of yours. I told your gorgeous husband that I'd have you watch while I screw his brains out. Then he can watch what I do to you, that brain of his all mushy. Every man I do ends up grinning like his brains have melted."

"I've got to tell you, Claudia, I'm surprised you're that experienced with men at your tender age. Shouldn't you be in school learning how to read? How old are you, fifteen?"

"I can read, bitch, and I'm eighteen."

"Yeah, right. From what I'm hearing you sound barely fifteen. I'll bet your mama had you when she was real young, and you ended up on the street, and that's where Moses found you. And here you are, a little girl acting all grown up, hooked up with that creepy old man."

"Shut up! You won't think you're so smart when Moses gets to you."

"Okay, if he didn't find you shooting up on the street, then how'd you meet him, Claudia? He follow you home, maybe butcher your mama?"

"I'm not fifteen and my mama was over forty when she died, you hear me? She was smart, a schoolteacher, but some tattoo-tongued gangbangers raped and beat her because she wouldn't screw their leader. She died."

"I'm really sorry about your mother, Claudia. You said she was a school-teacher?"

"Yeah, a math teacher, and she was real smart. I was sorry when she died, I really was. I mean, she could have flushed me down the john, right? But she didn't. You hear me, bitch?"

"You're screaming so of course I hear you. You're out of control, like a little kid throwing a tantrum. Why would she have flushed you? Where was your daddy?"

"My mama slept with this jerk who left her. There wasn't any daddy."

"Where'd you learn to talk so dirty, Claudia? From your mama or from that saliva-dripping old man you're with now?"

"My mama didn't cuss!"

"After she died, what did you do?"

"I took off. I wasn't going to let those freak social service people take me. And I picked up Moses, not the other way around. He was standing over this filthy old tramp, blood all over his hands and his old army fatigues, and those black boots he wears, and he was laughing his head off. I asked him why he beat the bum like that, and he told me the guy wouldn't share his Ripple. I figured someone like that could protect me, so I offered him some of my bourbon. All I remember is waking up in a motel room in the morning."

"What were you doing in Atlanta, Claudia? Running from juvie?"

"Nah, it wasn't Atlanta, but what do you care? I'm going to hurt you, lady, more now for dissing me and my mama."

Sherlock laughed. "Sure you are, Claudia. You sound like one of those playground bullies who's all mouth. Why don't you tell me where you are, and we can get together and talk things over before Moses gets you killed, or you end up in a state prison until your hair turns gray?"

"Next time we get together, I'm going to pull your tongue out."

"Now there's a real grown-up threat. You're young enough to still have a chance, Claudia. Stay out there and you'll end up a drugged-out hooker. All that booze will make you look as old as Moses in a few years. Is that what you want for yourself?"

"I'll tell you what I want, bitch. I'll tell Moses to do you first, to do whatever he wants, just for me. And I'll be there to watch."

Sherlock heard a man's voice, and a scuffle. "What are you doing, Claudia? Who is that?"

"Don't you hit me, Moses!"

There was a crackling sound, and the phone went dead.

Savich looked at her, watched her punch off the phone. "I'm going to call the Hoover Building, see if they've located these two specimens."

"I heard noise in the background. Lots of voices. Maybe they were in a restaurant."

Savich nodded. He was talking with the communications chief a few seconds later. "We did much better this time, Savich. It was a third-party provider, using a wireless prepaid card, but Sprint was able to track down the directory number and get us a location about twenty seconds before you lost the connection. It was a good, fixed signal from a GPS-equipped phone, so we have his location within ten meters. It's a Denny's on Atherton Street in Milltown, Maryland. Units should be there any minute."

Savich punched off the phone. "Cops are on their way to Moses's location. You were right, it is a restaurant, a Denny's. We'll know soon if they arrived in time. It sounded like Moses didn't know she was using his new phone. You can bet they headed right out." Savich sighed.

Sherlock gave him a long look. "You didn't tell me Claudia plans to screw your brains out."

"She's certifiable, and what makes it worse is that she's so young. Why would I tell you something that disturbing?"

"Marlin Jones was disturbing, Tyler McBride was disturbing, Günter Grass was disturbing. But Claudia? I feel sorry for her, because of her age. But you should have told me."

"You feel sorry? She and Moses dug out Elsa Bender's eyes, Sherlock. She helped pose Pinky's body over that skeleton at Arlington National Cemetery. She's a psychopath. The thought of her anywhere near you scares the sin out of me. There was no reason to tell you about their ridiculous fantasies. You shouldn't have talked to her, Sherlock. It was unprofessional."

"Unprofessional? Me? This ought to be good. Do tell me what you mean, Dillon."

"First of all, you answered my phone, knowing full well it could be Moses. That phone is our only link to him, and you should have asked me first. At the very least, you should have given me the phone when I stepped out of the shower."

"I happen to be a Federal agent who's on the case with you. You could treat me like a partner, like I'm someone you respect as a fellow agent. Hey, on a good day, maybe even all of the above."

"Dump the sarcasm. Of course we're partners. Well, actually, I'm your boss, and I'm your husband."

Whenever she got angry, Sherlock's face turned as red as her hair. She could feel the heat rising from her neck, that miserable red stain creeping over her skin, and that made her even angrier because she knew he could see it. "Oh, you want to protect the helpless little wife? The meek little thing who should keep her precious ears unsullied by prurient threats from a crazy teenager?"

"Stop, Sherlock, and listen to me. You are my wife and I would protect you with my life."

"And you're my husband, you moron, I'd protect you with my life, too. What does that have to do with this?"

"Because you enraged her, you baited her, and you have her promising to come after you. How could you do that? I can't believe you would pull something like that without discussing it with me first."

"Oh, I see. I was to say, 'Excuse me, Claudia, but I've got to ask my husband what to say before we talk.' That is so infuriating." She shoved him hard on his bare chest, muttering under her breath, "The old double standard. That garbage coming out of your mouth burns me, Dillon. Stop being a macho ass."

"Well, if I'm a macho ass, you're just going to have to live with it." He gave her a look of frustrated dislike, then stomped back into the bathroom.

She yelled through the door, "Because I'm a good cop, I goaded her into telling us about her mother, how she hooked up with Moses. You were listening, *boss*. And I would have kept her talking longer if Moses hadn't grabbed the phone from her."

Towel wrapped around his waist, Savich stomped back through the door, stopped right in front of her, and crossed his arms over his chest. He was doing it because he knew he looked tough and intimidating, something he was very good at. "I never said you weren't a good cop, but you crossed the line on this one. This was an ill-advised stunt. I'm saying that as your boss, so suck it up. Let's get dressed and get to work."

She fluttered her hands. "Goodness, do you think I can manage that without fainting dead away? Maybe I should have a glass of water first, put my head between my knees, maybe call Dix so the two of you muscle-bound yahoos can go out and chop some wood while you decide what to do."

He dashed his hand through his wet hair. "This is ridiculous. Sherlock, close it down or I'll beat your butt."

She assumed a martial arts position and beckoned him with her fingers. "This is no time to mess with me, macho boy. Try it and I'll flatten you."

She was wearing a thick oversized hotel bathrobe, wrapped nearly twice around her. Her feet were bare and her hair curled wildly around her head. Her face was red with rage. And she wanted to fight him. How had it come to this? He laughed even as he wrapped his arms around her waist, threw her over his shoulder, and tossed her onto the bed. He fell on top of her, pulled her arms over her head, and held her down.

He said an inch from her nose, "Stop sneering at me. I know threats don't work with you, so I won't bother. Why don't you tell me where you think we should start with all the info you extracted?"

It was terrible that she couldn't indulge her anger at him, but she recognized the olive branch — really more of a twig — and the fact was, business was business. She saved her anger for later.

"Get off me, you baboon, so I can breathe."

Savich rolled off to the side, but kept one leg on top of her.

"All right. My guess is that all that stuff Claudia told me probably happened in the past year or two. We have a number of details about Claudia's mother that must have led to an investigation. And maybe Claudia is her real name. So you need to fire up MAX and get on it. Now let me go before I get seriously upset and hurt you."

He leaned over and kissed her, still angry and frustrated, then rolled off the bed. He looked down at her for a long moment, brooding, before he walked back into the bathroom and shut the door.

He heard her laugh and yell, "Hey, Dillon, maybe you should call Director Mueller, fill him in on what I got Claudia to tell me."

Savich stood in front of the bathroom mirror, a razor in his hand. He'd heard every word quite clearly; Sherlock had a piercingly clear voice when she wanted to.

341

But beneath that laughter, he thought, she was still angry at him, perhaps as angry as he was with her. He sighed as he soaped up his face.

He was not in a happy place. He cut himself twice.

His phone rang again ten minutes later with the news that Moses and Claudia were no longer at the Denny's.

Savich called Jimmy Maitland to give him a report, then Dix to say they wouldn't make it for dinner. They had a lot of work to do.

CHAPTER 26

Sheriff Noble's house
Maestro, Virginia
Thursday evening

Rafe mowed across his corn on the cob without stopping. Rob, not to be outdone, managed an even wider swath of his own, four rows of kernels at a time. For a moment, Ruth thought he was going to choke. She clapped him on the back and handed him a glass of water, then gave him a thumbs-up when he sat back and smiled contentedly at his brother.

"Neither of you took a single breath," Ruth said. "That's remarkable. Next time I'm going to find really, really big ears of corn and test your limits."

Dix looked up from his own corn at his boys, then over at Ruth. The boys acted natural around her, not at all prickly, as they often did when they thought a woman was threatening to take their mother's place.

She'd known them since Friday night. It

was amazing how comfortable they all were.

Dix said, leaning back in his chair, "Do you know I can't remember ever felling an ear of corn in under six seconds?"

"We did it faster, right, Ruth?"

Ruth laughed. "I wasn't timing you but I bet you beat that. My older brother and I always competed to see who could be the grossest as well as the fastest. Drove our parents crazy."

Rob said, "Grandpa Chappy usually laughs when we do a gross-out for him, like stuffing chewed-up green beans in front of your bottom teeth and peeling down your lip. Uncle Tony gets all uptight and Aunt Cynthia looks like she wants to lock us in a closet."

"How about your uncle Gordon?" Ruth heard the words come out of her mouth before she even realized what she'd asked.

"Uncle Gordon? Hmm." Rob looked over at Rafe, then said, "Fact is, we've never been gross around Uncle Gordon. He always looks so perfect, you know?"

"So does your grandpa Chappy," Ruth said.

"It's not the same," Rafe said, shaking his head. "And when the two of them are together they're so busy fighting we might as well not even be there."

"Isn't that the truth," Ruth said.

"How about you, Ruth? What did you and your brother do that was real gross?"

"Well, my favorite gross-out was chugging a Coke while I was ice skating. You come to a fast stop in front of one of your friends and belch really loud right in their face."

The boys laughed. Dix knew that until tonight his sons had been putting up a brave front, trying to act as natural as they could while all hell was breaking loose around them — three people murdered in their town in less than a week while their father was the one responsible for finding out who killed them.

Rob stopped laughing first. He looked down at the pile of baked beans on his plate.

Well, impossible to ignore reality forever, Dix thought. He said easily, "Thanks for the visual, Ruth. When we go skating, no soft drinks allowed," but the boys looked thoughtful.

Rafe said, "I saw Uncle Tony scratch his armpit once, and when we were playing baseball, he was standing out in center field and he scratched —"

Rob cut his brother off. "Not in front of Ruth."

"You're right, Rob, too much information," Ruth said, and saluted him with her glass of tea.

Dix scooped another spoonful of green beans onto his son's plate. "Eat and don't smash them in front of your bottom teeth."

Rafe shot his father a wary look and said faster than Brewster could swing his tail, "I went to see Mr. Fulton, you know, see where we might stand with his hiring me, you know, when my report card comes out."

"This is a hardware store, right?" Ruth asked.

Rafe nodded. "Mr. Fulton said only six days had passed and nothing was any different at his store, and when would I have proof that my grades are up in English and biology."

Brewster was trying to climb Ruth's leg. She leaned down to pet his head and slipped him a bit of hot dog. But Brewster wasn't hungry, he wanted attention. He rubbed the hot dog on her shoe until she had to lift her feet off the floor to avoid him. The boys laughed until she scooped Brewster up and hugged him against her chest. "What are you up to, smearing hot dog all over my shoe, making everybody laugh at me? I thought you were my hero."

"Some hero," Rob said, piling more potato salad on his plate. "Brewster was so small when he was a puppy we were afraid we might roll over on him during the night and squash him."

Dix chuckled, one eye on Brewster. "He was hero enough to find Ruth. I've rolled over on Brewster myself and he's survived. Now, Rafe, what did Mr. Fulton say about the job?"

Rafe swallowed a mouthful of hot dog bun. "Mr. Fulton asked me to spell 'valedictorian.' That wasn't fair, Dad."

"Did you even attempt it?" Ruth asked.

"Yeah, I did. I missed the e in the middle. It wasn't fair," he repeated.

His father said, "I gather Mr. Fulton didn't hire you?"

"He told me to bring him my next report card. Then he'd speak to you again."

"Stup Fulton is full of surprises," Dix said to Ruth.

"Ah, he asked me what you're doing about all this violent stuff, Dad. I told him you and the three FBI agents are working real hard on it. He just harrumphed." He looked down at his plate. This time his voice was as thin as the kitchen curtains. "And there's the kids at school. They're saying that you're not as good as everyone says you are, that everyone in town's getting murdered."

"Well," Dix said, "you don't look banged up so I guess you didn't get into any fights."

"It was close," Rafe muttered.

"I understand. But you managed to walk away?"

It was Rob who said, "Sure, Dad. Right."

Ruth had noticed the bruise on Rob's knuckles. It couldn't have been all that bad a fight if his knuckles weren't skinned. She smiled brightly. "Hey, I saw a baseball and glove in the hallway. Who's the Barry Bonds?"

Rob said eagerly, "Me. Didn't Dad tell you I'm going to be the starting pitcher on the high-school team?"

"Sorry, Rob, I didn't, but I sure intended to." Not that Rob really cared whether he had, Dix thought as Rob rushed on. "The thing is, Ruth, I'm only a sophomore. Billy Caruthers started last year as a junior, and he's totally pissed the coach picked me."

Dix gave his son a long look.

Rob cleared his throat. "Ah, Dad, everyone says it. Okay, Billy Caruthers was being a jerk —"

Dix said, "Rob, remember how your mom once washed out your mouth with soap? That real strong soap that could peel the skin right off your hands?"

Rob stared down at his plate. "Yeah, I remember. It burned off all my nose hair."

"You got the soap twice, Rob," Rafe said, poking his brother's arm.

"You should have, too," Rob said, and lifted his fist toward his brother.

Dix said, "Boys?" in a quiet voice, and they stopped dead in their tracks. "Good. Rob, finish it up now."

"Okay, he was so mad he looked like he was gonna burst."

Dix gave him a thumbs-up. "I'll give that a pass."

Ruth raised her glass. "Here's to the next Derek Lowe."

"Hear! Hear!" Dix drank down the rest of his tea. "You guys ready for some bread pudding?"

Ruth perked up. "Bread pudding? When did you have time to make that, Dix?"

Rafe snickered. "Nah, Dad didn't make it, it was Ms. Denver, the physics teacher. She's been after Dad since the beginning of the school year. She's a really good cook, so Rob and I don't mind except —"

"That's enough, Rafe."

Rafe subsided, slouching back in his chair.

Rob said, "Dad, you are going to catch the killers, aren't you?"

Dix looked at his eldest son. "What do you think?"

Rob didn't hesitate. "I told the kids you'd have them in jail by Tuesday."

"Well, that's a motivator," Dix said, with a rueful glance at Ruth.

Ruth leaned forward, her elbows on the table. "I agree with you, Rob. I'm thinking Tuesday is about right. But you and Rafe both know it's not quite that easy."

"I'm thinking Monday, myself," Dix said, and folded his arms over his chest.

Ruth thought the boys would burst with pride at this macho display.

Rob said, "Dude! Dad, we're not kids. You can talk stuff over with us, really. Everyone at school is talking about Ms. Rafferty being killed in her bed, about how you found that student buried in Winkel's Cave." He paused for a moment and cleared his throat, but his voice was unsteady. "And about Mr. McGuffey. Oh man, that was really bad."

Dix's own voice wasn't all that steady, either. "Walt was a fine man. I really liked him."

Rafe said to Ruth, his voice still quavering,

"Mom always liked Mr. McGuffey. Last Thanksgiving he said Dad's turkey was as good as Mom's, but he couldn't do stuffing worth a damn. I told him you couldn't find Mom's recipe."

"I'll give you one, Dix," Ruth said, knowing they were skating on very thin ice. The boys seemed both hyper and scared, and trying not to show either. "Corn bread with water chestnuts and cranberries."

"I like water chestnuts," Rafe said. "But I like lots of sausage in my dressing, too."

Ruth beamed when Rob said, "Maybe we can try it your way, too, Ruth."

Dix's doorbell rang not long after the boys went to bed.

"You missed a great corn-on-the-cob gross-out," Dix said by way of a greeting.

"Let me get your coats," Ruth said, peeling off Sherlock's leather jacket. She paused, then took a step back. "What's wrong, guys? What happened?"

"Sorry," Savich said shortly. "Lots on our minds, no excuse."

He and Sherlock followed Dix into the living room. Savich held up his hand when Ruth opened her mouth. "No, Ruth, Sean's all right, we spoke to him earlier. He's already decided he wants a Yorkshire terrier whose name is going to be Astro."

Sherlock was still acting a bit stiff, but she tried, giving Ruth and Dix big smiles. "Last summer we talked about putting down Astroturf in the backyard for a very miniature miniature golf course. I guess Sean fell in love with the word."

But it had nothing to do with Astroturf or anything else, Ruth thought, glancing at the two of them. She looked from one carefully expressionless face to the other, saw the strain in Dillon's eyes, the red creeping up Sherlock's cheeks, which meant she wanted to kick someone — Dillon?

Dillon and Sherlock were the anchors of Ruth's professional life. She was immensely grateful to Dillon for bringing her into the Criminal Apprehension Unit eighteen months earlier. He was an intuitive, natural leader, tough as a rock, honorable to the core. Sherlock was funny and insightful, sharp and focused, and you could count on her no matter what. She had only one speed — full steam ahead. Ruth had never seen them like this before.

Then the light dawned. She said slowly, "I don't believe this, you guys have had a major argument, haven't you. Even if I told everyone in the unit, they'd demand I take a lie detector test, which no one would believe because they know I can cheat lie detectors in my sleep." She looked at the ceiling. "I'm ready to pass over, Lord, since I've now seen it all." She wagged a finger at Sherlock. "What did you do, Sherlock, drive the sacred Porsche?"

"Very funny, Ruth," Sherlock said. "You know, every time I've driven that car I've gotten a speeding ticket."

"Nothing's wrong," Savich said, his voice too loud. "Now, if you don't mind, we've got some serious stuff to talk about."

Sherlock nodded. "Here's the deal. We have to take off early tomorrow for Quantico because —"

"Before we go there," Savich interrupted her, "we need to tell you what MAX found out about Moses Grace and Claudia. Her last name is Smollett, emphasis on the last syllable."

Ruth sat forward, serious as could be now. "That's an English name, isn't it?"

Savich nodded. "Of all things, her mom was English. Her name was Pauline Smollett. She came to the U.S. when she was twenty-two. She was a high-school math teacher in Cleveland, and never married, at least in this country. From the police reports, she had a pretty colorful personal life, but she managed to keep it separate from her job. She raised a child, Claudia, out of wedlock by herself."

"What happened to her?" Ruth asked.

"She was raped and murdered by a gang."

Dix leaned forward, hands on his knees. "Police reports? How did you find the connection, Savich?"

"When I called, I told you we had more work to do," Savich said matter-of-factly, then added, his voice dropping ten degrees, "and that meant following up some information Claudia gave Sherlock."

Dix said, "Don't you mean — You actually spoke to Claudia, Sherlock?"

Sherlock's chin went right up, a fire burned in her eyes. "Yes, for quite a while. She called on Dillon's cell while he was in the shower." She looked at her husband, eyes narrowed, as if daring him to comment.

"She did indeed," Savich said smoothly. "After her mother's death, Claudia ran away from home. We had enough details for MAX to pull up a half dozen open cases with a similar profile, and that's how we found Pauline Smollett. It all fit.

"Claudia has a juvenile record of her own, and we matched her ID photo with

354

the picture of Annie Bender her mother Elsa gave us. Claudia looks just like her."

Sherlock continued. "Claudia Smollett was nine years old when she started shoplifting cigarettes and booze from the local 24/7. She got thrown out of school twice, once when she burned a boy with a cigarette, and again when she broke another kid's arm. Then there was the usual juvenile rage, throwing a textbook at a teacher, cursing out another, threatening her mother. She was a wild kid who probably wouldn't have made it even if her mother had lived.

"She ran into Moses Grace moments after he murdered a homeless man. They got drunk on bourbon in a motel, and the rest is history. Claudia said the word 'bourbon' with a Southern accent, and it seemed to me she ran into him somewhere in the South." She paused. "And Claudia isn't eighteen. She turned sixteen three weeks ago."

Dix pushed his fingers through his hair. "She's about Rob's age."

Savich, fiddling with one of the sofa pillows, nodded. "She's a child, a crazy, unrestrained child. It turns out my wife was right about the murdered homeless man. We found a report of a man beaten to death in an alley about eight months ago in Birmingham, Alabama. The police never found the assailant, but another homeless man said he saw an old buzzard in bloodied army fatigues, so my bucks are on Moses."

"Claudia told me Moses wears army fatigues and old black army boots, so it fits," Sherlock said. "We notified the Birmingham police, gave them what we've got. Unfortunately, they didn't have anything to give us in return."

"Did you trace the call, Dillon? Do you know where they are?" Ruth asked.

Savich said, "It's good news, bad news. Claudia called from a prepaid cell phone Moses purchased for cash at a Radio Shack this morning. He activated it from a pay phone in the parking lot. It's anonymous that way since there's no registered owner, but the signal was loud and clear. And since they were calling from a set location, we located them dead-on."

"Where?" Dix asked.

Sherlock said, "At a Denny's on Eighth Avenue and Pfeiffer Street in Milltown, Maryland. Even though the local cops got there in under five minutes, Moses and Claudia were gone. Evidently Moses had left Claudia alone with the cell phone.

When he came back she was still talking to me. I heard his voice, could tell he was angry at her for using it. So that means he knew we could find him. He hit the road fast." Sherlock sighed. "If only he'd spent a bit more time in the men's room, we could have joined them for dinner."

"Please tell me where the good news is in all of this?" Ruth asked them.

"Good news is we've got great descriptions, down to Moses's old black lace-up army boots, and Claudia wasn't exactly undercover. She had on low-cut plumber jeans, a skimpy hot-pink top, and a fake fur jacket. They made quite an impression on their waitress, who said Claudia was pretty but she wore too much makeup, and that the old guy looked like he'd spent a hundred years staked out in the sun.

"But the best information is from a waiter who was outside smoking a cigarette when Moses and Claudia left the restaurant. He was yelling at her, shaking the cell phone in her face before he shoved her into a van.

"The waiter had Claudia in his sights until the van disappeared from view. She waved at him from the passenger-side window. He doesn't remember much about the van — thinks it was a Ford, real dirty. He was focused on Claudia. We might get something more from him. I'd bet my next paycheck on it."

Savich said, "Our Denny's waiter is all set up to have Dr. Hicks hypnotize him tomorrow morning at Quantico, and we need to be there. I'm not certain if we'll be back tomorrow evening, depends on what shakes loose.

"Moses isn't stupid. He might have figured we could locate them even with a prepaid cell phone, as long as Claudia stayed on the line."

Sherlock picked it up. "And that would mean we'd speak to people at the restaurant who saw them. So they might lie low for a while. Still, every squad car in the area will have Claudia's picture by morning."

Ruth clapped. "Dillon didn't tell us what you'd managed to do when he called earlier. This is great, Sherlock. Keep it up and you'll break the whole thing wide open."

Sherlock said to Ruth, "Claudia wanted to talk to Dillon, Ruth. She wants to have sex with him, actually. Dillon was upset because he thinks I'm too delicate to hear the dirt Claudia dishes out."

Two pairs of female eyes went to Savich.

"There's more to it than that, Ruth, and Sherlock knows it."

"Ah," Dix said, sat back on the sofa, and crossed his arms over his chest.

"Ah, what?" Savich asked him, never looking away from his wife.

"So maybe all of this boils down to the fact that you want to protect her."

Sherlock turned on him. "From a crazy child on a cell phone? Dillon has no right —"

Dix spoke over her. "I'd probably feel the same way if Ruth were my wife. It's simply the nature of the beast — both of you must know that by now. It's just instinct."

Sherlock went on point, and Dix felt lucky Savich was sitting between them. "Women have the same instinct, macho man."

Dix cleared his throat. "Well, I'm glad we cleared that up without bloodshed. Would everyone just look at the time. Is it late, or what?"

There was a sprinkling of laughter, most of it from Ruth, Dix thought, then a pound of silence.

Ruth jumped in to tell them she and Dix had spent the rest of their afternoon with Gordon Holcombe. "We searched every space in his office, house, and studio, every record. He was cooperative, I'll say that for him. We even spoke to three of his former lovers on the phone. They were fine, all of them elsewhere at the time of the murders."

Dix said, "I'm going to talk to Gordon again tomorrow." He frowned down at his clasped hands. "I can't get past the fact that two of the victims were his lovers. Maybe he's told us all about the students, but Helen wasn't a student, now was she?"

CHAPTER 27

Quantico
Friday morning

At ten o'clock Dr. Emmanuel Hicks walked into Savich's small office in Quantico's Jefferson Dormitory and sniffed. "Pepperoni." He looked at the young black man slouched in a chair beside Savich. "From the Boardroom?"

The young man nodded. "Double pepperoni, Doc."

"Ah, my favorite, sometimes even for breakfast. My name is Dr. Hicks and I'm harmless." He shook the young man's hand. "This will be very easy for you, Dewayne, no discomfort at all as I'm sure Agent Savich has told you. We're simply going to help you remember all the details you've already got stored away on your hard drive." Dr. Hicks tapped his head, to which Dewayne answered, "Cool."

Ten minutes later, Savich pulled his chair closer to Dewayne's and laid his hand lightly on the young man's forearm.

"I'd like you to think now about the first time you saw the old man and the young girl in Denny's yesterday, Dewayne. You have them in your sights?"

Dewayne nodded.

"Good. Tell me what you see."

"She's taking off those big sunglasses and looking around. She's something — pretty, real pretty, and she knows it. She's flirting with everybody."

"What about the old guy?"

"He's sitting back in the booth, his arms crossed over his chest, and he's grinning. I don't think he does anything but grin. He's real old, you know, his face is all seams and wrinkles. She's maybe his great-granddaughter, I'm thinking, he's that old. She's looking through the menu, taking her time. The old guy, he doesn't even open the menu, just orders a hamburger."

"Melinda waited on them?"

"Yeah, that's right. When she came to the kitchen to place the order, she told us we should check her out. All us guys already had.

"She knows all the guys are talking about her. Man, it's nearly freezing outside and she's wearing this tiny top, showing off her belly button."

"She have a ring in her belly button?"

"Oh yeah, a little silver ring. And boy, her belly's sweet, a little baby fat, but sweet."

"Do you ever get close enough to hear them speak to each other?"

Silence, then a slow nod. "Yeah, I'm taking a combo meal, a surf 'n' turf thing, to this couple sitting two booths down from them. I sort of slow down, you know, because she winks at me, really winks, and gives me a big grin, tosses her head. She's got four gold earrings up her right ear."

"Do you hear anything they say before she notices you and winks?"

Dewayne nodded. "Something about a redhead — that was the old guy talking. He looks crazy, you know? Those army fatigues and those stupid army boots, all scuffed up, muddy, like he's been out on a battlefield, you know? I didn't know who this redhead was they were talking about, but I wanted to hear her talk some more so I walked slower. She says something like, 'I'm thinking the next stop should be a bank, Moses. What do you think?' And the old guy grins some more and shakes his head. 'I don't think so, sweetcakes.' Yeah, that's what he called her. I nearly laughed to hear that old buzzard call the little chick that. Then the folks hollered at me to get them their food, so that's all I heard. No, wait a second. I think he said something like, 'He's probably got himself all staked out like a goat, waiting for me to call.' "

Savich waited a beat, but there wasn't any more. He said, "That's excellent, Dewayne. Okay, now you go outside for the cigarette break. You're smoking when you see that pretty girl walk out of Denny's, right?"

Dewayne jiggled the change in his pocket. "Yeah, there she is."

"Tell me exactly what you see."

"She's pulled that fluffy jacket back on but it isn't long enough to cover her butt. Man, she's got a fine butt, really nice, and she's swinging it all over the parking lot. She knows I'm watching, even looks in my direction and smiles at me, but she's really not paying me much attention because she's talking on her cell phone, real intense now. Then the old guy comes roaring out of the restaurant, maybe because he sees her on the cell phone. He starts yelling at her. I thought he was going to hit her for a moment, and she says something like 'Don't hurt me.' He grabs the phone, still yelling, and pushes her into the van."

"Look at the van, Dewayne. Do you see it?" At the young man's nod, Savich continued, "That's it. I want you to look at the van now, not the girl. Tell me what you see."

"It's hard, man."

Savich waited.

"I'm still looking at her, hoping the old guy doesn't hit her. I watch her put those big sunglasses back on. Then she turns to look at me and blows me a kiss. Do you believe that chick? Okay, the van. It's an old Ford Aerostar, filthy white, makes me wonder what kind of slob that old man is to let his wheels get that dirty. It's one of those cargo vans — you know, windows on one side but not on the other. It's got a roof rack and sliding side doors."

"Is there anything on the side of the van except dirt?"

Dewayne frowned at Savich, jiggled his change. Savich said, "It's okay, take your time. Look closely, Dewayne."

Dewayne Malloy scratched his ear, began beating his right foot heel to toe on the floor, and continued to jiggle his change. He had incredible coordination, Savich thought.

"Yeah, Agent Savich, there's a picture of something, maybe a lawn mower. Yeah, that's right, a lawn mower."

Dr. Hicks thought for a moment that

Savich was going to leap to his feet for some high fives, but instead he asked carefully, "A lawn mower — like it's some sort of gardener's van?"

"Yeah, maybe. There's some writing under the lawn mower, but it's real dirty, I can't read it."

"You've got great eyes, Dewayne. Keep looking, don't think about anything except those letters. What color are they?"

"Black."

"Words?"

"Yeah, there are words, I think."

"Are they positioned right beneath the lawn mower?"

"No, they're kind of on a diagonal, you know, like they want to be a little bit different. And the letters are thick, with all those curlicues hanging off them."

"That's great, Dewayne. You've got fine eyes, you took everything in. Okay, now look at the first word. Can you see it?"

Dewayne shook his head. "Man, I'm sorry, but I can't read the words."

Savich patted the young man's arm. "That's okay, Dewayne. Keep looking at the van. Tell me what else you see, anything unusual."

"There's nothing else, only lots of dirt."

"Okay, the guy is driving out of the

parking lot. Can you see a license plate?"

"The old guy's really burning rubber, man, you can smell it. I didn't have time to look at the plates if I'd even thought of it. They're all dirty, too, just like the van. Wait a second. White. The license plate is white."

Savich questioned Dewayne for several more minutes, but Dr. Hicks finally laid his hand on Savich's arm. "His hard drive has crashed, Savich. That's it."

Savich nodded to Dr. Hicks, who told Dewayne how great he was going to feel in a moment, and woke him up.

Dr. Hicks shook the young man's hand, told him the Boardroom also served an incredible sausage pizza. Savich said, "You were a tremendous help, Dewayne. Thank you. How would you like to meet the director of the FBI and have him thank you himself?"

"Cool." Dewayne Malloy grinned up at Savich. "When can I meet him?"

"I'm calling right now," Savich said. "Then I'd like you to meet with our sketch artist."

Two hours later, Savich, Sherlock, and four agents sat around the table in the CAU conference room.

"One week ago, Moses and Claudia left

an old stolen Chevy van at Hooter's Motel as a decoy, as a lure to make us think they were in that motel room. They were trying to kill cops."

Sherlock said, "Bottom line, Dillon, Moses wanted to kill you. Killing anyone else was gravy."

"And you, too, Sherlock," Dane Carver said, "only a few hours later at Arlington National Cemetery."

"But I was the one who got lucky," Connie Ashley said. She looked good, Sherlock thought thankfully, even with her arm in a sling.

"My point is that they've probably been driving the Aerostar since then, and obviously had it in place near the motel. We now know from Dewayne's description that it has an out-of-state license plate. They could have left the area to buy or steal the van a few days before they took Pinky."

Ollie said, "Dewayne said the plates were white, right?"

At Savich's nod, he continued, "I'm thinking Ohio plates; they're the closest."

Savich said, "Pursue that, Ollie, would you? I doubt they drove farther than that for the van. Dewayne also told us there's a lawn mower on the side of the van, with some lettering, like a gardener's van."

Dane said, "They stole it then. I sure hope no one else is dead."

Sherlock said, "So we have the color and make of the van, and a big lawn mower on its side that might as well read 'Arrest Me.' That, and an old man who doesn't seem to change his clothes paired with a flashy blond teenager. How hard can that be?"

"You know what amazes me?" Ollie pointed to a glossy picture of a Ford Aerostar Savich had tacked to the board. "Moses didn't even bother painting over the lawn mower or the writing on the side of the van."

Dane Carver said, "The behavioral science folks have a take on that. They don't think Moses Grace believes anyone can touch him. He thinks he's smarter than everyone and can do as he pleases. Steve also said he may not be planning to get out of this alive. They think from the recordings he might be very ill, even dying."

Savich shrugged. "I hope he doesn't find out we made Claudia, that we have her picture."

Ollie said, "Maybe I'm pushing it here but I don't think Moses can read. The waitress said he ordered a hamburger, didn't even look at the menu."

"Good point, Ollie," Savich said. "The thing is, though, he rigged a pretty sophisticated bomb at the motel. It's true Claudia nearly brought it all down on him this time, but he just doesn't seem that ignorant to me."

Sherlock said, "Along with Claudia's old ID photo, we have the sketches our artist put together with Dewayne Malloy. The three waitresses recognized them immediately when we faxed them the sketches so we know they're right on."

The agents studied the drawings again.

"He looks like a cold old buzzard," Connie Ashley said. "Like no one human lives there. The real question is, who is Moses Grace? Where has he been for the past fifty years? We already know there's never been a felon by that name, or even a driver's license issued that fits him, so it's probably an alias. What do we know about him?"

Ollie said, "She's right. Someone who looks as old as Moses Grace ought to have a record. We can't find one, so that leaves decades of his life unaccounted for."

"Which brings us to his motivation, again, Savich," Dane said. "He wants to kill you because of this woman you supposedly hurt. She must be somehow connected to him, a relative, maybe. We've been through sixty-two cases of yours so far, even some that you were only marginally involved with. There were plenty of people who got hurt, including women, but there's not a trace of any connection to Moses."

Sherlock said, "Another question. Was there anyone else before he picked up Claudia?"

"Had to have been," Dane said.

Ollie said, "Look at Claudia — those eyes, cold and blank as the calculus blackboard in high school."

Savich handed around computer-scanned copies of Annie Bender's photo that Elsa Bender had given them. "Compare the photo to our artist's sketch of Claudia."

Ollie said slowly, "I know Elsa Bender told you and Sherlock Claudia looks like her daughter, but I don't see it. General coloring, yes, but that's it."

"That's because the photo of Annie Bender shows a real live person, one who feels and thinks and cares. This girl . . ." Dane Carver shrugged.

Savich said, "Maybe it's just time for us to get lucky, and the cops will spot the Aerostar. I've called Detective Ben Raven with the Washington PD. He's instructed them not to bring Moses and Claudia in by themselves. They might be the most dangerous individuals they'll ever see on the street." Savich fell silent. "I can't think of anything else to do except continue going through my old cases. The key is there, I know it. We'll give it a couple more days, and if we don't spot the Aerostar by Sunday morning, Mr. Maitland will call a press conference and give the media the sketches of Moses and Claudia."

Ollie said, "One more call to your cell might help. Wouldn't it be a gift from the Almighty if it ended that way?"

Agent John Boroughs laughed. "We should be so lucky. Ain't nothin' ever easy, that's what you told me when I joined the unit, Savich."

There was some laughter, which felt good to everyone. The meeting broke up. As Savich stuffed papers into his briefcase, Ollie asked him, "So what did Dewayne Malloy think of meeting Director Mueller?"

Savich grinned. "He said he was pretty cool, for an old guy. He was so juiced about helping us solve this crime, he asked if he should consider becoming an FBI agent. I told him to go for it."

Sherlock stood at the door of the conference room with the other agents, one eye on Savich and Ollie. "Listen to me, guys. I can take care of myself, even though Dillon doubts that. It's him these people are after. Please don't let him go off on his own. We have to keep him safe."

"That's enough, Sherlock." Savich spoke very quietly. The other agents glanced at him, nodded to Sherlock, and left them alone.

Sherlock knew this was as important to her as breathing. She looked him straight in the eye. "I told them the truth, nothing more. I intend to discuss this with Mr. Maitland as well. I'm thinking this is winding down, Dillon. I'm thinking we should stay in Washington, together, with all our people. I have this feeling that Moses and Claudia are going to try something very soon, and it's going to be directed at you. We want to be here and we want to be ready."

It was odd how often their instincts meshed. He closed his hand around her arm and said quietly, "You don't need to speak to Mr. Maitland about this. I was thinking the same thing."

She pulled away from him, started walking down the wide hallway before turning back to say, "Let's go get Sean. I spoke to Graciella before the meeting. She wants to come home."

"All right. I'll call Ruth, tell her what's going down here. We're only two and a half hours away if something happens in Maestro."

She gave him a crooked grin. "Much less by helicopter."

Dane Carver came trotting up to them, his cell phone still in his hand. "Interesting news, guys. The police found an abandoned white van with a lawn mower and the words 'Austin's Gardening Service' on its side in front of a warehouse on Webster Street. It looks like Moses didn't just ditch it — he set it on fire."

Savich sighed. "He knew we probably tracked that call Claudia made and might have a description of it. No point in waiting now. It could be they headed out of town."

Dane said, "But you don't believe it."

Sherlock was silent for a long moment, twisting a lock of curly hair around her finger, a habit when she was thinking hard. "No, Moses isn't about to leave, not until he takes his final shot at you."

Savich nodded. "Then we'd better get ready."

CHAPTER 28

Maestro, Virginia
Friday morning

At ten o'clock, Dix called Gordon's office at Stanislaus.

". . . I don't know why I need to tell you that, Dix. She's not a student here. I don't see the point in involving her. Listen, it was nothing, a brief fling, nothing to make the earth move for either of us."

"I can keep you nice and warm in my jail, Gordon, until you tell me what I want to know. Is the woman you left out Cynthia, Tony's wife?"

"Cynthia," Gordon said. If Dix wasn't mistaken, there was a hint of distaste in Gordon's voice.

"Well, good for you," Dix said. "That's a relief. Talk to me, Gordon." The silence dragged on. Dix said, "I'm thinking hand-cuffs would make a nice visual for all your professors and students —"

"No, Dix! You can't do that. I'm simply trying to protect a woman's reputation, nothing more. You think I would sleep with Cynthia?"

"A woman's reputation?" Dix asked. "Not a girl's? Could it be there was maybe even a thread of gray in her hair?"

"No, she's gorgeous and she'd sue me —"

Dix shook his head. "And here I thought Ginger would have the good taste not to sleep with a man her father's age. You never know, do you? At least it wasn't Cynthia. Now, that wasn't so hard, was it?"

Gordon finally gave it up. He told Dix he'd slept with Ginger Stanford two years ago, and all right, her mother, too, if they were interested, but the two of them lasted only a couple of months, hardly enough time to even regard it in the grand scheme of things.

When he paused to take a breath, Dix asked, "Who broke things off?"

"We ended up not liking each other very much. Ginger told me she'd expected more from me because she'd heard I was experienced, and that I didn't give her what she wanted. She told me to take myself to a sex education class. Can you imagine the gall? Sex education! Me!"

"And Gloria Stanford? Was she unreasonable in her demands, too? Like mother, like daughter?"

A ruminative pause, Dix thought. "She's immensely talented, you know that, Dix, but the fact is we were never really that attracted to each other. She never criticized me like her bitch of a daughter."

Before he punched off, Dix warned Gordon, "Don't even think about calling Ginger, Gordon. If you do I won't give you an extra blanket in your cell."

"Sheriff, Agent, what are you doing here?" Henry O was on his feet, the question out of his mouth the moment Dix and Ruth came into the office. "Oh, I see. You don't know anything more than the last time you were here, do you?"

Good, Dix thought, Gordon hadn't called. Henry O looked natty in a crisp white shirt and well-made dark gray wool trousers, belted high.

"Actually, Henry, we're here to arrest Ms. Stanford," Ruth told him. She gave him a little wave and kept walking, Dix behind her.

"Are you nuts? You don't arrest a lawyer; she'll sue your socks off. Wait, wait! Oh, lordie, Ms. Ginger, they rolled over me!"

"Hard to believe," Ginger Stanford said, rising slowly, dropping her beautiful black pen on the desktop. "It's okay, Henry.

They're not going to snap on the cuffs, I don't think, are you, Dix?"

Dix gently shoved Henry out and closed the door. "Good morning, Ginger. Time for you to tell us about your short, uninspired affair with Gordon Holcombe."

Ginger laughed. "Oh, sit down, both of you. You pried it out of him, did you? Yes, I slept with Gordon, and what a colossal mistake that was. No, simply a waste of my time. I really thought he'd be good. I can't tell you how many times he gave me this intense, hungry look, but he was just a fumbling old man. I gave him a couple of chances, then kissed him off. End of story. You don't actually think I had anything to do with those horrible murders, do you?"

Ruth asked, "Did you tell your mother about it?"

"Actually, I did. She only laughed and said she slept with him a couple of times herself, and agreed with me. Men of a certain age, she told me, usually aren't adventurous or innovative, just happy if everything goes smoothly. She told me she lost her rose-colored glasses long ago, that there are very few men who know anything, and if they do, they usually don't care, just hope for a fake orgasm to let them off the hook. She said the only thing she got from Gordon was a good interpretation pointer on Bartók's Sonata for Solo Violin." Ginger laughed.

"Why do you call your mother Gloria?" Ruth asked.

"What? Oh, Gloria. Well, the thing is she was gone practically all of my growing-up years, touring, you know. My dad checked out when I was ten, couldn't take his wife being gone, couldn't deal with me anymore, whatever. I was raised by two nannies, both of whom I still call Mom. She's always been Gloria. Don't get me wrong, I love and admire her, and she is my mother, when all's said and done. I'm here, aren't I?"

"Why did you move to Maestro when she did? What was it? Six months after Christie and Dix moved here?"

She cocked her head at Ruth, poured some water out of a Pellegrino bottle into a crystal glass and sipped. "Christie and I went to school together. We were close."

Dix pointed out, "But you had a very nice practice in New York City, didn't you?"

Ginger said at last, "You're a bulldog, Dix. Okay, there was a man in New York. It didn't work out. Yes, he was married and I was stupid enough to believe him when he swore the marriage was over. He set the fool's cap right on my head. I thought moving far away would make everything better — and it did, for the most part. May I ask why Gordon told you about me and my mother? Why is that any of your concern?"

Dix asked, "Were you angry that he slept with your mother?"

"Good heavens, no. Look, Dix, Gloria didn't see that many men after my father went walkabout. Gordon is a talented man, and he can be a real charmer. I had no reason to mind. It might even have turned out well for her if he'd been different. He probably slithered out the door because Gloria didn't fawn over him like he wanted her to, and why should she? She's not twenty-two years old and ignorant as a stump. She's more talented, more famous, and far richer than he'll ever be."

Ruth said, "You don't think Gordon broke it off because he thought your mom was too old for him?"

"Hmm, I never thought of that. What a thought, Gordon dropping her because she was too old? He said that? Talk about the pot and kettle." She grinned. "Well, duh."

Dix and Ruth left her office ten minutes after they'd entered it. Dix said to Henry O on their way out, "We forgot our hand-cuffs. Can you believe that? You keep an eye on Ms. Stanford for us, all right, Henry? Make sure she doesn't try to make a break for it."

Henry O stood tall. "You've got to pay me more if you want me to be your deputy, Sheriff."

CHAPTER 29

Maestro, Virginia
Friday afternoon

Dix and Ruth could hear Cynthia Holcombe's voice a good fifteen feet from Tara's front door. Dix placed a finger to his lips, stepped off the flagstone walkway before they reached the Gothic columns, and walked over the snow-covered lawn toward the side of the house. "The only person she yells at is Chappy. Well, usually. I'm betting they're in the library. Let's go see if I'm right."

It was forty-one degrees under a sunless, steel-beam sky, fat snow clouds huddled over the mountains in front of them. A library window was cracked open and Cynthia Holcombe's voice boomed out, loud and clear.

"You miserable old codger, there's nothing wrong with me, and Tony would never divorce me! We've been trying for a year to have a grandchild for you. And stop talking to my mother, she doesn't know anything about it. Another thing, I don't sleep with other men. How many times do I have to tell you?"

"She knew enough to tell me you don't like children. As for my poor son, he's at his wit's end, said you were lying to him, taking the pill on the sly and telling him you're all excited about getting pregnant."

"I'm not on the bloody pill! Why do you keep making these things up? Are you that bored? Why don't you consider getting yourself a life? At least go spew your venom on someone else for a change."

"Your mother insisted I couldn't trust a thing you said, she —"

There was the sound of glass crashing against a wall, then Chappy chuckling. Cynthia was panting as she yelled, "Anyone who listens to my mother deserves what they get, you hear me? You want the truth, old man? I'm beginning to wonder if I want to have a child with your weak-willed son! I can't believe he's even able to walk since he has no backbone. He lets you kick him around until I want to scream."

"Oh dear," Ruth said.

Dix said, "Not quite what I expected. Time to break it up before she connects a vase to Chappy's head. Then I'd have to arrest her, and that thought scares me."

Ruth put a smile on for Cynthia when she jerked the front door open. "Well, what do — Dix, hello. Do come in. Oh, you. So you're still here? Sorry, but I don't remember your name. You're some kind of police officer, too, aren't you?"

"Some kind, yes," Ruth said agreeably. "Agent Ruth Warnecki. I believe we had lunch together, what was it, two days ago? They say memory is the first to go."

Cynthia said, "Yes, I've heard that, too. But why would I even want to remember you?"

"Good one," Ruth said.

Dix said, "Ruth and I heard you and Chappy fighting from outside. You should have closed the library window."

Cynthia shrugged, looking completely unconcerned. "Well?"

Dix walked right at her, and she moved at the last instant so he wouldn't mow her down. He headed toward the library, Ruth at his side, Cynthia reluctantly trailing after them. The thing about the library, Ruth thought, looking around, was that it wasn't a room for books, it was a room for CDs, hundreds of them, scrolled labels categorizing them — jazz, blues, three or four dozen classical composers listed by name. What books there were appeared to be the oversized coffee table sort. Dix waved her to a deep burgundy sofa. He sat on a hundred-year-old pale green brocade chair next to her. Cynthia sat opposite them, looking like she'd rather be in a dentist's chair. Chappy wasn't in the room.

Dix said to her, "You and Chappy developed some new material. I never heard you insult Tony before. I'm sorry it's come to that, Cynthia."

"You're not married to him, Dix. You don't see him fold whenever Chappy so much as frowns at him. He can't imagine losing his position at the bank, as if that would ever happen."

"What'd you throw at Chappy?"

"Just some stupid blue bowl someone sent him from China."

Chappy said from the doorway, "The blue bowl was a very valuable ceramic fashioned during the Kangxi period of the Qing Dynasty, circa 1690." He strolled in as if he hadn't a worry in the world. "She shattered a three-hundred-year-old work of art that cost me more than a divorce from this viper would cost Tony."

"I suppose you're going to tell him what I said," Cynthia said, her expression a study of anger, frustration, and something

Dix couldn't pinpoint. He pictured the bowl in his mind, remembered how exquisite it was. If he were Chappy, he'd be cussing mad about it. He said only, "Was the bowl insured?"

"Sure, but who cares about the money?"

Cynthia jumped out of her seat, waving her fist at him. "That's the only thing you do care about, Chappy — money and control over everyone you know. Don't pretend to be a martyr and a victim." She turned to Dix. "He wants me out of Tony's life and away from here."

Dix shrugged. "So why don't you and Tony leave? You have alternatives, Cynthia. Do you really want to raise a child here at Tara?"

Cynthia shuddered as she said, "No, of course not, but what I want doesn't matter. Tony won't leave."

Chappy said, "No, my son isn't going anywhere, Cynthia." He turned to Dix and Ruth. "If this harpy won't give him a child, she can take off herself as far as I'm concerned, maybe screw Gordon's brains out on her way out of town."

"I don't think Gordon has the time," Ruth said. "He's pretty much occupied right now."

"Twister was never too busy for sex."

386

Chappy studied his fingernails. "Do you know that Gordon can tell you the name of any perfume a woman wears, his nose is that sensitive? Always amazed me." Chappy shook his head. "Tony's going to attend that memorial at Stanislaus, said it wouldn't look good if the local bankers didn't pay their respects."

Dix said, "We're going as well."

"Well, I'm not. Why should I? Twister will be there, some young sweetie sitting beside him, I'll bet, holding his hand and squeezing it while he cries. He can cry on demand, which always pissed me off."

Cynthia said, venom as thick as cream in her voice, "You've got to have a heart to cry, Chappy."

Chappy ignored his daughter-in-law. He said to Dix, "Are you going to take Twister off to jail?"

"We'll see."

"If I thought you were serious, I'd get him a lawyer." Chappy rubbed his hands together. "Twister wouldn't mind having some deep pockets in the family then, would he? What do you think, Dix? One of those O.J. lawyers? What about that little Shrek guy from Boston? Hmm, I could start checking this out, tell Twister what I'm doing." Chappy walked from the room whistling. He turned in the doorway and gave Ruth a little wave. "I'm going to find a new vase, maybe Japanese this time. Hey, Agent Ruth, I hear Twister asked you out to dinner. You going to go?"

"Depends on the restaurant," Ruth said easily.

"Wear pants," Chappy said. "It's your best defense." He strolled past the shards of the ceramic bowl without a glance.

"He's insane," Cynthia said. "Really, Dix, the old fool is quite mad. Imagine claiming I'm taking birth control pills when Tony and I are trying to have a baby. Imagine me sleeping with Gordon. Hasn't Chappy looked at his own son? Tony is very handsome, don't you think?"

"Handsome and weak?"

"I guess I shouldn't have said that, but Chappy makes me so mad and I mouth off just to get back at him. The reason he won't let Tony go is that he's Chappy's only ticket to immortality now that Christie's gone —" Cynthia shrugged, looked away from Dix.

"She's not merely gone, Cynthia, as in off finding herself or on an extended vacation. She's dead. And you know it."

Cynthia shrugged. "Yes, I suppose she is."

"As I said, the two of you should move away from this house and from Chappy."

"The thing is, I really don't want to leave Tara. Maybe Chappy will kick off soon and Tony will inherit all this."

"Don't hold your breath. I'd give him another twenty years. You and Tony should move to Richmond. Tony could head the bank there, hire a manager for the bank here in Maestro, and let Chappy torment him. When Chappy's out of the picture someday, you can move back to Tara, if you like."

Cynthia strolled over to the front windows, pulled back the heavy brocade curtain and looked out. Cold air flooded the room. She closed the window as she said over her shoulder, "Tony's afraid to leave, afraid he'll fall on his face if he does, or that Chappy will disinherit him."

She shrugged. "Christie could have talked him into leaving, but I can't. I wish she wasn't dead, Dix, I really miss her."

"You didn't appear to appreciate her all that much when she was here, Cynthia. Why the change of heart now?"

"I know better now, I guess." Cynthia turned away from the window and paced the full length of the twenty-five-foot library before she turned back again. "Are you here for lunch? Mrs. Goss didn't say anything to me."

"No, we're not here for lunch. For one thing, I wanted to ask you some questions about Chappy's whereabouts last Friday night."

"Goodness, that was when you found Ruth, wasn't it? Chappy was here late, that's all I know. What did he tell you?"

"That he was here, working in his office," Dix said. "How about Tony? Where was he?"

"Making me a very happy woman, at least after about ten o'clock Friday evening. He was at the bank all day, I suppose. He usually is. He left for a couple of hours after dinner. He didn't say where he was going and I didn't ask. When he came back, he had a bottle of champagne under his arm, a big smile on his face. He wanted to be with me right away, so we went upstairs to bed. I remember Chappy was home because he knocked on our bedroom door about eleven o'clock, demanding to know what I was doing to his son. I was glad I'm always careful to lock the door. That wasn't the first time he did that."

Dix didn't think Chappy had been interested in sex since his wife died so many years before. "He probably wanted to give the two of you grief. Tony didn't tell you where he went after dinner?"

"He probably went back to the bank. He tries to be anywhere his father isn't. I'd had another fight on the phone with my mother and I was fuming, not really paying attention to anyone." She yawned. "Fighting with Chappy always exhausts me. Maybe I'll drive to Richmond, do some shopping; it'll help me forget."

"You're not going to Erin's memorial?" Ruth asked.

"I really didn't know her all that well, now did I?" Cynthia yawned and rose.

"I don't know why I bother," Dix said some minutes later as they walked to the Range Rover. "Oh yes, Tony did work late at the bank last Friday evening, according to the security guard, and he was there all day, according to the employees and Tony's secretary. As for Chappy, Mrs. Goss claims he was gone during the day on Friday, but she doesn't know where he went. He never explains anything to anyone. I'll ask him about it directly."

"Have you heard anything from Richmond about who might have hired Dempsey and Slater to kill me?"

"Not a thing from either the field agents

or the Richmond PD. I'll give Detective Morales a call, maybe promise him you'll have dinner with him if he comes through. You like Italian, don't you?"

Ruth grinned. "It's a toss-up, Dix, between your stew and spaghetti Bolognese."

Erin Bushnell's memorial was held in the large auditorium in Gainsborough Hall. A dozen lavish wreaths were set up around the stage, and a two-by-three-foot color photograph of Erin playing her violin hung from the ceiling. She looked so young, Ruth thought.

The auditorium was filled to capacity. Dix would bet every student and professor at Stanislaus was there. Those who couldn't find seating were huddled against the walls and sitting on the steps in the aisles. He saw a lot of townies, too, sprinkled throughout the auditorium.

He and Ruth got lots of looks, some of them frowns, some tentative greetings. Erin's parents were a conservative-looking couple, pale and silent, unable, he imagined, to come to grips with their daughter's violent death. He'd met them, expressed his sympathy, when they first arrived. He had lost his wife, but he couldn't imagine what it would be like to lose a child. He thought of Rafe and Rob and felt his chest tighten.

They would never find out exactly what was done to their daughter, if he could help it. Drugged and stabbed, that was horrible enough without adding the rest. Dix could only hope the half dozen people who knew the truth would never have to let it out.

He spent the memorial studying the faces around him, and knew Ruth was doing the same thing. There were half a dozen eulogies, including a very moving one by Gloria Stanford, and another by Gordon, who looked barely able to control his tears. The Presbyterian minister from Maestro focused on God's providence and his belief in God's own justice for Erin, an idea that seemed to resonate with the six hundred plus people in the auditorium.

Dix saw Tony and Gloria Stanford sitting on either side of Gordon, Gloria holding his hand. He saw Milton Bean from the *Maestro Daily Telegraph.*

No one acted unexpectedly. The fact was, Dix felt brain-dead. He was tired of seeing everyone as potential suspects, and though he mourned Erin Bushnell's passing, he grew tired of hearing her praised beyond what most human beings would justly deserve at the age of twenty-two.

He thought of Helen, her body released by the coroner to her brother, who finally agreed to a memorial at Stanislaus the following week, and of old Walt, seemingly not important enough for a formal memorial, buried now in the two-hundred-year-old town cemetery on Coyote Hill. Dix had been surprised to see a small crowd of townspeople, his real friends, at the graveside service. Walt would have been pleased by that.

After the memorial Dix drove to Leigh Ann's Blooms for All Occasions and bought a bouquet of carnations. He and Ruth drove to Coyote Hill, and together they walked to Walt McGuffey's grave, a raw gash in the earth. Dix went down on one knee and placed the carnations at the head of the grave. "I ordered a stone to be carved for him. It should be here next week."

Ruth said, "I would have come to his funeral with you yesterday if you'd only asked me."

"You were on the phone to Washington. I didn't want to disturb you. And you're tired, Ruth, we both are. You've been through an awful lot. Now, it's cold out here. I don't want you to get sick. Let's go home."

She nodded, and it struck her that he'd

called it *home* — for both of them. That was odd, and a little scary, yet it made her feel very good. She'd lived with him and his boys for a week now, and it felt more natural every day. Dix was an honorable man, and he cared — about his boys foremost, about his town, about doing the right thing. As for how that long, fit body of his looked in low-slung jeans, she didn't want to think about that.

She wanted to talk to him more about Christie, but knew now wasn't the time. Not yet. She might not have known him for all that long, but she knew in her soul that if Christie was at all like her, she would never have left him or the boys. Not willingly. Something very bad had happened to Christie Noble, and everybody knew it.

As they walked back to the Range Rover, Dix felt her looking at him, but he couldn't see her eyes through the opaque black lenses of her sunglasses. She huddled in her bulky black leather jacket next to him on the front seat, her purple wool scarf around her neck, and pulled her matching purple wool cap nearly to her ears. Dix noticed she was wearing her own socks, not the nice thick ones Rafe had loaned her. He turned up the heat.

CHAPTER 30

They got home just before six o'clock. As Dix unlocked the front door, Ruth's cell phone rang and she turned away to answer it. After a couple of minutes, she punched off. "That was Sherlock. Things are coming together. She and Dillon are going to stay in Washington, unless, she promised me, we needed them in any way. I told her we're fine here."

He hurried since Brewster's nails were scraping madly against the front door.

"Brewster, hold on! Don't forget, Ruth, if he jumps on you, hold him away."

"Nah, Brewster won't pee on the person who fed him some hot dog under the kitchen table last night."

When Dix opened the front door, Ruth grabbed Brewster before he could climb her leg. She held him close, laughing and kissing his little face. He never stopped barking or wagging his tail.

"Oh dear," she said. "Brewster, how could you?"

Brewster looked up and licked her jaw.

"We'll get the coat to the cleaner's tomorrow. They'll be able to get the smell out — I happen to know this for a fact. And the leather won't stain."

Ruth laughed. "You little ingrate, what did you want that I didn't give you? A bun with your hot dog? Some mustard, maybe?"

"Well, hang it up," Dix said, pulled her against him, Brewster between them, barking his head off, and kissed her.

Dix pulled back almost immediately and pressed his forehead to hers. "Sorry about that. I didn't mean to . . . Well, yes I did."

He pulled Brewster away from Ruth, hugged him, then set him on the floor. To his surprise, Brewster didn't take offense. He sat looking up at them, his head cocked to one side, tail wagging.

Ruth felt a bit shell-shocked. She swallowed, cleared her throat. "Ah, I'm not sorry, either. Actually, I —"

"Dad!"

"What's that smell? Oh, Brewster got you, Ruth?"

"Yeah, he did, Rafe. Hi, guys. What'd you make for dinner?"

Rafe and Rob looked at each other. "Well, we were sort of waiting for you."

"Pizza," Rob said. "I can put frozen pizza in the oven."

"You mean," she said slowly, looking back and forth at them, "you guys let your father do all the work?"

"Well, sometimes ladies bring us food."

"We do laundry and clean our rooms."

"He doesn't have to cook so much, really. We'd be happy to eat pizza more often," Rob said.

Dix said, "I'm going to broil some fish and bake potatoes. Rob, Rafe, finish up your homework in the next hour."

"Oh yeah, sure, Dad."

"I don't have any."

"Like I'm going to buy that one. I want you both in your rooms, studying. No TV, no earphones."

"Dad?"

Dix heard a thread of something in Rafe's voice he hadn't heard in a long time. He wondered if the boys had seen him kiss Ruth. Better if they hadn't; it was too soon. "What is it, Rafe?"

Rafe shot a look at his brother, then looked down at his sneakers. "Mrs. Benson, my math teacher, was crying today. You know, she knew all three of the murdered people."

Dix picked up Brewster, stuffed him into his coat, zipped it halfway up, and brought both boys against him. "I know this is tough. You can bet it's tough for Ruth and me, too. I told you straight last night — I will catch the person behind these murders, I promise you that."

Rafe tried to smile. "By Tuesday." He pressed his face against his father's shoulder. "That's what I told Mrs. Benson. She swallowed hard and said she sure hoped so since she voted for you."

Dix said slowly, looking from one face to the other, "Is there anything else you want to talk about?"

Rafe hugged his father's waist. Rob was slower, stepped back so he could look squarely at his father. Dix saw, to his shock, that Rob looked no more than two or three inches shorter than he. When had he shot up like this? He was filling out, too, his shoulders less bony, his chest and arms thicker. "Tell me what's wrong, Rob."

Ruth stood silently, knowing she probably shouldn't be there, but that didn't help her feet move. She held still and kept quiet.

Rob stole a look at her. "I saw you kiss Ruth, Dad."

Rafe jerked back, stared at his father then at Ruth. "You kissed her? When?"

"A minute ago," Rob said.

"Yeah," Dix said, "I did. Maybe I didn't plan it, but I did."

"Well, if you really didn't mean to . . ." Rob said, and looked closely at his father.

"That wasn't exactly the truth," Dix said. "I wanted to, although I knew I shouldn't, but I did anyway. Either of you got a problem with that?"

There was a moment of charged silence, then Rob whispered, "It's Mom."

Dix had known this moment would come, sooner or later, when a woman finally came into his life. In the days after Christie disappeared, Dix had wandered around in a fog of pain, too busy trying to find her to try to sort things out with the boys. When his brain began to clear some weeks later, he realized the boys very much needed to talk with him about their mother. He also realized he needed them as much as they needed him. What he gave them was as much honesty as he could. In return they got into the habit of always telling him what they were feeling. At least he'd believed that was the case. As for himself, he'd let his own pain stay buried, for the boys' sake, and they slowly adjusted, accepted what couldn't be changed. Until now, when his kissing Ruth had finished their unspoken agreement.

Dix ran his hands through his sons' hair, love, pain, and guilt sweeping over him, nothing new in that. But now Ruth was added to the mix.

Rob said again, "It's Mom."

Dix said, "I know, Rob, I know. But your mom's been gone for almost three years now."

Rafe said, "Billy Caruthers — you know, that jerk on the baseball team I beat out as pitcher — he was shooting his mouth off about how he bet Mom ran off with a guy she met at the gym. I don't believe it — but if that's true, maybe she'll come back."

Hard, raw anger roiled in Dix's belly. "You know that didn't happen, Rafe."

Rob's eyes blurred with tears, but his voice was steady. "Yeah, I know. I told him Mom wouldn't do that, and that's when we got into a fight."

Rafe said, "And Uncle Tony told us that maybe she got real sick and didn't want us to see her die, and so she left. But if that's true, Dad, why didn't she write and tell us?"

"Your uncle Tony told you that? When was that, Rafe?"

"Maybe three months ago."

Rob nodded. "I asked Uncle Tony if she had cancer, but he said he didn't know, but it had to be something bad, something that couldn't be cured."

They simply didn't want to accept that their mother was dead. Dix well understood denial because he'd felt the same thing many times himself. "Listen to me, your mother would never have left us, never. No sickness, nothing would have made her up and leave without a word. Why didn't either of you tell me about this?"

Rob wouldn't meet his father's eyes. He shook his head, his eyes on Brewster. "It's Ruth, Dad. We told you because of Ruth."

"I see. I didn't plan to kiss Ruth, but it happened. At some point I have to move forward with my life, with my feelings, hard as that is for all of us. Your mother would want that. I wish you'd come to me when you heard these things and not kept them hidden deep inside. I thought we were well beyond that."

Rob whispered, "You believe Mom's dead because that's the only way she'd leave us for this long."

There was silence in the entrance hall. Dix looked at his boys. He'd told them the truth since the beginning, but he knew they didn't want to accept it, and he, because he'd hated their pain, hadn't pushed it that hard. Well, only the stark truth would do now. And so he said, holding them both away so he could look at them, "Let me say it again, your mom wouldn't have left us for a single day, you both know that. I pray every day that I'll find out what happened to her because all of us need to know. I'll never stop looking, never.

"I know she's dead, Rob, know it in my head and in my heart. Since your mother left — No, let me be clear about it. Since your mother died, I've tried to love you with her love added on to mine, and believe me, that's enough love to reach all the way to heaven. And that's where your mom is. And every once in a while, I feel her close by, and I know she'll always be here for us.

"You know I've searched and searched for any clue to help us find out what happened to her but there haven't been any. I'm more sorry than I can say about that. Something bad happened to your mom, and I wish I'd been this straight with you sooner. I was dead wrong. I see now that we have been trying to keep the truth buried deep because it hurts so badly. We won't do that anymore. It's not fair to any of us. You've both been very brave, and I am so very proud of you."

Dix straightened, looked over at Ruth, then down at his sons. "You saw me kissing

Ruth and it upset you. I understand that. Truth is, I like Ruth very much. I have no idea what she thinks of me, but I do know she's smart and nice and she really likes you delinquents. Can we keep things loose? Is that good enough for the time being?"

"Ruth isn't Mom," Rafe said.

"Of course not. Ruth isn't anything like your mother, but the thing is, she doesn't take a thing away from your mother, doesn't make her any less special to you or me or anyone who knew her and loved her. Do you understand?"

The boys looked stony.

"Actually, Ruth is exactly like your mom in a couple of important ways. She's tough and she's good all the way through." Dix handed Brewster to Rafe. "You don't need to study right now. Here, take the Doberman out for a walk until I call you for dinner."

Dix and Ruth watched them toe off their sneakers, put on boots, jackets, and gloves, and head out. The front door slammed behind them. At least that was normal for them. They heard them yelling to Brewster, and that was normal, too. He turned to Ruth. "Do you want to go sponge off that beautiful leather jacket?"

Ruth looked at him, bemused. "You really think I'm tough?"

"Maybe. Though I wouldn't mind being caught in a dark alley with you." He laughed. "When you get through with your jacket, you want to help me whip up a salad and save us all from a frozen pizza?"

CHAPTER 31

Washington, D.C.
Friday night

Savich's cell phone played the opening lines of *Bolero* at 9:15 that evening. He was tucking Sean in for the night, reminding him again about what it was like to take care of a puppy. He kissed him good night, then walked into the hallway.

"Savich."

"Savich, Quinlan here. An explosion just rocked the Bonhomie Club — might be the boiler, we don't know yet. There's lots of smoke, people are hurt, and panic's going to hurt more."

"Is Ms. Lilly all right?"

"Yes, but she's not about to let a fire burn all her jazz records. I don't know yet about Marvin and Fuzz."

"Keep her out of the club, Quinlan. I'm on my way."

Savich forced himself to be calm. He looked back into Sean's room, saw that he was well tucked in under his favorite blanket, Robocop next to him. He quickly walked back in, kissed his boy again.

Sean gave a little snort in his sleep.

Savich found Graciella and Sherlock in the kitchen eating popcorn and drinking Diet Dr Pepper. When Sherlock saw him, she jumped to her feet. "What happened, Dillon?"

"James Quinlan just called from the Bonhomie Club. There's been an explosion. Maybe the boiler blew, he didn't know, but people are hurt. It sounds like a mess. Ms. Lilly's all right, just really mad, I bet. I've got to go down and help."

"It might not be the boiler, Dillon, and you know it. It might be Moses Grace."

"It might be, but it doesn't matter. Those are our friends there, Sherlock."

"We'll both go. And we'll keep our eyes open. Graciella, we'll be back when we can."

They heard Graciella yell from behind them, "Be careful!"

They heard the sirens two blocks from Houtton Street, a "border" neighborhood five years before, now slowly gentrifying.

Emergency lights flashed, lighting the sky like Bat signals. They saw fire trucks parked sideways on the street and up on the sidewalks, firemen running toward the club, hoses and axes in hand. A media van screeched to a stop close to the police cars and fire trucks, hoping the cops wouldn't have time to order them out. Houtton Street was blocked off, as well as the side streets. The first line of police was trying to hold back gawkers, reporters, and cameramen. Behind them, others were helping patrons streaming out of the club, stumbling, dirty, coughing, yelling for their boyfriends, their wives, whoever. Reporters stuck microphones in any face that came close enough. They blurted out their questions, happy and eager to ask about the disaster, maybe get their spot on the late news. There were a good hundred people jostling about, many of them dressed for a Friday night at the club, many of them bystanders who had gathered to look or to help. Savich pulled the Porsche directly in front of the club, where six cops had kept a space clear, probably for the chief of police, or maybe some politician who'd called ahead to do a sound bite showing his interest in and compassion for this largely black area. Before the cops could yell at him to move, Savich jumped out and flipped out his shield. "Agent Dillon Savich. What's happening?"

Officer Greenberg, one meaty fist aimed

at a reporter who'd managed to break through his line, panted, "An explosion of some kind in the club. Not a big one, I don't think, but there's lots of thick black smoke, which helped feed the panic. You know what happens when folks try to stampede out of a club like this. So far I've counted maybe a dozen injured. Almost everyone is out, but there's still the fire to contend with and making sure no one is trapped in all that poisonous smoke. Hey, get that guy with the microphone back! Sorry. It's taking a while, Agent Savich, but we're getting things under control. I know it still looks like pandemonium but you should have been here ten minutes ago. Stay back!" he yelled at three reporters who'd seen Savich and were trying to get to him.

"Blowhard sharks," he added when their flashes went off. "You'll probably be on the news, Agent Savich, everyone knows who you are. You need to talk to Detective Millbray. He's in charge along with Detective Fortnoy. I'll get you to him, otherwise you'll never find him."

"Savich!"

Agent James Quinlan ran to him, grabbed his arm. He was filthy, his suit jacket ripped, and he had a small cut over his eye. "Glad you got here so fast. I shouldn't have scared you. It's not as bad as I first thought. More smoke than anything else. But that explosion was so bloody loud, it shook the whole building. Ms. Lilly's all right, frothing at the mouth about the club, as you can imagine, and about her white dress. Fuzz the bartender is okay, just inhaled some smoke. He's helping get people out. An ambulance took Marvin the bouncer to the hospital. I think he went down in the panic to get out of the club. The paramedic said he'll be all right."

"Where's Ms. Lilly?"

"I saw her and a fireman hauling out boxes, probably her records and accounts. There she is, over by the firemen, telling them what to do." He grinned, his teeth very white against his smoke-blackened face.

Savich almost didn't recognize Ms. Lilly. Her beautiful white satin dress was ruined. But she was yelling, and that was a huge relief. He waved to Officer Greenberg. "Hold on a moment, I'll be right back."

Savich grabbed Sherlock's hands and pulled her close so she could hear him. "I want you to hang back, keep your eyes open for Moses and Claudia. Maybe we're being paranoid, but you know what I think about coincidences. I'm going to ask the detective to have three officers surround you, just in case. If you spot Moses and Claudia, yell at the top of your lungs, okay?"

She nodded. At least she wouldn't have to worry about being trampled trying to get through the throngs of people. He left her leaning against the driver's side of the Porsche, her SIG held loosely at her side, looking through the jostling crowd. She watched Officer Greenberg lead Dillon and James Quinlan through the hordes of club goers, cops, and firemen to where a bull of a man was closely studying a device in his big hands, his back to the chaos. He was wearing a long wool coat, one of those big Russian fur caps on his head.

Savich tapped Detective Millbray on the shoulder. He turned quickly, started when he saw Savich, then studied his shield. He looked faintly puzzled, then, "Hey, I know who you are, Agent Savich. Ben Raven's worked with you, right? He's around here somewhere. That girlfriend of his, the reporter with the *Post*, she's been bugging everybody. At least she got some blood on her, pulled somebody out from under a chair. I'm Ralph Millbray."

Savich introduced Detective Millbray to Agent James Quinlan. "Quinlan isn't just an FBI agent. He performs here one night a week on his saxophone."

"That's some combination, Agent Quinlan."

Savich said immediately, "Please send a few of your guys over to guard that red-headed woman standing against the Porsche at the curb. It's critical. I'll explain later."

Quinlan and Savich watched Detective Millbray quickly assemble four cops and dispatch them to surround Sherlock.

"Thank you, Detective. What have you got?"

Detective Millbray handed Savich the device. "Would you take a gander at this harmless-looking little gadget. It's a piece of a cell phone, used as a homemade detonator. It's a pretty popular item in the Middle East, as you probably know. Turns out the blast didn't cause all that much damage, but it created enough of a rumble and spewed out enough thick black smoke to scare the crap out of everybody. Whoever went to the trouble and tossed the bomb could have put a much bigger charge on it. It was just enough to set off the mad stampede. It almost looks like some kind of sick stunt, like someone wanted to close the place down."

"It wasn't about closing this business, Detective," Savich said. "When Agent Quinlan called me, I knew it could have been Moses Grace. He knows I perform here on occasion and am friends with Ms. Lilly. That's why I asked for protection for Agent Sherlock. She's my wife."

Detective Millbray grew very still. "You mean that crazy old guy every cop in the city is looking for? And that teenage girl?"

Savich nodded.

Detective Millbray shouted for his sergeant and stepped away for a moment. When he returned, he said, "I've told him to tell everyone the perpetrators might still be here. And I've told him who it might be. If he knew this place, knew the owner was important to you, then why did he just flirt with this pissant little bomb and not make it a full-bore disaster?"

Another plainclothes detective stepped up. "I'm Detective Jim Fortnoy. I've called for more police. We're going to do a sweep for those two."

Savich nodded, then turned back to Detective Millbray. "You asked me —"

He heard Sherlock yell. She was swinging her SIG upward, to a point beyond his right shoulder. She yelled, "Dillon, get down!"

She fired off two shots as she ran toward him, the four cops running behind her, their guns out, firing up at the two-story building.

But Savich wasn't looking over his shoulder, he was looking at his Porsche. He thought of the bomb Moses had left at Hooter's Motel. There were a dozen people milling around the Porsche, and he knew as surely as he knew his name what Moses had planned. He cupped his hands around his mouth, yelled as loud as he could, "Run! Get away from the Porsche! There's a bomb! Run!"

Fortnoy and Millbray shouted with him even though they didn't understand. Wasn't Moses Grace in the building behind them? But there was no return gunfire.

No one hesitated. Nerves on hair triggers from the terror in the club made them scatter fast.

Detective Millbray grabbed Savich's arm. "Why do you think there's a bomb there? Your wife and the police have been shooting up at that building. What's happening, Savich?"

Savich heard the roar as his Porsche exploded into a ball of flame. There was an incredible concussion and a wave of heat that sucked up all the air. The power of the blast flung the dozen people closest outward, forcing them to the pavement or hurling them into one another. Savich heard screams, and a policeman yelling for everyone to stay down and remain calm. Savich, flanked by half a dozen cops, ran toward them. He fell to his knees in front of a young woman lying motionless on the sidewalk, and touched his fingertips to the pulse in her throat. Thank God, she was alive. He yelled for a paramedic. After an eerie moment of quiet, firemen started to rush toward the burning Porsche, some pulling their fire hoses, others pulling people to safety, carrying those who couldn't walk.

It was a nightmare landscape — the screams, the moans, the weeping, the roaring orange flames that gushed into the night air, the struggle to control panic and fear.

Savich whirled around, yelling Sherlock's name. He'd seen her for only an instant when she ran toward him, looking up, firing her SIG. He saw her then. Her wool cap was gone, her hair streaming about her shoulders looking like it was on fire in the surreal glow of the orange flames.

Then she was there, right in front of him, her face black, her heavy coat ripped. "I thought I saw him up in a window on the second floor. He was aiming down at you. Some of the cops went up there to look." She hugged him close, her hands patting him all over. "You all right?"

He nodded against her hair.

She pulled back, studied his face. "He blew up your Porsche. He wanted me to go out with it. Do you think he could have detonated it from that window up there?"

"We'll find out soon." For a moment, he couldn't speak. It had been so very close. "I can't tell you how grateful I am that you saw someone up there. It saved your life." That actually sounded calm, he thought, as he stared down at the most important person in the world.

Then she grinned up at him, filthy and beautiful. "You were the psychic about the car bomb. Where do you think Moses went?"

"Millbray and Fortnoy have half the cops in Washington on it."

After fifteen minutes of chaos, people began to sort themselves out, growing calmer once their loved ones were close and safe. Many simply left, grateful to be alive, afraid of more explosions. Paramedics went from group to group, leading the injured to waiting ambulances. Television cameras were everywhere, the spectacular footage of the explosion's aftermath already on the airwaves.

"Savich!"

Savich looked up to see Ben Raven running toward them, Callie Markham behind him, her coat flapping around her boots. "I'm here with Sherlock. We're okay."

Ben was panting, sweat running down his face. "All right. Good. What an unholy mess. I just put a man, probably with internal injuries, into an ambulance. A kid, here to check out the scene, got hit in the head with a piece of metal. I think he'll be okay. Damn, Savich, your Porsche. Your beautiful Porsche."

"You sound like you've just lost your best friend," Callie said and punched him in the arm. "Get a grip here, Ben, it's only a car. What's important is that Dillon and Sherlock are okay. I've never seen anything like this, but the cops are dealing. It's amazing how well they're dealing."

"But I never got to drive it."

Savich said, "Moses Grace and Claudia might still be close by, but I doubt it. Too risky. He had to be close enough to set up the Porsche, and Sherlock spotted him up in that window. He must have picked the moment to drop the bomb in the car and walked away, not that difficult with all the people milling about. He must have been waiting for me to walk back to it. Until Sherlock spotted him." It hit him again, a cold shot to the gut. He looked at Sherlock, pulled her so tight against him she couldn't breathe. Her coat was still warm, and her hair smelled like dirty smoke.

"I'm all right," she whispered. "Really, I'm okay." She relaxed against him, stroked her hands up and down his back.

"I'm an idiot. We shouldn't ever have come here. You were right, it was a setup. If you hadn't seen Moses and run toward me, you would have been killed, you and those cops with you."

Ben and Callie looked at each other. Slowly, Callie pulled out her tape recorder and began speaking into it quietly.

"Please, Callie, off the record," Dillon said.

He watched her until she nodded and turned off the recorder.

Savich turned to look at the smoldering ruins of his Porsche, his pride and joy since his dad had given it to him on his twenty-first birthday. Now it was nothing but twisted metal and black smoke. He saw a plate-size chunk of red metal sitting askew at the edge of the sidewalk.

"I'm sorry about your Porsche, Dillon."

"Don't be an idiot." Savich pulled her close to him. He felt something wet under his right hand, and his heart dropped to his feet.

"Sherlock, what's wrong, what's —"

"Oh dear," she whispered, swallowing hard. "I guess maybe I didn't clear the minefield."

Savich jerked off her coat, saw blood staining her right arm.

Savich picked up his wife and carried her to the paramedics, who were packing their medical supplies away in the back of an open ambulance. John Edsel, not a day over twenty-five, tall and buff as a surfer, immediately snapped to. "Hey, what's this? Hold on, Gus, we got more business." John motioned for Savich to ease Sherlock down on a gurney. He lifted her legs.

"No, please, Dillon, let me sit up. The last thing I want is to be flat on my back."

Savich sat her on the edge of the gurney, held her against him as he spoke to the paramedic.

Edsel nodded. "Agent, you're going to have to let her go. Take two steps back, that's all the room I need. Let me take a look. You said she's been wounded in this arm before?"

Savich nodded. "Yeah, a knife wound a few years back when she didn't move fast enough."

"Why didn't you move fast enough?" John asked her as he cut away her sweater to see the wound.

Sherlock knew he was trying to distract her, but sudden throbbing pain hit her so hard she nearly passed out. She'd forgotten how pain like this could slam down like a hammer on bone. She tried to keep focused on the present. "I guess I didn't work out enough so I was slow. Dillon was really angry, took it out on me at the gym when I was well enough, worked me so hard I sweated off my eyebrows. Now I'm so strong I could lift that ambulance. Don't worry, I'm not going to pass out."

"Oh I see, you're an FBI agent, too. You guys sure lead exciting lives. Was that your Porsche that got blown up? Okay, this isn't too bad, Agent, your coat really protected you. Whatever hit you wasn't flying too fast. You're going to need a couple of stitches. Let's get you to the hospital."

John paused to look over at the twisted, smoking ruin. "A real pity about your

Porsche. Okay, you ready to lie down, Agent?" John turned her on the gurney and helped her to lie down, but he was looking over at the Porsche carcass, shaking his head.

CHAPTER 32

Washington, D.C.
Late Friday night

It was close to midnight when Ben Raven brought them home in his Crown Vic. Sherlock, full of pain meds, her right arm in a sling, was singing the theme to *Star Wars*, but she was so loopy it wasn't coming out right. She said good night to Ben and let Dillon carry her inside the house. After they had told Graciella what happened, Savich carried her upstairs. He sat her on the side of the bed and started to undress her when his cell phone rang.

Sherlock stopped singing, whispered, "It's midnight, right on the dot. He has a sense of timing, doesn't he?"

She watched Dillon nod as he drew a deep breath, saw his control settle in. He let the cell phone ring three times, then nodded to her, and Sherlock dialed the Hoover Building on their land line to alert them that Dillon was on with Moses Grace.

Savich said, "Quite a splash you made, Moses."

"Lit up the night, didn't we? And there you and your little wife were. I like that, shows me how important I am to you. Claudia and I had a ball watching all those yahoos blast out of that club, screaming, pushing, knocking each other over. People are so rude, aren't they? Good manners only on the surface. No such thing as right and wrong when it comes down to survival. I picked the Bonhomie Club just for you, what with all your friends there. I knew you couldn't stay away.

"And sure enough, here you come roaring up in your shiny red car, just like I knew you would. Claudia saw you jump out and practically licked her lips."

The old man cackled, hiccupped, and swallowed phlegm. Savich could almost see him rubbing his veiny hand over his mouth. "Hey, a pity about your pride and joy, boy. I believe I had a tear in my eye when it went up in flames.

"Claudia says we're getting to know each other too well, you know that? Your little wife spots me up in that window. Surprised the hell out of me when she started yelling and firing her gun. She nearly got me, but Claudia pulled me away in time." The old man sighed. "Then you had to guess what was going to happen.

"Claudia was bummed that your little cutie wasn't plastered against your Porsche when it blew. She wanted to see her fly through the air, like the pieces of your car."

Savich let the contempt blast out. "Yeah, you screwed up again, just like at the motel. But you're an old man, Moses, lost your edge because you're so sick and weak. You know something else? You're a liar, a pathetic, twisted liar."

"Huh? What're you talking about, boy? We was playing games, we didn't really want to blow your flesh away from your bones, not at Hooter's, but if it happened, well then, fun time would have been over, wouldn't it? What's this about me lying to you? I ain't never lied to you, boy."

"Oh yeah you did. You claimed I tortured a woman, made her scream, and then you said I murdered her. That's a lie. I never tortured anyone, never murdered anyone, man or woman. Only you and that psychopath Lolita you're with do that. Why'd you make something like that up, Moses? Are you so pathetic you have to make up ridiculous crap like that to feel important?"

Savich heard the roll of phlegm, heard the old man's breathing hitch and bubble, then his voice exploded through the phone. "I didn't make up anything, you bastard! You showed her no mercy, and you're not going to get any!"

Savich bore down, his voice snarly. "You're a liar, Moses. Why are you lying?"

"You waited until she was free, and then you murdered her. I'm going to make you sorry for that. Tell you what, boy, I'll be sure you know who she was before you die. Just before. Everything up to now was for fun, but not any longer. Now I'm going to get to you and I'm going to make you suffer like she did. You're going to pay." The phone disconnected, cutting off in the midst of an awful hacking cough.

Savich slipped his cell phone into his shirt pocket and turned to his wife. "He sounds like he's drowning. You called Agent Arnold, let me call Mr. Maitland so he can get enough cops out when we find out where Moses is. Then I'll get you out of those clothes."

She touched her hand to his cheek. "That was very well done, Dillon. Did he tell you enough?"

"Yes, I think I know everything I need to, and not only from what he told me.

Moses repeated that I killed the woman he's connected to. Think about it, Sherlock. Moses planted a bomb in my car tonight, right in the middle of dozens of police. No one saw him at the motel or at the cemetery, or anywhere near the Denny's, though he had to have been near. Who have we ever known who could pull off something like that? Make people see what he wants them to see, not what's really there, him included."

She stared up at him. "Only Tammy Tuttle."

"Bingo," he said. "She may have learned at his knee."

"But we looked at her file. We found no connection."

"And we were wrong."

She got to her feet. "Agent Arnold will call back in a minute, then we're going to nail that crazy old man." She placed her fingertips against his mouth. "No, don't undress me and don't argue. We're in this together. I'm not going to keel over on you. Hey, I might even sing you another song."

At ten-thirty Saturday morning, Savich opened his front door to see Ruth with Brewster nestled in the crook of her arm,

Sheriff Dixon Noble and his sons standing behind her, grinning.

"Well, this is a surprise. Now, Ruth, I told you guys last night everything's all right. You shouldn't have come, you —"

"Be quiet, Dillon, just be quiet. I've been so worried, I had to see for myself. Where's Sherlock?" Then Ruth threw herself against him, Brewster between them, barking manically. "The news reports, Dillon, all those awful clips we saw on TV. It looked like a scene out of hell. Please tell me Sherlock is okay."

"She's fine, I promise."

"Okay, okay. We couldn't stand it. We had to make sure."

"In other words," Dix said, stepping forward to shake Savich's hand, "you could have been lying to Ruth, could really have been stretched out in a hospital bed, riddled with bullets and burning metal.

"Truth is, we were as worried as Ruth. She was convinced you were being stoic, said she'd belt you one if you weren't upright and smiling when we got here. Your Porsche — on the news they showed you pulling up in front of the club, panned to all the insane chaos, then they showed the Porsche burning. Some sight that was."

"All right, Brewster, come here."

"Be careful, Savich, you know how he is," Dix said.

"Yeah, I will." Savich let Brewster lick his chin, then held him slightly away. But Brewster didn't pee.

Rafe said, "We just walked him thirty minutes ago, so I guess his tank's empty."

"I'm convinced he has an auxiliary tank," their father said.

Rafe said to Savich, "Rob says you can get any girl you like when you drive a car like your Porsche."

"Yeah," Dix said, "it's all over for him now, boys. Tough break."

Sean walked into the entrance hall, his mother behind him. He stopped and stared at Brewster, who was wildly licking his father's face. He smiled.

Ruth saw the sling. "Omigod, Sherlock, Dillon said you hurt your arm, but just a little bit. What happened?"

Sherlock said, "I'm fine, really. It was a piece of flying metal, hardly touched me. Hello, Rob, Rafe, Dix. It's great to see you guys. Come in, come in. Oh dear, Dillon, quick, move Brewster off the carpet, he's peeing."

Half an hour later, the four adults sat around the kitchen table, drinking coffee and tea and eating raisin-stuffed scones from the new Potomac Street bakery, Sweet Things. The three boys had consumed half a dozen scones and were now in the living room with Graciella and Brewster, who occasionally barked and butted his head against Sean's hand.

Graciella sat on the sofa, mending a sweater, smiling at the boys and the most adorable dog she'd ever seen.

Ruth said to Savich, "You baited him again. You thought you could break him down."

Savich shrugged. "I wasn't getting anywhere finding out who he really is. There simply hasn't been a case in which I had to kill a woman. But after the bombing and Moses's call last night, Sherlock and I think we finally know."

Ruth sat forward, her elbows on the table.

Savich must have seen something in Sherlock's eyes because he rose, got a pain pill from the kitchen counter, and held it to her mouth. When she'd swallowed the pill, he sat down again, raised his teacup to toast Ruth. "Are you ready for this? The woman was Tammy Tuttle."

Ruth froze, said to Dix, "That was before I came into the unit, but I heard all about her, how she had this power to make people see what she wanted them to see."

"Mass hypnosis?" Dix asked, an eyebrow up. "You sure? That's pretty out there."

Savich nodded. "You're telling me. But we had a real hard time tracking her down even though we had her in our sights on two occasions. Thank God Tammy Tuttle couldn't trick everyone. When she got close enough to me, for whatever reason, I recognized her. Moses had only one fact right — I did nearly shoot her arm off. She was going to kill two teenage boys she and her crazy twin, Tommy, had kidnapped. I had to shoot her in the shoulder, which led to her losing an arm. She escaped from the hospital when she recovered and came after me. She wanted me real bad, like Moses."

Sherlock said, "Dillon didn't kill her, though. His sister was staying with us at the time. Tammy took her right out of our house and drove to the barn on the Plum River in Maryland where it all started. She managed to save herself, killed Tammy. We arrived when it was all over."

"Your sister," Dix said to Savich, "she's all right?"

"Oh yes."

Ruth took a bite of scone, savored it. "I want to marry the guy who made these."

Savich said, "Arturo weighs three hundred pounds."

Ruth grinned. "Okay, so maybe he's not perfect. So Moses Grace is what? Tammy Tuttle's grandfather?"

"Maybe. It's interesting. Moses hasn't mentioned Tammy's twin, Tommy. I wonder why not."

Sherlock said, "The only family we know of is Tommy and Tammy's cousin, Marilyn Warluski. She owns the barn on the Plum River, which is how MAX found the Tuttles. Marilyn wasn't a criminal, simply a bit on the slow side, I guess, and malleable, or she'd simply been beaten down by her cousins. They used her, manipulated her, but she survived. We're all praying she knows something about him, maybe can tell us what Moses Grace's real name is."

Savich said, "I remember asking Marilyn about Tommy and Tammy's parents, and she told me their mom was dead. She didn't know who their dad was. I didn't ask for more because there was too much going on. It makes sense that Moses Grace might be their grandfather. They had to get their crazy genes from somewhere. Moses sure fits the bill."

Dix asked Savich, "No luck tracking

Moses after his call last night?"

"Our guys located where the call came from again — the parking lot of another Denny's, this one in Juniperville, Virginia, about a forty-minute drive from here. It appears he and Claudia are fond of Denny's, but it took too long to identify the phone and triangulate the signal again. They were gone by the time the squad cars got there."

Savich added, "I'm convinced Moses has a pretty good idea how long it takes us to track him through a cell phone. He keeps using them because it gives him a kick to have cops racing to a particular spot only to find he's done a vanishing act."

"Then you'll have to find him another way," Ruth said.

"I do have a couple of ideas," Savich said, but he didn't elaborate.

Sherlock squeezed his hand. "Dillon asked Dane Carver to find Marilyn Warluski. Last we heard she was in the Caribbean, so Dane is checking all the islands first. Unless she's in hiding for some reason we don't know about, it shouldn't be long."

"There's another thing," Savich said as he drank more of his tea. "When I speak to Moses, his grammar can be appallingly bad, but other times it's perfect. I'm thinking he's playing a game with me, trying to make me think he's illiterate, but then he forgets and speaks normally. His Southern accent fades in and out, too. I really doubt he's the fourth-grade dropout he pretends to be."

Rafe and Rob came into the kitchen with Sean running between them, Graciella behind them, grinning like a proud parent. Rob said, "Agent Savich, we heard you talking about this Marilyn Warluski person, how she owns a barn near the Plum River and you're looking for her. We asked Graciella how to spell it, then we Googled her on Graciella's laptop. There's a Marilyn Warluski who lives in Summerset, Maryland, at Thirty-eight Baylor Street. We called up a map of Summerset, and it's about ten miles north of the Plum River. We could have dialed her number, but Graciella thought we'd better tell you first. She said it'd be nice of us to leave something for you to do."

Savich rose, walked to the boys, and hugged them close. They heard him say over Graciella's laughter, "You guys better teach Sean everything you know, all right?"

Ruth looked at Dix. "If the boys heard that, then this isn't exactly what you'd call a private conference. Maybe they'd like to go outside with Graciella. I'm thinking a nice bribe is in order. Okay, Sherlock?"

Ten minutes later, Graciella was out the door, three boys at her heels, headed for the ice cream parlor on Prospect Street.

"Okay," Savich said, sitting down again, "it's time for you to give us an update on your Maestro investigation."

"We've had to back off the embalming angle," Ruth said. "There's no way to track it to a specific purchase. The fluid is available everywhere, even traded as a street drug. Some people are suicidal or stupid enough to soak marijuana in it as a replacement for PCP.

"As for the BZ gas, I found out that even though they load a chemical like that into conventional bombs for warfare, it's easily available to the public. Rob and Rafe could order it online. I checked some scientific journals on MEDLINE, and the drug seems to be an industry standard for research on some types of neurotransmitters. Thousands of labs around the world have a supply. Like embalming fluid, trying to track down purchases of BZ to Maestro is daunting.

"I did find out that when I was in the cave I didn't necessarily have to breathe it in. It's a contact hazard, too. I could have easily absorbed it through my skin if enough had settled on something I touched."

Sherlock asked, "So where are you guys going to take it from here?"

"We're starting to look for evidence of an undiscovered serial killer. We've checked a fifty-mile radius around Maestro for persons reported missing over the past five years and found nineteen."

Sherlock said, "That sounds like a lot. Did you check it statistically?"

Dix nodded. "Yes, it's almost fifteen percent higher than average for a predominantly rural area in Virginia. Most of them were young, and some of them may have been runaways. We got ahold of Helen Rafferty's calendars, all safely filed in her office, and tried to match the dates the people were reported missing with Gordon's out-of-town appointments."

Ruth added, "Naturally, these are short distances, no overnights really necessary, meaning Gordon could have simply driven to a neighboring town, spotted the victim he wanted, and taken her."

Dix said, "But we did find half a dozen trips out of town that overlapped with the disappearance of teenagers and young women in their early twenties. Of course, they could be coincidences."

Sherlock tapped her fingertips on the table. "If a killer traveled to those towns to take someone, he could have been observed, maybe even seen with a victim."

"Yes, of course," Ruth said. "Dix sent several deputies out of town today to speak with the police in the towns around Maestro. We want them to know all the details about what's happened in Maestro and what happened to Erin. They need to take a fresh look at all those cases, and talk to the families again."

"You think it's Gordon?" Sherlock asked.

Dix said, "It's a tough call, particularly since he was my wife's uncle, but Helen's death especially points to someone local, someone who knows all the players."

Ruth said, "For all his protestations, all his tears about Erin and Helen, Gordon was the closest to them."

"At this point, there's still no smoking gun," Sherlock said. "You accuse Gordon, he'd get all huffy, even laugh at you, and he'd never speak to you again."

"We need to develop something else," Dix said, "some physical evidence, maybe a witness."

Savich said, "In other words, you're talking about lots of good old-fashioned police work. We've got personnel to help you canvass those towns you mentioned. I can call the Richmond SAC, Billy Gainer, to coordinate it with you."

"Yes, that would be great."

When Graciella brought the boys back, all of them on a sugar high from triple-scoop ice cream cones, Ruth decided it was a good time to head out. Sean got it into his head that he would be going with them, which required ten minutes of distracting him before they could leave.

CHAPTER 33

Summerset, Maryland
Saturday afternoon

The day was sunny and cold. The weatherman swore there would be no more snow until Tuesday, but no one believed it. Savich and Sherlock arrived in Summerset, Maryland, at three o'clock, and ten minutes later found 38 Baylor Street. Savich pulled Sherlock's Volvo into the small driveway of a single-level tract house in a subdivision that had been folded into Summerset thirty years before.

"She's been renting this house for a little over two years, since she turned twenty-three," Savich said, studying the small lot with its straggly oak trees hanging partially over the house. "The man who owns it is a big-time woodworker and furniture builder. He employs her, too."

Savich knocked on the freshly painted front door, framed by pretty pansy-filled flower boxes. There was no answer, no sound of footsteps. Savich knocked again.

After a moment, he stepped back. "Okay, let's check the garage. She drives a '96 Camry. If it's not there, odds are she's not home."

There was a window in the electronic garage door so Savich didn't need to try to raise it. No Camry.

Sherlock scratched her arm through the sling. "She could be anywhere."

"Yeah," he agreed, "she could. But you know what? I don't think Marilyn's an anywhere kind of person. I've got an idea. Let's go see if I'm right."

A short time later Savich pulled onto a two-lane pothole-riddled asphalt road. Sherlock looked at the forest of maple trees, their branches naked and waving in the cold wind. "This looks familiar. You know, I'll be glad to revisit the barn. It ended right there, all of it."

He remembered the long-ago afternoon like it was yesterday. "We won that day. Those two boys they kidnapped won, too."

Sherlock said matter-of-factly, "It's ironic how Moses Grace has some things right and others dead wrong. It's obvious he did all his research in the newspapers."

"Yes, and he imagined the rest. Good heavens, would you look at this."

The huge old barn, abandoned for

decades, no longer looked dilapidated and derelict. The once peeling clapboards were freshly painted a bright red and reflected the afternoon sun that speared through the maple branches. The garbage and machine parts that had once littered the outside of the barn were gone. Instead, there was a gravel path leading to the two large front doors.

Sherlock said, "It doesn't look like the same place. You think Marilyn's done all this?"

"Who else? Look, one of the doors is propped open. She must be here." Savich was smiling as he pulled the huge door wide. Sunlight poured in from the west. It was amazing, he thought, staring. It must have taken days to clear out all the moldy hay, the rusted equipment, the wooden troughs. The black circle painted in the middle of the floor that he remembered so clearly was gone. There was no dirt floor, either. It was covered with plywood. The walls had been Sheetrocked and painted, and the windows had glass in them again. The old barn smelled as fresh as the outdoors, with an overlay of new paint, sawdust, and wallpaper glue.

They walked back toward the tack room, noticed the dropped ceiling with new hanging lamps that sent out huge circles of light. The stairs at the far end of the barn leading up to the loft had been replaced and painted. They looked solid.

He heard a woman humming and called out, "Marilyn? Is that you?"

The humming stopped. A voice called out, with just a dollop of healthy fear in it. "Who is it?"

"It's Agent Dillon Savich and Agent Sherlock, FBI. Do you remember me?"

A young woman dressed in ancient paint-stained jeans, a big Plum River sweatshirt, and paint-splattered sneakers strode forward, a paintbrush in her hand. The overweight, slump-shouldered, defeated young woman with the stringy hair and frightened eyes they both remembered had vanished. This woman was healthy, her eyes bright, hair clean and pulled back in a ponytail. "Mr. Savich? Is it really you? Oh my goodness, it is! And don't you look fine!" She threw her arms around his neck and jumped up to lock her legs around his waist. She reared back a bit and grinned at him. "Oh, this is just dandy. Remember that overnight letter I sent you from Aruba? I told you how glad I was that Tammy didn't kill you?" She leaned down and gave him two big smacking kisses. "I never thought I'd see you again."

Savich gently grasped her wrists and pulled her hands from around his neck. "Marilyn," he said, laughing, "it's not that I don't appreciate your greeting, but this is my wife, Agent Sherlock. You remember her, don't you? She's got her arm in a sling right now, but if she didn't, she'd be over here pulling you off me and hugging you herself for how you helped us."

Marilyn twisted in his arms. "Oh hi, Agent Sherlock. Why aren't you Agent Savich, too?"

Sherlock grinned at the woman whose legs were still wrapped around her husband's waist. "Well, you see, Marilyn, there's already one Agent Savich. Trust me, the FBI doesn't need two. Besides, my maiden name makes bad guys think twice if they want to tangle with me."

"Sherlock," Marilyn said, rolling the name in her mouth. "Yeah, I like that." She hopped down and stepped back, smiled up at Savich. "It's been quite a while, Mr. Savich."

"And lots of good changes, too," Savich added.

Marilyn nodded. "I took a nine-month course at the Center for Architectural Woodworking in Baltimore two years ago, learned all about drafting shop drawings, jigs and templates, joinery, machining, stuff like that. Then I found out about this old gentleman who has a shop right here in Summerset. He's totally awesome, an old-style craftsman, really famous in the area for his furniture making. So I managed to talk him into taking me on. Buzz Murphy's his name. He's a nice old guy. He's teaching me everything he knows. And now we're almost partners. He's going to sell me his shop when he retires." She paused. "Well, now the old coot wants to marry me — like that's going to happen.

"I'm not poor anymore, Mr. Savich — well, not as poor as I used to be. And I'm not a fat old frump, either. I work out and only eat french fries twice a week." And she lifted up her oversized sweatshirt to show them her midriff as she twirled around.

Sherlock laughed. "You look great, Marilyn, maybe too great, so I want you to stay away from my husband." She waved her hand around her. "This is quite a project — look at how much you've accomplished."

Marilyn beamed at them. "Doesn't it look great? It's taken months and months. When I need something done and it's too much work for me, I find someone who's good at it. Barter's the greatest thing going if you have a skill to trade. You can build your own business that way."

She waved toward a grouping of four mahogany chairs. "See those chairs I made with Buzz? I really like the Chippendale design." Marilyn was so excited she was nearly dancing.

"That's a late eighteenth-century British design. Look at the elaborate splats — boy, does that ever take concentration and a gentle touch — and the ball-and-claw feet, you bust your butt to get those beauties."

"They're incredible," Sherlock said. "So very finely made."

"Buzz helped me with the splats, but I did the last two all by myself. Bet you can't tell which are mine, without his help."

Savich studied each of them, ran his hand over the intricate splats of one chair, then smiled at her. "No, I can't tell. You're really good, Marilyn."

"Thank you. I've already got the old tack room done. It's going to be my office. My living area is going up in the old hay loft. I'll have it done in a couple of months, then I'm moving out here.

"I decided I don't want Buzz's shop or his house, just all his tools and equipment and clients, but I haven't broken that to him yet since he's been attached to that shop for thirty years. But my shop will be here. There's plenty of work space, all I need. And the light, would you look at all the wonderful light!"

Savich was coming to terms with how much she'd changed. Not only her appearance, but the air of hopelessness that had clung to her, the fear — it was all gone. She was no longer that terrorized girl the Tuttles had abused. In her place appeared this solid young woman.

Savich took her hand, knowing he was going to scare her again, and hating it. "I don't want to needlessly frighten you, Marilyn, but we need your help. It has to do with Tammy."

Her hand jerked in his, but he held it tight. For an instant, she looked panicked.

"No, it's okay. Both Tammy and Tommy are long dead, you know that. It's about someone close to them. We're looking for an old man who knew Tammy, maybe her grandfather."

"But why? They're all dead, aren't they? You swear Tammy's dead, don't you, Mr. Savich?"

"Of course she's dead," he assured her. "But there's a vicious old man out there who's as insane and violent as Tammy was.

445

He wants to avenge her by killing me. And he wants to hurt Sherlock. Help us, Marilyn. Tell us who he is."

"Moses Grace?" she whispered, her face now pale, the old fear back in her eyes. "That old man everyone's talking about? And that teenage girl he's got with him? Claudia?"

Savich nodded.

"Oh God, do you think he knows about this property?"

He said matter-of-factly, "No, I have no reason to believe he does. The location of this barn wasn't in any newspaper accounts. And believe me, Marilyn, if he'd somehow found out about this place, he'd have been here months ago. He doesn't know. Believe me."

"Okay, that's a good thing. But you think Moses Grace is Tammy's grandfather?"

"Yes, he may very well be. He's too old to be her father."

"I don't want him to kill you, Mr. Savich." She nodded at Sherlock's sling. "Did he do that?"

"Yes, he did," Savich said.

"You're right about it not being Tammy's daddy. He left when she and Tommy were real young."

"Okay. You told me your mother and

Tammy's mother were sisters or half-sisters. Tell us what you remember about any other relatives, Marilyn — names, where they lived, whatever."

"It's hard to talk about them, Mr. Savich, but I'll try." She waved them toward the mahogany chairs again. "Sit down, sit down. Okay. Good." Then she stopped talking. She stretched her legs out in front of her and stuffed her hands in her jeans pockets.

She said finally, slowly, as if the words were being pulled out of her against her will, "Dalton, Kansas, that's where I grew up with my mom. Tammy and Tommy lived with their mom in Lucas City, a little farming town maybe fifteen miles away. There weren't ever any daddies around that I can remember. But both moms had been married, I'm sure of that. Tammy's mom was Aunt Cordie. Cordelia Tuttle — Tuttle was her husband's name, but like I said, he was long gone. My daddy's name was Warluski, so my mom was Marva Warluski. My old man took off before I was even born.

"My mom used to say that Cordie had the brain of a mushroom and was meaner than a copperhead snake, just look at Tommy and Tammy, carbon copies of her.

Whenever Tommy and Tammy beat me up, my mom said it was okay as long as I still had my neck because I had to toughen up.

"I used to hide when they came to visit." She paused for a moment, her face twisted. "They always found me, and they walloped me anyway. My mom called me a wuss."

"Do you remember other aunts or uncles?"

Marilyn shook her head. "My mom never spoke of any. Aunt Cordie didn't, either."

"And both your mom and Tammy's mom died, is that right, Marilyn?"

Marilyn's eyes popped open. "Yes, Mr. Savich, they died when we were all teenagers. That's when Tommy and Tammy took me away, told me I had to do exactly what they said or they'd put me in a hole filled with snakes."

"How did they die?"

"Tommy said they broke into this old lady's house to take her social security money, but she wouldn't tell them where she kept it. A neighbor heard the old lady screaming and called the police. They ran out of there, the cops chasing them, and one of the cops shot out a rear tire. Mom couldn't hold the car on the road, and they hit a tree. Killed them both."

Sherlock felt a wave of revulsion and

swallowed. Marilyn spoke so matter-of-factly about it. She saw Dillon's expression hadn't changed, but his dark eyes were darker and hard. He said, "Think now what your mom's maiden name was."

"My mom's name was Marva Gilliam."

"Was that Cordie's name, too?"

"Aunt Cordie — yes, she was Gilliam, too, because they were sisters, not half sisters."

"Good. Very good. So she was Cordelia Gilliam. Did your grandfather and grandmother ever come around?"

She closed her eyes again. "I don't ever remember a grandmother. But Granddaddy — yeah, I remember him. He never stayed with us, only with Aunt Cordie. I was maybe six years old when he came. Something must have happened because he suddenly left. Maybe he did something bad and had to run. He was mean, Mr. Savich, as mean as Aunt Cordie and Tommy and Tammy. He'd hit Tammy upside the head, then he'd cuddle her and stroke her hair. It scared me to death. It wasn't right, I see that now. What he'd do when he cuddled Tammy wasn't right."

"Did you ever see him again?"

"After my mom was killed he came real late one night, to Tommy and Tammy's house. We were packing because the social workers were coming and we had to get out fast. He stuffed a whole bunch of money in Tammy's hands, and then he kissed her, with his mouth open, patted her face, and left. I remember Tammy ran out after him. She didn't come back for maybe an hour." Marilyn looked at Savich. "I haven't thought about that in years. I really didn't realize . . . but Tammy was maybe fifteen then. Did he have sex with her, Mr. Savich?"

"Don't dwell on it, Marilyn. Did you ever hear his first name?"

"Both my mom and Aunt Cordie called him Papa. I heard him tell Tammy to call him Malcolm. So I guess he had to be Malcolm Gilliam. Do you know what? I just saw him in my mind. He was handsome, real good-looking, but old, you know?

"Once, about six months later, I remember Tommy and Tammy talking about him. Tammy waved this postcard in front of my nose, said it was from her granddaddy. I said he was my granddaddy, too, but she laughed, said I didn't know Granddaddy like she did. She said he sent the postcard all the way from Montreal."

"How did he know where they were, do you remember?"

"I don't know, Mr. Savich. They didn't talk about that."

"Were there other postcards or letters?"

"Yeah, some, along with wads of cash, for three or four years, then they stopped."

Savich leaned over and patted her hand. "You have helped us immensely. Thank you."

Because Marilyn was so proud of her new home, Savich and Sherlock drank some sodas with her and ate a couple of her favorite Fig Newtons. She showed them the table she was making to match the beautiful chairs. The last thing Marilyn said to Savich when she walked them to Sherlock's Volvo was, "I'm sure sorry about your Porsche, Mr. Savich. I saw it blow up on TV. Now you've got to ride in this stuffy thing."

Savich patted her cheek, kissed her lightly. "As soon as I can I'm going to go out and get myself something you'll really like."

"Then make it one of those new Corvettes, red of course. Unless you have enough money for a Ferrari."

They waved until both she and her barn were out of sight. When they drove onto the country road again, Savich said, "Malcolm Gilliam. I'll bet you anything his parents were named either Moses or Grace or a combination of the two."

CHAPTER 34

Richmond, Virginia
Saturday afternoon

The Saturday-afternoon traffic was sluggish as they approached Richmond, people hanging out of their cars, enjoying the break in the weather.

Dix exited the downtown expressway and worked his way over to West Grace Street to the Richmond Police Department headquarters.

"There's some irony in the street name," Ruth remarked.

For a Saturday afternoon there was lots of activity, more than Dix had seen since his days in New York. They passed a woman sobbing into her hands, a man ranting about his mechanic cheating him, and a cop filling out papers next to a teenager who looked scared to death. Dix was thinking he should have left Rob and Rafe in the car with Brewster, but then Detective Morales came forward, his hand outstretched. After the introductions, the detective led them to the second floor. He eyed the boys and spoke quietly into his cell phone.

Rafe whispered to his brother, "Hey, would you look at that scar? How cool is that? Bet he was in a gunfight."

Detective Morales said over his shoulder, "Yep, a bunch of Colombian drug dealers were holed up in the warehouse district, and we stormed the place. This is my souvenir." He ran a finger lightly over the pale scar. "My wife thinks it's pretty cool, too.

"Ah, Linus, these two hotshots are Rob and Rafe Noble. While I'm dealing with their dad, Sheriff Noble, and Special Agent Warnecki, I'm hoping you could break away from chasing down bank robbers to give them a tour of our fine facilities."

Officer Linus Craig couldn't have been over twenty-two, Ruth thought as she shook his beefy hand. He had to be six-five, maybe two hundred and fifty pounds on a light day. She'd wager he'd played football in college, probably offensive line. His broken nose hadn't healed quite straight, and he had the sweetest smile. He grinned at Rob and Rafe, shook their hands, then leaned close to the boys. "You guys want to see the lineup room? It's down the hall in the detective division. Hey, I'll hang some numbers on you, let you live the experience. We can see how tall you are, too."

The boys didn't give them a backward glance. Detective Morales, dark-haired and dark-eyed, already sporting a five-o'clock shadow, laughed as he led them to a small conference room down the hall. "I've got three teenagers of my own. They wanted me to put them in a cell overnight. I settled on the lineup thing. They didn't stop talking about it all day." He opened the door to the conference room and gestured them in.

"A nice setup you've got here," Dix told him as he accepted a cup of coffee.

"The place is brand-new, up and running in 2002. None of that smell city police stations have, that combination of dampness, cheap room deodorizer, and eau de criminal. Not yet. It's the best part of having new digs. So you're an FBI agent," he said without pause to Ruth. "How'd you and Sheriff Noble hook up? You guys married? Those your boys?"

"No, we're not married," Dix said easily. "We just met a week ago when this all started, Detective Morales."

"Call me Cesar."

Dix nodded, sat forward and clasped her hands in front of him. "I'm Dix, and this is Ruth. Ruth is the agent Dempsey and Slater fired on last Saturday night. We met with Ruth's boss in Washington this morning, and I'm real glad to find you here at work today, to meet you personally."

Ruth said, "We both know about weekend work, Sheriff. The devil never sleeps."

Dix said, "Sorry to tie up your staff with the boys, Cesar. It's been a rough week for them, with people they know dying, our own house getting shot up. I wanted to show them we're dealing with it, calm them down a little, and I didn't want to leave them alone."

"I understand," Morales said. "Officer Craig can handle the kids, and I've got time to fill you in on what we're doing."

"You mentioned you're working on some information from someone called Eddie Skanky?"

Detective Morales nodded. "Yes, I've also got two of my detectives working the usual stuff — credit cards, phone calls, bank accounts. They've leaned on Dempsey's girlfriend and their business associates — you want to call them that — but lowlifes like that never have anything to tell you unless they're up on charges and need some leverage to deal down.

"Eddie Skanky is a local thug who's been sent up twice by Detective Marilyn Honniger. She got him again on a parole violation and he's promised to put his nose to the grindstone if she doesn't toss him back in jail. Seems he knew Slater and Dempsey, both in prison and out. We're waiting for him to give up a name."

"A name would be a good start," Dix said, "but we have to be sure he's not pulling a name out of the newspaper to stay out of prison."

"Some of the people who were close to the victims are prominent, respected people," Ruth explained. "Let's hope he brings in something solid, or they'll laugh at us."

"I understand," Detective Morales said. "I hear everything, and I know some of those people are relatives of yours, Sheriff. I'm glad I'm not in your shoes on this one."

Dix sighed deeply, muttered under his breath, and said, meeting Morales's eyes, "Yes, it could get real messy. I pray no one in the family is involved, mostly for the boys' sake. I wouldn't want to have to tell them something like that. But we'll deal with whatever comes."

They left a short time later, dragging Rob and Rafe, who didn't want to detach themselves from Officer Craig. Dix unlocked the Range Rover to a hysterically barking Brewster, and everyone settled in. Ruth waited until the boys were plugged into a computer game before she said quietly, "I like Detective Morales. I'm glad we stopped here to meet him. It makes a difference when you know the other person. He's a straight-up guy. He'll come up with a name for us. I just don't know if it will be in time." At his raised eyebrow, she said smoothly, "By Tuesday."

Dix grinned as he checked the boys in the rearview mirror, and murmured, "They're still dealing with losing their mother. I hope we're wrong about Gordon."

"Hey, Dad, did I tell you how Officer Craig took us to booking? Showed us their fancy new fingerprinting machine? It's newer than yours."

Rafe said, "He showed me how to look like a real rough character in the lineup booth, how to slouch and turn my sneakers up on the edges."

"The lineup, huh? Maybe next time Officer Craig can dump you in a holding cell, lock you up for a couple of hours so you can keep company with some of the city's more upstanding citizens."

The boys hooted and settled back into their game. If a wild cacophony of gunshots and car crashes counted as settling in, Ruth thought.

Dix passed an old truck, nodded to the farmer who waved him ahead, and eased the Range Rover around him.

CHAPTER 35

Washington, D.C.
Sunday night

Savich and Sherlock sat in the Volvo in their driveway, the engine idling, heater running. Savich stared at his laptop. MAX was in satellite communication with the communications center in the Hoover Building. A large-scale map of the Washington, D.C., area appeared on the screen.

Sherlock said, "It's ironic, isn't it? Our neighbors to the north had Malcolm Gilliam in custody for nine years. If they'd only kept him incarcerated none of this would have happened."

"I wish he'd been in prison rather than in a mental hospital," Savich said. "It's a pity the Canadian Supreme Court ruling in 1991 changed their criminal code. They made it easier to escape criminal culpability by claiming insanity."

"But still," Sherlock said, "he brutally kills two people in Quebec and they let him out in nine years?"

Savich rolled his shoulders and stretched. "Once his lawyers managed to convince a jury he wasn't criminally responsible because he was hallucinating and delusional at the time of the crimes, it wasn't lawful for them to hold him in custody any longer. Something about cruel and unusual punishment."

"Unless," Sherlock said, "they could prove he still posed a risk to the public. He must have learned the rules really well." She looked at MAX's screen for a moment and panned the map westward. "So, Dillon, if they deemed Moses was no longer a danger to the public, the Institut Philippe Pinel couldn't monitor him after he was released?"

"He was scheduled to see his multidisciplinary support group weekly, but he was legally free to leave. So he hacked off his locator bracelet, skipped out and came back to the U.S. two years ago. Then we lose track of him until he picks up Claudia and beats that homeless man to death eight months ago in Birmingham."

"You know he must see Claudia as another Tammy."

"Probably. Claudia is the same age as Tammy was. And now the two of them have gone on their own killing spree."

Savich opened a JPEG file on MAX. "You haven't seen this photo yet, Sherlock. It was taken three weeks before Moses's trial."

She leaned over to stare at the photo of a rather distinguished-looking, middle-aged man with thick gray hair, a thin ascetic face, and an aquiline nose. His nicely worn tweed suit made him look like a banker. "You'd never know it was Moses Grace," she marveled out loud. "The description everyone at Denny's agreed on was that he looked ancient. It hasn't been much more than a dozen years since this photo was taken."

Savich nodded and began to massage her neck and shoulders to ease the tension. "It'd be nice, though, to have a photo from when he got out of the Canadian institute after nine years. We're still working on that."

She studied MAX's screen again. "He's aged thirty years, and not well, since this was taken."

"He's very ill, Sherlock, and maybe that's got a lot to do with how old and worn he looks. He was being treated for pulmonary tuberculosis reactivation at Philippe Pinel. They didn't finish treating him before he skipped out. When I told

Dr. Breaker his symptoms, he said it sounded like the infection had progressed to the cavitary stage — destroyed enough tissue to form big holes in his lungs. Dr. Breaker thinks he's in the end stages."

"I guess more people were exposed to tuberculosis back then. So a disease he probably got in childhood is going to do him in. At least there'll be some kind of justice for him."

"If this satellite link to the communications center holds up, we'll be helping him get justice sooner than that," Savich said.

"I sure hope so, Dillon, or we'll never get any sleep."

"We still have some time before midnight," Savich said. He pulled her onto his lap, kissed her behind the ear, and smoothed her soft hair with his hand. "Rest a moment. It's only been two days since you got your arm sliced up."

He looked down at his Mickey Mouse watch. "Moses called at exactly midnight the last time. We won't stay out much later than that. Dane and Ben should be here about now."

At midnight sharp Savich's cell phone rang. He pulled out of his driveway and next to the curb, and let the car idle again. He gave everyone a thumbs-up and answered it.

"Hey, Moses, how you doin'? Coughing up lots of blood? Nearly dead, aren't you, old man?"

Savich had surprised him. There was a long silence. Savich needed him to say something, to identify himself.

"Now, boy, you know my Claudia wouldn't let that happen. I'm plenty fit enough to take care of business with you."

Before Moses finished his sentence, a flashing yellow dot appeared on MAX's Washington map, pinpointing his location. He was moving. Sherlock magnified the map with a keystroke, nodded to Savich, and pointed straight ahead. The Volvo accelerated smoothly.

"Still think you're going to kill me? Not a chance, old man," Savich said.

"We'll see, won't we, now that I know where you live." He cackled, and Savich could hear liquid rolling around in his mouth. "You want to know how I found out your address? I found it at Ms. Lilly's before I set off that little bomb. Claudia thought since we missed your cute little wife, we ought to get down to business and try again real soon, so I wanted to let you know you can't hide anymore. It was quite a scene there for a while Friday night, wasn't it?"

Sherlock motioned for a left on Clement

Street, and Savich turned smoothly. Dane Carver and Ben Raven listened in on their cell phones in the backseat to radio communications from the Hoover building. They were relaying Moses's location by voice to all the agents converging on him.

"You caused quite a furor, Moses. Say hello to Claudia for me, will you? That's Claudia Smollett, isn't it, from Cleveland, Ohio? She looks pretty in her pictures. Are you sure you're anxious for me to meet her?"

They heard Moses's muffled, angry voice. "Damn, Claudia, he's made you. What am I going to do with you if you don't listen to me?"

The flashing yellow dot disappeared from the map. Moses's phone was in a dead spot, without GPS signal. Then it flashed on again, bright as before, to the collective relief of everyone in the Volvo.

Savich said, "I wouldn't be too upset with her, Moses. She's not the only one who's been careless. You're not really Moses Grace, are you? Moses was your daddy's name and Grace was your mama's. Do you think your parents would be pleased you're doing all this killing using their names? Looks to me like they were real nice people."

There was a sharp hitch in Moses's breath, followed by a violent hacking cough. Finally he managed to say, "Well, well, well. Was that a guess or has our Boy Scout been doing his homework?"

Sherlock gave Savich a thumbs-up and mouthed, *Two minutes.*

Savich said, "Why don't I talk while you choke on your own blood, Moses? Your name is Malcolm Gilliam, born in Youngstown, Ohio. You flunked out of engineering school, then spent some time in Canada. You've really got to work on that illiterate hillbilly shtick, by the way."

"You gonna tell me how you found out about me?"

Savich only laughed at him. "You did a good job keeping that mental hospital stretch in Canada to only nine years. How'd you manage that?"

He heard blood and phlegm bubbling up in Moses's throat. He swallowed convulsively but the bubbling sound remained. "Well, you know, boy, I started taking Zenadrine to lose some weight, and damned if I didn't start hearing voices. Terrible thing, my lawyers said, terrible thing. But do you know those do-gooder morons still kept me in that damned mental ward for nine years? *Nine years* I had to play a role and

465

do every damned thing I was told to do! I'll tell you, it took everything in me to play them right, to give them all the answers they wanted on their idiot tests, but now it's over, and here I am, boy, your worst nightmare."

Sherlock whispered to him as Moses spoke, "He's driving south on Andover. Right now he's crossing Delancy Street, heading into a residential area. He's only six blocks from us. Dane, Ben, you guys got that?"

"Who you got with you, boy? About time we finished this chat, anyway. I know how you like to try and get cute triangulating my cell phones even though I beat you every time."

Savich had to keep him on the line a little longer. "It's Sherlock, Moses, no one to be afraid of. Besides, we're old friends, seeing as how you're Tammy's granddaddy."

Moses's surprise was palpable in the silence. This time Savich could hear a touch of fear in his voice. "How the hell do you know that?"

"I know all about you, Malcolm. Last time you saw Tammy and Tommy, you gave her a wad of cash, then took off for Canada."

There was silence, and finally Moses

whispered, "You butchered my poor Tommy, and you shot off Tammy's arm. Only one person left who knew about that — Marva's little girl, what's her name? Marilyn. Here I thought she was already dead. Never liked her, whiny little bitch, but Tommy liked to have her around. Well, I'm going to find her, let Claudia have a go at her before I cut her heart out." The last word caught in a spurting cough.

Savich looked at Sherlock, who whispered, "He's only a couple of blocks ahead, driving slow."

"You got Claudia with you? She listening to us?"

"My little cutie's right here."

"Is she holding a box of Kleenex for you to catch the blood you're spewing? Too bad about your tuberculosis, Moses."

"I'm going to blow up your house, boy, you hear me? I'm going to blow you and your little wife to hell."

Moses clicked off.

Savich saw the dark blue van at the same time Dane and Ben did. Moses was driving around Jackson Park, a small square dotted with old maple trees, deserted now in the cold winter night. Only a few lights were on in the houses surrounding the square.

Dane whispered into his cell, "We've got

him dead ahead. Everyone come in silent. Wait for my signal."

The van suddenly accelerated. They realized they'd been spotted, but it was too late. It was way too late.

"Gotcha, old man." Savich punched down on the gas, heading straight for the van. Ben and Dane leaned out, fired multiple rounds at the van's back tires.

Both tires exploded.

Claudia leaned out the passenger window, returned fire.

The van swerved madly, struck a parked Toyota, then bounced off. Moses jumped the curb and turned the van into the park, skimming between two skinny maple trees. The doors flew open and he and Claudia leaped out, carrying what looked like AR-15 assault rifles. They ran in opposite directions through the small park, taking cover behind trees.

FBI vehicles started pulling up all around the park, tires screeching, headlights filling the park with glaring light.

Savich was out of the Volvo, yelling, "Down, everyone down!"

Automatic gunfire from the park sprayed the area in a wide circle. Savich heard a grunt, yelled without hesitation, "Bring them down!"

For a minute the gunfire was intense, blasting into the park from all directions. Savich heard Claudia yell, watched the AR-15 spin out of her arms as she fell to the ground. She tried to crawl away, holding her side.

They were close enough to hear Moses coughing, curses spewing out of his mouth as he fired. There was a brief silence when they heard him slam in another clip, and he fired again.

Lights came on in the houses around the square. There were no shadows left anywhere. Claudia hissed out a yell and crawled back to her assault rifle. As she grabbed up the weapon, one of the sharpshooters found her in his sights. There was a loud report as her head exploded and she fell back, dead.

The shooting abruptly stopped because Moses was no longer firing and was no longer in view.

He wasn't anywhere.

Savich began to run to where he'd last seen Moses bent nearly double with the force of his coughing, fanning his assault rifle, firing until another clip was empty.

He yelled, "Hold your fire!" He was within six feet of where Moses had stood, saw the spent shells but nothing else. He heard a cough and turned sharply to his left, ran toward it. "I can hear you, Moses. In a second I'll be able to see you, too. You're not as good as Tammy was."

A bullet fired, went wide. Savich saw Moses Grace in the next moment, the assault rifle hanging limply in his hand, bent over, moaning, hacking up blood. A large bloodstain was spreading across his belly. Suddenly a fountain of blood gushed out of his mouth. Savich walked over to him and took the rifle out of his hand. "Everyone can see you now, Moses. It's over." Savich yelled over his shoulder, "All clear."

The old man heaved up more blood. He was covered with it now, streaming down his chin. Savich watched him weave, then fall hard to the ground on his side. He groaned as he rolled over onto his back. His eyes stared straight up, locked onto Savich's face.

His face twisted as he tried to speak, his bloody chest pulsing in frantic breaths. Savich came down on his knees beside him. His blood-drenched mouth opened, and when Savich leaned down close to him, he tried to spit on him. But he no longer had any breath. If he was still aware of where he was, the last thing he saw was twenty FBI agents standing over him.

Savich felt for a pulse in his neck, then shook his head. For a long moment, he stared down at the mad old wreck of a man.

Jimmy Maitland dropped to his knees beside Savich. "Dear Lord, I didn't know there was this much blood in a human being. Thank God it's over. Step away, Savich, he's infected."

Mr. Maitland rose, Savich coming up slowly to stand beside him. They watched all the men and women high-fiving each other. Mr. Maitland shouted, "Okay, boys and girls, let's get this nightmare wrapped up."

They could hear sirens in the distance. Mr. Maitland said to Savich, "The media will be here any minute. I hope to God they never find out how you pulled this off. You know what? Even I don't know how high up the chain of command this one went." He clapped Savich on the shoulder.

Savich grinned at him. "Worked like a charm, didn't it?"

Ten minutes later, Jimmy Maitland watched the forensic team carefully bag the bodies of Moses Grace and Claudia Smollett. The police cordoned off the area to keep the homeowners away. Men and women tumbled out of media vans, armed with microphones and cameras. Mr. Maitland watched Savich hug Sherlock and help her into the Volvo. Then he walked around to the driver's side and climbed in. He imagined Savich wincing as he turned the key, and smiled. Then he squared his shoulders and turned to deal with the media.

CHAPTER 36

Maestro, Virginia
Sunday noon

The boys had wolfed down their first hamburger and baked potato before they stopped talking about the lineup at the Richmond Police Department. It wasn't until they were building their second hamburgers that Rob started a new topic. "The ice was great on the pond this morning, Dad. We all raced and I won, easy."

"You only beat me once, Rob, and that's because you cheated. And the other kids were all twelve years old."

"What about Pete? He's a senior, older than me."

"He's a spaz, can't figure out which foot is which."

Ruth and Dix sat back, half listening, watching the boys eat and argue, mostly both at the same time.

Dix said, "The amazing thing is I can remember when I ate just like that with my brothers."

473

She nodded, but she was thinking, and Dix saw it. "We did a lot of good work this morning, Ruth. Give your brain a rest for a while."

"I can't."

Rob said, "Hey, Ruth, do you skate? You think you can beat my little brother? If you do, you can race against me."

"And the winner of that race will go against me, right?" Dix asked.

"Okay, Dad, with maybe a handicap."

"And maybe a blindfold," Rafe said.

"You're that good, are you?" Ruth asked him.

"Beat my boys and see."

Ruth grinned as she passed the mustard for the new round of burgers.

Dix noticed that Rob didn't dig into his hamburger right away, and that was unusual. "What's up, Rob?"

Rob carefully laid his fork down on his plate. "I don't know, but something's wrong, Dad, with you. I think you're all wound up. You and Ruth both."

"I suppose that's the truth," Dix said. He imagined he knew where this was going, and he didn't want to stop it. He said nothing, only nodded.

"Rafe and I were talking." Here Rob

shot a warning look at his brother.

"Yes?"

"Well, maybe . . . Nothing, Dad. We can talk about it later." Rob pushed his chair back, grabbed his hamburger, and shot up. "We're going to go sledding now." He waved his hamburger. "I need my strength. Thanks for lunch."

"Wait for me, Rob!"

"Be careful," Ruth called after them.

Dix opened his mouth to demand to hear more, but he didn't. They heard things, and they must be imagining even worse things. Rob was right, both he and Ruth were wound up. A discussion with the boys could wait until they were all ready for it, and he wouldn't be ready for it until everything was resolved.

"They must blame me," Ruth said, surprising him. "It's easy to think that if I hadn't come here, none of this would have happened."

"Well, if they think that, they're wrong and they'll come to realize it. They're fair and they're bright. The best thing we can do for them is to put an end to all this as soon as we can. Then we'll help them deal with it, Ruth. It'll just take some time."

His cell phone rang.

"Sheriff Noble."

Ruth watched Dix's face as he listened. When he punched off, he said, "That was Cesar Morales. He doesn't have a name for us."

"That sure makes me want to pop out with a profanity. All right, Dix. Cut the tease. Why did he call?"

"It turns out Dempsey's girlfriend has been spending lots of cash. They pinned her with it and she finally told the detective that Tommy gave her nine thousand dollars in cash to keep safe until he and Jackie got back from a job."

Ruth's heart speeded up. "Did she give up anything that would help us find out who gave Dempsey the money?"

"As I said, Cesar didn't have a name. But Tommy told his girlfriend it was for a job he was doing for a woman." He paused, and grinned. "What he said, exactly, was that the job was for a crazy bitch at the music school in Maestro."

CHAPTER 37

Maestro
Sunday evening

Dix pulled into Gordon's driveway at six o'clock that evening. He turned to Ruth as he unfastened his seat belt. "You armed?"

"Oh yes."

B.B. climbed out of his cruiser to meet them in the driveway. "Sheriff, Agent Warnecki. Somebody with the boys, Sheriff?"

"The boys went over to the Claussons' for dinner and Foosball with their friends."

"Are you going to arrest him, Sheriff?"

Dix said, "We'll see, B.B." He turned to scan the house as he murmured to Ruth, "When Christie disappeared, everyone in the department became the boys' substitute mothers." He turned back to B.B. "We've got all our ducks in a row. Now, where did he go this afternoon?"

"He drove to Tara about two o'clock, then came back here maybe an hour ago. Looks like he turned on every light in the house."

It did indeed, Dix thought, scanning the house. "I want you to stay in your car, B.B. If for some reason Dr. Holcombe leaves the house before we do, give me a call."

"Especially if he's running around waving a gun," Ruth added.

Dix took Ruth's arm, and they walked up the stone pathway to the front door. Gordon answered the door looking like an aristocrat in a gray cashmere turtleneck sweater and black slacks. Elegant and worldly, but exhausted, his eyes hooded and dull.

He knows we're here for him, Dix thought, *he knows.*

Gordon paused in the doorway, staring at them. "Dix, Agent Warnecki. It's Sunday; to what do I owe this pleasure?"

"We'd like to speak to you, Gordon."

Gordon looked over Dix's shoulder. "I've seen your deputy outside. I hope you don't want to bring him in, too."

"No, my deputy is guarding our backs." Dix walked into the entryway as Gordon gestured them in.

"We've got some things to discuss with you, Gordon, like who hired Tommy Dempsey and Jackie Slater."

"Who? Oh, those men you killed in the car chase. Oh, all right. Come on in then, it's not like I can stop you." Gordon waved them into the living room.

Dix and Ruth watched Gordon walk to a drink trolley on the far side of the room, lift a brandy bottle, an eyebrow arched. "Either of you want a drink?"

Ruth and Dix shook their heads. Dix said, "No, we're fine."

Ruth looked around the large open space, all windows and rich oak, dominated by a large grand piano at the far end of the room. The walls were covered with musical scores, beautifully framed — all of them, she knew, originals penned by the composers themselves. It was a comfortable room, elegant and subtle, filled with earth tones and oversized leather furniture. A fire burned brightly in the stone fireplace.

They watched Gordon pour himself a liberal amount of brandy, splashing some of it over the side of the snifter, as if he'd already had too much.

"You have a lovely Steinway, Dr. Holcombe. I noticed it when we were here before."

"Yes, you saw everything, didn't you, when you searched my house?" Gordon walked to the eleven-foot black grand piano and laid a hand lightly on the keys.

"Did you know that Steinway fought at the Battle of Waterloo?"

They shook their heads, and Gordon sighed, sipped his brandy. "Who cares?"

Dix said without preamble, "I don't think I've mentioned yet, Gordon, that we know who hired Dempsey and Slater. Or perhaps you already know?"

"How would I know? Tell me, Dix."

"Helen Rafferty."

His hand jerked, and more brandy spilled out of his snifter. "Helen hired those two thugs? Why, for heaven's sake? To kill Agent Warnecki here? Helen didn't even know her last Saturday. That makes no sense, Dix."

"No, Helen didn't hire them to kill Ruth. She hired them to kill Erin."

"What did you say? *Kill Erin?* That's crazy. Why would Helen do such an insane thing? No, I was thinking it was that boy lover of Marian's, Sam Moraga. I heard he wanted Erin but she didn't want him." He stopped dead, stared at them. "Wait a minute, here, Dix. This means you no longer think I killed Erin? You think I'm innocent?"

Dix said, "We know you didn't hire them, Gordon. Our apologies for believing you did."

"We also know Sam Moraga had nothing to do with Erin's murder, either," Ruth said.

"So you're blaming Helen? I don't understand any of this, Dix." He leaned heavily against the grand piano.

Dix said, "We're cops, Gordon. It's our job to keep asking questions until all the pieces fit together. And for a while there, all the pieces pointed right at you. But in the end, they didn't fit when it came to your killing Erin and Walt. Truth be told, Gordon, we think you really loved Erin."

"Yes, yes, of course I did, Dix. She was filled with light, filled with love." For a moment, they were afraid he would burst into tears. He got hold of himself and managed to look contemptuous. "So you've been going down the list. Very well. Tell me what you think Helen had to do with it."

"Ruth and I spent the afternoon combing through Helen's bank records. We found three large withdrawals she made in the past three weeks, in cash. We've been through her telephone records as well. She called Richmond twice, Tommy Dempsey's number specifically. There was one call from Dempsey's number to hers, last Thursday. Helen may have been a good receptionist, but she wasn't an experienced criminal. She left a trail."

"She hired those men to murder my Erin? But that can't be right, Dix. She always supported me, helped me. I think she loved me. Why would she do such a thing?"

Ruth said, "It's not so hard to figure out, is it, Gordon? Helen saw that Erin Bushnell wasn't like the other students you took as lovers. She realized that Erin was the first woman you really loved, the one who might be with you for the long term, not just until she graduated. Helen had made herself accept that you turned her away because of your infirmity — that's what she called it — your need for stimulation and even inspiration from those talented young woman. So Helen was able to accept them, because they were temporary. Only she was a constant.

"But then you met Erin and everything changed."

Gordon gulped down brandy, coughed, wiped his brimming eyes. "I would have given Erin anything. Anything."

"Yes, we know, and so did Helen. And she couldn't live with that. She snapped."

"I still can't believe it. How could someone like Helen find two criminals?"

Ruth said, "We called Helen's brother, Dave Rafferty. We asked him if Helen ever mentioned either of the men. He's a high-school teacher, and he remembered he'd had Dempsey's younger brother in a class. He was a troubled kid whose older brother was in and out of prison. Dave thought he'd probably talked to Helen about him. So she must have tracked the older Dempsey down."

Dix continued, "We think it was Helen who told them about Winkel's Cave, as a good place to hide Erin's body. Otherwise, they would have had no way of knowing about it. Did you or Chappy ever take Helen there?"

Gordon said, "I don't remember. Maybe Chappy took her there. I never liked that cave when we were boys, it was Chappy's place."

"Helen knew about that entrance, she knew about the cave chamber. We think they chose how to kill Erin all on their own, though. Did you know they used a hallucinogenic drug to disable her, and after they killed her, they embalmed her and posed her? Did you know that, Gordon?"

He looked like he was going to faint. "They embalmed her? Like morticians do?"

Ruth nodded. "Morticians and insane people. We know that Dempsey's stepfather worked in a funeral home. He must have hung around the place, watched the process. So Dempsey did something to really confuse things. He and Slater embalmed her, and as a final touch, posed her to make it look like a ritual killing rather than a contract killing, in case she was found too soon. And that part of it worked like a charm. It was an excellent distraction. We were led to believe a ritual serial killer might have murdered Erin Bushnell. We thought there might be other victims, and spent some time and effort looking for them — including all your former student lovers. And because they are all alive and well, it didn't really settle comfortably that you were some maniac serial killer."

Gordon's face went white. "You believed I was capable of that? A killer who did that over and over?"

"They made it look possible," Ruth said. "But we know now it isn't."

Dix said, "Whatever else Dempsey and Slater were, they were savvy when it came to their own survival. Until they made the mistake of coming after Ruth."

Gordon sat down on the piano bench, then looked over at Ruth. "However did you get away from them in that cave?"

"That's a good question. I know that if they realized I was there they would have killed me. They killed Walt, so there is no doubt they would have killed me, too. We believe that after I inhaled or touched the drug they used on Erin, I fell and struck my head. Still, I must have gotten my wits together enough to find my way out of the cave without them seeing me, maybe after they left. And I must have wandered through the woods until I collapsed near Dix's house."

"But that's at least four, five miles from Winkel's Cave."

Ruth shrugged. "Neither Dix nor I can figure any other way I could have ended up in his woods."

"She's in excellent shape," Dix said, bringing Gordon's attention back to him. "So even while she was hallucinating and sick, she could have wandered for hours. We figure Dempsey and Slater must have told Helen about finding Ruth's car, with her wallet locked inside. So they knew she was an FBI agent. I'll bet that shook them, because they had to believe she knew what they'd done. I imagine they searched for her for hours."

Dix continued, "Helen must have contacted them when she learned that I found an unconscious woman in my woods who couldn't remember what had happened to her. It didn't seem like they had a choice, really, so they risked coming to my house Saturday night to kill her. The only thing they didn't count on was dying."

Gordon was shaking his head. "I still can't believe someone as devoted and kind as my Helen would have hired men like Dempsey and Slater. No, I think this is all a ruse to try to trap me somehow. I know you believe I hired them, maybe with Chappy's help since he knows so many people in Richmond. That's what you believe, isn't it?"

Dix said, "Oh no, Gordon, you're being the actor here. You do believe Helen did it because she called you on Wednesday night and told you what she'd done. And that's why you strangled her."

"That is insulting and ridiculous! You ask anyone, Helen had to come into my office to swat flies! I couldn't kill anyone."

Ruth said, "We know Helen called you Wednesday night — again, Gordon, her phone records. She probably told you all about it when you went over to her house to see her. Was she remorseful, tearful, Gordon? Truly upset about the death and pain she'd caused? Did she intend to tell everyone and ruin your life? Did you kill her in a rage, for revenge, or was it more cold-blooded than that? I go for cold-blooded, myself, because you strangled her in her sleep, when she couldn't see you, when she was at her most vulnerable. Were you trying to protect your reputation and your cushy little wood-paneled job?"

Gordon slammed his fist down on the keyboard. "I don't want to talk to either of you any more about this! You accused me of murdering Erin, you've had me watched continuously, you've searched my house, my office, my e-mail, for God's sake. And you have found nothing! And through all this I have cooperated with you. And here, after all that, you have the gall to come to my house and accuse me of murdering Helen. You have no proof of anything!"

So much for a distraught confession, Dix thought.

But Gordon wasn't through. "You are right about one thing, Dix. If what you say about Helen is true, then there is nothing left for me. Everything will come out now, no hope for it. I will have nothing — not Erin, not my reputation, my career, my good name. It's only a matter of time before the board of directors of Stanislaus very civilly demands my resignation. Can you imagine how Chappy will delight in that? Of course you can. You have ruined my life, Dix, ruined it!"

Gordon stuck out his hands. "So arrest me, find yourself a grand jury to indict me. You know it's impossible because I didn't kill Helen and so you can't have any proof that I did. You think I'm stupid and weak or you wouldn't even have come here.

"Damn you both. Get out of my house. Don't come back unless you come to arrest me."

It was as if he'd yelled out all his passion. He slumped forward, looking ineffably weary. He whispered, not looking at them, "Please leave. I want to be alone to mourn Erin, and Walt and Helen. I'm tired to my soul. I want to go to bed."

CHAPTER 38

Tara
Maestro, Virginia
Monday morning

Ruth and Dix sat facing Tony and Cynthia. Chappy sat in his big winged patriarch's chair, his fingertips tapping.

Dix looked around at Christie's family, who were preternaturally silent. He didn't think he'd ever been in their company when one of them wasn't insulting or complaining about one of the others. He sat as silently as Ruth, tapping his foot, waiting for one of them to speak about Gordon. Of course they knew everything. It was all over Maestro.

But no one said a word.

Dix finally said, "So which one of you is going to tell me where Gordon went off to?"

Chappy shrugged. "Can't imagine why you'd think any of us would have a clue, Dix." Chappy sat back and folded his hands over his belly. He chuckled, shook his head. "So old Twister's gone into the

489

wind, has he? Milt at the post office called me this morning, said your deputies were banging on doors trying to find him, but it seems he's a ghost. How did you let that happen, Dix? Didn't you have a deputy watching his house?"

"We know a driver with Flying Cabs picked Gordon up on the street behind his house and drove him to Elderville. He was dropped off in a residential neighborhood. No one we've spoken to in the area knows him, no one saw him. Someone else must have picked him up from there."

"Good for him, I say," Cynthia said, and toasted all of them with her last bite of muffin.

"Uncle Gordon was free to go, Dix. And you don't really have any proof against him, do you?" Tony asked. He sat forward, clasped his elegant hands between his knees. "Who cares if he took off? If you find out where he is, you still can't bring him back."

"He left because there wasn't anything here for him anymore, Dix," Cynthia said. "He was ruined. He couldn't face the humiliation, so he left."

Dix said, "That's certainly putting the best face on it, Cynthia. The fact is, though, Gordon is no more accomplished a criminal than Helen Rafferty was. He knows he's left tracks. That's why he snuck off while he could."

The silence returned, none of them meeting Dix's eyes.

Dix looked at Tony. "I find it interesting that you didn't bother to tell me all of Gordon's accounts were closed out. I don't suppose you helped him with that, Tony? I certainly can't imagine Chappy doing it."

"It isn't against the law to give a man his own money," Tony said.

Dix looked at each of them, wondering if there were words that would convince them. He didn't think so. They were finally together on something, not set against one another. He gave it a try anyway. "I know Gordon wouldn't have had the knowledge or the wherewithal to plan something like this."

Chappy chuckled. "Evidently old Twister's got unplumbed depths. Who would have thought it possible?"

Tony asked, "Who cares if someone helped arrange transportation, money, ID, whatever, for him, Dix? It's not against the law."

Chappy grinned. "Hey, maybe I did it for old Twister."

Dix shook his head. "Chappy, you're the only one I wouldn't suspect of that. You can't be in the same room with Gordon without your tearing into each other. I wouldn't have thought you'd do anything for Gordon except visit him in jail, joking about a file in a cake."

Chappy rose slowly to his feet. He shook a finger at Dix. "Are you nuts, Dix? Gordon and I are brothers. All we've ever done is have some fun with each other."

Ruth said, "You know where he is, don't you, Chappy?"

Chappy smiled down at her. "He was going on about killing himself, the little pissant. I wasn't going to let my own brother do that, not after we lost Christie, Dix. And he's not going to spend the last years of his life rotting in prison, either. Not unless you can prove what he did and, of course, find him. Naturally, I have no clue where he is, Agent Ruth."

Dix said, "So I gather Gordon won't be coming for a visit anytime soon. If he does, I think we'll have to notify the Justice Department about a fake passport, won't we?"

Dix rose together with Ruth. "Chappy, you never cease to surprise me. I'd like to bring the boys over sometime soon. This has been a difficult time for them. Would that suit you?"

"That would be nice, Dix," Chappy said. "Real nice."

CHAPTER 39

Greyhaven Inn
Great Bear Road
Maestro, Virginia
Monday lunchtime

"Sorry we're late, guys, but we had a little business with Chappy, Tony, and Cynthia."

Sherlock grinned up at them and Savich rose to hug Ruth and shake Dix's hand.

"You two look like you could use a little more sleep," Dix said. "You had a wild time last night."

"True enough," Savich said. "We slept in this morning."

"At least until Sean jumped on the bed and began a war dance," Sherlock said.

Once they were all seated and had ordered, Dix looked around the large room with a huge quarried gray stone fireplace at one end and beams overhead.

"This is one of the best-kept secrets for lunch in Maestro. Wait till you taste the vegetarian minestrone, Dillon." He raised his coffee cup. "To a conclusion, of sorts, to the trouble in Maestro."

Ruth grinned. "We solved it, Dix, so don't sound so down in the mouth."

Savich sat back and looked from one to the other of them. "All right. So tell us about this business at Tara."

Dix nodded. "Well, when we spoke earlier, I told you how surprised we were at how well Gordon stood up to us. We really hoped we could break him down but it didn't happen."

Ruth sighed. "We hoped to get a confession, and I swear we hit him with everything we had for maximum impact."

Dix said, "You could see it in his eyes when we told him Helen was responsible for Erin and Walt's deaths. He knew, Helen had told him all right."

Ruth said, "Dix, I'm thinking now it was Chappy who told him how to handle us. Gordon never seemed that strong to me." She shrugged. "It's Chappy's doing. And it's possible Chappy did more than get Gordon out of town."

"It wouldn't surprise me if Chappy has somehow covered up any evidence there was, too," Dix said.

"You're certainly giving Chappy a lot of credit, Ruth," Savich said.

Ruth said, "I'm just saying Chappy's

helped him more than once. Chappy helped him escape."

"It's not just Chappy," Dix said. "When Ruth and I went to see the family this morning, it turned out to be all of them."

When Dix finished explaining, he waved a carrot stick at Ruth. "And that's why," he said, "our FBI agent here is convinced Chappy is behind Gordon's great escape. We'll be patient," he added, "but you know, as far as I'm concerned, unless we find proof, Gordon can stay gone."

Savich thought Dix wanted Gordon to stay gone, proof or not.

Their food arrived, and talk turned to the boys. Over a dessert of warm fresh apple pie Ruth said, "Okay, guys, tell us exactly how you managed to track down Moses Grace and Claudia."

Sherlock looked over at her husband. "Well, it's like this. What Dillon did wasn't quite what you'd want to get out. In fact, the lid is on as tight as we can make it. So consider yourselves privileged."

Dix's eyebrow shot up. "Whatever did you do, Savich? If it needs to stay among the four of us, you've got my word on that."

Savich nodded, set his fork on his plate. "You know that when someone calls nine-one-one, the dispatcher gets the callback number and the location of the person almost instantly, regardless of the carrier. Bottom line, we reprogrammed all the cell towers in the Washington, D.C., area to switch any call to my cell phone to the Hoover Building as a nine-one-one call. We fastened MAX to the dashboard, all ready for Moses to call. When he did, we had a nice dancing yellow dot showing us exactly where he was.

"The programming was manageable, but getting permission to work with the cell phone providers to reprogram their networks was the hard part. But Moses helped us out. When he bombed the Bonhomie Club he became a domestic terrorist threatening the nation's capital. Some very important people in the executive branch wanted him stopped immediately, and that turned out to be quickly fatal for him."

Dix said, "So anyone calling your number would have had their voice recorded and their location displayed in the FBI building. Is that legal?"

"Not usually," Savich said, smiled, and took another bite of apple pie.

CHAPTER 40

Winkel's Cave
Monday afternoon

They stepped through the cave opening with no hesitation this time and climbed downward, pressing close to the right side of the cavern, well aware of the precipice two feet to the left.

Ruth stepped into the cave chamber where Erin Bushnell had lain and shone her head lamp all around. "How nice, this place doesn't seem all that scary anymore. It's nice now."

"It's nice because it still smells like a crime scene. All right, Ruth," Dix continued patiently, "you refused to tell me anything until we were here. This has to qualify. Do you think you can tell me what we're doing here?"

"We're here for some treasure hunting, Dix. We're here for my Confederate gold. I keep thinking about my treasure map. It said the gold was beneath the niche. When I saw the deep crevice and realized parts of this cave are cut well below us, I started to wonder whether they meant that literally. The soldiers may have found a lower crevice or cavern and buried the gold there."

"Why go to that much trouble?"

She walked to the deep niche, went down on her knees, pulled out her pick, and began tapping the earth. She said over her shoulder, "They didn't want anyone to find the gold, even if they found the cave. That's why they left the map incomplete."

He stood behind her, watching, saying nothing.

They both heard it — not the sound of rock but the dull sound of wood. She looked up at him, her smile lighting up the dim chamber. "Is this great, or what?"

She began digging with her pick, and Dix dropped to his knees and began pulling away the loosened earth. Within moments, they felt rotten wood planks, and soon they uncovered a depressed floor some three feet square.

Once Dix had pulled up the last plank, Ruth lay on her stomach and angled her chest down into the hole, Dix's Maglite shining down. "I wondered how they could do this, but now I understand. It's a natural passage they boarded up, like a hole into a low-ceilinged basement in a house. The drop is only about five feet. I wondered how they could get the gold bars down there so easily, and this is how." She jumped to her feet and wiped her hands on her jeans. "Let's go down there, partner."

Once Dix and Ruth stood in the middle of the chamber, they panned their flashlights around the small space. "Look," Ruth said. "That narrow passageway probably leads back to the underground river and that cliff at the cave entrance."

"The cave floor must slope up very fast," Dix said. "It dead-ends here in this chamber. Look how the floor keeps going up. At the back wall, I'll bet it's only about three feet tall."

"All that's surely nice," Ruth said, "but where's my gold?"

Dix said, "I guess there's no reason to think the Rebel soldiers would leave the gold out in plain view, not after they went to all the trouble of lugging it down here and covering that hole in the ceiling."

A few minutes later, at a height of about four feet, Dix's fingers pressed against something rough in a crevice in the west wall. He pounded his fist against it and heard the echo of wood. "There's something here, Ruth," he called as he felt excitement fill him.

They quickly uncovered more wood planks. Dix looked at Ruth, raised an eyebrow. Ruth nodded to him and smashed her pick through the rotted wood. It splintered inward.

Dix leaned over her shoulder, shining his Maglite into the blackness.

"Oh my." Ruth crawled into a space too small to stand in, laid the Maglite on the floor. She knelt in front of a low pile of what looked like bricks covered in dust. She ran her sleeve roughly over it. They stared at six rows of gold bars, four deep, lined up perfectly by those soldiers long ago. Sitting next to the bars was a very old leather satchel.

Ruth touched the gold bars, but her eyes went to the satchel. Gently, she pulled it out, carefully unfastened it. Inside was a small leather-bound notebook. "It's not a diary, there aren't any pages. There are a dozen or so letters here." She ran her fingertips over the folded sheets. She unfolded one near the top of the pile. "It's a woman's handwriting. Her name is Missy and she's writing to her husband." She looked up at him. "He's got to be one of the soldiers who stole the gold."

Soon they both sat cross-legged on the cave floor, the stacked gold bars unnoticed behind them, looking through the packet of letters. "They're all to Lieutenant Charles Breacken. Wait a moment, not this one." She picked up the last letter in the pile. "It's from him. He never got to send it. I wonder why he left it here?"

She read:

It was brutally hot today and still all we have to wear is wool. There's a battle coming, everyone knows it's coming, but no one wants to talk about it. I don't know when I'll see you again, Missy, but perhaps next month. I'm glad your parents are there to help you on the farm. Is your father still drinking too much?

We are protecting something of value we managed to steal from the Confederates, who were taking it to General Lee in Richmond. They are searching for us. We are determined they shall not have it. Elias stumbled across a cave for shelter, and I am writing this letter to you by candlelight deep inside the cave. If we prevail, my darling Missy, we will have done a great service for the Union. When next we meet, I may be Captain Charles Breacken.

I've got to go now. Elias just came in, said the Rebels are getting closer. I'm needed. Kiss our daughter.

> Your loving husband,
> Charles

Ruth said in a whisper, "He was a Union soldier, an officer."

"And he never got home to his wife and daughter," Dix said. "He died."

"All of them died, but they didn't give up the gold," Ruth said. "I wonder how the map ended up in an old book in that attack in Manassas? Why did Charles leave his satchel here? It obviously meant a lot to him."

"Maybe," Dix said, "he was killed right here, outside, near Lone Tree Hill."

He pulled her against him. "Well done, Ruth. You did it. Mr. Weaver's going to be a very happy man. You're pretty smart, you know that?"

She kissed him in reply.

National Intelligence Briefing
The White House
Tuesday morning

The director of National Intelligence jiggled the ice in his glass, a sure sign he was pleased about something. "With respect to item six, Mr. President, the FBI domestic wireless telecommunications operation has been decommissioned with no disruption of emergency nine-one-one service. The single FBI agent injured by gunfire will fully recover."

The president sat back in his leather chair and steepled his fingers. "And operational security remains intact? We can expect no blowback on any possible civil liberties questions?"

"That is correct, Mr. President. And we believe the swift conclusion has indeed given the message we discussed."

"John, I'd like you to write a letter under your own signature commending Special Agent Dillon Savich for his briefing and the successful execution of his plan."

"Of course, Mr. President," the director said. "Now to item seven, the request for new countermeasures on the Afghan border."

EPILOGUE

That summer

Ruth Warnecki knocked on the front door of a small tract house in a subdivision of Midlothian, Virginia. Linda Massey answered the door with two boys, both under the age of four, clinging to her jeans, and a baby nestled in the crook of her arm. She gave Ruth a harried smile. "I hope you're not selling encyclopedias," she said. "This crew is still a little young and no one else has the time."

"No, I'm not selling anything," Ruth said. "I do have a story to tell you about your family that goes back to the Civil War. I think it might interest you."

Linda Massey, the closest surviving descendant of Lieutenant Charles Breacken of the Union Army, was five hundred thousand dollars richer.

Ruth left an hour later, feeling so fine she clicked up her heels. She waved to Dix, who was leaning against his Range Rover, waiting for her. She gave him a huge grin and a thumbs-up.